TROUBLE

TROUBLE

A SHADOW SLAYERS STORY

NELLIE H. STEELE

A Novel Idea Publishing

*For Roger, who has always been an avid supporter of my work.
Thank you!*

ACKNOWLEDGMENTS

A HUGE thank you to everyone who helped get this book published! Special shout outs to: Stephanie Sovak, Paul Sovak, Michelle Cheplic, Mark D'Angelo and Lori D'Angelo.

Finally, a HUGE thank you to you, the reader!

CHAPTER 1

*B*lack clouds rushed across the sky as they pushed toward the coast. The choppy waters crashed against the rocks below. Thunder rumbled in the distance as lightning streaked across the dark afternoon sky, creating a jagged path from heaven to earth.

The crease in Celine's brow deepened as she eyed the ominous clouds. Her full lips formed a frown as her blonde locks danced in a wind gust.

The impending inclement weather matched her mood. Dark. Stormy. Brooding. She reflected on the cause: Marcus Northcott. It was always Marcus Northcott.

It had been almost two months since he had helped her retrieve Damien and Michael from one of the Alterra universes. And almost two months to the day from when he had issued his ominous warning to her.

The conversation echoed through her mind for the umpteenth time. As she had stepped toward the border to their time band, he had grabbed her arm and pulled her away.

"What are you doing?" she demanded.

"Stopping you from making the biggest mistake of your life," he'd told her.

He warned her not to return to her world. This world. She had scrutinized every word of the conversation upon her return though she had not shared it with anyone else. In the days and weeks that followed, Celine examined every occurrence, small or otherwise, searching for the meaning behind his words.

While she found none, the conversation remained at the forefront of her mind. She may have dismissed the conversation entirely if not for the source. Marcus Northcott did not make idle threats. Nor did he behave rashly. His actions during that moment had been odd. Yet she found no reason for his words. None so far, she reminded herself.

Celine rubbed the smooth black stone clutched in her palm. She stared down at it, tearing her eyes from the stormy horizon. She held Marcus's soul marker, giving her control of his soul. She narrowed her eyes at it as she considered the task ahead.

"No time like the present," she murmured as she slid the blackened stone into her jacket pocket.

Celine strolled along the path that clung to the cliff's edge as she approached the seaside house. She stared at it, hovering on the edge of the woods that sheltered her from its sight. She'd visited Marcus shortly after her return from Alterra. She'd demanded to know the meaning of his warning. He'd denied there was any, claiming he only attempted to persuade her to his side as he'd done time and time again throughout the centuries.

Celine did not believe him. But in the days immediately following the revelation that she held his soul marker, she didn't expect him to be forthcoming. Perhaps time had cooled his temper. She would soon find out.

Celine stalked toward the house and climbed the steps

leading to the covered porch. She pounded against the door until a dark-skinned man opened it. "Hello, Miss Celine," he said in his South African accent.

"I need to see him," Celine answered.

Dembe, Marcus's manservant and ally, motioned for her to enter the foyer. "He is in the sitting room, Miss Celine."

"Thank you, Dembe," Celine answered with a nod before she proceeded through the open archway.

"Ah, Celine," Marcus said from the armchair across the room. "Back again?"

Celine set her jaw as she eyed him.

"I don't suppose you've come to return my soul marker, by any chance?" he continued before sipping his brandy.

She narrowed her eyes. "No, Marcus."

"Hmm," Marcus mumbled as he swallowed the amber liquid before standing to retrieve another glass. "Too bad. Though one can always hope. Brandy, dear?"

"No, Marcus, I am not here for a drink or a pleasant chat."

Marcus twisted to offer her a smirk. "Another pity, though I cannot say I expected one."

"You know why I'm here."

He replaced the stopper on the glass decanter and took another sip of brandy. "No doubt to accuse me of something."

"You say that as though you're innocent."

He shrugged as he settled back in his chair. "If the shoe fits, as they say."

Celine narrowed her eyes further. "The shoe isn't even your style, Marcus, let alone size."

He rolled his eyes at her. "If you've come for another argument, I decline to participate. Celine, I have had quite enough of this."

"You're just miffed because I still hold your soul marker," she said with a sly smile.

He frowned at her. "What is it you want, Celine?"

"To know why you insisted it was a mistake for me to return to this time band."

"I've already told you though you refuse to listen."

"Yes, yes, I know your story. It was merely a ploy to throw me off balance. A carefully crafted move in yet another attempt to best me."

Marcus bowed his head to her. "My dear, you have answered your own question."

"I don't believe you," Celine snapped.

"Why? Surely those dimwitted companions you cling to so vehemently concur."

"It's what I think that matters," Celine answered as she stalked to the window. She crossed her arms and stared at the darkening skies.

"Ohhhh," Marcus sang. "I didn't realize you hadn't told them. What an interesting development."

"I didn't say that," Celine said as she spun to face him.

He smirked at her. "You didn't have to, my dear."

Celine set her jaw. "Perhaps you were bluffing. Nothing more than a desperate attempt to win a losing battle."

Marcus offered her an unimpressed glance but gave nothing more away. "Only time will tell, dear Celine."

"So far time has suggested nothing portentous."

"Then why return to question me?"

Celine set her jaw, glowering at him.

"And why have you not confided in your beloved Grayson? Or dear Damien? Or even faithful Alexander? Oh, Celine, it appears your dark side is showing."

"This conversation is over," Celine growled. She spun on her heel and stormed from the room, slamming the front door as she exited the house.

"Was it something I said?" Marcus called after her.

Fury burned through her as she tramped back toward her

house. The storm inched closer. Winds gusted, bending trees, and rustling the newly forming leaves. Thunder rumbled overhead. A few large raindrops pelted the ground.

Celine hurried toward the large gothic house on the hill before the onslaught of a downpour. The war with Marcus had cost her much over the centuries. And it showed no signs of slowing. Unless Marcus's warning was fake, it would continue. What would it cost her this time?

Marcus's final words rang in her ears as she reached the front door. Why hadn't she told anyone? It was a question she'd pondered before, though she had never answered it. Perhaps now was the time to confide in someone.

Celine stepped into the foyer as rain poured from the skies. Thunder boomed overhead, sending a shiver through the foyer's only other occupant. Damien Sherwood jumped at the loud noise as his eyes slid upward. He winced. "I really hate this house in a storm," he moaned.

Celine offered him a reassuring glance. "How about a distraction to take your mind off of it?"

Thunder crashed again and Damien gulped. He nodded his head as he offered Celine a wide-eyed glance. "Yes, please. Chess?"

"Video game?" Celine suggested.

Damien's eyes widened. "Wow, you really do want to distract me!"

Celine shrugged. She tossed her head toward the outside beyond the front door. "It looks like this one's going to be a rager."

Damien rolled his eyes. "Oh, wonderful," he lamented as they climbed the stairs and navigated the halls to his bedroom.

Damien dragged a second chair over to his gaming setup as Celine turned everything on. "Got a pick?" she asked as she perused the games.

"Not really," Damien said.

"Your choice."

Damien raised his eyebrows at her.

"What?" Celine responded to his stare.

He narrowed his eyes at her. "First you offer to distract me with video games and then you let me pick the game. What's going on?"

Celine shrugged. "There's a terrible storm coming, and you hate storms in this house. Just trying to distract you. Relive some old times."

"When you were Josie, you'd let me pick the game when you wanted me to do something I didn't want to do, or you wanted to tell me something bad."

Celine laughed. "That's not true," she said with a shake of her head.

"It is!" Damien insisted.

Celine pursed her lips. "Fine," she answered with a shrug. "I'll pick the game." She selected one and they collapsed into the chairs behind them as they waited for the game to load.

They played in silence for fifteen minutes before Celine spoke. "So, how have you been feeling? Fully recovered?"

"Yeah," Damien answered. "Fully recovered. Only the odd nightmare now and again about the Alterra version of you."

"Still having nightmares?" Celine questioned, her eyes remaining fixed on the screen.

"Not often," Damien said as he pounded on the controller. "Just a few lingering ones."

Celine arched an eyebrow at the statement but didn't respond. Damien glanced sideways at her. "It's not concerning."

"I'll be the judge of that," Celine answered.

"I'm fine, Celine," Damien insisted. "And it's not surprising. Alterra Celine was frightening!"

"You said she helped you!"

"Yeah, after scaring the life out of us. She literally pulled a guy backward like a magnet and tossed him into a chair. Restraints magically appeared to keep him there and then she squashed his face up and demanded to know the truth before she rendered him mute!"

"Okay, okay, my alter ego has struck fear into your heart. Lingering nightmares seem like a bargain compared to your declining health."

Damien paused the game. He grabbed Celine's hand and squeezed it. "I'm fine, Celine. Millie checks me almost every day. No ill effects, no recurring problems, no permanent damage."

Celine smiled at him and returned his hand squeeze. "And I have you to thank," Damien added.

Celine returned her gaze to the frozen screen in front of her. "And Marcus."

Damien groaned. "Ugh, let's not bring him into this. We've had a peaceful two months. Let's hope the trend continues."

Celine remained silent. Damien stared at her. "What?" he inquired.

Thunder rumbled overhead and lightning flashed through the sky as raindrops continued to pelt the window.

"Celine?" Damien questioned. "You're starting to scare me."

Celine faced him, pulling her eyes up to meet his. She shrugged as she searched for the words. "I need to tell you something, but it has to stay between us."

"Of course," Damien said, his brows pinching with concern.

Celine nodded as a moment of silence passed between them before she launched into her tale. "When we were in the in-between…" Celine began.

Damien leapt from his seat and paced the floor behind

the chairs. "I knew it! I knew it! He did something, didn't he? I knew we never should have left you alone in there with him! Thank God Gray had that red vial!"

"Damien, please," Celine entreated, "sit down."

Damien spun to face her. "What did he do? Did he try to take you? Did the red vial save you?"

Celine shook her head. "No, sit down. I need your full focus on this."

Damien sank into the chair. "When we were in the in-between," Celine began again, "after Michael went through, I stepped toward the barrier, but Marcus stopped me. He dragged me away from it and told me not to come back. He said he was stopping me from making the worst mistake of my life."

Thunder punctuated Celine's last remark. "That was creepy," Damien answered, his eyes floating upward to the ceiling. He shook his head before responding. "That bastard!" he exclaimed. "He's always working an angle."

"No," Celine countered. "Something was off. He said he couldn't allow me to return. He warned me not to. I'd chalk it up to Marcus being Marcus, but his behavior was odd. He was nothing like Marcus. He was bothered, almost panicked. Marcus is never panicked."

Damien's brow furrowed as he considered the information. After a moment he suggested, "Perhaps it's some elaborate trick just to win?"

"It didn't seem like a trick."

"Nothing's happened since we've been back, though, right?"

"No," Celine admitted. "And Marcus denies having meant anything by it."

Damien glanced at her, his eyebrows rising toward his hairline. "You've spoken to him?"

Celine nodded. "A few times, actually. He maintains his

innocence in the entire ordeal. Claims it was exactly what you said, Marcus being Marcus and trying to win."

Damien stood and resumed his pacing, running his fingers through his hair. "If he says it was just him being him, then there's more to it. He's a proven liar."

"I agree," Celine answered. "Yet we've gone two months with relative peace."

"Well, of course. You've accused him of causing trouble so now he's deliberately not causing any just to prove you wrong."

Celine scoffed at the statement. "If only that worked, D," she lamented. "I've accused him of causing trouble numerous times in the past. It never stopped him from continuing, even if he could prove me wrong."

"So, what could it mean?" Damien questioned.

Celine shrugged. "I'm not sure."

"Was there anything else that he said? Anything else you remember?"

Celine shook her head. "No. Just that he couldn't let me return because it would be the biggest mistake of my life. He cursed giving Gray the red vial when I started to be pulled back to our world and then followed me back through the barrier."

"What did Gray say about it?" Damien questioned.

"I didn't tell him," Celine admitted.

"What? Why?"

"There is enough bad blood between Gray and Marcus, this would only add to it. And for what? So far nothing has happened."

"But you can't let it go? You don't think it's nothing."

"No, which is why I told you. You're the only one who knows. Until we figure this out, please don't say anything to Gray. I don't want him upset over potentially nothing."

"I won't say anything, though I'm not sure this is the

wisest course of action. Your premonitions are rarely wrong, Celine. If you think there's something to this, there's something to it."

"But what?" Celine questioned. "What was Marcus trying to warn me about?"

CHAPTER 2

Thunder cracked overhead, causing Damien to wince again. "Why does that happen every time you make a statement like that? It really, really makes it seem so much worse."

A knock sounded at the door. "Yeah?" Damien called.

Gray poked his head inside. "There you are," he said, spotting Celine across the room.

"Here I am!" Celine answered. She waved the controller in the air. "We were just playing a few video games to ease Damien's storm jitters."

"Don't let me stop you. I just wanted to let you know I'm home," he said as he crossed the room.

Damien collapsed onto the chair next to Celine. He swallowed hard as he clutched the controller. "You okay?" Gray questioned. "You look a bit pale."

"Oh, I'm fine. All good. Couldn't be better," Damien babbled. Celine recognized the characteristic behavior of a nervous Damien. With her recent admission, Damien's mind bubbled with turmoil. Hiding a secret was not his strong suit.

"He's just upset because I've beaten him yet again," Celine

covered as she unpaused the game and struck the final, fatal blow to Damien's on-screen avatar. The character groaned as it slumped to the ground on the monitor and a success message whipped across the screen declaring Celine's win.

Damien offered a tight-lipped smile as Gray raised his eyebrows at the scene.

"Seems like you two are having fun," he answered with a chuckle.

"I sure am," Celine answered. "I'm not sure the same can be said about Damien."

"I'm letting you win," he offered.

Celine arched an eyebrow at the statement.

"Are you using magic?" he questioned.

She chuckled as Gray squeezed her shoulders and kissed her cheek. "I'll leave you two to it. Have fun. See you later for dinner."

"Yep, see you then," Celine said with a smile.

Gray disappeared from view, closing the door behind him. Damien slumped in the chair next to Celine, resting his head against the back. "I do not understand how you cover that well."

"According to Marcus, it's my dark side."

Damien rolled his head to face Celine. "You don't have a dark side, Celine."

Celine shrugged at him. "He has a point. I've been keeping this a secret."

"But not because you want to harm people! It's because you DON'T want to harm people. Which means it can't be a dark side."

Celine inhaled a deep breath.

"Why aren't we telling Gray again?" Damien questioned.

"I don't see the sense in telling Gray. He'll chalk it up to Marcus's bad behavior and it will only add to the animosity between them."

"And that's a bad thing because?"

"I would like to minimize the fighting between us and Marcus."

Damien raised his eyebrows at her statement. "Not for Marcus's sake. For ours. Things have been quiet, almost peaceful. Why risk the status quo?"

"What about Alexander?"

Celine shook her head. "Neither of them," she responded. "Not until we have a better handle on this."

"Celine, I'm not certain we can handle this alone."

"So far there's nothing to handle. I only told you because it's been playing on my mind. I can't shake the encounter."

"Which means there's something to it," Damien interjected.

"But until we have some idea of what, what is the sense in disturbing everyone?"

"Getting their help?" Damien suggested.

"If I thought they'd have something meaningful to add to the conversation I wouldn't object. But I can't see how they can. If they'd sensed anything, they'd have told us."

"Unless they're playing things close to the vest, like you."

"I just want a week or so to figure this out before we tell everyone."

"Celine, you've had two months to figure it out!" Damien exclaimed.

"But I didn't have you to help me," Celine replied with a grin.

"Oh, sure, butter me up. Expect that'll work, do you?"

"It was worth a try."

He wagged his finger at her. "I should be mad at you for keeping this from me for two months."

"Are you?" Celine asked with a wince.

Damien rolled his eyes. "No. I can never stay mad at you."

He sank into the chair again and grabbed her hand. "But why did you?"

Celine's jaw dropped as she shook her head. "Seriously? You nearly died, D!"

"But I'm fine!"

"You weren't! It took you weeks to fully recover. And even after that, you still had the nightmares."

"Still…"

"D, I wasn't going to drop this on you until I knew you were fine."

Damien nodded and waved his hand at her to dismiss his concern. "Okay, okay. We'll spend the week going over everything."

"Okay."

"And if we come up with nothing, we tell Gray and Alexander."

"Deal."

He smiled at her. "Now," he said, snatching the controller from the table, "let's play again and see who beats who this time."

* * *

Damien wandered down the stairs into the foyer. His eyes focused on the large portrait hanging above the enormous fireplace. The likeness of Celine circa 1791 stared back at him. A freight train of thoughts charged through his brain as he stared at her lifelike but painted blue eyes.

Dozens of ideas pulled his mind in every direction. Celine had confided in him about a warning issued by Duke Marcus Northcott. The ominous tale echoed in his head. She'd withheld the information from him while he recovered from his trip to Alterra. The physical toll the journey took on his and Michael's bodies lasted for weeks.

During that time, Celine suffered alone. He shook his head as he stared up at her portrait. Not anymore. He'd dig through even the slightest clue to make sense of the warning. And to head off any trouble. Celine's assessment was correct. They had lived in relative peace for several weeks. Was this merely the calm before the storm? Or could they be entering a new phase of tranquility now that Celine held the Duke's soul marker?

He hoped for the latter, but he'd prepare for the former. With a sigh, he tore his eyes from Celine's likeness and wandered toward the sitting room. A brandy before dinner might slow his racing mind.

He strolled through the partially ajar doors, finding Michael inside. With his feet on the coffee table, Michael stared into the glowing fireplace. A blank laptop sat on his lap and papers were strewn on every surface surrounding him.

Damien poured two glasses of brandy. He sauntered toward Michael, holding the drink out to him. Michael glanced up at him before grabbing the glass. "Thanks," he said, raising the glass before he took a sip.

"Busy, huh?" Damien asked as he sank into a chair across from Michael.

"Something like that," Michael answered. His gaze fell to the amber liquid in his glass.

Damien craned his neck to glance at the paperwork covering the table. He grabbed a sheet and spun it to face him, perusing its contents. It outlined the creation of a new branch of Carlyle Industries in Bucksville. Shortly after their arrival in Maine, Michael had proposed the location to allow him to stay close.

Damien returned the sheet to the disheveled pile before scanning the others. Signature flags were stuck in various spots, requesting Michael's autograph to approve the details. Every line remained blank.

"New branch paperwork!" Damien exclaimed.

"Yep," Michael answered.

Damien narrowed his eyes at the man across from him. Michael's responses conveyed a hidden problem. Some issue kept him from executing the contracts and getting the ball rolling for the newest Carlyle Industries location.

"Exciting," Damien ventured, testing the waters.

Michael didn't respond, instead sipping his brandy.

"You haven't signed them yet," Damien noted.

"I'm still reviewing the details."

Damien pursed his lips at the statement, narrowing his eyes. The paperwork had been messengered weeks ago. He'd assumed Michael's recovery sidelined him from reviewing the particulars. But with them both fully recovered, it surprised Damien that Michael hadn't made short work of the review, corrected any issues, and signed off.

"Some problem?" Damien questioned.

Michael shrugged and took another sip of his brandy. He glanced up at Damien. "I just want to be sure."

"Sure of the details?" Damien inquired. "Or sure you want to stay?"

Michael snorted. "How do you always read people that easily?"

"It's not that big of a surprise," Damien responded. "You're hesitant about signing the papers. You're never hesitant. You jump right into everything. So, something's wrong and I'd doubt it's the details about the branch."

"No, it's not. The details are spot on. Exactly what I requested."

"So?"

"So, I want to be sure staying is right."

"What's holding you back? Tired of the constant drama and danger?"

"Something like that."

"Come on, man. We've been through a lot together. Tell me what you're thinking."

"You're right. You deserve the truth. It's not really the whole danger thing. It's more…"

"Yeah?" Damien prompted.

Michael shook his head and rose from his seat. He stalked across the room and refilled his brandy. After another sip, he offered more explanation. "That last one took a toll, man."

"Yeah," Damien admitted, "it did. And we're only human. Are you still having issues from it?"

"No," Michael answered as he sank back onto the couch. "I'm back to normal but…" His voice trailed off.

"But?"

"I don't know." He stared into the dancing flames in the fireplace.

"But you're worried the next one will leave a lasting issue? Or worse?"

Michael considered his question. "Maybe. It's not just that. I'm not sure I can go back to a normal life but, honestly, I'm starting to question if staying was the right choice."

"I get that this is a big responsibility. And that there's a ton of danger involved, especially for us as humans but… come on, man, we're a team, right?"

"Are we?" Michael questioned.

"I thought we were," Damien responded without hesitation. "We're family."

"You're family. I'm not. Why am I here? Should I be? Maybe I shouldn't have stayed."

"Come on, Michael! Celine would always protect you. She came to Alterra for both of us, not just me. She'd have gone for you alone. You have to realize that."

Michael nodded. "Yeah, yeah, I know she would. And I'd do anything for you both, too. I just…"

"Feel like the third wheel," Damien finished for him, familiar with the sentiment.

"Exactly."

"But you shouldn't!"

"Explain that one to me, buddy, because I'm not as clever as you to see how this is working. When we're in the thick of things, it's not so bad. But as soon as everything dies down, it just hits me. Celine is married to Gray. We live with Gray's family. I'm not family. I'm not tied to you or her in any way. It feels weird. Like I don't belong."

"Well, hell, neither do I, then," Damien countered.

"How do you figure that? You're Celine's family."

"Not really," Damien lamented, his gaze falling into his glass.

"Oh, come on, now who's having the pity party? You're her cousin."

"It's not a pity party," Damien replied. "And I was Josie's cousin. Not Celine's. I'm not related to Celine at all."

"She considers you family."

"She feels the same about you," Damien answered. "And so do I, by the way. Just because we don't share any blood, doesn't mean we're nothing to each other. We're a team. We're family by choice."

Michael raised his eyebrows. "I suppose you make a decent point. Though I still maintain your familial connection is a bit better established than mine. I can feel the daggers coming from Gray's eyes every time he looks at me. I'm the guy Celine dated while she was someone else for twenty-five years."

"He'll get over it. Plus, in every time period we've met him in, he hates us. And you haven't been Celine's ex in any of those other situations. Hell, he even hated us in a parallel universe where we had never met Celine."

Michael chuckled at Damien's assessment. "Excellent point."

"Yes, it is. So, let's stop second-guessing everything and just take life as it comes. Besides, with the exception of Gray, the rest of his family likes you. Avery likes you."

"I'll take it under consideration."

"Good. And maybe we'll take a second look at that caretaker cottage. Perhaps you'd feel better if you had your own space," Damien suggested.

"Deal. I'll look at the cottage and I'll keep what you said in mind."

"Dinner?"

"I'm skipping. Got a lot of paperwork to review."

"And hopefully some signing to do," Damien said with a grin as he set his glass on the table and rose from his seat.

Michael chuckled at him but offered no further response.

Damien strolled from the room into the foyer. His eyes slid up to Celine's portrait as he crossed. He sighed. Two problems in the span of a day. What else was new, he ruminated? In Bucksville, when it rained, it poured. Michael's final reaction suggested he remained undecided. Would Michael choose to leave? Would Marcus Northcott's warnings come to fruition?

He veered into the hall leading to the dining room. As he approached the double doors, he hesitated before continuing past them. He'd grab a tray of food and take it to his room. He'd lost his appetite and he doubted his ability to make polite conversation as his mind continued to churn.

Beyond Marcus and Michael, his own words rang in his head. "I don't belong either," his voice echoed over and over. A sinking feeling grew in the pit of his stomach. Did he belong? He clung to the thin tether connecting him to Celine.

He was her cousin. Sort of. Was it enough to stay? He couldn't leave Celine. But did she prefer him to? Did she crave returning to her old life? One that did not include him. Perhaps he provided a constant reminder of her life as Josie. A life she may prefer to forget.

He closed his eyes and shook his head in an attempt to shake the thoughts from his mind as he slipped into the kitchen. Mrs. Paxton, the housekeeper, bustled about in the large area, preparing the family's dinner.

"Hello," Damien called as he strolled through the door.

"Oh, Mr. Sherwood," Mrs. Paxton answered. "Something I can do for you?"

"No. Nope," Damien replied as he opened a cabinet and pulled a tray down. "I'm just going to grab my dinner and head to my room."

"I can do that for you."

"No, it's fine!" Damien exclaimed as he waved her away. "I've got it. You can keep on with whatever you were doing. I didn't mean to interrupt. And, please, I know I've said it before, but call me Damien. Mr. Sherwood was my dad."

"No interruption at all. I could have brought it up to you though."

"I only just decided. I'm suddenly tired. I'm just going to eat in my room. I'll bring the tray down as soon as I'm finished."

"If you leave it outside your door, I'll retrieve it."

Damien considered it. He hated to make the woman traipse through the halls to get his tray. But he wasn't sure he wanted to run into anyone in his current mood. "I may take you up on that. If I'm not down here by six-thirty, it'll be outside my door."

"Fine by me. Just leave it in the hall and I'll gather it up before I finish up tonight."

Damien nodded and offered a tight-lipped smile as he

loaded his full plate onto the tray and exited through the back entrance from the kitchen in an effort to avoid running into anyone.

He snaked through the back halls on his way to his bedroom. A sigh of relief escaped his lips as he enclosed himself in the confines of his bedroom without anyone spotting him.

Now his mind was free to roam through the list of troubles it had created.

* * *

Michael stared at the papers scattered around him. With a sigh, he began collecting them one by one. There was no sense in leaving them sprawled across every surrounding surface. He'd read them a hundred times. He knew the details by heart. He understood the responsibilities, the workload, the position he'd take on as President of Carlyle Industries Northeast.

It wasn't a bad position. In his current job as Vice-President of Marketing, he enjoyed fewer perks, less control over the company's vision. Had the position been offered to him before the life-changing events took place last year, he'd have accepted in a heartbeat. Now, he struggled to welcome the new title.

On one hand, he couldn't imagine leaving Bucksville. Too much had happened. And even though Celine wasn't his Josie, the woman he thought he loved a year ago, he still felt an attachment toward her. He probably always would.

And not just her. There was Damien, too. Their wild battles with the dark forces in the world had bonded them for life. He couldn't just walk away from Damien. Could he?

Then again, could he really stay? Did he actually belong here? He lived with strangers, practically. Celine was not

Josie. He and Damien had only become friends because of the extraordinary circumstances they'd lived through. And Gray detested the sight of him. How long before they asked him to leave? And then what?

One notion burned through his mind as he flicked the manila folder closed after stuffing the contracts inside. What right did he have to stay?

CHAPTER 3

Celine pushed through the doors to her bedroom suite.

Gray fiddled with his watch clasp before sliding it from his wrist. "Did you get Damien's nerves settled?"

"The storm's passed. He should be fine now," Celine answered.

Gray glanced at her with narrowed eyes. "He is odd."

Celine cocked her head, offering a half frown to him. "Don't say that."

"I can't help it. A grown man afraid of storms is odd."

"He's not afraid of storms. He just doesn't like this house during one."

Gray raised his eyebrows as he prepared his response. Celine beat him to it. "He just moved in. And it's not been the most peaceful experience from the time he followed me from New York. Give him time to adjust. He'll get used to it."

Gray's expression softened as he scooped Celine into his arms. "He did go above and beyond when we lost you. I suppose he deserves some slack. He's earned it."

Celine smiled up at him as she slid her arms around his

waist. "Both he and Michael did. It nearly cost them their lives."

"Millie says they're doing fine. No lasting effects, right?"

"Thank God," Celine murmured. "I wouldn't have been able to live with myself if anything had happened to them."

"It didn't," Gray reminded her. "And with your control over Northcott's soul, we may actually have a moment's peace to enjoy."

Celine forced a smile at the statement. Gray leaned in to brush her lips with his before he pressed his forehead against hers.

"How about lunch out tomorrow? I'll be working in town all day."

"Diner?" she suggested.

"Your taste in food is abominable," Gray said with a grimace.

"Their food is good!" Celine countered. "The fries are excellent."

"I think you've kept some of Josie's tastes," he teased.

"I have not. I've always liked their fries! Even long before I was Josie."

"I suppose the taste of them hasn't changed since before you were Josie. I'm certain they're using the same oil to cook them."

Celine offered a wry glance. "Very funny, Gray. Your humor hasn't changed since before I was Josie."

"Neither has my love for you," he said before another gentle kiss.

"Which is why we'll be eating at the diner tomorrow," Celine answered with a giggle.

"I can't say no to you. The diner it is, my dear."

* * *

Celine strolled through town in the cool late morning air. Gray clouds floated through the sky, obscuring the sun. A chill tinged every gust of wind. She shrugged her cardigan tighter around her as she shoved her hands into its pockets. The harbor bell sang as the waves rocked against the coast.

She quickened her pace as she spotted Gray's familiar form outside the diner attached to the local hotel. "Fancy meeting you here," she said as she approached him.

"I came to check the place out. I heard the French fries are outstanding."

Celine offered him a half-smile as he pulled the door open for her. "Shall we?" he said as she slid past him and into the small café.

They selected a table near the open entrance to the hotel lobby. Celine glanced through the open doorway at the hotel's desk. An older man fiddled with some paperwork behind the counter. She smiled at the sight.

"I see Mr. Cunningham is still working at the inn."

Gray glanced over his shoulder. "Yes, he is. And I'm fairly sure he's the one who outed you to your friends last year. You can thank him for the sudden appearance of Damien and Michael."

"I suppose I should since we needed their help."

"I couldn't be happier with the way it turned out," Gray admitted, reaching across the table to squeeze Celine's hand.

The waitress arrived to take their orders, then collected their menus and departed with a curt, "Won't be long."

"Did you find Damien?" Gray inquired as the waitress left.

"No, not yet. He hasn't emerged from his room."

"That's odd, isn't it? Perhaps he's ill."

Celine shrugged. "If he's not up by the time I get back, I'll check on him."

"I'm surprised you haven't beaten down his door already. He missed both dinner and breakfast."

She bit her lower lip. Damien's absence likely stemmed from his desire to avoid Gray given the information she'd imparted yesterday. At least, that's what she assumed. Although if he was also avoiding her, she'd have another worry. "I'm trying to give him his privacy," she sidestepped. "Let him really settle in."

"How's that going?"

"Maybe I should have checked on him this morning," Celine admitted with a sigh as worry grew within her.

"That sounds more like you," Gray said with a chuckle as the waitress returned with their food.

Celine snatched a French fry from her plate and bit into it.

"Were they worth it?" Gray questioned.

"Definitely," she answered.

They continued their meal with light conversation. An icy gust of air blew through the diner as the hotel's exterior door opened and banged shut. Celine shrugged her sweater tighter as the wind penetrated through her.

The bell sounded at the front desk. Within a few moments, Bill Cunningham's familiar voice reached Celine's ears. "Help you?" he asked in his old Maine accent.

A woman's voice answered him. "Yes, I'd like a room. I have an undecided departure date. Will that be a problem?"

A crease formed between Celine's eyebrows. She froze at the sound of the voice, setting her burger down as she leaned toward the door opening.

"Shouldn't be," Bill responded. "Got a room available with no bookings for at least two weeks."

"Great," the woman answered. "That should work."

"What's wrong?" Gray questioned as he eyed Celine's odd behavior.

"That voice," Celine answered. "Sounds like…" Celine's eyes widened and her jaw dropped open as she stared through the opening. She straightened in her seat, a perturbed expression on her face.

"Like who?" Gray inquired. Celine didn't answer. "Celine?"

Celine leaned in toward him. "Josie's mom," she whispered.

Gray arched an eyebrow, glancing around the corner and into the hotel lobby.

"I think I will!" the woman said. "I'm starving!"

"Just leave your luggage there. I'll have it taken up to your room. Enjoy your lunch."

"Oh, shoot!" Celine breathed. "She's coming in here. I've got to get out of here."

"What? Now? You haven't finished your lunch."

"Yes, now, Gray. Obviously, Monica hasn't informed me she was coming. What is she even doing here? I'd rather not run into her…" Celine's voice cut off as the woman appeared in the doorway.

Celine shut her eyes for a moment as she realized escape was now impossible.

The woman scanned the room, her eyes settling on Celine. "Josie!" she exclaimed. A smile spread across her face as she took a step toward the table.

Celine faked surprise as she leapt from her seat. "Mom?" she questioned, her voice an octave higher. She forced a chuckle out and a smile onto her face. "What are you doing here?"

"What? I can't surprise my baby girl with a visit? I haven't seen you in months!" She stepped toward Celine, her arms outstretched for a hug.

Celine allowed herself to be pulled into the embrace. She squeezed the woman tightly before releasing her. As she let go, she slid her wedding ring from her finger, palming it in her right hand. When she stepped back, she slid the wedding band into her cardigan pocket.

"Oh, I've interrupted," her mother answered, glancing at Gray.

Celine offered a nervous laugh. "Just a business lunch. Mom, this is Grayson Buckley," Celine said, motioning toward a now-standing Grayson. "Gray, this is my mom, Dr. Monica Benson."

"A pleasure, Dr. Benson," Gray said as he shook her hand. "Welcome to Bucksville."

"Thank you, Mr. Buckley," Monica answered. "What a lovely town. Buckley? Bucksville? Any connection?"

"Gray, please. And guilty," Gray answered. "My family founded the town."

"How interesting! So, the Buckleys have been here for generations!"

"Indeed, we have," Gray answered.

Celine glanced between them as she shifted her weight from foot to foot. She forced another smile as an awkward pause filled the space between them.

"Why don't you join us?" Gray offered.

"Oh, no, I've interrupted your business meeting. I don't want to butt in."

"No interruption at all!"

"Thank you so much for your hospitality, Gray, but I'm exhausted after my trip. I hoped to grab something light and take it to my room to settle in."

"Are you sure?" Gray questioned.

"Positive. Though I hoped to catch you for lunch tomorrow, Josie. Are you available?" Monica asked as she glanced at Celine.

"Oh, yes. I'm available," Celine answered. "Meet back here around noon?"

"That sounds great! I'll see you then!"

"Okay!" Celine said in an overenthusiastic tone.

Monica stepped away from them before she twisted to face Celine again. She grabbed her arm and squeezed it. "Sorry for not texting, Jos. I wanted it to be a surprise."

"You succeeded! I'm surprised!" Celine answered with a nervous laugh.

Monica chuckled as she squeezed Celine's arm again. "It's good to see you, Josie." She offered another smile before she wandered to the counter to peruse a menu.

Celine collapsed into the chair across from Gray. With her jaw set, she focused on her plate as she picked at what remained of her food.

"You okay?" Gray asked, his eyebrow raised at Celine's behavior.

"Just perfect," Celine answered as she bit into a fry.

"You may want to try a better portrayal of 'okay,'" Gray suggested. "Your mother is stealing glances over here at every opportunity."

"Why is she here?" Celine whispered.

"I suppose she missed you and Damien," Gray offered.

"That's another strange thing. She comes without calling or texting. She just shows up! And then she doesn't even mention Damien. Don't you find that odd?"

Gray shrugged. "I don't even know the woman so I can't help you there."

Celine sighed. "Trust me, something's off."

"And it's made you very jumpy."

Celine widened her eyes at him. "Gray! The last thing we need right now is Josie's mother wandering around town. Do you realize how difficult this may become to hide what's going on here?"

"Why not tell her?"

Celine narrowed her eyes and offered an unimpressed

glance. "That should go over well. Hi, Mom, great to see you. By the way, Josie, the girl you raised, was a mere shell holding me, Celine Devereaux Buckley, a centuries-old witch, until I reawakened. Just FYI! How's your burger? Aren't the fries great?"

"Perhaps that's not the best way to break it to her."

"There's no good way to break it to her, Gray. She can't know."

"Damien and Michael survived it."

"Damien and Michael are scraping by. And they are not Josie's mother."

"We'll get through it, and she'll go home. It's only tempo-rary, Celine." He reached for her hand across the table.

Celine pulled her hand away and into her lap. "Not a good idea. She doesn't realize we're married."

"If she has any deductive powers, she ought to realize I am in love with you in one glance."

"Let's hope she's devoid of those powers. The last thing we need is her questioning our relationship or sticking around longer than expected because of it. Especially with Marcus still running around town."

"He hasn't caused you any trouble, has he?"

"No," Celine answered. "But still... he's unpredictable. Which is the last thing we need with Monica Benson in town."

"With any luck, she's just in town for a few days to visit with her lovely daughter and her nephew, take a bit of a vacation and she'll be on her way soon."

"Fingers crossed."

"Finished?" Gray asked as Celine finished the last of her fries.

"Yes. I should get going and warn Damien."

They stood and Gray tossed a few bills onto the tabletop. "I suppose a kiss is out of the question."

Celine offered him a single, stony glance in response.

"Well, then, I shall look forward to one in the confines of our home tonight. Until then, goodbye, Josie," he said with a wink.

"Goodbye, Gray," she answered. "I'm going out through the hotel."

Celine glanced toward her mother. The waitress was delivering her a takeout container. Celine took the opportunity to disappear into the hotel lobby. She hastened across the small entryway and pushed outside into the cool spring air.

She gulped in a few breaths as she hurried down the sidewalk away from the hotel and café. Her mind spun out of control as she scurried toward the Buckley estate. Why had Monica Benson shown up without warning? How would they hide the truth from her? What would Damien say when she dropped this bombshell? Why hadn't Monica mentioned Damien at all?

She hoped Gray's assessment proved correct and Josie's mother's visit was short-lived. With any luck in a few days, Monica Benson would be headed back to New York none the wiser to her daughter's new life.

Celine veered off the road and onto the winding drive cutting through the Buckley estate. A sense of safety enveloped her as the tall trees closed around her.

As the drive grew steeper, Celine swung onto another path leading to the beach bordering the property. She breathed deep as the ocean came into view. The smell of salt filled her nostrils. The waves crashed onto the beach, pulling the smaller rocks further out with them as they receded.

Celine listened to the rumbling of the rocks as they rolled down the shore, allowing the sound to fill her mind as she sought to slow her racing thoughts. With her arms crossed, she stared out at the waves.

"Fancy meeting you here," Damien's voice called, interrupting her meditation.

"D!" she exclaimed. "I missed you at dinner last night and breakfast this morning. Everything okay?"

"Yeah, just… busy."

She narrowed her eyes at him. He was hiding something. She'd have to delve into that after delivering the surprising news. They needed to focus on a plan while Monica was in town.

Her hesitation prompted Damien to continue. "I'm just… with what you said about the thing in the in-between, I've been really thinking it through. And avoiding Gray. So, I don't tell him. And then there's the thing with Michael…"

Celine interrupted him. "Thing with Michael? What thing with Michael?"

"Oh, ahhh…" Damien stammered. "Probably shouldn't tell you but I will, just don't say anything, okay?"

Celine nodded. "Of course."

"He's been having second thoughts about staying here."

Celine raised her eyebrows at the admission. "He's hesitant about signing the papers for the branch creation. He feels like he doesn't belong. I just… he does, right? You think so, right? Because I do. I really don't want to lose my friend."

Celine grabbed his arm and squeezed it. "He belongs," she assured him. "He'll come around. We'll make sure."

Damien nodded. "Cool, thanks." He stared out across the sea for a moment and swallowed hard. "I belong, too, right?"

"Yes! Of course, you do! What kind of question is that, D?"

Damien shrugged. "I don't know. While Michael and I were talking last night, he said he wasn't connected to any of us. And I said neither was I. And then that thought just plagued me all night."

"So that's why you missed dinner and breakfast," Celine concluded.

Damien nodded.

"D, that's ridiculous. You're my cousin. You're my family."

"But I'm not. I'm Josie's cousin. And Josie's not real."

Celine shook her head and grasped his hand. "I will always consider you my family, D. Now, no more of this nonsense. Deal?"

Damien chuckled. "Deal."

"I need to talk to you about something…" Celine began when a new voice entered the conversation.

"Well, well, well, if it isn't the dynamic duo of Celine and her trusty sidekick, Damien," Marcus called as he strolled down the beach toward them.

Celine rolled her eyes and sighed under her breath. Marcus was the last thing she wanted to deal with at this moment. She glowered at his approaching form.

"What do you want, Marcus?" she asked.

"Oh, merely to say hello. Perhaps have a chat about the weather."

"Oh, yeah right," Damien barked. "Here to make more threats? Offer another ominous warning?"

A smirk crossed Marcus's face and he arched an eyebrow. "Ah, I see we've shared the tale with dear Damien."

"I'll ask again, what do you want, Marcus?" Celine questioned.

"Such hostility. And for no reason. I'll chalk it up to your nerves, dear. And leave you both to your brooding. Au revoir, dear Celine."

"Listen, buddy," Damien began, waving his finger at Marcus as he stepped in front of him, stopping his departure.

Celine grabbed his arm to pull him back.

"Careful, Damien," Marcus warned. "As entertaining as I

find you, my patience has its limits." Marcus sidestepped him and continued down the beach.

"That guy has some nerve," Damien complained as Marcus strolled down the beach and away from them.

"Let him go," Celine answered. "We have another problem to deal with."

Damien shook his head. "I'm fine. And we'll handle Michael, too. He'll get through it. And we'll solve your issue. I've been giving that some thought…"

"No, not those," Celine interrupted. Damien stopped speaking and stared at her. "Josie's mom is in town."

Damien's eyes widened and his jaw fell open. "What?!" he exclaimed. He paced in a circle among the rocks, running his fingers through his brown hair. "Aunt Monica? Are you serious?"

"Unfortunately, I am. She showed up at the hotel today while Gray and I were having lunch."

"You didn't know she was coming?"

"No! I would have told you, D."

"Oh, this is terrible. Just terrible!" Damien lamented. He stood with his hands on his hips, shaking his head at the latest turn of events.

"A sentiment I agree with," Celine replied.

Damien continued his head shaking. "There's no way I can keep all these secrets from her. None. Zero probability."

"You're doing okay with keeping the secret about the Duke's warning from Gray."

"Yes, because I have literally avoided seeing him since I've found out!"

"I don't expect you'll get away with that with Monica," Celine said. "She's asked about lunch tomorrow." Given their conversation earlier about Damien's misgivings regarding his familial connections, Celine omitted the fact that Monica failed to mention Damien to her at all.

Damien clamped his hands onto his head. "Oh no," he murmured. "Tell her I'm sick."

Celine's eyebrows shot skyward and she opened her mouth to respond but Damien cut her off. "No, no, don't tell her that, that'll make it worse. Tell her I'm busy. Really busy. Tons of work. Can't get away."

Celine cocked her head at him. "First of all, telling her you're too busy for lunch also won't solve the problem. She'll hear 'I'm drowning in work' and make sure she checks on you to ensure that you are all right."

"True," Damien said.

"And second, I don't think you can use that excuse for the duration of her stay. Which sounds like it may be lengthier than either of us would like?"

"Really? Did she say how long?"

"She didn't, but I overheard her with the hotel clerk saying her plans were open-ended."

"Ugh," Damien groaned. "Are you kidding me?"

"I'm not."

Damien remained silent for a moment. "Man, I hope that guy doesn't spout off about you being Mrs. Buckley like he did to me and Michael! We'd never explain that away."

"Yes, that is definitely a complication we do not need."

"So, the plan is we tell her nothing, right?" Damien inquired.

"That's my plan, yes," Celine admitted. She brandished her bare left hand. "I pulled the wedding ring off before she could spot it, introduced Gray as a business associate, and left it at that."

"Why can nothing ever go right? First Marcus's warning,

then Michael and now this." Damien shook his head for the third time.

Celine reached out and took his hand. "We'll get through it. Just… don't give too many details. Maybe she's just in town for a visit since it's been almost a year since we moved and she'll leave shortly after she sees both of us."

Damien knit his brows. "Aunt Monica… just in town on a quick visit to see both of us… Doesn't that seem… implausible?"

"I thought so, too, but what else could it be?"

Damien shrugged. "I don't know but why not text or call? Tell us she'd like to see us or that she's planning a trip up. Why the sudden appearance out of nowhere?"

"It's odd to me, too, but we've never lived this far from her. Perhaps it is just some kind of maternal instinct. A need to see her children. It's been almost a year."

"I guess we'll find out." Damien kicked a stone across the beach. "And I just got used to calling you Celine. Now I've got to remember to call you Josie again."

Celine chuckled at his predicament. "You have an entire day to practice."

Damien rolled his eyes. "An entire day on pins and needles worrying I might say something wrong to Aunt Monica. I really love Aunt Monica, but I really don't want to have lunch with her tomorrow."

"Let's just hope it solves the problem. With Marcus Northcott slinking around, I'd really rather Monica be as far away from this as possible."

"That bastard would spill the beans just to watch the fallout," Damien said, his eyes narrowing as he stared down the beach in the direction Marcus had departed.

"It's not that. Don't get me wrong. I do NOT want Monica finding out about all this, but," Celine responded, "she was Josie's mother for twenty-five years. I don't want anything happening to her. I do not want her to become collateral damage in the war with Marcus."

"Do you think this may be what he was referring to?" Damien questioned.

"His warning? That Josie's mom was coming to town?" Damien nodded and Celine shook her head. "That doesn't seem like Marcus. Returning here because Josie's mom was coming is the biggest mistake of my life? Doesn't add up."

"No, you're right, it doesn't. That seems a bit extreme. Even if this all goes sideways and she finds out about you, I can't see that being the biggest mistake of your life."

"Marcus always regarded my marriage to Gray as the biggest mistake of my life. Whatever is coming, he'd equate it with being more extreme than that. A human learning the truth about me wouldn't even rate on his scale."

"Back to the drawing board, I guess," Damien said with a shrug.

"Let's take a walk before we go back to the house," Celine suggested.

"Best idea I've heard all day," Damien responded.

The pair strolled down the beach, avoiding any further discussion about Monica Benson. For much of the walk, Damien remained lost in thought. Celine interjected comments here and there, receiving only minimal responses from Damien.

They climbed through the sea cave and up to the pathways winding through the pine trees. The pair spent the better part of the afternoon on a winding pathway back to the house.

Raindrops drove them inside as another spring storm passed through the area. As large drops splashed on them, they made a dash for the house, slipping inside just as the deluge began.

"Whew, good timing," Damien said with a chuckle. "Oh, or did you do that?"

Celine giggled. "No, I keep telling you I don't control the weather."

"Well," Damien conjectured, "you do, sort of. Every time you fight with Marcus, the skies get cloudy, and thunder starts."

"That's different," Celine said.

Gray descended the stairs into the foyer. He lifted his eyebrows at the scene between them. "Laughing and joking? Have you told him yet?" he questioned.

"Huh?" Damien asked, his eyes going wide. "What? No! No, Celine hasn't told me anything. There's nothing she told me at all. Nothing. There's no secret or anything."

Gray crinkled his brow at Damien's babbling. Celine realized the reason: his nerves.

"Yes, I told him."

Damien shook his head as he began to reply. Celine continued before he could. "He knows Monica is here."

"Ohhhhh," Damien said as realization dawned on him. "Yeah. Oh, yes, about Aunt Monica. She told me, yes. Not good."

"Celine feels the same," Gray replied, his brow still furrowed at Damien's responses.

"With any luck, lunch tomorrow will do the trick and she will be on her way after a brief visit," Celine answered.

Gray arched an eyebrow, glancing at Celine's hand. "Let's hope so. I detest seeing that ring off your finger."

Celine winced as she dug into her sweater pocket and retrieved her wedding band. "Sorry, slipped my mind after I left the diner." She slid the band onto her left ring finger. "Better?"

"Much," he said with a kiss to her cheek. "Cocktail before dinner?"

"Sure," Celine answered.

"No, nope, not for me. I need to check my email and finish some code. And I've got a few projects. I really should run."

"Okay," Gray answered. "See you at dinner."

"Yep! Or not. I may not come. I don't know. We'll see. I'm pretty busy. Really, really busy," Damien said as he inched backward toward the stairs. He started his journey upwards still facing Celine and Gray. He stumbled up a step before regaining his balance. "Okay, see you later!" he shouted as he spun and raced up the stairs.

Gray followed his retreating form with a puzzled stare. He shook his head as Damien disappeared around the corner at the top of the stairs. "He is odd."

"He's nervous. The Monica thing threw him."

"Is it wise to let him speak to her?" Gray asked as they entered the sitting room.

Celine accepted the brandy he poured her as she answered. "I'm not sure there's much choice."

"She didn't mention him, perhaps it's avoidable."

Celine's brow wrinkled as she turned pensive. "I am surprised Monica didn't mention Damien at all, though I'm sure it was just a slip of her mind. She didn't inform me of her plans. So, she may have been surprised when she ran into me."

"Perhaps leave him out of your lunch tomorrow."

Celine shook her head in response. "Celine, the way he babbles, he'll almost certainly say something you'll both regret."

"I'm not going to tell Damien she didn't even ask about him."

"Why? It may relieve him."

"No. He's… that's not a good idea."

"He's what?"

Celine took another sip of her brandy. "He's feeling like he doesn't belong because we're not actually related. I'm not going to tell him his aunt, the person he is actually related to, didn't even ask about him."

Gray rolled his eyes. "He's being a bit ridiculous, wouldn't you say?"

"No, I wouldn't," Celine countered. "Both he and Michael have been through a lot. He's just started to process the idea that we're not related."

"You braved Shadow World and crossed to another universe with Marcus Northcott to save his life. He can't possibly believe you don't want him here."

Celine shrugged. "I think he realizes that deep down, but he's allowed to have a misgiving here and there."

"Just as long as he doesn't have a misgiving in front of Josie's mother and cause you more trouble than you need."

"Believe me, Gray, my fingers are crossed."

* * *

Celine scanned the cloudless horizon as the sun climbed in the morning sky. The waves lapped at the rocks below her, quieting overnight as the weather improved. Perhaps the better weather signaled a better turn in events.

While Marcus's words rang in her mind, she pushed them to the side. She had two other problems facing her. Michael's wavering regarding his decision to stay could prove problematic. While he had the right to make his own choice, his departure would upset the balance Damien depended on to bring normalcy to his situation. And while Damien's friendship with Alexander was budding, the loss of his fellow human friend may prove devastating. Beyond that, the lasting effects Michael endured from witnessing the events he'd experienced could not be monitored easily if he returned home.

Celine sighed as she turned her mind to the more immediate problem. In a few hours, she and Damien would meet with Monica Benson for lunch. While she felt love and tenderness toward the woman who raised her during her second childhood, the revelation of her true form may prove too much for her mother. And place Monica in a similarly dangerous position like Michael.

With any luck, their lunch today would produce no extraneous questions. She hoped Damien's nerves remained in check so Monica's suspicions were not raised.

Celine tore her eyes from the horizon and stalked into the trees behind her. She wandered the pathways with no direction in mind. After fifteen minutes of meandering, a house rose in front of her beyond the trees.

Celine continued toward it and knocked at the front door. After a moment, Alexander greeted her. "Celine! What a lovely surprise. Come in!"

"Thanks, Alex," Celine answered as she stepped into the foyer.

"Tea?" he offered. "I was about to have a cup."

"Please," she said with a smile as she strode toward the sitting room.

She eased into an armchair as Alexander poured her a cup of steaming hot tea. She took a sip before speaking. "How have you been?"

"I'm doing well. And you? How are you coping with the Duke's presence?"

"All's quiet on the western front," Celine answered.

"But?" he prodded.

"With Marcus one never knows," Celine admitted. "I suppose we're all a bit on edge still."

"Is Damien?"

"Damien is almost always on edge."

"We were getting together for chess almost every evening. I haven't seen him in several days. Is there anything amiss?"

"Oh," Celine answered with a nod. "Yes. Josie's mother is in town. She arrived yesterday."

Alexander puckered his lips.

"Damien's been understandably nervous about meeting with her today. He's been avoiding everyone."

"I see. I assume he is afraid of saying something he shouldn't?"

"Yes," Celine admitted. "Monica isn't aware of anything going on here. And we'd like to keep it that way. Damien is afraid he may spill the proverbial beans to her with a slip of the tongue."

"Poor boy. He does tend to babble when he is nervous."

Celine smiled over her teacup at his assessment. "Which makes him more nervous," she said with a chuckle.

"Perhaps he should avoid his Aunt Monica. Feign illness?"

Celine shrugged. "I'm not certain that will work."

"It will make her suspicious and more determined to speak with him," Alexander assessed.

Celine nodded. "Which is why it's best to just go to lunch and hope for the best."

"Though the plan does little to settle Damien's nerves."

Celine shook her head as she sipped her tea.

"I suppose you'll have your hands full for a few days at least. I shall miss my chess buddy."

"He may need your chess games more than ever," Celine responded.

Alexander smiled at her. "I won't complain. I do enjoy them."

"So does Damien. And I enjoy the budding friendship between you. It's good he's got someone to talk to outside of me."

"He seems to be adjusting well," Alexander noted.

Celine nodded in agreement. "He is. Though he still has his hiccups."

"Anything to be concerned with?"

"Nothing much. Apparently, Michael is questioning his decision to stay, which of course led Damien to question his."

"Why?"

"Michael pointed out he had no real connection to any of us. And, in kind, Damien concluded he didn't either."

"He is your cousin."

"He is Josie's cousin, which he feels may not be the same."

Alexander arched an eyebrow as he considered the statement. "To be clear," Celine added, "I do not feel that way."

"Have you told him?"

"Yes, I have."

"And?"

"It seems to have settled him. At least I hope so."

"I shall reinforce that to him if given the opportunity."

"Thank you."

"Of course, Celine. I understand you would be devastated if he decided to leave."

"Yes, I would be. He's my family, blood or not."

"Have you spoken with Michael about his decision?"

"No, but I plan to. I don't want to push. It's complicated between us."

"If there is anything I can do, please ask."

"I will, thank you. Though the best course of action may be to support Damien and let Damien support Michael. They've been through a lot together. They have the biggest connection."

"Yes, they have been. Perhaps that is what's prompted Michael to reassess."

"I'm sure. This life isn't easy, especially for a human. But

Damien will be devastated if he leaves, so I'd like to prevent that."

"I'll keep my fingers crossed he decides to stay. For Damien."

A moment of silence passed between them before Celine spoke again. "Anything else new?"

"Thankfully, no."

"You haven't noticed anything… odd? Out of the ordinary? Off?"

"Uh-oh," Alexander murmured.

Celine glanced at him. "What?"

"That question suggests something is wrong. Or that you suspect it is."

"No, it doesn't," Celine countered. "I'm just checking."

He raised his eyebrows at her statement.

"It's true! We've had almost two months of relative peace. I'm waiting for the other shoe to drop."

"Always suspecting danger is lurking around the corner?"

"With Marcus skulking around, yes."

"He hasn't caused you any trouble, has he?"

"Not yet. But if he's about to, I'd prefer to know. Hence the question."

"Understood," Alexander replied. "And in answer, no. I have not sensed anything."

"Good."

"Perhaps this war has finally wound down."

"Let's hope," Celine replied.

They settled in for a second cup of tea and a game of chess before Celine departed to ready herself for her lunch with Damien and Monica Benson.

As Celine returned to the main house on the wooded path, she spotted Damien hurrying toward her. Her stomach dropped and a lump formed in her throat.

"There you are!" he shouted from a distance.

Celine quickened her pace. "What's wrong?" she questioned as she hurried toward him.

Damien puffed with exertion as they met on the path. He bent over, placing his hands on his thighs as he caught his breath. Celine placed a hand on his back and leaned over toward him. "D, what is it? What's happened?"

CHAPTER 5

Damien heaved out another breath. "It's almost time to go to lunch! I thought you were ditching me."

Celine breathed a sigh of relief as she straightened. "Of course not, D."

Damien pulled himself upright. "Whew," he said. "Sorry, got nervous there for a second."

"We have over an hour!" Celine said.

"Yeah, but still… I couldn't find you and then it got later and later. I guess I just panicked. Sorry." He gave her a sheepish glance.

Celine wrapped her arm around him. "It's fine. I was having tea with Alexander."

"Oh! Oh, that's nice. Yeah. I missed my games with him. After our conversation, I was afraid I'd say something wrong."

"He mentioned missing your games."

"Yeah, I'll get down there soon. Maybe tonight or tomorrow. With Aunt Monica in town, I may need the distraction."

"Alexander will be happy to provide it."

They began their return walk to the house. "You haven't gotten any texts from Aunt Monica, have you? Maybe canceling our lunch?"

Celine pulled her phone from her pocket and swiped at the screen. "Nope, nothing," she confirmed as she shoved the phone back into her pocket.

"Darn," Damien said with a frown.

"D, it'll be fine," Celine assured him.

Damien ceased walking and ran his fingers through his hair. He glanced around, avoiding eye contact with Celine. "I'm going to say something wrong. I just know it. There's so much going on that we can't explain. So much has happened. I just…" He threw his hands in the air.

Celine grasped his arms and pulled them down, sliding her hands around his and squeezing. "D, it's fine. You won't say anything wrong."

"What if something I say leads her to find out about you? Like who you really are?"

Celine heard the barely discernible quiver in his voice revealing his deep-seated worry.

"Then she finds out who and what I really am," Celine answered. "And she'll accept it, or she won't."

"I don't want to be the reason that happens," he said.

"It doesn't matter if you are, D."

"It does."

"To me, it doesn't."

"So, you won't hate me forever if Aunt Monica finds out everything and it's my fault?"

"No, of course not."

A small half-smile formed on Damien's lips.

"Don't get me wrong, I'd prefer to avoid that," Celine replied. "But if you say something and she ends up finding out…" Celine paused and shrugged. "Well, that's the way it is. I'm not going to hate you."

He breathed out a long breath. "Okay, good. I mean, I'd like to avoid Aunt Monica finding out, too. But I feel better realizing if she somehow figures it out because I say something stupid, you won't hate me."

"I could never hate you, D. Now, let's go get this lunch out of the way so you can relax."

"Yeah, I'll relax when Aunt Monica is on her way back home. I love Aunt Monica, but she couldn't have picked a worse time to visit."

"Well, she could have visited when I was missing," Celine suggested.

"Okay, smarty-pants, yes, she could have picked a worse time, I guess."

Celine chuckled as they emerged from the woods and approached the house. "I'm just going to change and be right down."

"Sounds good. I'll be here."

"I hope so," Celine said as she climbed the stairs. "I'd be mad if you ditched me."

"No chance, Celine, no chance."

Celine wound through the halls to her suite. She shut herself inside and stood perusing her closet. She pulled a few items out and scanned them before returning them. With a sigh, she shoved items aside as she searched for the perfect outfit. Her nervousness approached Damien's level of jitters as the clock ticked closer to the meeting.

She preferred Monica to be none the wiser to the entire tale of Celine Devereaux Buckley. Would they pull it off, she wondered? She hoped they could, she ruminated, as she pulled a light pink tunic sweater from her drawer.

She donned it before brushing her hair and slicking on pink lip gloss. She strode toward the door before she paused. With a shake of her head, she retraced her steps and headed to the jewelry box on top of her dresser. She slid her wedding ring from her finger and placed it inside before closing the top and stalking from the room.

"Ready?" she asked as she descended the stairs toward a waiting Damien.

"Nope," he answered, "but there's no stopping it."

"If it's any consolation, I'm also looking forward to the end of lunch."

"Then let's go get this done!"

They drove the short trip into town. Damien eased the car into a space a block from the cafe. He blew out a long breath as he turned the ignition off. "Last chance to run," he said as he glanced at Celine.

Celine chuckled. "Come on, D. It'll be okay."

She slid out of the car and joined Damien. They made their way to the cafe and entered, finding the seating area empty.

"Maybe she went home," Damien suggested as they selected a table.

"No such luck," Celine said as the familiar form of Monica Benson appeared in the doorway leading to the hotel lobby. She smiled and waved.

Monica caught sight of them and smiled. Celine detected a note of surprise in her expression as she spotted Damien. "Hi!" she exclaimed as she approached them, her arms outstretched for a hug.

"Hi, Mom," Celine said, giving her a squeeze.

"Damien!" Monica said, turning to him. "I'm so glad you could come, too! I wasn't sure if I'd see you today."

"Of course, Aunt Monica," Damien said as he pulled her in for a hug. "Celine… er, I mean, I cleared my schedule once Josie told me you were in town."

"Well, I'm sorry to throw the unexpected monkey wrench into your schedule, but on a whim, I decided I had to see my babies."

They dropped into their seats around the table. Monica perused the menu. She glanced over it at Celine and Damien. "I hope you two are eating," she said as she noticed their closed menus.

"Yeah, sure," Damien answered. "I know what I want. We eat here a lot."

Monica raised her eyebrows. "Not too much, I hope. You both need good home-cooked meals."

"We eat a lot at home, too," Damien said with a nervous chuckle. "Most times. But when we eat out, we eat here. There's not a lot of restaurants in town."

The waitress interrupted any further babbling on Damien's part.

"Oh boy, can't wait for those fries," Damien continued after she left.

"So, how are you both settling in?" Monica inquired.

"Perfect," Damien answered. "Couldn't be better. Not that we weren't happy in New York. We were. But we're happy here, too."

Monica smiled at him. "That's good. Everything okay, honey?" she asked, noting the nervousness in his voice.

"He's fine," Celine answered. She patted his hand. "He had some unfinished work I pulled him away from."

"Oh, I'm sorry, honey," Monica answered. "Though you do need to take a break sometimes. I've always said you throw yourself into your work far too much."

"You're right! You got me! That's it, just concerned about work."

"And a move like this is also taxing," Monica added. "Relocating can really throw you. There're always unexpected things that crop up. There's the adjustment to a completely new life, new town, new people."

Damien offered another nervous chuckle. "Yep," he said as he gulped from his water glass.

"So, Mom," Celine began, "how long do we get to see you for? I'm surprised your surgery schedule isn't fully booked!"

"Well, that's why I didn't call or text ahead of time. It was all very last minute. On a whim, I just decided I needed to see my babies. I called Dr. Reynolds and he very graciously offered to cover for me."

"On a whim?" Celine questioned. "That doesn't sound like you."

Monica shrugged as their food was delivered. "What can I say, I missed you."

The waitress set the food down in front of each of them. Damien took the opportunity to shove a fry into his mouth. Celine assumed he hoped it kept him quiet. She suppressed a chuckle. After his fry, he gulped more of the water, freshly poured by the waitress.

"So, who's Celine?" Monica asked.

Damien choked on the water. "What?"

"When I said I wasn't sure if I'd see you, you mentioned someone named Celine. Who is she?"

"A friend," Celine answered.

"Yep, right. A friend, that's right."

Monica arched an eyebrow at Damien. "Only a friend?"

His face pinched in confusion. "Yes, of course. What else would she be?"

Monica offered a slight smirk. "A girlfriend, perhaps?"

Damien glanced at Celine, his jaw agape as he formulated his response. Celine shook her head and responded for him. "No, just a friend, Mom."

Monica shifted her gaze between them. Her attention prompted a further explanation from Damien. "She's right. She's married, actually. To Grayson Buckley."

"Oh, I see," Monica responded. "And Grayson Buckley is the man you were at lunch with yesterday, right, Jos?"

"Mmm-hmm," Josie murmured as she poked at her salad.

Monica knit her brows in thought as she considered the information. Silence fell between them for a moment. Damien's leg bobbed up and down under the table. Celine slid her hand onto his knee to steady it.

"Neither of you mentioned buying a house, have you found a new place yet? Your old place wasn't on the market very long at all!"

"No, it sold really quick!" Damien answered.

Monica nodded. "So, have you bought a place? I'd love to see it!"

"Ahhhh," Celine hesitated. "We haven't bought anything yet."

"Oh," Monica responded. "Well, where are you living then? Oh, please don't tell me you're living in a motel or something."

"No, nothing like that," Celine assured her.

"I'd love to see your rental! Any chance it might be rent to buy?"

Celine swallowed hard. "Well…" she began as Damien cut her off.

"We're living with the Buckleys," he spouted as he shoved another fry into his mouth.

Celine closed her eyes for a moment at the admission. This wouldn't bode well, she suspected.

"What?" Monica questioned, her eyes wide and her eyebrows high on her forehead. She set her fork down on her plate as she prepared a follow-up comment.

"It's temporary," Celine assured her.

"Josie, it's been almost a year. How temporary could this be?"

"Property is difficult to come by in Bucksville," Celine offered. "So temporary can be relative." She shrugged and returned her attention to stabbing pieces of lettuce with her salad fork.

Monica leaned back in her chair and crossed her arms. She narrowed her eyes at the pair of them. Celine felt the weight of the woman's stare. She recalled a similar sensation after they had been caught sneaking in after curfew.

"Is there anything I should know?" Monica prompted after a moment.

"Know?" Damien questioned. "Huh? I don't know what you mean!" He pushed the food around on his plate with his fork.

"You two are acting awfully strange. I'm beginning to suspect there's something you aren't telling me."

"There's nothing we're not telling you. The Buckleys were kind enough to open their home to us," Celine responded.

"And it's huge! We barely see each other! Like ships passing in the night," Damien added.

"I'm sorry but I find it odd that these Buckleys would open their home to you after just meeting you."

"They're very nice people," Damien replied.

"Uh-huh," Monica murmured. "Given how strange the two of you are acting, I'm going to say this straight out. I hope there's nothing going on between either of you and these Buckleys."

Damien's fork clattered to his plate. "What?" His leg resumed its panicked bobbing. "That's crazy."

"Is it?" Monica questioned. "The first name you mention is another man's wife." She turned her attention to Celine. "And you seemed awfully chummy with Mr. Buckley yesterday. The very married Mr. Buckley."

Damien chuckled. "Yes, absolutely, it is. Totally ridiculous."

"Josie?" Monica inquired.

"I can't believe you're asking me this," Celine answered.

"That's not an answer."

"I am NOT having an affair with a married man, Mother," Celine answered. "You raised me better than that."

"Yes, I did. And I am glad to hear it, but I still find the situation very strange. I'm not certain I approve at all."

"You should come to dinner there," Damien burst out. "Then you can see it's all on the up-and-up. Nothing scandalous at all. No affairs or anything tawdry. We have separate rooms almost a house away from them."

Monica cocked her head at the suggestion. Celine held her breath, hoping she'd decline. In seconds, her hopes were dashed. "All right. Even if there is nothing going on, I'd like to learn more about the people my children are living with."

"Tomorrow night, then?" Damien suggested.

"Shouldn't you check with the Buckleys?"

"If they aren't okay with it, we'll text you," Damien offered.

"All right, tomorrow night, then."

They finished lunch avoiding any other delicate questions about their situation. After hugs, kisses and promises of seeing each other the next day, Celine and Damien departed from the cafe and headed for their car.

They slid inside. Damien slumped against the steering wheel, banging his head against it. "I can't believe I invited her to dinner. I can't believe I called you Celine. Like five seconds in and I mess up. Ugh!"

"I can't believe she accused one or both of us of having an affair."

Damien frowned. "Well, technically, you are involved with Grayson Buckley. And, technically, he is married."

Celine twisted to face him. "Yes! To me!" she exclaimed.

"Also, technically true."

"Very funny, D."

"Ugh," Damien groaned again. "I'm sorry. I'm such an

idiot. I don't know what I was thinking. Why did I invite her to dinner?"

"You're not an idiot. You thought it would prove to her that nothing's wrong."

"This is going to make it so much worse," Damien lamented.

"While I agree it may be uncomfortable, it may not make things worse. We may be able to pull this off. Charlotte, Avery and the kids are out of town which makes this easier. It'll be just us, Mom and Gray."

"Yeah, that won't be uncomfortable at all."

"Perhaps we should invite Alexander."

"That's a great idea. Maybe she can accuse you of having an affair with him, too!"

Celine shot Damien a wry glance. "He's not married, so I'll only be in partially hot water."

"How can we explain where Celine is?"

"Business trip?"

"Yeah, good idea. Celine's away on business."

"I guess we should go inform Gray and Alexander. It'll take Gray the next twenty-four hours to get over the fact that we'll need to pretend not to be married for Josie's mother."

Damien fired the engine. "Yep, let's go give him another reason to hate me."

Celine chuckled as they pulled from the spot and Damien aimed the car at the Buckley estate. Within minutes, he eased the car to a stop near the front door.

"Gray!" Celine shouted as they stalked into the foyer. "Gray!" Only silence met them. Celine shrugged. "Guess he's not home yet."

"Good, it buys me some time before he wrings my neck."

"He's not going to wring your neck. Though he won't be happy. Perhaps we should…" Celine's voice trailed off as her gaze focused on an object on the foyer table.

"What? Try Alexander and see if we can strong-arm him into our ridiculous plan to snow Aunt Monica into believing we've got no involvement with the Buckleys?" He paused, waiting for an answer but received none. "Celine?"

"What's this?" she questioned.

Damien followed her gaze, finding a long nondescript white box tied with a satin navy ribbon on the table. Celine sauntered over to the table and ran a finger along the box.

"There's a card," Damien said as he teased it from under the ribbon. "It has your name on it."

Celine glanced at the card in his hand. Her name appeared scrawled on the envelope. She grabbed it from between his fingers and slid the envelope open. She pulled the small card from inside and read it.

You're still the one for me.

She turned it over searching for a name but found none. "From Gray?" Damien questioned.

Celine shrugged as she pulled the ribbon off the box. "There's no name." Celine shook the lid off the box, finding a single, long-stemmed red rose inside.

"Must be. Aww, he sent you a rose, that's sweet."

Celine lifted it from the box. "Ouch!" she squealed. A drop of red blood appeared on her fingertip where the rose's thorn pierced her skin. She sucked away the droplet, her finger already healing from the small wound.

"Whoa!" Damien exclaimed, his eyes going wide.

The rose shriveled and blackened. Its petals decayed and its leaves curled, becoming brittle and brown.

CHAPTER 6

Celine grimaced at it. She shoved it back in the box and slammed the lid on. She gathered the box and card.

"What are you going to do with it?"

"Toss it," Celine said. "And then we'll head to Alexander's and convince him to do a little play-acting at tomorrow's dinner."

"Sounds like a plan."

* * *

"Let me get this straight," Gray said as he paced the floor of the sitting room, a brandy in his hand. "You decided the best course of action was to invite Monica Benson for dinner here so we can all pretend Celine is Josie, I'm married to someone else and convince the woman that there is nothing going on between us?"

"That's not exactly how it happened but more or less, yes," Damien responded.

"Would you mind explaining to me why you thought this was a wise course of action?"

Damien shrugged. Celine answered for him. "It doesn't matter. We were backed into a corner of sorts and it's now the course of action we have. And it's not that bad of an idea."

Gray's eyebrows shot skyward. "Not that bad of an idea? The woman saw us together for ten minutes and suspected something was going on between us. What will she imagine is happening after she witnesses us together for an entire night?"

"After you profess your undying love for Celine, who is out of town on business, she won't imagine anything!" Celine countered.

"Until she spies a romantic glance across the table."

"Perhaps you should avoid any glances across the table, romantic or otherwise, cousin," Alexander suggested.

Gray glowered at the suggestion. He folded his arms across his chest. "This is a terrible idea."

"If we cancel, it will appear even more suspicious," Celine argued.

"What if Gray doesn't attend?" Alexander proposed.

"Again, suspicious. The whole point of this was to be transparent and show nothing's going on here," Damien said.

"Except there is!" Gray countered.

"But we won't tell her that," Damien said with a roll of his eyes. "Here is Josie's bedroom, a million miles away from Gray's, and here is Gray talking about his lovely wife, Celine, who is out of town. And here is Josie and Gray together with no spark between them at all."

"You see, Gray, simple," Alexander said with a grin.

"I cannot believe you are supportive of this plan," Gray complained.

"I don't see another choice. And I will do anything to support Celine and Damien."

"Ugh!" Gray exclaimed, tossing his hands into the air in frustration.

"There's a very simple solution to this," Michael suggested from his armchair near the fire.

Gray raised his eyebrows. "Oh? Perhaps you'd care to enlighten us."

Michael stood from the chair and sipped his brandy. "We'll tell your mom we're back together. Simple."

"I fail to see how that solves the problem," Gray spat.

Michael rolled his eyes. "If she thinks we're back together, she'll be so thrilled she won't even question your relationship with Gray."

"Thrilled?" Celine repeated.

"Your mother loves me, and you know it," Michael shot back.

Celine collapsed to the couch, her brows furrowing.

"He's got a point," Damien chimed in. "Aunt Monica does love Michael. He's the only boyfriend of yours she ever liked!"

Michael shot a brazen glance at Gray. Celine remained silent for a moment. "Okay, fine," she agreed at length.

"Celine…" Gray began.

She shook her head and held up her hand. "It draws attention away from us. She'll buy it. And once she does, perhaps then we'll be off the hook, and she'll stop prying."

"Yeah," Damien agreed. "Remember the end-game here is just to get Aunt Monica to stop asking questions and go home before she finds out that Josie is Celine who is a centuries-old witch and married to you, a centuries-old warlock."

"Would that really be so bad?" Gray questioned.

"I'm not sure we should find out if it is or isn't. I don't want her hurt, Gray!" Celine exclaimed.

Gray shook his head. "Fine, fine. We'll all play along and

hope she doesn't figure it out." Gray poured himself another brandy and sipped at it as he stared into the fireplace.

"Good," Damien said with a grin.

"With that settled, care for a game of chess before I return home?" Alexander asked Damien.

"Sure!"

Celine finished the rest of her brandy. "I'm going to leave you all to it. I'm heading up." She approached Gray and kissed his cheek. "See you later."

He tugged her arm as she turned to leave. He kissed her cheek. "See you soon," he said with a wink.

She smiled and nodded at him. "See you all tomorrow," Celine said.

She stepped into the foyer and pulled the sitting room doors closed behind her before she crossed the large space and climbed the stairs. As she navigated the halls, her mind twisted and turned through their situation.

With each passing moment, they fell deeper and deeper into their web of lies. How long would they need to continue these lies? Was it the best course of action? Perhaps they should tell Monica and let the cards fall where they may.

Celine sighed as she slogged through the door into her and Gray's bedroom suite. She pushed the doors closed and leaned against them. She shook her head. No, she ruminated, they couldn't tell Monica. She didn't want to face that. She couldn't predict her reaction. Others had reacted badly to the news. Some of them never recovered. Even if Monica could accept it, she didn't want the woman who spent twenty-five years as her adopted mother learning the truth about her.

Damien and Michael had accepted what she was, but it may prove too much for her scientifically-minded mother. In addition to disturbing her, it may cause her to view Celine in a different manner. In a sense, she may consider it like losing her child. The woman did not deserve that. She'd provided a loving, stable home to her throughout her life. She didn't deserve to be informed her child, Josie, did not exist.

With another sigh, Celine rubbed her thumb around her ring finger. She shut her eyes for a moment as her thumb found only a bare digit. Her head thudded against the door as she realized she'd forgotten to don her ring after returning from the lunch meeting.

Celine crossed the sitting room and entered the bedroom. She stalked to the jewelry box and pulled the wedding band from the box. As she slid it onto her finger, she acknowledged the dull pounding at her temples. As Josie, she'd been no stranger to tension headaches. As Celine, it surprised her to experience one.

She stared at the gold band around her finger. The throbbing in her head intensified. A tremor shook her hand. Celine curled her fingers into a fist before releasing it and wiggling her fingers. She expanded her fingers and gawked at her now-steady hand. Had she imagined the quiver?

She must have, she convinced herself. Likely a reaction to her tension headache. Though that, too, seemed to have eased. The stress of keeping secrets from Monica was likely catching up to her. She'd kept plenty of secrets in the past. None of them involved hiding something from someone she loved.

Once the visit from Monica concluded, Celine assumed everything would settle. At least she hoped so. For now, she craved rest.

* * *

Celine sprinted through the halls. Her upswept hairstyle escaped its pins as she darted down the hall and around a corner. She gasped for breath as she hurried through a random door. She closed and locked it behind her. She spun and pressed her back against it as her chest heaved up and down.

She glanced down, noticing her clothes for the first time. She ran her hand down the silk gown. Her brow furrowed. The style was from a bygone era. Why was she dressed like this?

Her mind flitted to another issue. She pulled her hand from her dress's fabric and held it in front of her. The gold of her ring glinted in the moonlight streaming from the window. Her hand trembled uncontrollably.

She gasped as she attempted to steady it. She found herself unable to stop the tremors. She grasped her left hand with her right and squeezed, pulling it against her body.

A noise caught her attention across the room. Celine glanced up and squinted into the darkness. The sound of a man's shoes clicked across the hardwood floor. A figure stepped forward into the moonlight. Hidden in the shadows, his face remained unidentifiable.

"Who's there?" Celine inquired.

She received no response.

"Marcus?" she inquired.

The crinkle in her brow deepened as she felt her hand move involuntarily. Her left hand pulled away from her body and reached toward the man's shadowy figure. It shuddered and shook as her fingers stretched toward him.

Celine gasped as she fought the uncontrolled action. She spun and flung the door open. With a terrified glance over her shoulder, she stumbled into the hallway. She raced further down the hall, meeting a dead end.

With her panic growing, she retraced her steps, rushing past the room she'd entered moments ago. As she approached the corner she'd rounded earlier, she found it closed.

Celine searched the wall for an opening but found none.

She spun around, her eyes darted frantically as she sought another escape. The wall at her back shoved her forward. With a sickening scraping, the wall pushed her toward the room her mysterious assailant occupied.

The wall at the other end pressed closer to her, too. It left her with no alternatives but to slip back into the room with the shadowy figure. She stepped inside as the walls slammed into each other. A brick wall met her gaze as she stared at the now-closed-off doorway.

Black clouds obscured the moon, plunging the room into darkness. Hands closed around her shoulders, warm breath wafted across her neck. Celine froze, her body stiff. Her hand trembled again as it reached for the man behind her. Her quivering fingers touched warm skin.

As the clouds sailed through the sky, moonlight filtered through the window. Ethereal white light streamed down onto her assailant. Celine twisted to glance over her shoulder. As his features began to form, she filled her lungs for a scream.

* * *

Celine shuddered as her eyes focused. She swallowed hard and glanced around. She stood in an unused bedroom several halls away from her own bedroom suite. Her face scrunched in confusion. How had she gotten here? She did not recall rising from her bed and wandering the halls to this place.

Thunder rumbled overhead and lightning lit the room for a moment. She spotted a figure out of the corner of her eye. Celine whipped around to face it. She saw only her reflection in the full-length mirror propped in the corner. It must have been her own movement that she spotted.

She took another glance around the room as she wrapped her arms around herself. She rubbed her arms as she shivered against the chill in the room. Her mind pondered the reasons she may have wandered to this room. She had never sleepwalked before, though she must have now. But why here? Perhaps she had roamed the halls aimlessly, she figured.

After spotting nothing, she shook her head and padded to the door. She jumped as her feet touched the cold marble floor in the hallway outside. She hurried onto the runner covering the floor and began her journey back to her bedroom.

As she walked, a dull ache returned to her temples. She rubbed at them. Her sleepwalking hadn't helped with her tension headache, she lamented, as she crawled back under her covers.

She squeezed her eyes shut as the dull pain continued to throb. Hopefully more sleep would help, she ruminated, as she drifted back to sleep.

* * *

Damien strode down the path toward the cliffs overlooking the ocean. With his mind a jumble, he hoped the soothing rhythmic sound of the waves and the fresh air would help to clear it. Thoughts pushed and shoved for attention as he strolled under the canopy of pine and deciduous trees. He struggled to focus on one train of thought.

He sighed as he shoved his hands into his pockets and selected one issue to dwell on: Celine's recent admission about the Duke's warning. What did it mean? Perhaps there was nothing to it, he considered. He shook his head. Not likely. Marcus Northcott was not the type of man who made idle threats. They had learned that over and over. If he said it, he meant it. But what was he warning her about? Why warn her at all?

He searched the depths of his mind for the meaning behind the odd admonition or anything related to it. After their return from Alterra, his recovery had been painfully slow. At least for his taste. Both he and Michael suffered from a lack of stamina, bouts of tiredness, and low body temperatures for three weeks. Perhaps he'd missed some clue while preoccupied with his own recovery.

Celine had spent much of her time fussing over him, keeping him company and ensuring he developed no long-term issues. She hadn't been away from him much, so she couldn't have experienced anything odd and forgotten to mention it to him.

Damien emerged from the woods. The ocean expanded across the horizon at the cliff's edge. He studied it as he listened to the waves pound against the rocks below. Another storm passed through last night, leaving the ocean angry this morning. He shuddered as he recalled the rumbles of thunder overhead as he attempted to sleep.

Attempted, he lamented. He hadn't gotten much rest at all. And not just because of the storm. His mind turned to the other prominent issue plaguing him: Monica Benson. A myriad of questions surrounded this issue, too.

Why did Aunt Monica arrive unannounced? The surprise trip went against every prominent trait she possessed. What would cause her to pick up and travel to Maine without even mentioning it to Celine or him?

And how would they keep their circumstances a secret? Damien rolled his eyes at his own behavior yesterday. As nervousness consumed him, he managed to bungle the lunch and invite a suspicious Aunt Monica to the Buckley residence.

As a result, they now planned to pretend Celine was Josie who was again dating Michael, that Gray's wife was out of town and that, besides living there, they had no serious connection to the Buckleys. Would they pull off the complex subterfuge? Would this manage to convince Aunt Monica that no intimate connection existed between Celine and Gray?

Damien hoped so. Admitting the truth to her was not an option. Things were too complicated to explain. He barely grasped it.

He recalled the conversations leading up to the lunch meeting. Celine also preferred to keep the woman in the dark. "Josie's mother" she had called her. He supposed that was the best term. After all, she'd had a mother as Celine. The woman died birthing her, but she'd still had a mother. Monica was Josie's mother, not Celine's.

This reminded him of his own tenuous connection to Celine. Or rather, his lack of connection to Celine. Michael questioned his reasoning for remaining in Bucksville. Perhaps he should do the same. Maybe he didn't belong either. Celine made him feel welcome and wanted. Maybe she felt sorry for him. Perhaps she preferred not to tell him to go home and let her return to her own life.

If Aunt Monica found out the truth, she certainly would advise Damien to return home. Once she realized Josie was merely a vessel carrying Celine inside her for twenty-five years and was aware of the constant danger that surrounded Celine, she'd insist Damien leave with her for his own safety.

He didn't want to leave. Though he wasn't sure how he'd argue with her over it. With no familial connection, he wouldn't have a leg to stand on with Aunt Monica. Despite being a grown man, he felt powerless to say no to her without good reason.

He hoped he could hold it together through the dinner to convince her all was well. Perhaps then she would return home, satisfied her children were safe and well.

A hand pressed against his back and rubbed up and down.

He jumped as he swiveled to face the person. "Hey!" Celine said with a smile.

He blew out a sigh of relief. "Celine! Whew! You scared me."

"Sorry. You okay? You looked lost in thought."

"I was, yeah," he said as he returned his gaze to the ocean.

"Feel like sharing?" she asked.

Damien shrugged as he formulated his thoughts.

"Uh-oh," Celine groaned. "That bad, huh?"

Damien ran his fingers through his hair with a sigh. "No, there's just so many things going on. I can't figure anything out on the Duke's warning. Then again my mind is consumed with the dinner I stupidly got us roped into tonight."

Celine slipped her arm around Damien's waist and gave him a squeeze. "We'll get through it," she said.

"Man, I hope so," Damien voiced. "If Aunt Monica finds out…" His voice trailed off.

"I prefer her not to know either. I'm afraid of her reaction, to be honest. And I don't want her hurt or disillusioned in any way."

"Yeah, all of the above for me, too, but also, I don't want her insisting I leave here."

Celine took a step back and glanced up at him. "Why would she make you leave?"

"If she finds out about what you are, she'll obviously figure out we're not actually related. And then she'll insist I get away from you and all this danger."

Celine pursed her lips. "D, you know I still consider you family."

"Yeah, I know," he said, "but the fact of the matter is: we're not."

"We are in every way that matters. Please tell me you realize that."

Damien remained silent for a moment until Celine prompted him again. "D? You do realize we are family, right? And that I don't want you to leave. Not at all."

He sighed before he responded. "Yeah, I do. I just… I don't want to leave either." He wrapped his arm around Celine and gave her a reassuring squeeze. "You're stuck with me. Unless Aunt Monica drags me home."

"She can't make you leave. You're not a child anymore."

"No, I'm not, but… I just don't want her mad at me. Ugh, the best outcome is we pull this off and she goes home none the wiser."

"I agree. That would be the easiest. Perhaps it's the coward's way out and I should just tell her, but… I just keep picturing the expression on her face as I say the words. And it's not good. She was so distraught when she admitted I was adopted, it would destroy her to realize…" Celine left the statement hanging between them.

"Yep," Damien concurred.

"On top of that, I'd rather she not hang around. Especially with Marcus lurking around every corner."

"And his ominous threat hanging over our heads."

Celine nodded in response, silent for a moment. "Well, let's hope tonight resolves all our problems," Celine said. "See you later?"

"Sure. Where are you off to?" Damien inquired as she started down the path.

"To see Celeste," Celine called. "It's best if she stays away from the house for a few days until Monica is gone."

"Good idea," Damien answered. "Good luck!"

Damien stared at Celine's retreating form as she continued down the cliffside path. He returned his attention to the horizon. After a moment, footsteps approached. A half-smile formed on Damien's face.

"Change your mind?" he asked as he spun to face the

approaching person. "Oh!" he shouted his expression changing in an instant from coy to concerned.

Marcus Northcott smirked at him. "Damien, fancy meeting you here."

"What do you want?"

"I am merely enjoying a stroll and taking in the picturesque views."

"On the Buckley property?"

Marcus raised an eyebrow. "Do you imagine they'd mind?"

"Yeah, I think they would. Especially if they knew about your threat to Celine."

"Threat? I've made no threats."

"Yeah, right. Your little stunt in the in-between suggests differently."

Marcus stalked closer to him, placing himself inches from Damien's face. Damien swallowed hard as he struggled not to back down. "I did not threaten Celine. Though consider yourselves warned regarding any incidents that may occur in the near future."

Damien's lips moved but he failed to form a response. Marcus pushed passed him, knocking him sideways. Damien stumbled a step before recovering.

Marcus twisted to face Damien as he continued down the path. "Oh, Damien?" he called. "Do be careful near the cliffs. One misstep could cost your life." He offered him another smirk before he strolled away.

A chill passed over Damien and he swallowed hard. Did Marcus Northcott just threaten him?

CHAPTER 7

*C*eline strolled down the seaside path toward Celeste and Teddy's home. The dull ache in her temples had amplified after her conversation with Damien.

Worry consumed her over Damien's state of mind. His upset over their lack of shared blood troubled her. She'd work harder to make him feel more welcome and at home with them.

Of course, his agitation wouldn't subside until Monica Benson returned to New York. With any luck, that would occur soon. Their ridiculous plan of pretending everyone wasn't who they really were for the dinner party seemed almost comedic, like something out of a sitcom. If the stakes were not so high and hiding the truth from Monica was not so important, she may have laughed at their silly plan.

Still, she ruminated, Damien's assessment proved correct. With Marcus Northcott's unexplained warning, they must convince Monica to leave. And quickly. Then she could turn her attention to Damien's difficulty accepting their relationship, Michael's restlessness and Marcus's threat.

Celine ceased walking. Her eyebrows pinched as she

glanced around. No longer on the path near the cliffs, she had wandered into the woods. She stood off the path near a large oak tree. She did not recall walking here. She must have been so lost in thought, she'd not paid attention to her wandering.

She winced as a sharp pain shot through her left arm. She pulled her hand from her jacket pocket and studied it. It trembled for a moment before ceasing its involuntary movement.

The stress of concealing her identity was taking a physical toll. She should tell Damien. No, she concluded, she couldn't. Not before the dinner party tonight. It would only add to his distress. She would wait and share it with him once they had successfully pulled off the subterfuge. Perhaps by then, the symptoms would disappear as the situation wound down.

She corrected her path and continued toward Celeste's house. She climbed the stairs to the porch and knocked at the front door. Celeste greeted her moments later.

"Celine! What a nice surprise. Do come in!" Celeste waved her into the foyer and motioned toward the sitting room.

Celine sauntered inside and plopped onto the sofa. A sudden wave of exhaustion passed through her, and she stifled a yawn.

Celeste eyed her. "Tired?"

Celine shrugged. "A little," she admitted.

"That's odd. Is something wrong?"

"Yes and no," Celine admitted.

"What is it, baby sister?" Celeste inquired as she pushed a lock of hair over Celine's shoulder.

"It's nothing major, but Josie's mother is in town."

Celeste's eyebrows shot up at the admission.

"Yeah," Celine answered at the gesture. "It's best if she

doesn't realize the truth, so we're all tripping over ourselves to keep it a secret."

"Oh?" Celeste questioned.

"It's all rather melodramatic," Celine admitted. "But we're having her at the house for dinner this evening in an effort to mislead her into believing Josie and Damien are living there temporarily while we look for a home."

"What does Gray have to say about that?"

"He's not pleased," Celine admitted. "Particularly since she's already practically accused us of having something going on, though she believes he's married to someone else. And in an effort to sway her away from that theory, Michael suggested we tell her we are back together."

"Josie and Michael, you mean," Celeste said.

"Right."

An entertained smile formed on Celeste's lips. "No, I cannot imagine Gray is happy with this plan."

"He isn't, though it's likely the best one we have to smooth things over and get Monica Benson on her way back home."

"Why did you invite her for dinner? That seems rather a terrible thing to have done."

"I didn't," Celine answered. "She showed up two days ago with no warning and asked to go to lunch. Damien and I met her yesterday and in a panicked moment after she accused us of strange behavior, he invited her to dinner to prove nothing was wrong."

"He really is terrible at lying, isn't he?" Celeste replied.

Celine nodded her head. "He is," she confirmed. "And in any other situation, I'd praise him for his honesty, but in this one, it's made rather a mess."

"Hmm," Celeste murmured.

"Anyway," Celine said with a sigh, "it may be best if you

stay away from the house for a few days until we sort this all out."

"Do you imagine she'll buy your little charade?"

"I hope so. Alexander is attending, perhaps he can divert some of the attention from the rest of us."

"I see. And how will you explain Gray's supposed wife's absence?"

"Business trip," Celine responded.

Celeste arched an eyebrow. "Well, I wish you luck with your deception. I hope it works in your favor."

Celine smiled as she climbed to her feet. "Thanks," she said as she embraced her sister. "I'll keep you updated."

* * *

Damien wandered the path back to the house. The encounter with Marcus Northcott ricocheted through his mind.

While he denied threatening Celine, he then proceeded to reiterate his warning, more or less. And on top of that, he made a veiled threat aimed at Damien.

The Duke's last statement rattled around in Damien's brain. He imagined falling from the cliff to the rocks below, his body broken by their sharp edges. The idea sent a shiver up his spine. Perhaps he shouldn't go near the cliffs for a while, he pondered.

He should tell Celine, he decided. Then he shook his head. No, he couldn't add to her distress before the dinner party. He'd tell her. But not until after the Aunt Monica situation was resolved.

* * *

Michael pulled on his blazer and straightened his tie. He considered the task that lay ahead of him. His eyes flitted to the folder of paperwork laying on the side table across his room. Unsigned paperwork was stuffed inside.

Michael's eyes lingered on the folder. He reached to his jacket's inside pocket and withdrew a pen. He stalked across the room and flicked open the folder. After shuffling to the last page, he uncapped the pen and pressed the tip to the paper.

Michael froze. With a shake of his head, he capped the pen and returned it to his jacket pocket. He couldn't bring himself to sign it. Why, he wondered?

He stared at himself in the mirror above the dresser.

"You're never this indecisive," he said to his reflection.

Yet, still, in this situation, Michael couldn't manage to pull the trigger on the Northeast deal. What held him back?

He turned his mind to the situation awaiting him downstairs. He'd seen the car pull up and Mrs. Benson climb from inside it. She stared up at the gigantic mansion before ducking in through the front door.

He wiggled his eyebrows. He could pull this off. His feelings may have changed once he learned Josie was Celine, but he still cared about her. He cared about all of them.

"So, why can't you admit that and just sign the damn papers?" he asked himself.

Because you don't belong here; you're nothing to them, his brain suggested.

With a shrug and a shake of his head, Michael pulled the door to his room open. He didn't understand what held him back but if he continued to experience this reluctance, he didn't see what choice he'd have but to leave.

For now, though, he had a job to do.

* * *

Celine smoothed her dress as she stared in the full-length mirror. She caught sight of her gold wedding band glinting in the light. She scowled as she slid it from her finger. Her eyes squeezed shut as the dull ache thudded against her temples.

When she opened them, she caught sight of a flash of burgundy in the mirror. She blinked and did a double take as she focused on her baby pink sheath. She glanced behind her, searching for the source of the color but found none. Her eyes must be playing tricks on her, she assumed, as she stalked to her jewelry box and dropped the ring inside.

This night couldn't end soon enough, she lamented. She rolled her shoulders back before she strode from the room and down to the sitting room. There she found Damien sipping a brandy. He poured himself a second as she entered the room.

"Brandy?" he asked while pouring her a glass before she responded.

"Thanks," she said as she collected it.

"To pulling this off and ending this nonsense," he said as he clinked his glass against hers.

"From your lips," she replied.

She sank onto the couch. Her fingers tapped the glass as they waited for the dinner party to begin. Damien sat across from her, his leg bobbing up and down.

"There isn't enough alcohol in this house for tonight," he said.

The comment elicited a small chuckle from Celine. It was short-lived as the front door opened. "Right this way, ma'am," Henry's voice resounded.

"That's our cue," Celine announced as she stood.

"Here goes nothing," Damien said as he joined her.

"Thanks, Henry," Celine said as she entered the foyer.

"Oh, you're welcome, M..." he began as Damien cut him off.

"Yeah, thanks a lot, we appreciate it. We'll be seeing you." He wrapped his arm around the man and guided him to the front door, practically shoving him out.

"Evening, Mr. Sherwood," Henry said as he nodded his head at him and crinkled his brow at their reaction.

"Hi, Mom," Celine said.

"Hi, honey," Monica answered, giving her a kiss on the cheek and a hug.

"Come in!" she responded, motioning to the sitting room.

"Drink?" Damien inquired as they entered and closed the doors behind him. He poured a sherry for Monica, handing it to her before he eased onto the couch next to Celine.

"Thank you, hon. Wow, this house is impressive."

"Told you it was huge!" Damien said. "We barely see people most days it's so big. We just wander around like we live here alone. Barely even see the Buckleys." Celine gave him a discreet tap and he nervously sipped his brandy.

"When we met for lunch yesterday," Celine began, "you picked up on a strange vibe between us."

"I still do," Monica replied.

Celine took a deep breath and shot a glance at Damien before continuing. "Well, the truth is, we are hiding something. Not intentionally, we just weren't planning on telling anyone yet. It's not a deep, dark secret or anything. But the thing is..."

The doors to the foyer swung open, interrupting Celine's speech. Michael appeared in the doorway. He scanned the room, his eyes settling on Monica. A coy smile crossed his boyishly handsome face. "Mom," he cooed in a smarmy tone.

He strode toward a surprised Monica. She set down her drink and stood to greet him. Her eyebrows shot up and a slight smile formed on her face. "Michael?!"

"In the flesh," he said as he grabbed her hands and squeezed them. "You look great! I swear you don't age."

She chuckled. "Oh, Michael, you're such a flatterer. What are you doing here?" She shot a stunned glance to Celine.

Michael pushed between Damien and Celine as they took their seats. Damien hopped to an armchair as Michael and Celine settled on the couch. Michael wrapped his arm around Celine with a grin. "Didn't you tell her yet, babe?"

Celine glanced at him with a fake smile plastered across her face. "Not yet, I was just about to."

"Tell me what?" Monica asked, her tone rushed with excitement.

"Michael and I..." Celine began.

"Jos and I are giving it another try," Michael burst with a grin.

A smile crossed Monica's face. "Oh, really? That's fantastic news! Josie, why would you want to keep that from me?"

"Well..." Celine started.

"We're taking it slow," Michael answered for her. "We want it to work this time. We just didn't want to have anyone's preconceptions about us ruin it."

Monica offered an understanding nod. "Isn't the long-distance difficult, though?"

Michael shook his head. "Carlyle Industries is opening a branch here. When I ran into Josie here, I realized it was meant to be. Destiny. I'm planning to take charge of the new branch and relocate."

The entrance of Gray and Alexander interrupted further conversation. Celine sprang from the couch as they entered. "Mr. Buckley! Good to see you!" she exclaimed.

"Good evening," Gray answered as he headed toward them. "Welcome to my home, Dr. Benson. It's a pleasure to see you again." He offered a handshake before motioning toward Alexander. "This is my cousin, Alexander Buckley. Alexander, this is Josie's mother and Damien's aunt, Dr. Monica Benson. I hope you don't mind my taking the liberty to invite Alexander to dinner with us."

"Not at all, Mr. Buckley."

"Gray, please," he interrupted her.

"Gray," she repeated with a smile, "it is, after all, your home. Thank you for welcoming me into it. I hope I'm not imposing, but I was curious to see where my children are living." She turned her attention to Alexander. "And it's a pleasure to make your acquaintance, Mr. Buckley."

"Oh, please call me Alexander," Alexander said.

"Oh, what a charming accent. You're from the UK?"

"Born and bred, yes," Alexander answered.

"When did you move here?"

"Oh, quite a while ago," Alexander answered. "Though my accent remained."

Gray wandered to the drink cart to pour brandies for himself and Alexander as Michael pulled Celine to sit next to him on the couch.

"We're so pleased to have Josie, Damien and Michael living with us. They help fill up the house," Gray mentioned.

Monica turned her attention back to Michael. "You're living here, too? I didn't realize."

Michael nodded. "I am, yes. It's nice to be so close to Josie," he answered, giving her a kiss on her cheek.

Gray glowered at him as he handed a brandy glass to Alexander. "This may be worse than watching her work with Northcott," he breathed.

"That's quite a comparison, though I am uncertain it applies."

"Oh, it applies. And at least she hates Northcott."

"Let's hope it's only for one night," Alexander answered before sauntering toward the group.

Gray raised his voice. "Perhaps we should head into the dining room."

Monica knit her brows at the announcement. "Oh! Shouldn't we wait for Mrs. Buckley?"

"No," Gray answered. "She's out of town on business, so it'll just be us."

"Oh, what a shame, I hoped to meet her."

"Perhaps another time," Gray answered. "Shall we?"

The group set their drinks down and stood to depart as the sitting room doors burst open. Celine's eyes widened at the sight. She swallowed hard as the woman spoke.

CHAPTER 8

In a breathless voice, Celeste said, "Oh, I do hope I'm not late. I rushed right home when I heard the news!" Her full lips curled up into a devilish grin.

She crossed the room, giving Gray a kiss on the cheek. "Darling, it's so good to see you." She turned her attention to Monica. "And you must be Mrs. Benson. What a pleasure to meet you."

"Mrs. Buckley, I presume?" Monica answered as she extended her hand.

"Celine, please."

Alexander was the first to recover from his shock. "We were about to head into the dining room."

"Of course," Celeste answered. "Please, follow me, Mrs. Benson."

"It's doctor, dear," Gray interjected.

Monica chuckled as she wrapped her arm around Celeste's. "Oh, Monica, please!"

"What a pleasure to meet Josie's mother and Damien's aunt..." Celeste's voice trailed off as she led Monica from the room.

Gray shot Celine a glance. "Why did you invite her?" he whispered.

"I didn't!" she shot back. "In fact, I told her NOT to come."

"Perhaps we shouldn't dally," Alexander prompted.

"He's right, babe, we should go," Michael said.

"If you call me that one more time, I'm going to blast you with a fireball right after this is over," Celine warned.

"And I'll be right behind her," Gray added. "It's a little over-the-top."

"I'm trying to make this look legit!" Michael argued.

"And, by the looks of it, it's working," Damien added.

Michael offered an imperious expression.

"It won't be if we don't go," Alexander suggested again.

"Coming?" Celeste inquired as she appeared at the door.

Everyone plastered a smile on their faces before following. "Of course, dear," Gray answered.

They filed into the dining room. Celine plopped into a chair next to Michael as her head continued to pound. Celeste relinquished her seat at the head of the table to Alexander in favor of sitting next to Gray and across from Monica.

Mrs. Paxton delivered their meal and left them to dine. Celeste and Michael dominated the conversation with Alexander chiming in as needed to fill in any gaps. Celine shot Gray a discreet glance partway through the meal as Celeste yammered on about a fake trip to a ski resort she and Gray had taken. She clapped her hand across Gray's forearm as she choked out her comical tale between giggles.

On the positive side, she noted, their plan appeared to be working. She eyed Monica, who chuckled at Celeste's fake story, thoroughly entertained and most likely bamboozled by Celeste's act.

As the meal wound down, Celeste excused herself. "If you

don't mind, I am exhausted from my trip. I'll retire early and allow you to catch up. Gray, coming?"

"Right behind you, dear. Monica, your company was a pleasure."

"It was," Celeste agreed. "I hope we'll see you again soon."

"Oh, thank you both for your hospitality. I enjoyed the dinner so much."

"Think nothing of it," Celeste answered with a grin. "We so enjoy having everyone here. Why, they are just like family." She motioned toward Michael, Celine and Damien.

"I, too, shall say my goodnights," Alexander chimed in. "Monica, such a pleasure meeting you. Goodnight, everyone."

"Goodnight, Alexander," Celeste said. "Let me walk you to the door."

She disappeared with Alexander and Gray in tow. Everyone stood for a moment in awkward silence before Celine elbowed Michael. "Oh, wow," he said with a fake yawn, "I'm exhausted, too. I think I'll head up and leave you three to catch up."

"How kind of you, Michael, though you always were so well-mannered."

"I'm so pleased we got to catch up. Will we have another chance to see each other before you head home?" Michael inquired.

"I'm not certain, I do need to be getting back, so in case we don't see each other, it was a pleasure seeing you again, Michael. Good luck with the new branch, though I'm certain you'll make it a success. And please take care of my baby."

Michael wrapped his arm around Celine and pulled her close. "Of course. You have my word on that. Well, if I don't see you again, have a safe trip home."

"Thank you."

Michael excused himself. "Shall we go to the sitting room?" Celine suggested.

"If you don't mind, honey, I'm going to head back to the hotel. I'm exhausted! It must be the travel."

"Oh, of course," Celine answered. "I'll get the car for you."

"I'll get it!" Damien offered. "Meet you in the foyer." He dashed out the door, leaving Monica and Celine alone.

Monica smiled at Celine as they followed Damien's disappearing form into the foyer. He returned a few moments later. "Henry'll be right around with the car," he puffed.

"Thanks, honey," Monica said. She smiled at them both. "It's good to see you both so happy. The Buckleys seem like lovely people. And you both seem to fit in well here."

"We do," Celine assured her.

"Yep. Like a glove. Better, actually. Like we belonged here. Or…"

Celine nudged him with her elbow into silence. "We're both very happy here."

Monica pushed a lock of Celine's hair behind her shoulder as she nodded. "Well, I realize you're both very busy, but I was hoping to spend a bit more time with you. Perhaps a girls' trip this Saturday? Shopping in Portland, maybe? I hear it's a lovely spot to shop!"

Celine smiled at her. "Sure. Portland's a great place to shop."

"Sounds like a plan. Sorry, honey," she said to Damien. "Unless you'd like to join us for shopping."

"Pass," Damien said without hesitation. "No way. I'll leave the shopping to the experts."

Monica chuckled. "I figured."

"Do you have plans for the next few days until Saturday?" Celine questioned.

"Not really," Monica answered, "but I realize you're both busy with work. I'm not here to impose and I can entertain myself."

"You're not imposing, Mom," Celine said. "I've got a few

things happening on Friday, but maybe tomorrow I could pop into town and show you what Bucksville has to offer. We've got a really quaint shopping district. Maybe you can find a souvenir for Dad and Dr. Reynolds. You probably owe him big for the last-minute cover."

"Good point," Monica said. "Well, if you have the time, I won't say no to spending some extra time with my baby."

"Sounds like a plan," Celine responded. "I'll meet you around eleven tomorrow?"

"Great!" Monica said. Gravel crunched in the driveway outside. "Sounds like my ride." She reached out and pulled Damien into an embrace. "Mmmm," she said as she kissed his cheek. "I'm so glad you invited me, honey."

She turned to Celine. "I'll walk you out," Celine offered as Monica gave her a hug. Monica grasped her hand as they strolled from the foyer.

Damien waved as they stepped through the door. A sigh of relief escaped his lips as the door swung closed. He squeezed his eyes shut as he refocused his mind after the trying dinner experience. A drink was in order, he decided. He could nurse one as he waited for Celine to come in from sending Aunt Monica on her way.

Damien plodded through the sitting room doors.

"Need a drink, buddy?" Michael questioned.

"Hey, whew, you startled me. I thought you went to bed. And yes, absolutely, I do."

Michael chuckled as he poured a brandy for Damien and handed it off. "I circled back, figured we'd want to celebrate our victory." He clinked his glass against Damien's before taking another sip.

"Yeah, seems to have worked like a charm," Damien agreed as he sank onto the couch. "Aunt Monica is so glad to see we're happy and settled and yada, yada. Sounds like she's planning on going home after this weekend."

"Sticking around that long, huh?" Michael inquired.

"Seems so," Damien answered. "She made a shopping date with Celine on Saturday, but it sounded like she might go home after that."

"Perfect," Michael responded. "Looks like we pulled it off. Celine's just got to get through that shopping trip."

"Yep. And tomorrow. She's heading into town to keep up the appearance of normality and show 'Mom' around tomorrow."

Gray and Celeste slipped through the doors. "Is she gone?" Celeste inquired.

"Celine's walking her out. She should be gone any minute," Damien confirmed.

"Did she buy it?" Celeste questioned. "Is it finished?"

"I'm not certain, but it seems it may have done the trick," Damien responded. "She said she's happy to see us so settled and all that."

"Wonderful," Celeste said with a devilish grin. "It seems my acting skills are still up to par."

"Don't hurt your arm patting yourself on the back, Celeste," Michael replied. "You were hardly the main attraction."

"Oh, I suppose you imagine the credit goes to you for your performance as the doting boyfriend."

"If the shoe fits," Michael said.

"Let's stop arguing over who pulled this off and hope this problem is solved," Gray interjected.

"Does it appear to be?" Alexander asked as he slipped into the sitting room.

"Damien believes it may be. We're waiting for Celine. She's walking Monica out."

Alexander frowned. "She isn't here?"

"No," Gray answered. "Monica must be talking her ear off out there."

"I saw the car pull down the drive before I returned."

Damien crossed to the large window overlooking the front of the house. "He's right. The car's gone."

"So, then where's Celine?" Gray questioned.

Damien pulled the doors to the foyer open and strode out. He swung the front door open and stepped onto the gravel drive. No sign of the car, Aunt Monica or Celine existed. He spun in a circle as he scanned the area. "Not out here," he announced as he came back through the door.

"Perhaps she went upstairs already," Gray suggested.

"That doesn't seem right," Damien disagreed, "but maybe."

"I'll check," Gray said as he hurried up the stairs. He returned moments later. "She's not in our suite, nor either of your rooms. I checked the kitchen, too, not there."

"So, where is she?" Damien exclaimed as he leapt from his seat on the couch.

"Did she head into town with Monica?" Michael suggested.

Damien dug his phone from his pocket. "I'll text her," he said as he typed furiously with his thumbs.

A gust of cool air blew through the sitting room as the foyer door banged shut. "That must be her," Gray said as he strode to the door.

"Evening, Mr. Buckley," Henry's voice said. "Just wanted to let you know Dr. Benson is back at the hotel, safe and sound."

Damien narrowed his eyes at the statement. Henry made no mention of Celine. "And Mrs. Buckley? Did she go with you?" Gray questioned.

"No, sir," Henry answered. "Left her right out front after she said goodbye."

Damien joined Gray in the doorway. "You left her outside. She didn't go with you."

The man's forehead crinkled. "Naw," he answered. "Something wrong?"

"No, Henry," Gray answered. "Thank you for letting us know."

"Of course, Mr. Buckley." He nodded his head before spinning on his heel and heading out to the car.

"What's going on?" Michael asked as he joined them.

"Celine didn't go with him," Gray answered.

"So, then, where the hell is she?" Damien questioned.

"Just calm down," Gray shouted. "Let's think this through."

Damien stalked around the room, his finger perched on his lips. His mind spun out of control. With the Duke's haunting warning at the forefront of his thoughts, he imagined the worst. The Duke had kidnapped her once. Had he done it again?

"Calm down?" he shouted. "Are you serious? Celine is gone. Again! Don't tell me to calm down."

"We don't know she's gone. She could be anywhere," Gray responded.

"That's exactly the point!" Damien argued.

Michael offered Damien another brandy. "Sit down, buddy. Let's take a minute."

Damien snatched the glass from his hands with a sigh. "You've got to be kidding me," he murmured as he dropped onto the couch.

"I'm with Damien," Celeste chimed in. "This is unlike Celine. She'd want the support of her family after a trying evening."

"I can't believe I'm saying this, but I agree with Celeste," Damien said.

"Where would she go?" Alexander posed.

Damien leapt from the couch to resume pacing. "Mind-clearing walk in the woods?" Michael suggested.

"At night?" Damien asked. "No." He shook his head. "I hate to even say this but… what if she didn't go willingly?"

The group remained silent at the suggestion.

"Why is no one saying anything?" Damien blurted. "The Duke is in town. And he…"

"Let's not panic," Gray interrupted.

"Right," Michael agreed. "Let's have a look around. See if we can find her."

"Gentlemen, I suggest we go in pairs," Alexander said.

"Good idea. Alexander, you're with me," Michael replied.

"We'll head toward my home," Alexander suggested.

"Perfect. Damien and I will head toward the cliffs and check her swing," Gray answered. "Celeste, you stay here. If she returns here, text me."

"All right," Celeste agreed.

Damien sped out the door with Gray trailing behind him. "Slow down, Damien," Gray said.

"We have to find her."

"I'm anxious to find her, too, but…"

"No buts," Damien argued.

They hurried down the path to the cliff's edge, calling for Celine as they went. No responses met their shouts. An empty horizon stared back at them as they emerged from the wooded path at the cliff's edge.

Damien's shoulders slumped. "Come on, Celine. Where are you?" he murmured.

"Let's try the gazebo," Gray suggested.

"Okay," he answered with a nod.

They hurried down the cliff-front path toward the gazebo overlooking the ocean. Damien squinted into the distance as they approached it. In the moonlight, he detected movement. His step quickened as he hoped Celine provided the source of the motion.

"Celine?" he called as he closed in on the gazebo. He received no response.

He raced up the path with Gray following close behind. As he rounded the gazebo, he spotted her blonde hair blowing in the breeze. "Celine!" he exclaimed.

He slowed as he climbed the step onto the gazebo platform. "Celine?" he questioned again.

The swing inside glided back and forth in a lazy dance. Celine's form sat slumped in the seat. Her limbs hung limply. Her head leaned to the side, lips parted, blank eyes staring straight ahead.

CHAPTER 9

amien's eyes widened, and he gulped as he glanced at Gray. "Celine?" he squealed, his voice cracking with concern. Gray stopped the swing's rhythmic motion as Damien knelt in front of her. He took her hand in his and squeezed it. He blinked and swallowed hard again as he noticed the rise and fall of her chest. The steady movement cast aside his worst fears about her.

"Celine!" Gray shouted. He grasped her shoulder and shook her.

She continued to stare ahead, her eyes still focusing on nothing. "What's wrong with her?" Damien croaked.

Gray grasped both her shoulders and wiggled her again. "Celine, wake up," he insisted.

Her eyes blinked in slow motion and her mouth closed. She sniffed and her forehead wrinkled. Her eyes darted around as she swallowed. She squirmed in her seat.

"Hey, Celine," Damien said with a smile at her. "You okay?"

She nodded as she continued to glance around. "Why did you disappear like that?" Damien continued.

"I didn't," Celine answered.

"Celine, what's wrong?" Gray inquired.

She pursed her lips and glanced up at him. "I think we need to talk."

* * *

Damien handed Celine a glass of brandy as everyone settled in the sitting room. They'd walked her back from the gazebo after finding her unresponsive there. After feeding a fib to Celeste about a mind-clearing walk and sending her on her way, Celine sipped at the amber liquid before beginning her explanation. Her left arm ached as though she'd lifted a heavy object and her head felt like a rubber band squeezed it.

She considered the most recent event. She had no memory of wandering to the gazebo after her mother departed in the car. Her situation was deteriorating faster than she expected. The cause still escaped her.

Gray squeezed her shoulder. "Take your time."

She took another sip of her brandy. Damien sank onto the couch next to her. The expression on his face betrayed the depths of his worry.

Celine inhaled and blew out a long breath. "Okay," she began. "Sorry for frightening everyone."

"It's okay," Gray answered. "Just tell us what's going on. How did you get out there?" Gray paced the floor in front of the fireplace as he awaited an answer.

"I've been losing time," Celine admitted.

The confession stopped Gray in his tracks.

"You've what?" Alexander questioned.

Celine nodded at him. "Losing time, yes," she affirmed.

"For how long?" Gray inquired.

Celine shrugged. "For a few days. It's happened three times."

Gray shut his eyes and shook his head. "Celine, why didn't you tell us before?"

Celine pursed her lips. "Hey, give her a break, she's had a lot going on," Damien began.

Celine waved at him to stop. "It's okay, D," she said. "I didn't realize until now."

"You said it happened three times, but you didn't realize?" Gray asked.

"In retrospect, after a time loss as severe as tonight's, I do. But when they occurred before, I didn't realize what was happening."

"Tell us about them," Alexander prodded.

"Wait, back up," Michael interjected. "What do you mean you've been losing time?"

"One minute I'm one place and the next thing I realize, I'm somewhere else and I have no idea how I got there or how much time has passed," Celine explained.

Michael nodded. "Okay, and this happened before tonight, too? How did you not realize?"

"The first time it happened, I was asleep. I woke up in another bedroom. I figured I sleepwalked during a nightmare."

"And the second time?" Damien asked.

"I was lost in thought. I was walking outside, and my mind was preoccupied. I figured I just didn't pay attention to where I was going and ended up veering into the woods instead of staying on the path.

"What were you preoccupied with when you lost time the second time?" Gray inquired.

Celine sighed. "Celine?" he prompted.

She frowned before continuing. "There was an incident between Marcus and me in the in-between before we returned."

Gray grimaced. "How did I know he'd factor into this?" he grumbled.

"Incident?" Michael inquired. "What did he do? Damn it! I knew we shouldn't have left you in there alone."

"Same thing I said," Damien lamented.

Gray knit his brows. "You knew?"

"I told him a few days ago."

"You've got to be kidding me," he groused. "You waited weeks to tell anyone, and your first choice was Damien?"

"Hey!" Damien exclaimed.

Celine rubbed her temples. "Please can we stop bickering? I didn't think anything was going to come of it, but I couldn't get it out of my head. So, I told Damien. But now with the time loss, I'm worried there may be more to this than I originally thought."

Damien wrapped his arm around Celine's shoulders. "Sorry, Celine. Just take your time."

"I agree with Damien," Alexander said. "Let's not jump to conclusions before we've heard what Celine has to say."

Celine winced as she moved her left arm around and let her hands drop into her lap. "After Michael and Damien left us alone there, Marcus had some sort of… moment," she said. "He grabbed me and tried to convince me not to come back here."

"Surprise, surprise," Gray murmured.

"I would have chalked it up to Marcus being Marcus, but something disturbed me about his behavior."

"I'm not understanding how this is any different from his normal behavior," Michael admitted.

"Marcus's normal bad behavior is carefully crafted. This seemed… panicked, hurried, sincere."

Gray guffawed. "Please do not use that man's name and the word sincere in a sentence together."

Celine sighed. "It's the best way I can describe it. He told me not to return and said it would be the worst mistake of my life."

"I'm with Michael," Gray cut in. "This is nothing more than his normal ploys."

Celine leapt from the couch and paced the floor. "That makes no sense, Gray."

"Why not?"

"Why give you the red vial to return me if he planned to convince me to leave?"

"Perhaps he intended it to have the opposite effect and made a mistake with the formula," Gray suggested.

Celine shot him a glance. "Marcus doesn't make mistakes. Anyway, either way you slice it, he warned me not to return and claimed it would be the biggest mistake of my life. Things have been relatively calm, but I couldn't shake the warning."

"So, you told Damien," Gray said.

"Yes, a few days ago I confided in Damien."

"And?" Michael prompted.

"And nothing," Celine answered. "Monica showed up and our attention shifted."

"Yeah," Damien confirmed, "we didn't spend a lot of time discussing it. I was so focused on not screwing things up with Aunt Monica that I didn't spend my usual amount of time fixating on it."

"I assumed any symptoms I experienced were related to stress I felt over her visit."

"Symptoms? Beyond the time loss?" Alexander questioned.

"Yes," Celine nodded. "Tiredness, a dull headache and an achy arm." She rolled her left shoulder again.

"Have you spoken to Mille about it?" Gray asked.

"Not yet," Celine admitted. "I will as soon as she returns from her trip."

"Perhaps you should text her," Gray suggested.

"I doubt she can do anything from where she is. She'll be back tomorrow night. I'll speak with her about it then."

"Good," Gray answered.

"Man, that guy is really something else," Michael said as he leapt from his seat on the couch.

"I agree," Gray answered.

Celine furrowed her brow. "Marcus? This doesn't fit his M.O."

"Wreaking havoc and causing you pain doesn't fit his M.O.?" Gray questioned. "You've got to be kidding! This is typical behavior for him. I'm surprised he waited so long!"

"Why warn me first?" Celine inquired.

"Why not? It put you on edge for weeks before he struck," Gray said.

"And I still hold his soul marker. Why antagonize me now? I assumed the relative calm and peace between us was a direct result of that."

"Perhaps he assumes he'll soon have control back once the adjudicator finishes its repose," Alexander suggested.

"That won't be for at least another month," Celine answered.

"So, he's getting a head start," Gray snapped.

"You must admit, Celine, it's not surprising if this stems from Marcus," Alexander said.

Celine slumped her shoulders. "No, you're correct. He's the most likely suspect."

"We'll have to determine what it is he's doing to induce this and stop it," Alexander replied.

"Perhaps Millie can help with that, too," Gray suggested.

"Yes, let's hope so. In the meantime, would you mind going over your symptoms again?" Alexander prodded. "In detail and with a timeline."

Celine recounted the details to them again. As she

concluded her tale, Damien sank onto the couch and buried his head in his hands. "Ugh," he groaned. "Here we go again. This guy never stops."

"Welcome to the last two centuries of our lives, Damien," Gray answered. "I'm going to call Millie and have her come home early."

"She's due back in less than forty-eight hours, Gray, I'm not sure she'll get back any sooner even if you summon her. Besides, I'm meeting Josie's mom tomorrow in town anyway, so even if she gets back early, I may be tied up."

"Do you think that's wise?" Michael questioned.

"Yes, I do," Celine answered. "We're on the verge of convincing Monica Benson nothing is going on. We've got to keep up the act. I'm hoping after our shopping trip in Portland on Saturday, she'll be on her way."

"Portland?" Gray questioned. "Celine, he's right, this isn't a good idea."

"Canceling on her may make the situation worse."

"You shouldn't go alone. Damien, go with her."

"That's probably a super terrible idea," Damien answered. "If I go, I'll probably say something to ruin the whole thing."

Gray narrowed his eyes at Damien. "Oh, for heaven's sake, pull yourself together and deal with it."

Celine shook her head. "Even if he wanted to, Monica asked for mother-daughter time."

"I doubt she'd object to her nephew tagging along," Gray argued.

"It would seem odd and with Damien's inability to lie, it's a disaster waiting to happen."

Damien nodded in agreement. "She's right."

"Perhaps your doting boyfriend," Gray growled, scowling at Michael.

"I'd love to, but again, Celine is probably right. Monica may get suspicious."

"I thought she loved you," Gray retorted.

"She does," Michael answered. "But if she asked for mother-daughter time, she's going to insist on getting it. If she doesn't get it Saturday, she'll stay until she does."

"He's right. Michael tagged along on a mother-daughter lunch once. It ended with a spa day two days later since Michael 'ruined our girl time.'"

Gray sighed. "That woman can't leave soon enough."

"It seems we shall have to let Celine handle Josie's mother," Alexander said. "Though if you experience any symptoms, particularly those that could lead to a time loss..."

"I'll make my excuses and get home as quickly as possible," Celine finished. "Though there doesn't seem to be any apparent warning signs."

"I'll stay in town tomorrow. If anything happens, text me and go to the office. I'll meet you along the way," Gray said.

"Okay," Celine agreed. "I don't plan to be long with her tomorrow. Saturday may be another story."

"Let's hope Sunday's story is Monica Benson is on a train and heading home," Michael said.

"Fingers crossed," Celine said.

Gray crossed to her and wrapped his arm around her shoulders. "You should rest."

She nodded in response.

Damien approached her. "Get some rest, Celine," he said as he hugged her. "We'll figure this out, okay? We'll stop him."

Celine nodded. "Thanks, D." She twisted to face Michael and Alexander. "And thanks to you both."

"Of course, Celine," Alexander answered.

She and Gray left the room. Celine trudged to their bedroom suite, changed and crawled into bed. She hoped the rest improved her situation. Gray stroked her hair. "Get some rest, Celine. I love you," he whispered.

With her eyes closed, she grasped his hand and squeezed

a silent "I love you" before she drifted off to sleep.

* * *

Damien stalked through the woods with no direction in mind. His brain wandered through the latest developments as thoughts tumbled around his head. Last night, they'd found Celine unresponsive. She'd wandered to her gazebo and sat on her swing without having any knowledge of traveling there. She also complained of a headache and an achy arm.

The strange and seemingly unrelated symptoms disturbed him. In the past, these physical symptoms often stemmed from the Duke. He was certain the vile man was at the heart of this issue, too.

Why did he continue to torment Celine? She'd assumed when she returned from Alterra with his soul marker they may experience some break in the madness. Not even that could stop the maniac from his heinous torture.

What was his endgame, Damien wondered? What did he hope to achieve with his latest sick ploy? Perhaps he hoped to wrangle his soul marker back from a weakened Celine. Yes, that was a possibility. He had no guarantee the adjudicator would return it to him. If he could get Celine to give it to him, that would solve his problem.

Damien shivered as he recalled the odd-looking adjudicator. The strange, winged creature with its black eyes that turned red when angry terrified him. But not more than the Duke did, he ruminated.

He emerged from the woods. His eyes focused on the structure in the distance. He squinted at it. His wandering mind drove his feet to seek out the source of the troubles. He stared at Marcus Northcott's residence in the distance. Perhaps he should approach it. Confront him.

CHAPTER 10

*D*amien took two steps toward the house before he ground to a halt. He pursed his lips. This was a terrible idea, he chided. No, his mind challenged, Celine needed help. She was on her way into town to meet with Monica to attempt to assuage any misgivings the woman had about her children's move to Maine. She was shoving aside her own pain for the good of all of them. He should do the same. He'd been alone with the Duke before. They'd even had a conversation once. He could handle this.

He nodded and took another step toward the house. On the other hand, he reflected, as his leg dangled in the air before he took another step, during that time, the Duke had tossed him like a rag doll against a stone wall and nearly killed him. And he'd just made a veiled threat against his life yesterday.

Damien twisted away from the house. His first assessment was correct. This was a terrible idea. With a deep sigh, he kicked a stone in front of him in frustration as he retreated to the tree line.

Helpless, that was the word to describe him. He could do

nothing to help Celine. He couldn't make her symptoms stop, he couldn't confront the source, he couldn't even help ensure Aunt Monica returned home none the wiser to their odd lifestyle.

He lamented this lack of power over the situation as he wandered along the trail. A few moments later, he stared at another structure peeking between the trees. The white columns of Alexander's house rose to meet the gabled roof overhanging the front door.

An involuntary smile crept across his face. Here was a solution that wouldn't get him killed. He'd go to Alexander's for a game of chess and a strategy session. Perhaps between the two of them, they could come up with a plan to help Celine.

With a new purpose, he strode toward the house.

* * *

Celine wandered down the driveway toward town. She'd chosen to walk rather than drive. She hoped the cool air relieved some of the dull, pounding pressure in her head. Despite remaining undisturbed throughout the night, her headache showed no signs of waning.

Tension crept into her shoulders with each step. While Monica hinted at returning home, Celine hoped her current condition did not deteriorate enough to cause her to change her mind. And the original question remained. Why did Monica drop in unannounced? Something still felt off to her. It added to her already strained mood.

She stepped from the driveway onto the road into town. The sea air wafted across her skin, giving her a chill. She swallowed hard as she pressed on toward Bucksville. Soon the quaint buildings of the seaside town surrounded her.

Her cell phone chimed in her pocket. She withdrew it and

peeked at the notification. A new text message from Gray flashed across the screen: *How are you feeling? Everything okay?*

She smiled at the message despite the throbbing in her head. After swiping across the screen, she typed a message back: *Okay so far! Wish me luck!*

Gray's good luck message popped on the screen before she toggled off her phone's display and shoved it back into her pocket.

She caught sight of the inn ahead with its wooden sign swinging in the breeze and the old-fashioned streetlight out front. It surprised her not to find her mother already waiting out front.

As she focused on the door, she missed the man approaching her from the side.

"Celine!" Marcus greeted her.

She closed her eyes as she swallowed her annoyance. When she opened them, she focused on his form with narrowed eyes. "What do you want, Marcus?"

"I hoped to have a discussion with you," he said, leaving the statement hanging between them.

"I'm busy," she snapped.

He raised his eyebrows at her. "Oh? Hot date, as they say?"

"None of your business, as they say," she shot back.

He narrowed his eyes at her as he considered her statement.

"Hi, Josie! Oh, I hope I'm not interrupting," Monica's voice sounded behind them.

Marcus eyed the woman up and down before softening his features and grinning at her. "Not at all!"

Monica smiled at him. "Dr. Monica Benson, Josie's mom!" she said as she stuck her hand out.

"Duke Marcus Northcott," Marcus answered, grasping her hand and bending forward to kiss it.

"Duke? As in the royal title?"

"Yes, as in I am in line to the throne," he replied.

The pounding in Josie's head worsened. Monica glanced at her. "Well, I hope I haven't interrupted. Josie and I were about to do some shopping."

"Oh, how delightful, though I dare say you'd do far better in Portland than Bucksville of all places."

"We have a trip planned for Saturday," Monica answered. "Though I'm sure I'll enjoy visiting the quaint shops here, too."

"Quaint, they are, yes," Marcus answered. "Well, I suppose I should let you explore."

"Oh, no, please finish your business. I just wanted to let Josie know I was ready."

"We were finished," Celine answered.

"Yes, the remainder of our conversation can wait. It is not pressing. I should not wish to rob a mother of her daughter's company."

Monica offered a broad grin. "How kind of you, Duke. Aren't you quite the charmer!"

"I would like to think so, yes," he said with a jovial chuckle that turned Celine's stomach.

Monica offered a giggle over the comment before responding. "Well, it was a pleasure to meet you."

"The pleasure was most certainly mine. Enjoy your stay. I do hope we shall see each other again." He faced Celine. "What a lovely mother you have, dear. We'll talk again soon."

He turned on his heel and strode away from them. Monica pushed a lock of hair over Celine's shoulder as she smiled at her. "What a charming man!"

Celine forced a smile onto her face. "Shall we shop?"

Monica offered her a coy smile. "Sure, honey." Monica threaded her arm through Celine's. "Lead the way."

Celine led her down the street toward the shopping

district. They stepped into the first shop, containing a variety of handmade items perfect for a tourist's souvenirs.

As Monica studied a hand-crafted wooden lighthouse replica, she side-eyed Celine. "So, how are things going with Michael?" she inquired.

"Good!" Celine replied, sounding a bit too enthusiastic.

Monica arched an eyebrow at Celine's response. "Good? That's it? No juicy details you'd like to share with your mother?"

Celine shrugged as she faked exploring a set of seashells in a jar. "We're taking it slow. Things are going well. We're just trying not to get ahead of ourselves and make sure this is right for both of us."

Monica nodded. "I wondered when you two broke up if you were being short-sighted but it's your relationship. I didn't want to presume to know what you were feeling."

Celine offered a brief smile before continuing to peruse the store's selection.

"I suppose if things don't work out, you may have another opportunity lined up already."

Celine crinkled her brow, keeping her focus on a set of stuffed lobsters in a basket. "Huh?"

Monica offered another coy smile as she picked up a stuffed moose with gangly legs and waved him at Celine. "I'd venture to say your friend, Duke Northcott, is interested in you."

Celine held back a sigh. "He isn't my friend. He's not interested, and Michael and I are in a good place."

Monica cocked her head. "I think the lady doth protest too much. Are you, perhaps, interested in him?"

"No," Celine said flatly. "I told you, Michael and I are doing well."

"You broke up once before even though things were going well. You have some misgivings that held you back. They may crop up again. Don't get me wrong, hon, I think you make a great couple. But it's not my life and if he doesn't make you happy, then he's not the one."

Celine nodded. "That's why we're taking things slow."

Monica smiled at her and rubbed her back. "Is there something holding you back?"

"No," Celine answered as they stepped out of the first shop and moved to the next one.

"Are you certain?"

"Yes," Celine answered.

Monica narrowed her eyes at Celine over the rack of windbreakers emblazoned with the town's name.

"What?" Celine asked, noting her stare.

"You don't seem overly enthusiastic about your relationship with Michael and I'm just wondering why."

"I got back together with him, didn't I? That's pretty enthusiastic, isn't it?"

"I'm just wondering if there isn't someone else on your mind."

Celine met Monica's gaze. "I'm NOT interested in Marcus Northcott."

"No, you've made that much clear. Though I still think he's interested in you. And, quite frankly, you could do worse than a Duke."

Celine held back rolling her eyes as Monica continued. "You're not holding back because of Grayson Buckley, are you?"

Celine frowned at her. "I thought we put that to rest, Mom. There is nothing going on between me and Grayson Buckley!"

"I believe you! Though that doesn't mean the idea isn't tempting."

"He's married. To a very charming woman," Celine answered.

"That doesn't mean he won't go looking outside his marriage, Josie. You're a pretty girl. I'm sure he's noticed that."

"He is very much in love with his wife," Celine assured her. "And I am not interested in an affair with a married man."

They meandered down the sidewalk to the third shop. Monica slipped her arm around Celine's waist. She kissed her hair. "Good. I don't want to see you brokenhearted. And that is a sure-fire way to a broken heart."

Celine nodded in agreement without speaking.

"And you've got much better prospects outside of a married man," Monica continued as they stepped into another shop. "I still say that Duke is a charming man."

They continued their shopping before settling at the cafe for a late lunch. Celine's head still pounded as she sipped at her soda. She stifled a yawn.

"Did I tire you out?" Monica asked as Celine stared into her fizzy drink.

"No, sorry," Celine answered. She offered a sheepish glance at Monica. "I stayed up too late playing video games with Damien last night."

"Ah," Monica said, "still at those, huh?"

"We are," Celine answered. "We normally play in the evening, but since we dined later last night, we didn't get the chance, so we stayed up a little too late. We're both paying for it today."

Monica slid her hand across the table and grasped Celine's. "It's nice to see you both so happy. I was worried when I came up about what I may find."

Celine offered her a genuine smile. "We are," she said with no hesitation.

Monica squeezed Celine's hand. Her eyes filled with

tears. "Would it bother you terribly if we canceled the shopping trip Saturday?"

"No, Mom, not at all. Not that I won't miss you but it's fine."

Monica pulled her lower lip up and the corners of her mouth turned down in an awkward half-smile, half-frown. "I've taken up enough of your time. I'm sure you both have lots of work."

Celine squeezed Monica's hand. In their attempt to not reveal their true lives to Monica, had they made her feel unwanted? "You're not intruding," Celine insisted.

"No, I know. You've made me feel very welcome. But I do need to be getting back. I checked the train schedules, nothing runs out of town on the weekends. I'd be here until Monday."

"Not enjoying the quiet life in Bucksville?" Celine questioned.

Monica chuckled. "I'm very much enjoying the town and seeing my babies. But I did plan on returning before Monday."

"Dad expecting you?"

"Yes, and I'd like to relieve Dr. Reynolds earlier than later."

"It's too bad Dad couldn't come up," Celine lamented.

"He wanted to, but this was so last minute. He couldn't get anyone to cover his classes. Maybe at Christmas," Monica suggested.

Celine nodded her head. Her father's position as a prominent college professor made traveling for pleasure during a semester almost impossible. "Well, I suppose we'll plan on a Christmas shopping trip," she said.

Monica smiled at her. "That sounds perfect! The stores will be so pretty then!"

"So, you'll be leaving tomorrow morning?" Celine inquired after their food was delivered.

"There's a train out tomorrow afternoon," Monica answered. "I was hoping to get one more lunch with my baby."

Celine smiled and nodded. "I'll tell Damien," she began when Monica interrupted her.

"Oh, no."

Celine furrowed her brow and cocked her head at the answer. Monica continued her explanation after a nervous chuckle. "It's not that I'd not be happy to see him again before I go, but I really hoped to spend a bit more time alone with you, Josie."

"Okay," Celine answered.

"I'm sorry, that sounds terrible, but..."

Celine cut her off. "No, it doesn't. I'm sure Damien won't mind. He is, as always, up to his eyebrows in work. He may even be relieved he doesn't have to come up with an excuse to ditch us."

Monica chuckled at Celine's statement. "Then it's a date. A girls' lunch tomorrow to replace our girls' shopping trip. It's a poor substitute but..."

"It'll be fine. We'll have more of a chance to talk than we would shopping."

Monica smiled and nodded at her. They finished their lunch making chitchat. Celine pulled Monica into a hug before she set off for home, leaving Monica at the inn.

As the town disappeared behind her, she pulled her phone from her pocket. With a swipe, she pulled up her text app. She sent a quick message to Gray to tell him she was heading back, safe and sound. She sent a second message to Damien, passing along the same information.

Unsurprisingly, Damien answered first. *Awesome... how'd it go? Any disasters? I'm at Alexander's working on your problem. Meet here?*

Celine smiled at the message. As always, Damien threw himself into whatever problem was on their plates. She returned his message: *Sure, see you soon...no issues, will talk when I see you.*

A message from Gray popped onto the screen as she sent her response to Damien. *Good... see you at home. Get some rest.*

She answered and told him she was meeting Damien at Alexander's. She toggled off her phone and continued toward the Buckley estate entrance. She planned to meet everyone at Alexander's. After she made another stop first.

Her eyes narrowed as her mind focused on her destination. After twenty minutes, she reached the edge of the forested trail. Marcus's seaside home rose in the clearing. Celine stormed to it. Without hesitation, she climbed the steps leading to the porch. She threw the door open and stalked through the foyer and into the sitting room.

CHAPTER 11

$\mathcal{M}$arcus read a book in an armchair near a roaring fire. "Ah, Celine!" he said as she strode through the door. "All finished with mommy dearest?"

Celine narrowed her eyes at him. She fought to steady her trembling arm. Marcus stood and continued, placing his finger on his lips in a dramatic display of thought. "Oh, or should I say Josie?"

"Leave Monica Benson alone," Celine spat.

Marcus rolled his eyes and stared at Celine. "Oh, really, Celine," he chided, "I barely said two words to the woman. I was perfectly pleasant to her."

"I don't want you to say even one word to her."

"Fine. Perhaps next time I shall just call you by your real name and let the chips fall where they may."

"There had better not be a next time," Celine insisted through clenched teeth. "Leave Monica Benson alone." She spun on her heel and stalked from the room.

"She seemed a lovely woman!" Marcus shouted after her.

Celine slammed the door shut behind her, drowning out any further conversation. With a sigh, she descended the stairs and strode down the path, heading toward Alexander's home.

She approached the stately house and let herself in through the front door. She veered toward the sitting room where she found Damien and Alexander pouring over a desk topped with open books.

"Solved it yet?" she asked.

"Hey, Celine!" Damien answered. "How was lunch? I'm dying to know. You said no issues but still, I feel like that was cryptic enough that it meant there was an issue, and you didn't want to say."

Celine offered a half-smile at his exuberance. "No issues, really. In fact, Monica may be leaving sooner than we expected."

Damien raised his eyebrows at her, prompting her to continue.

Celine shrugged. "She canceled our shopping trip and asked for one more lunch before she left tomorrow afternoon."

Damien's jaw dropped. "Really? Tomorrow afternoon?"

"That's what she said. She realized there were no trains over the weekend and preferred to leave before Monday."

"Whew, one more lunch to get through. I hope we make it."

"You're off the hook," Celine answered.

Damien's eyes grew wide. "Really?!" he exclaimed.

"Yep," Celine answered. "She hoped you weren't hurt by her request of a mother-daughter lunch. I assured her you would not be."

"Heck no!" Damien admitted. "I love Aunt Monica and I'll miss her, but I will be more than happy to skip lunch. I don't trust myself. I'll say something stupid, and she'll be here for two months."

"I'll tell her you said goodbye but are up to your eyeballs in work."

"It's not really a lie," Damien asserted.

Celine glanced at the stack of books spread across the desk's top. "So, it seems," she answered. "Have you found anything?"

"That depends," Alexander chimed in.

"On?" Celine asked as she sank onto the couch.

"Your answers to a few questions," Damien said. "First, a recap of any and all symptoms. I know you've been over it and over it but as soon as we started looking through stuff, I started to question everything."

Celine chuckled at his tendency to second-guess. "It started with a dull headache."

"Where?" Damien inquired.

"At the temples," Celine answered, touching both sides of her head. "Like a tension headache."

"And an achy arm, you said?" Alexander inquired.

"Right, an achy left arm," Celine answered.

"And then the time loss," Damien continued.

"Yep. Once when I was walking which I chalked up to distraction. Once while I was asleep which I assumed was sleepwalking. And the last time last night when I wandered to my swing. Which I couldn't explain away." Celine shrugged and threw her hands in the air.

Damien did a double take. "Is the trembling hand new?"

Celine glanced up at it. Her left hand shook. "No, I've had a tremor in it off and on since this started."

Damien jotted notes on a notepad near an open book. "Okay," he said as he scrawled across the page, "headache, body aches, tremor in left hand, time loss. Anything new?"

Celine nodded again. "My hands are numb. That just started today. Left is worse than the right, but they're both numb and tingly, like when your leg falls asleep." Celine wiggled her fingers and snapped her hands open and closed as she described it.

"Does that relieve it at all?" Damien inquired as she shook her hands.

"No, not at all. So have you found anything that fits?"

Damien scribbled a few notes on his paper. "Well," he began, "yes and no." He poked at a book lying open on the desk. "This one describes a spell where the victim loses time, but it doesn't mention any physical symptoms."

He shuffled the books around before he held up another. "And this describes a poison giving pain in the limbs, however, no time loss, headaches or numbness is described."

"In short," Alexander summed up, "we've found references to all the symptoms you're suffering from, however, we've not found a single source that gives all of them. The tingling hands adds a new twist."

Damien nodded. "Yep, what he said. Perhaps it's a combination of spell and poison."

"How was the poison administered?"

"Have you had any contact with the Duke?" Damien questioned.

Celine rolled her eyes. "Yes," she admitted.

Damien widened his eyes and raised his eyebrows.

"He cornered me in town today. And, of course, Monica happened upon us, so he took it upon himself to introduce himself to her."

Damien winced. "Bet that went over well."

"Oh, it did. She's convinced he's a charming man."

Damien shut his eyes and shook his head. "Man, he really has her fooled."

"Marcus's antics with Monica Benson aside, was there a time when he could have slipped you a poison?" Alexander inquired.

"No," Damien answered for her as he rubbed his chin.

"No, we met on the beach just after Aunt Monica arrived, but he never got close to her. So, he couldn't have given it to her then."

"Was there another opportunity?" Alexander posed.

Celine lowered her eyes. "I met with him before that. The day I told you about his warning, D. I met with him just before that."

"Celine!" Damien chided. "You shouldn't go near him!"

Celine shook her head as she leapt from the couch to pace. "I wasn't that close to him then, either. And I didn't have any symptoms directly after that."

"How long after did the symptoms appear?" Alexander questioned.

Celine scrunched her brow in thought. "A few days," she responded. "I noticed the headache the day we had lunch with Monica. I figured it was tension, though I was surprised if that was the case."

"So, a few days after you met with the Duke," Damien repeated. "And after lunch with Aunt Monica. Hmm. When did you notice the headache? After the lunch or during?"

"After," Celine answered. "I had it when we discussed the plan to pretend Michael and I were back together."

Damien snapped his fingers. "The food. Could it have been in the food?"

Alexander pursed his lips. "Hmm, perhaps."

"It would have required the cooperation of the waitress," Damien continued.

"An easy feat for a man like Marcus Northcott," Alexander answered.

"True. Okay, so working theory, this poison," Damien said, pointing at a book, "or something similar was slipped into Celine's food."

"Unfortunately, this theory does little to help us,"

Alexander pointed out. "The food is gone. We cannot test it for any poisons."

"Damn it!" Damien exclaimed.

"Perhaps it wasn't the food," Alexander suggested after a few moments in silence.

"What then?" Damien inquired.

"Has there been anything else out of the ordinary?"

"Other than the sudden arrival of Monica Benson?" Celine joked.

"You don't think…" Damien began before stopping.

"No," Celine answered before he could continue. "I don't think Monica had anything to do with it. I don't even think she was an unwitting pawn in the game."

Damien nodded, content with the answer for the moment. "So, was there anything else? Anything we're missing?"

"An unusual visitor? Outside of Monica," Alexander added with a chuckle. "A strange package, perhaps? A new acquaintance you've met in the past few days?"

"No, nothing," Celine began as she stalked across the room. She shrugged. "Outside of the arrival of Monica, everything's been quiet…" Her voice cut off.

"What is it?" Damien inquired.

Her brow furrowed and she spun to face them. "The day we had lunch with Monica," she began.

"Yeah?"

"It likely happened that day," she said. "And I did receive a strange package!"

Damien's face lit up in understanding. "The rose!" he exclaimed.

Celine nodded. "Yes, the rose. Its thorn pricked my finger."

"A rose?" Alexander inquired. "From whom?"

"The note didn't say. It came in a plain white box with a

blue ribbon. The note said 'You'll always be the one for me.' I assumed it was from Gray."

"But it must have been from the Duke!" Damien said.

"Do you still have the rose?"

"No," Celine said. "We tossed it. After it jabbed my finger, it wilted."

"I wonder if it's still in the trash. Perhaps we can examine it for traces of poison," Alexander suggested.

"One way to find out!" Damien said.

"Shall we?" Alexander inquired.

"After you!" Damien answered.

The two men proceeded across the room toward the foyer. "You coming, Celine?" Damien asked as he approached the door.

Celine did not move. With her back to them, she did not answer. "Celine?" he inquired again.

Silence met him. He glanced to Alexander before returning his gaze to Celine's still form. "Celine? You're starting to scare me."

He crossed the room and rounded her unmoving figure. "Celine?" he whispered.

His brows knit as he faced her. Celine stood motionless; her lips slightly parted. Her eyes stared straight ahead.

Damien's expression became pained. "Celine!" he shouted. He grabbed her shoulders and shook her. She failed to respond in any way. Her muscles stiffened though her facial expression remained unchanged.

Damien offered a pleading glance to Alexander. "We have to help her!"

Alexander studied her statue-like posture. "I'm not certain we can, Damien."

"We have to do something!"

Celine's lips began to move. They bobbed up and down as

though she attempted to speak, though no words came out. "She's trying to speak," Damien reported.

"Yes," Alexander responded. "Though I'm not sure she's speaking to us."

Celine's eyes focused above her, as though she stared up at someone taller than her.

Without warning, Celine spun on her heel and sauntered toward the foyer. Damien lunged toward her. "No," Alexander cautioned as he held Damien back. "Don't touch her."

"What? Are you kidding me? We have to help her!" Damien cried.

"And we will. Right now, there is nothing we can do for her. But what we can do is determine where she is going. Perhaps that will give us a clue to what's happening and why."

"We snapped her out of this last night," Damien contended.

"Did you? Or did she merely come out of it while you were there? You said she didn't respond at first," Alexander answered.

Damien stared after Celine's form as she crossed the threshold into the foyer.

"Damien, we cannot pull her from whatever trance she's in by force. This is the best thing we can do. With any luck, we'll learn something from her wandering. At the very least, we can prevent her from harm."

Damien pursed his lips and nodded. "Okay," he breathed.

Damien raced into the foyer as Celine pulled the front door open. A cool breeze swept in as Celine stepped into the waning warmth of the late afternoon air. Gravel crunched under her feet as she crossed the drive and continued toward the wooded path.

"Where are you going, Celine?" Damien mumbled as they followed her.

She entered the woods. "She's not going to her swing."

"No, it appears not," Alexander concurred.

An expressionless Celine continued to lead them down the forested path. She stared straight ahead as she walked, her head never moving.

"It appears she's heading for the house," Alexander said after a few more moments.

"Yeah," Damien agreed.

The trees cleared and the main house rose in front of them. Celine veered from the path, crossing the lawn to the front door. She pawed at the handle as she stared at the door. On her third attempt, her hand pushed the lever down and the door swung open. Celine strode inside and continued into the foyer.

Damien and Alexander slipped in behind her, pushing the open door closed. Celine stalked across the foyer and climbed the stairs. She wandered through the upstairs hallways in a seemingly random pattern.

"Where the heck is she going?" Damien inquired in a low voice as she slipped into a closed-off wing of the house.

"It should prove interesting to find out," Alexander whispered back.

Celine continued her rambling walk down the center of the hall in front of them. Without warning, she ceased walking. She stood still for a moment before she turned ninety degrees and approached a door. She pushed the door lever. The door creaked open on its hinges. A boom of thunder sounded overhead.

"Really?" Damien questioned as his eyes slid upward. "Every time something creepy is happening there's got to be a storm."

Celine stepped over the threshold and into the room.

Damien followed, glancing around. A sheet-draped bed sat against the left wall in the large room. White sheets covered other bulky objects on the room's fringes.

The only uncovered item stood against the far wall. A large full-length mirror reflected the room. Celine wandered to the bed. She ran her hand across the sheet as though searching for something, though her eyes never glanced downward. After a moment, she spun and approached the mirror.

She stared into its reflection. For the first time, it appeared she saw something. She cocked her head and fingered a lock of her hair before using both hands to sweep it upward. She held the style in place with one hand as she rubbed at the base of her bare neck.

Her eyes flitted to the side, and she straightened her head as she made eye contact in the mirror with Damien. "Damien?" she questioned.

"Yeah? Celine, are you okay?"

She spun to face him, her eyes wide and her jaw slack. "Damien Carlyle? Whatever are you doing here?"

CHAPTER 12

"Huh?" Damien questioned. Why would Celine ask what he was doing there? And why did she call him Damien Carlyle?

Alexander stepped between them. "Celine? Are you feeling all right?"

"Alexander!" she exclaimed. "I didn't realize you had returned already! Welcome home."

"What is she talking about?" Damien whispered behind Alexander.

Alexander continued without answering him. "Yes. I returned from Paris early."

"Paris?" Celine questioned. "I thought you went to London."

"Oh, yes," Alexander answered. "That's what I meant. I have been planning a trip to Paris."

"How lovely, though I hope not too soon. Another overseas journey would prove taxing."

Alexander narrowed his eyes at her statement. "Yes," he murmured.

"Any idea what's going on here?" Damien hissed behind him.

"No," he murmured over his shoulder. "But for the first time, she's noticed we're here. I'm trying to keep her talking."

Damien nodded in understanding as he approached Celine. "Hi, Celine. Say, how long's it been since we've seen each other?"

Celine pondered the question. Her brow furrowed in thought. After another moment, a pained expression came over her face.

"Celine?" Damien questioned. She doubled over, grasping at her temples.

"Celine!" he shouted again. He rushed toward her and grabbed hold of her as she crumpled in his arms.

Damien sank to the floor with Celine's limp form in his arms. Alexander joined him, kneeling next to them on the floor. Celine moaned as she settled into his lap. Her eyelids fluttered open, and she glanced around.

"D?" she questioned. "Alex?"

Alexander clasped her hand. "Yes, Celine, we're both here."

"What happened? Where are we?" She pushed to sitting as she glanced around the room.

"Back at the house. Easy, are you okay?" Damien questioned.

"Yeah. Other than my pounding head and my tingly hands, I'm fine. How did we get here?"

"Well, that's a bit of a long story," Damien answered. "Are you sure you're okay?"

Celine nodded. "Yes, I'm fine. What happened?"

"What's the last thing you remember?"

Celine screwed up her face. "Talking about the rose at Alexander's."

"Then what?"

"Nothing," Celine answered.

"Let's move you somewhere more comfortable and I'll tell you everything," Damien suggested.

"Okay," Celine agreed. Alexander pulled her to standing and they walked Celine to the sitting room. After settling her with a brandy near the fireplace, Alexander excused himself, intent on finding the rose they discussed earlier.

Damien recapped the events of the past twenty minutes to Celine.

"So, I just froze and then wandered to a random bedroom here?" Celine questioned.

Damien nodded. "Yeah, pretty much. And you called me Damien Carlyle. You seemed surprised I was here. And you thought Alexander had just returned from London. He said something about Paris, and you said another overseas journey would be taxing. It was weird."

Celine's brow pinched. "And you said I was searching for something on the bed?"

Damien shrugged. "I'm not sure. You ran your hand over the sheet covering it like you were trying to grab something."

"What?" Celine questioned.

"Do you have any memory of what happened during the episode at all?"

"No," Celine answered. "Not even speaking with you and Alexander. Nothing between talking about the rose and waking up on the floor of that bedroom."

Damien leapt from his chair and paced the floor in front of the fireplace. The doors to the sitting room burst open and Alexander entered. He waved a rotted object trapped inside a plastic bag in his hand. "Success!" he declared.

"You found it?"

"We did. After a great deal of digging, Mrs. Paxton and I located the box and its contents."

"Careful," Damien said, "we don't want anyone else poisoned or cursed or whatever."

Celine approached them and stared at the rose. "You're still the one for me," she mumbled.

"What?" Damien asked.

"The red dress, the ruby necklace, the cave," she blurted. She blinked a few times after the words tumbled from her mouth and stared at Damien and Alexander, a shocked expression on her face. "Where did that come from?" she questioned.

"Not sure," Damien answered. "What did you say? It seemed like random words."

Celine shook her head. "Uhhh," she murmured as she tried to recall them.

"The red dress," Alexander began.

"Right," Damien said. "The red dress, something and a cave."

"Necklace," Celine repeated.

"Yes, that's it!" Damien exclaimed. "The red dress, the ruby necklace, the cave. And you have no idea why you said that?"

"No, none," Celine admitted. "Though at least I remember saying it."

"Yeah, that's a plus," Damien agreed.

The sitting room doors opened, and Gray entered the room. "There you are. I was beginning to worry. I went to Alexander's and found the place empty. I thought something may have happened."

"Something did," Celine admitted.

"Oh? Trouble with Monica?" he questioned as he poured a brandy.

"No," Celine answered. "That situation seems to be resolving. She canceled our shopping trip, schedule one last mother-daughter luncheon tomorrow, and plans to leave on the late train."

"And just in the nick of time," Damien said.

"Yes, before you spill the beans," Gray replied.

"No," Damien countered. "Before Celine's behavior gets any worse."

Gray crinkled his brow. "We've had an interesting incident," Alexander explained. "Celine lost more time, though in this instance, Damien and I followed her. She wandered to a room here in the house. She caught sight of us in a mirror and began to speak to us as though it was another century."

"And I can't remember any of it," Celine added.

"Yeah, and just now she started babbling what seems to be a series of random words."

"Add that to my thudding headache and numb, tingly hands and we've got a recipe for disaster."

"Thank God I called Millie."

"Is she coming home early?" Alexander inquired.

"Yes, this evening." Gray checked his wristwatch. "She should be here in about three hours."

"Good," Celine said as she sank into her chair.

"Will that man ever stop?" Gray questioned rhetorically.

"What does he gain from this?" Celine asked.

"To keep you off balance. To weaken you. To weaken all of us," Gray explained.

Celine shook her head. "I don't see it."

"You can't honestly think he's innocent," Damien said.

"I didn't say innocent. But not at fault in this instance, perhaps."

"Oh, please. This has Marcus Northcott written all over it."

"Something doesn't add up for me."

"Let's keep an open mind, shall we?" Alexander suggested. "When Celine has a gut feeling, it usually has substance."

"Fine, we'll keep an open mind," Gray answered. "But I'll keep my money on Northcott."

* * *

Dr. Amelia Gresham stepped into the foyer as she pulled her umbrella shut. She dumped it into the umbrella stand before peeling off her damp trench coat and hanging it on the hook.

"Millie," Gray greeted her. "Good to have you back."

"Thank you, Gray. It's too bad the weather didn't hold out for my return."

"Yes, sorry to call you back early, but the situation with Celine needs your attention."

"It's all right," Millie answered. "The conference wasn't that interesting."

"No intriguing new medical discoveries?"

"Compared to what I deal with here? Hardly," Millie said with a chuckle.

Gray signaled for her to enter the sitting room.

"Well, hello everyone," Millie said as she greeted the room full of people.

"Welcome home, Millie," Alexander said.

"Thank you. I suppose you're the only one excited to see me, since you're the only person besides Gray I won't be examining."

"You can skip me, too," Damien answered. "I'm fine. Celine needs you more than I do."

"Same," Michael echoed.

"I'll be the judge of that, Damien and Michael," Millie answered. Millie glanced around the room. "Speaking of, where is Celine?"

"Here," Celine answered from behind her. "Really, Gray, give the poor woman a chance to get through the door before you're asking her to examine me."

Millie chuckled. "Oh, really, I'm fine. I've spent far too long crammed into a train seat. I'd like to stretch my legs. Now, Gray's told me a little about your symptoms. Can you expand on it?"

Celine sank onto the sofa next to Damien. "It started with a dull headache, then an achy arm, then time losses, followed by tingly numb hands and more strange behavior."

"Mmm-hmm," Millie said as she checked Celine's pulse and looked into her eyes.

"We believe this may have something to do with the symptoms," Alexander said as he waved the bagged rose in the air.

Millie wrinkled her brow at the object. "How does a rose fit in?"

"It was delivered to me the day the symptoms began," Celine explained. "It pricked my finger. A few hours after, I started to experience the symptoms."

"Poison?" Mille questioned.

Alexander nodded.

"Yes," Damien added, "we found a poison that causes some of her symptoms, though not all of them."

"Can you squeeze my hands?" Millie asked Celine. "Good," she responded as Celine squeezed them successfully with both hands. "And the headache, has it increased in intensity or stayed the same?"

"Increased."

"So, the effects are worsening," Millie repeated.

"Yes. The time losses are becoming more frequent and longer as well."

"And the other strange behavior?"

"She spoke to us during one of her time losses. She talked strangely, like she was in another century," Alexander explained. "And earlier she uttered a several random words."

Celine nodded. "Though I recall that."

"What were they?"

Damien flipped a page in his notebook and read, "The red dress, the ruby necklace, the cave."

"Interesting. Have you any idea the meaning of the phrases?"

Celine shook her head. "No, none. I'm sure I've had several red dresses and several necklaces. And there are countless caves in the area."

"Yes, they are sufficiently vague. Perhaps your subconscious has more to share."

"Hypnosis again?" Damien inquired.

"Yes," Millie confirmed. "And I'd also like to get a blood sample in addition to studying that rose."

"Okay, just let me know when," Celine answered.

"Now, if you wouldn't mind," Millie responded.

"Sure," Celine said with a shrug. "But if you'd like to freshen up first…"

"No, I'll grab my bag and be right back. I'll worry about relaxing after my trip when you're not suffering from a headache." She winked at Celine before she disappeared from the room.

"Hopefully we'll soon have some answers," Gray responded as he paced the floor.

Millie returned in a few minutes with her physician's bag. She withdrew a needle, two vials and a tourniquet. After wrapping the tourniquet around Celine's upper arm, she drew vials of blood from her left arm.

"All right," she said as she stowed them in her bag. "Let's try the hypnosis if you're ready."

"Sure."

"Do you want us to leave?" Damien inquired.

"That's up to Celine."

"It's fine if they stay. Perhaps something I say will trigger a lead for their search."

"All right, then let's proceed," Millie answered.

Damien squeezed Celine's hand. "Good luck. See you on the flip side."

She returned the gesture and offered a smile before settling back into the couch.

"Okay, Celine. You know the drill. Relax, listen to my voice and keep your focus on my pendant," Millie said as she dangled a sparkly necklace.

Celine focused her attention on the twirling pendant. Its gems caught the light, reflecting it and bending it into a rainbow.

"That's right, Celine, just relax. Listen to my voice and concentrate. You're beginning to feel very relaxed. Your limbs are heavy, and your eyes are starting to close as you drift off."

Celine's body relaxed as her eyelids drooped before closing. Once her eyes closed, Millie pocketed the pendant and continued. "Are you relaxed, Celine?"

"Yes," Celine murmured.

"Good. I'd like to discuss the physical symptoms you've been experiencing of late. Do you know the cause of them?"

"No."

"You've experienced several blackouts where you've lost time. Do you recall any of the events that occurred during these episodes?"

"No."

"Nothing? No details at all? Think, Celine. Is there anything you can recall from the episodes where you lost time?"

Celine's brows knit. Her breathing became labored, and she balled her fists. "Red," she choked out.

"Red? Explain, Celine," Millie questioned.

"Red," Celine repeated. "The red dress, the ruby necklace, the cave."

"That's the same thing she said before," Damien whispered.

Millie nodded. "Celine, what red dress? What are these objects you're discussing? What is their significance?"

"The red dress, the ruby necklace, the cave. The red dress, the ruby necklace, the cave. The red dress, the ruby necklace, the cave," she repeated in an endless cycle.

"She's stuck on that," Michael said. "Can we redirect her some way?"

"The red dress, the ruby necklace, the cave. The red dress, the ruby necklace, the cave. The red dress, the ruby neck..." Celine's voice stopped mid-word. Her head cocked to the side and her eyes snapped open. "Hello."

Damien's eyes widened and he glanced around the room. His brow crinkled. "Who's she talking to?"

"Shh," Millie chided.

Damien held up his hands in apology. "Celine, who are you talking to?" Millie questioned.

Celine did not answer the question. "A gift?" She responded. She arched an eyebrow and smiled. She rose from the couch and stalked across the room. The group followed her path.

"Should we follow her or what?" Damien whispered.

"Celine?" Millie questioned. "Celine, do not walk out that door."

Celine hovered at the open doorway. She stared straight ahead into the foyer. Seconds later, she stepped through the door and began to cross the space.

"Should we pull her out of it?" Gray asked.

"Perhaps we should follow her again," Alexander suggested. "We can always try to reverse course if she exhibits some negative effects."

"What if we can't?" Damien questioned.

"We may not be able to at this point, anyway," Michael

added. He pointed at Celine's stiff form as she climbed the massive stairway across the foyer to the second floor.

"So, we follow," Gray answered.

The group followed Celine as she wound through the halls to a familiar spot. "This is where she brought us earlier," Alexander said in a hushed tone.

Celine twisted the handle and pushed the door inward. It creaked open as it swung into the room.

"Yep, same creepy, creaky door," Damien answered.

They filed in behind Celine as she entered the room. She stalked to the bed. Her hands reached down and caressed the surface before she appeared to clutch something. She pulled the invisible object to her chest and wandered to the mirror across the room.

"What is she doing?" Damien questioned as he eyed her.

She stood in front of the mirror. Her closed fists reached toward her shoulders. She stared at her reflection as she twisted her head to the side. She wrapped one hand around her waist as the other reached across her chest.

"Looks like she's modeling a dress," Michael suggested.

"Oh, yeah. The red dress?" Damien questioned.

"Who knows, it's invisible."

"I don't like this," Gray chimed in. "We should stop this."

"I agree," Millie answered. "We're learning nothing from this, and I do not want to endanger her any further."

Millie approached Celine as she twisted at various angles in front of the mirror. "Celine," she began. "I'm going to count backward from ten to one. When I reach one, you will wake up." Millie began her slow count backward. She reached one and snapped her fingers. Celine did not respond.

CHAPTER 13

"Uh-oh," Damien said when Millie's attempt to rouse Celine failed.

Michael raised an eyebrow. "No kidding."

"Celine?" Millie questioned.

"Millie, get her out of this," Gray insisted.

Millie held two fingers to Celine's neck and pressed. "Her pulse is steady and normal."

"I don't give a damn about her pulse, I want her out of this."

"Gray, I can't! She's non-responsive! All I can do is monitor her vitals."

"The mirror!" Alexander exclaimed.

"The mirror?"

Realization dawned on Damien's face. "The mirror, yes! The last time she was in this weird trance, she spotted us in the mirror. She started talking to us and then she snapped out of it."

Millie studied the mirror then stepped toward it. She appeared in its reflection. Celine snapped her head toward Millie. "Who are you? What are you doing here?"

"Celine, I'm Dr. Amelia Gresham. You know me, we're friends."

The crease between Celine's brows deepened. "I do not know you. A female doctor?"

"Yes, we're old friends. Come away from the mirror, Celine. Give me what you hold in your hands."

Celine snapped the imaginary object away from Millie. "No, the dress is mine."

"Yes, it is. And it's very lovely, but let's put it down, shall we?"

Celine puckered her lips as she considered it. She returned her gaze to the mirror. Her head tilted as she gazed into it.

"Celine," Gray said as he stepped toward the mirror. "Celine, let Millie help you."

"Gray?" she questioned as he appeared in the mirror's reflection.

He smiled at her. "Yes, darling, it's me. Come away from the mirror."

Her brow furrowed as she considered his request. Her eyes flitted between her body and Gray's reflection. Gray motioned for her to follow him. She swallowed hard as she offered a slow nod.

She twisted away from the mirror and reached for his hand. As she extended her arm, her breathing increased, becoming labored. She snapped her head back toward the mirror. A pained expression crossed her face and she winced, grabbing her head.

Gray reached for her, and Damien rushed toward her. She shot upright before they could grasp her and flung her hand out toward the mirror. A bright blue ball of lightning shot from her open palm. It struck the mirror. An explosive boom ricocheted off the walls and the mirror shattered into pieces. Broken glass crashed to the floor. A few stray shards hung in the mirror's frame, their edges jagged and sharp.

Everyone ducked reflexively. When Damien raised his head, Celine lay sprawled on the floor.

"Celine?!" Damien exclaimed as he rushed to her side.

Gray reached her first and pulled her into his arms. "Celine?" he asked as he tapped her cheeks with the back of his hand.

Celine's eyes fluttered open. "Gray?" she questioned.

"Hey," he said with a smile.

Damien grasped her hand. "Celine, are you okay?"

"Yes, I'm fine." Her eyes darted around the room, taking in her surroundings. "How did I get here?"

"You led us here while hypnotized," Millie answered as she knelt next to Celine and took her pulse. Damien stood and backed away to allow Millie to examine Celine.

"This is the same room you led us to during your last episode," Alexander added.

Celine pulled herself up to sitting. "Easy, Celine. How are you feeling?" Millie inquired.

"Okay. My head is throbbing, and the numbness has gone further up my arm but other than that I feel fine."

"Is there anything you remember about the incident?" Millie questioned.

Celine considered it for a moment before answering. "No, nothing since you started to hypnotize me."

"So, we've learned nothing new," Gray groaned, throwing his hands in the air.

"Not necessarily," Damien answered.

* * *

Damien took a few steps back from Celine as Millie began to check her vitals. What had happened to her, he wondered?

She'd somehow gotten lost during the hypnosis session. She'd again managed to lead them to this bedroom. She'd mentioned something about a dress. Was it the red dress she'd babbled about moments before her journey through the house? What was she seeing in the mirror?

Damien's eyes rose from Celine's floor-bound figure to the broken mirror. Shards of glass were scattered across the floor. A few pieces of glass still clung to the frame.

Damien stared at them. Something was odd. He spun to look at the other members of their party. Alexander and Michael stood behind him. They weren't moving. He twisted back toward the mirror. Something in the mirror was moving, though. What was it?

Damien stalked toward the glass. He squinted at it. Red flitted in and out of the shard he focused on. He shifted his gaze to another piece. The red fabric floated through it. It disappeared and reappeared in a shard across the mirror's back.

The conversation behind him faded to the background as Damien followed its movement. He lost sight of it as it passed to an area missing any glass. As his gaze fell to the floor, his eyes went wide.

In the jumble of mirror fragments strewn across the hardwood floor, red fabric glided around. It appeared in several, drifting in and out, spiraling around in the remnants of the mirror.

Damien's brows knit as he considered the meaning behind what his eyes detected in the mirror's remains.

Behind him, Gray lamented the hypnosis being a waste since Celine could provide no additional details about her experience.

"Not necessarily," he answered, his eyes unwavering from the show unfolding in the mirror's shards.

"What?" Gray questioned.

"Yeah, we haven't learned anything," Michael agreed.

Damien cocked his head as he stared at the broken glass. "Anyone else seeing this?"

"Seeing what, Damien?" Alexander inquired.

"The movement in the mirror," he responded. Damien pushed a few pieces of glass around with his foot as Alexander approached him.

"Oh my word," he gasped as he stared at the pieces.

Michael joined them, along with Gray. "What in the world?" Michael questioned.

"Or not in this world," Damien corrected.

"Astute assessment. I am not certain what we are seeing here," Alexander answered.

"Mirror world?" Damien suggested in question form. He pushed a few more shards around, trying to piece together the puzzle.

"I'm not certain," Alexander admitted.

"The red looks like satiny fabric," Michael said.

"Could it be the red dress Celine's been rambling about?" Damien asked.

"Perhaps. What is it doing? Why is it moving?" Alexander inquired.

Damien twisted his head as he continued to move shards around in an attempt to restore the bulk of the mirror on the floor.

"Falling?" Michael suggested.

"Floating?" Gray proposed.

Damien pushed a few more pieces together. Celine groaned across the room as she grasped her head. "Celine?" Gray questioned, returning to her side.

Alexander followed him as Damien continued his mission. He bent toward the floor and shifted a few pieces with his hands. "See anything?" Michael questioned over his shoulder.

"I'm not sure," Damien murmured. He concentrated on the larger pieces, shoving the smaller shards aside since they were too hard to place.

Michael peered over his shoulder. "Concentrate on the bigger pieces," he suggested.

"That's what I'm doing. You can help, you know."

"I wouldn't be much help, I'm terrible at puzzles. I'd be more of a hindrance than a help."

Damien continued to slide pieces around until he'd almost formed the center of the mirror. His lips parted as understanding dawned on him as the scene unfolded in the splintered reality. He opened his mouth and drew in a breath, preparing to declare success when the image in the mirror shifted.

The reflected room darkened. The red dress ceased its motion. A shadow crossed in front of it. A hand reached toward him. A low growl filled his ears.

Damien gasped as the hand seemed to reach through the mirror toward him. He cried out as he scrambled backward on his hands and feet.

"Whoa, man, what the hell?" Michael questioned as Damien backed into him and knocked him to the floor.

A reverberating clap resounded through the room and black smoke poured from the mirror. Seconds later, the mirror crumbled to blackened ash.

Michael's eyes widened and he stared at the dissipating black cloud as it rose to the ornate ceiling above. "What the hell was that?" he mumbled.

Alexander joined them, staring at the scene in front of them. He stooped near the remnants of the mirror and sifted a handful of ash through his fingers.

"The... the..." Damien gulped before trying again. "The mirror just exploded in a big cloud of black smoke."

"D?" Celine questioned. "Are you all right?" She struggled to get to him while Millie and Gray held her back.

"Easy, Celine," Millie cautioned. "You were just in extreme pain."

She shook them off. "I'm fine," she answered. "The moment the mirror exploded, my headache sank back to normal levels."

She crawled over to Damien. "I'm fine," he assured her. She settled next to him and stared at the blackened ash on the floor.

"Did you manage to note anything before the mirror disintegrated?" Alexander questioned.

Damien nodded. "Yes, I was just about to call you over to look when that happened," he said as he gestured to the piles of black powder. "Dancing. The red fabric was a dress. Celine was wearing it. At least, I think it was Celine."

"Dancing?" Michael questioned.

Damien nodded again. "Celine was dancing with someone."

"Who?" Alexander inquired.

Damien shrugged. "I'm not sure. I never saw his face."

"Gray?" Alexander suggested.

"No, it wasn't Gray. Even from behind, I could tell it wasn't Gray. It wasn't me, or you, or Michael. It wasn't even the Duke."

"You're sure?" Gray questioned.

"Yes, I'm sure," Damien answered.

"And then the mirror just exploded?" Michael inquired.

"No," Damien countered. "No." He swallowed hard.

Celine placed her hand on his shoulder. "What happened, D?" she prodded.

"Celine stopped dancing. The man disappeared. Everything got dark and then a hand started to reach out at me. It seemed like it came right out of the mirror for my throat.

And it sounded like someone was snarling at me. I jumped back and that's when the mirror exploded."

Millie joined the group and studied the ash. "Do you happen to have a handkerchief?" she inquired of Alexander.

"Of course," he answered as he removed one from his pocket and handed it to her.

"Thank you," she answered as she scooped the powder onto it. "I'd like to analyze this."

"Excellent idea, doctor," Alexander replied.

"Perhaps we should reconvene in a more comfortable location if we plan to continue our discussion," Gray suggested.

"Good idea. This floor is about as hard as it looks," Michael complained.

The group reconvened in the sitting room minus Millie, who collected the sample of Celine's blood and the rose and departed to begin her analysis on the items in her on-site lab.

"Tell us again what you saw, Damien," Alexander prompted.

Damien took a sip of the brandy Celine delivered to him before he recounted the story. "Celine was dancing in a red dress with someone I didn't recognize, though I couldn't see his face. They stopped and he disappeared. Then everything went dark and the next thing I knew a hand was reaching through the mirror for my throat. That's when the mirror exploded."

"What did the man look like?" Gray questioned.

"Ummm, taller than Celine but shorter than you. Medium build, medium brown hair."

"That's it?" Gray barked.

"That's all I saw of him! I didn't see much!" Damien exclaimed.

"It's fine, D," Celine said as she placed a hand on his shoulder. "Just relax and tell us anything you remember."

He gulped down another sip of the amber liquid as he nodded.

"What was the dancing like?" Alexander inquired.

"Old-fashioned, like a waltz or something."

"And the dress?"

"Red," Damien exclaimed. He combed his fingers through his hair as his leg started to bob.

"D, relax, it's not a test."

Damien sprang from his seat and paced the floor. "No, if it was a test, I'd pass it. I was good at academics!"

"Pull yourself together, Damien," Gray warned.

"Back off, man," Michael said, stepping toward Gray.

"That's not helping," Celine warned. "From either of you."

Michael backed off and Gray held his hands up in defeat. "I just think you're being a bit reactionary. It's just a few questions."

"It's not! This could define what's going on with Celine. I don't want to mess something up that sets our progress back."

Celine narrowed her eyes at him as he ran his fingers through his hair again. "There's something else," she said.

"Yes, I'm sure there's some other detail of the dress that I've forgotten," Damien responded.

"No, not that," Celine said. Celine approached him and placed her hand on his shoulder. He jumped, startled by her touch. "Something about that scene disturbed you. What?"

Damien swallowed hard and chewed his lower lip before he answered. "I'm not sure," he admitted. "I just got an overwhelming sense of terror when that hand reached for me. Like my life was over."

"Come sit down," Celine said. She pulled the almost empty brandy glass from his grip and passed it over to Gray, nodding toward the decanter as a signal to pour another. "It's okay, D. You're safe, but I understand how frightening the circumstances were. Take your time."

Damien nodded as he accepted a refreshed glass of brandy from Gray. He took a deep breath and patted Celine's hand. He swallowed a sip of the brandy and took a second deep breath. "Okay," he said with a nod. "The dress. Red."

"Length?" Celine questioned.

"Long, floor-length."

"Old-fashioned or modern?"

"Uh," Damien hesitated.

Alexander pulled his phone from his pocket and tapped at it. After a moment, he handed it to Damien. "What style fits the closest?" he inquired.

Damien stared at the screen. An array of dresses from the 1700s to the present filled the screen. He scrolled through them. "Uh," he mumbled again as he studied the picture.

"Best guess, D," Celine said. "You don't have to be accurate to the decade."

"A lot of these look similar, it's hard to say," he murmured. He settled on a selection of three dresses. "Something like these, though. I'm not sure I can be more specific than that."

"Okay, that's good. That narrows it down quite a bit," Celine answered. Alexander peered over his shoulder at the dresses. They ranged from the 1830s to the 1850s.

"Yeah, only three decades," Damien retorted.

"When you've lived as long as I have, that narrows it down enough," Celine joked.

Damien chortled at the joke.

"So, we've identified the dress from somewhere between 1830 and 1860," Alexander announced to the rest of the group.

Gray narrowed his eyes at Alexander. "Are you thinking what I'm thinking?"

"Probably," Alexander responded.

"It's not good," Gray replied.

"Not at all."

"Someone want to clue the lowly humans in on the not-so-good news?" Michael asked.

"They're talking about an incident that occurred in 1842," Celine answered. "At least, I assume we're talking about Tobias Greene."

"I really wish you wouldn't mention his name, Celine," Gray said.

"Who's Tobias Greene?" Damien inquired.

"A terrible man," Alexander said.

"What, like the Duke?" Michael asked.

"No, not quite," Celine explained. "He's different. He's…"

"If it's all the same to everyone, I prefer we didn't discuss this. If that man is involved, the less they are involved the better," Gray said, motioning to Michael and Damien.

"Oh, come on, you can't sideline us!" Damien argued, leaping from his seat.

Gray spun to face him. "Do you recall that sense of foreboding terror you just experienced?"

"Yeah," Damien answered.

Gray stalked toward him. "Take that feeling, multiply it by one hundred. Imagine that hand grasping your throat. Dark eyes boring into your brain until it hurts. You feel your windpipe collapsing but you don't yet die. Your flesh begins to crawl. You begin to feel like you are burning from the inside out. You're rendered useless, but you don't die. Instead, you are caught in this endless loop of pain, agony and fear." He ended his speech standing nose to nose with a wide-eyed Damien. "That is a fair description of an encounter with Tobias Greene."

Damien swallowed hard and collapsed to the couch behind him.

"He's right," Alexander agreed. "This isn't something you should involve yourself in. If it is, indeed, what is happening."

Celine grasped Damien's hand. "Let us handle this."

"Handle it how?"

"That I don't know," Celine admitted.

"Perhaps Millie's analysis will help," Alexander suggested.

"Let's hope," Celine answered.

"And soon," Gray added.

"Until then, I suppose we are at a standstill. We have no idea if a poison is inducing this and how to reverse it," Alexander said.

"Well, not a standstill. In the meantime, it's vital I meet with Monica tomorrow and ensure she leaves. If Tobias is here, or close, she's not safe here."

"If," Alexander repeated. "This could be anything or anyone."

Gray remained silent for a moment. "I suppose you're correct. My money's still on Northcott," Gray answered. "Though I'd prefer you not leave the house at all given our latest theory."

"Our latest assumption," Celine corrected. "We're not certain it's Tobias. And it's just for a lunch. In less than twenty-four hours, Monica should be on her way, and we can tackle this problem with all our resources."

* * *

Damien wandered into the east wing. Given the setting sun, the light in the wing waned as the sun sank in the western sky. Most rooms in this wing were unused. An eerie silence hung in the space. The darkened halls were lit only by bright light streaming from an open door near the hall's end. It added to the ominous feeling of the space.

Damien approached the open door and peered inside. A

variety of medical and scientific equipment lined the walls in the large room. Previously a bedroom suite, Millie converted it to a lab space after her arrival in Bucksville.

Millie peered into a large microscope before jotting several notes on a paper clipped to a clipboard. She stood and crossed to a centrifuge as she finished her notation.

"Knock, knock," Damien said as he rapped his fingers against the door jamb.

"Damien!" Millie greeted him as she peered over her glasses. "What are you doing all the way over here."

Damien offered a nervous chuckle. "Yeah, quite a walk," he said as he stepped into the room. "Just figured I'd stretch my legs and see how your work is going."

Millie opened the machine and withdrew a vial of blood. She prepared a slide of it to view under the microscope. "That bored, are you?" she quipped as she focused the microscope.

Damien shrugged as he glanced at the variety of equipment. "Interested," he answered. "I'd like to help Celine."

"Did you make any progress with the scene you witnessed in the mirror shards?"

"Yes and no."

"That sounds noncommittal. Care to share?"

"I pinpointed the dress I saw Celine wearing to sometime in the early to mid-1800s. Which caused everyone else to think it might be related to some guy named Tobias Greene."

"Tobias Greene?" Millie questioned. She ceased her perusal of the blood slide and stared at Damien.

"Yeah, heard of him?"

"Yes," she admitted. "Though not much. None of them like to talk about it. It's my understanding he was quite a brutal man with some sort of hold over Celine. I'm afraid I don't know much more than that. Though their reluctance to discuss it suggests it was very traumatic."

"Yeah, the little Gray told me seems to agree with that line of thinking. They suggested Michael and I stay out of it and hoped you'd make some progress so they could discuss a course of action to reverse whatever Celine suffered from. So, on that front, here I am to see if you've made any progress."

Millie nodded. "I have made progress, though I'm not certain it's helpful yet." Millie switched a slide on the microscope then adjusted the knobs. She waved her hand toward the microscope. "Have a look."

Damien peered into the eyepieces. He waited for his eyes to adjust to the magnified view. Red cells floated around the circular space. "What am I looking at?" Damien inquired.

"Those are blood cells. Normal red blood cells from my own body."

"Okay?" Damien answered as he pulled away from the microscope.

Millie switched the slide and adjusted the knobs. She motioned for Damien to view the new slide. He positioned his eyes over the two eyepieces and focused. His brow furrowed as he viewed the new sample.

Damien peered into the microscope. Distended red blood cells floated around. Among them, black cells with odd spikes mixed. "What is…"

Millie cut him off. "Keep watching," she said.

Damien continued to stare into the microscope. After a moment, one of the black, spiky cells latched on to a red blood cell. Within moments, the blood cell withered, wrinkling like a raisin. The black cell consumed it, turning the healthy red cell into a new warrior in the war being waged on the slide.

Damien stood straight and whipped to face Millie. "What is that?" he asked.

"That is a sample of Celine's blood. You'll notice first the red blood cells appear slightly different from ours. Distended. Likely the result of her immortality."

Damien nodded. "And the black stuff?"

"The poison," Millie answered. She picked up the plastic bag containing the withered rose. "A match to the sample I pulled from the rose's thorn."

"It's… it's attacking the cells," Damien said.

"Correct. It attacks them, kills them, then converts them to assist in its takeover of the sample. The same thing occurs if I expose a sample of my blood to the poison. Only it happens much faster."

"Faster?"

"Yes, being mortal, my cells appear weaker than Celine's. Had you or I touched that rose, we'd likely be dead already."

"Dead? Could this kill her?"

CHAPTER 14

$\mathcal{M}$ille shrugged her shoulders at his question. "Hard to say. As you can see, it appears the poison is spreading. Though without continuing to monitor it, we don't know if her cells will eventually fight back."

"But you said…"

"Mine would not." Millie produced a third slide and placed it on the stage. Damien peered in. Black cells littered the view. "That is a sample of my blood only hours after being exposed. There are no red cells left."

"Won't this eventually happen to Celine, too?"

"I'm not certain. As you can see, her sample still contains a large amount of healthy red cells, even after exposure to the poison for a longer period than my blood was exposed to it. In short, this poison would kill a human, rather quickly, I'd wager. What it will do to Celine, I remain uncertain."

Damien frowned. He didn't like uncertainty. "What is this poison? Is there any antidote?"

"Another thing I am uncertain about," Millie admitted. "I've never seen a similar cell structure. It's no poison I am familiar with."

Damien's shoulders slumped at the answer. Millie raised a finger as she continued. "Here is something interesting, though." She swapped slides on the microscope's stage again. "Take a look."

Damien peered into the eyepieces again. The field appeared gray like a film covered it. Black cells crept around. "Is this the poison from the rose?" Damien inquired.

"No," Millie answered. "That is the ash from the mirror. Some mirror particles still remain."

Damien faced her again. "The black things are attacking the mirror pieces."

A smile crossed Millie's lips and she nodded. "Yes. In a similar way that the poison attacks blood cells. It's almost like this is a supercharged poison... only for mirrors."

"That's bizarre," Damien said as his mind whirled at the newest discovery.

"Yes, it is. Though you'll find life with the Buckleys provides little normalcy," Millie answered.

"Yeah, no kidding. I haven't been here over a year and there is no shortage of bizarre."

Silence passed between them for a moment before Damien spoke again. "Is there anything I can do to help you? I'd like to come up with something to help Celine."

"Not at the moment, no," Millie admitted. "I have a few experiments I'd like to try before I call it a night. Perhaps after I've gathered more data, we can have a discussion and determine the next course of action."

"Okay, sounds like a plan," Damien answered.

"Wonderful. And thank you for the offer. We'll talk in the morning."

Damien nodded in agreement before he left the room. He wandered through the darkened halls back to the lived-in part of the house. His mind raced as he strode to his door. His fingertips caressed the knob before he shook his head.

He'd never sleep. Celine had retired early, citing her headache as the reason. Michael excused himself for a mind-clearing walk on the property. Alexander had likely returned to his home. And Gray... well, never mind Gray. Damien preferred not to spend his time with Gray at the moment.

Perhaps he could bump into Michael on the grounds and find some company and a distraction from his wayward thoughts. With his plan set, Damien released the door handle and threaded his way through the halls to the foyer. He exited into the cool evening air. Stars already twinkled overhead, and a waxing crescent rose steadily into the sky.

Damien wandered to the cliffs overlooking the ocean. He stared out over the horizon. No sign of Michael, he noted. After a few moments spent in contemplation, he meandered down the path with no direction in mind.

Damien sauntered through the wooded area he'd visited so many times before. It brought him no peace this time, though. His worry for Celine consumed him. Could the poison kill her? No, he reasoned, not Celine. But what if? His mind let the question dangle.

He continued walking, his mind a jumbled mess. He stopped as he approached a clearing. A house rose in the distance. The seaside house stood like a beacon against the night sky. Lit from within, its rosy glow cast long shadows all around it.

Damien narrowed his eyes at the house. Judging by the position of the lights, Duke Marcus Northcott was home. Damien's jaw tightened as an image of the man formed in his mind. He almost certainly had a hand in this. He had warned Celine not to return and now he was thrusting more pain upon her as punishment for not bending to his will.

Perhaps he should confront him. Damien took two steps toward the house before he stopped. No, this was a terrible idea. And one that he'd never hear the end of if Celine found out. That is if he lived through the experience.

Damien spun on his heel and left the Duke's house behind. He returned to the house and navigated to his bedroom. After changing, he crawled into bed for a long night of tossing and turning.

* * *

Michael shoved his hands into his pockets as he strolled down the beach. The chill in the night air made him wish he'd have brought his jacket. The temperatures here were much cooler at this time of year than at his previous home. Home, his mind pondered. Was this his home?

Not really, he decided. He had no connection to these people. They weren't his family. Would he prefer to return to the family fold?

Michael stared out across the ocean as he pondered the question. His family life was unconventional at best. Growing up rich had its perks. It also had its downsides. Turmoil reigned within his household. Not the kind of turmoil he dealt with now. Social turmoil. There was a constant battle between his parents, power struggles between other family members, betrayals, arguments, and more drama. Did he want to return to that?

Maybe. He was used to it. He'd spent thirty years living with it. He belonged with them. Right?

Michael shook his head. He couldn't leave now. As usual, trouble brewed. Beyond the issue with Monica Benson's arrival, Celine suffered from some sort of illness.

He'd wait until after that issue subsided before he broached the subject of heading home. He still wasn't certain, but he was leaning toward returning to the Carlyle fold and leaving the Buckleys behind.

* * *

Damien arose from a restless sleep to find the sun streaming through his window. He rolled onto his back with a groan. He felt drained with little energy to face the day. His eyes wandered to the bright sunshine outside. He considered rolling over and catching another hour or so, but he decided against it.

He wanted to know if Millie had made any progress. And he wanted to check in with Celine before she headed into town for her lunch with Monica. He hoped the lunch marked the end of that saga. He loved Aunt Monica, but her presence here, especially with an ill Celine, made things difficult.

Damien crawled from his bed and headed for the shower to help wake up before he pulled on his clothes. He emerged from his room into an empty hallway. With his hands shoved into his pockets, he descended to the main floor and made his way toward the dining room for breakfast.

As he crossed the foyer, Celine emerged from a far hallway.

"Hey," he greeted her.

She offered a closed-mouth smile. "Hey, D," she said. "How are you feeling?"

"I should be asking you that," he replied.

"I still have the dull throbbing in my head and both my arms are tingly. Other than that, I feel okay."

He nodded. "Will you be able to make lunch with Aunt Monica?"

Celine nodded. "Yes," she answered. "And let's hope that ends that situation so we can focus on this one."

"Hey, who is this Tobias Greene guy?" Damien inquired.

Celine raised her eyebrows. "Stop avoiding, D," she responded.

"Avoiding?"

"My question. How are you feeling? You didn't answer. And I haven't forgotten it."

"I'm okay," he answered.

She raised her eyebrows further at him. "I'm a little tired," he added. Her crystal blue eyes still gazed at him. He swallowed hard. "I didn't sleep much."

Celine pushed a lock of hair from his forehead. "Too much going on in that brain of yours?"

"Something like that," he answered with a nervous chuckle. His mind flitted to his conversation with Millie. Did Celine know what was happening inside her body? Had she spoken with Millie? Should he tell her? Perhaps it was a distraction she didn't need before her lunch with Monica. His mind swirled.

"Come on," Celine said, "let's get you some breakfast."

"I'm okay," he said as she hooked her arm through his and pulled him toward the dining room.

"I'm sure you are. But some breakfast isn't going to hurt you." She waited a moment before she continued. "Any nightmares?"

"No. I guess I didn't sleep enough for Alterra to creep into my dreams."

"I meant from your experience yesterday."

"Ohhhh," Damien said as understanding dawned.

"You were disturbed after the mirror exploded. I just want to be sure you're okay."

Just like Celine, Damien thought. "Yeah, I'm okay. I mean, I don't want any more mirrors to explode from some weird mirror poison, but I don't feel that sense of dread I had immediately after."

"Good," Celine answered as they reached the dining room. Her brows knit as Damien poured a cup of coffee. "Mirror poison?"

"Yeah," he answered. "Have you talked to Millie yet?"

"Not yet," she admitted. "What did I miss?"

"I spoke with her last night," he answered as he filled a plate with eggs after handing his coffee mug to Celine.

"And?"

"And she had reviewed the samples. She said the ash from the mirror looked like it was a poison eating it away."

"Hmm," Celine answered as they settled at the table. "Anything else?"

Damien shoved eggs in his mouth. "Mmm," he said with a full mouth. "Nope." He kept his eyes trained on his plate, unwilling to glance up at Celine.

Celine narrowed her eyes at him. "Nothing else? Or nothing else you want to tell me? Especially before I have lunch with Monica."

Damien gulped his coffee, cursing its heat level as he swallowed. He lifted his eyes to Celine's face. She cocked her head at him, her icy blue eyes burning a hole through him. "She said she found some kind of poison-like substance on the rose. She couldn't identify it. She exposed it to her blood, and it obliterated it. It looks like it was doing the same to your blood but at a much slower rate. She wasn't sure if it was capable of destroying your blood sample in the same way as it did hers."

Celine nodded and pursed her lips. "I'm sorry," Damien said. "I... I didn't want to say anything to upset you, especially before the lunch but..."

Celine waved her hand at him. "I'm okay, D. I have a feeling you're more upset than you're letting on."

Damien swallowed hard. "I'm worried, Celine. Those poison cells ravaged Millie's cells in a matter of hours. What if..."

Celine interrupted him. "It didn't do that to me, D. It's been days and I'm still okay!"

"But..." Damien protested.

"But we have time. This poison is moving much slower than it would in a human. That buys us some time to figure this out. As soon as I get back from lunch with Monica, I imagine you and Millie will have a slew of plans!"

"Way to put the pressure on me," Damien groaned.

Celine chuckled at his less-than-genuine complaint. She knew Damien's mind would work overtime. "Allow me to take some pressure off," she said with a wink. "You and Millie may want to ask Alexander. He's good at this type of stuff, too. Between the three of you, you may be able to make quick work of identifying the poison, or something close."

Damien nodded. "Okay, I'll check with him."

"D," Celine said.

"Yeah?" he asked as he stared at his plate, pushing the eggs around it in a circular motion.

"D," she repeated until he glanced up at her.

"We'll figure this out, okay? I promise."

He offered her a half-smile. "I'm gonna hold you to that."

She returned his smile as she climbed from her seat and approached him. She wrapped her arm around his shoulders and rested her head against his. "Don't work too hard," she cautioned him before she strode from the room.

He took another sip of his coffee as Celine disappeared through the doorway. "Yeah right," he mumbled to himself. They needed a plan. And they needed one fast. They couldn't risk Celine's life. He glanced at his watch as he tried to decide if he should check in with Millie first or head to Alexander's house.

He decided he'd get an update from Millie before retrieving Alexander to brainstorm ideas. Perhaps they could have a solution by the time Celine returned from her lunch. He took a last sip of his coffee before he strode from the table with a clear destination in mind.

* * *

Celine winced as she crossed the foyer. Her headache throbbed at her temples. Was it worsening? At this moment, it seemed to be. Perhaps it was the stress of the upcoming lunch with Monica. She swallowed hard as she paused to steady herself.

After a moment, the throbbing subsided, settling to a dull ache again. She wiggled her now-tingly shoulders before she continued across the large space.

"Good morning," Gray greeted her from the stairs above.

"Good morning," she answered.

"You were up early."

"Nervous energy I guess."

"How do you feel?"

She shrugged. "My head aches and my arms are numb but other than that I'm okay."

"I wish you didn't have to go into town today," Gray said as he rubbed her shoulders.

"I'll be okay," Celine responded.

"I have no doubt," Gray answered. "But I'd prefer you here, safe, under the watchful eye of Millie and Alexander."

"Hopefully I won't be long."

"And you'll come straight back?"

Celine nodded. "Yes. And then we'll start working on fixing this problem," she said, waving her hands in the air.

Gray nodded. "I'm going into town this morning. If you need me, I'll be right there. Okay?"

She smiled at him as he wrapped her in his arms. "Okay."

"I'll be home right after lunch to help with that."

"See you then."

"You bet," he said with a wink before he leaned in for a kiss.

"Get a room, guys," Michael teased as he descended the stairs.

Gray rolled his eyes before he kissed the tip of Celine's nose. "See you later," he whispered as he gave her a final squeeze before pulling on his coat and disappearing through the door.

"You see Damien around?" Michael inquired as he stepped onto the foyer floor.

"I just left him in the dining room."

Michael nodded. "I'd like to check on him after yesterday."

"I appreciate that," Celine said.

"How's he handling it?"

"In typical Damien style. He's worried about other things and his mind is working overtime."

"Sounds about right," Michael responded. "Well, I'll head there and see if I can make any headway settling his mind."

"Thanks," Celine said with a tight-lipped smile.

"Yeah, no problem. Damien and I are friends. I'm concerned about him."

Celine nodded. A wistfulness passed over her. If Michael left, she'd miss him. So would Damien. He was an integral part of their team. But that was a problem to deal with later.

"Hey, good luck today with Monica," Michael said. "Not to sound like an ass, but I hope she leaves soon and safely."

"Thanks," Celine said with a chuckle.

"Wouldn't want to have to dig deep for my award-winning acting skills again," Michael said with a grin as he backed away from Celine.

She grinned at him while shaking her head. Yeah, if Michael left, she'd miss him.

* * *

Celine strode under the canopy of trees. Bright light filtered through the branches to the pavement below. She neared the end of the Buckley drive and stepped onto the road leading to town. She'd chosen to walk rather than drive. With her headache and tingly arms, she preferred not to be behind the wheel of the car. Nor did she want Henry driving her to town. One slip of his tongue calling her Mrs. Buckley may ruin the entire plan.

With the weather promising to provide a beautiful spring day, Celine enjoyed the walk. She breathed in the sea air, hoping it eased the throbbing in her temples. As the little town came into sight, she stepped onto the sidewalk, passing several buildings before she reached the cafe attached to the hotel.

Celine entered and found Monica already waiting at a table tucked into a far corner. Monica smiled and stood to greet her with a hug as she approached.

"Hi, honey," she said after kissing Celine's cheek. She offered Celine a wide-mouthed grin. Celine recognized it as one she used when she was nervous. Perhaps she was reconsidering her departure, Celine ruminated.

"Hi, Mom," she said, giving her arms a squeeze before sitting down at the table.

The waitress arrived to deliver menus and they ordered after a few moments. "So," Monica said, still grinning and leaning forward with clasped hands. She breathed out a long breath. "I hope Damien wasn't upset it's just us girls."

Perhaps that was why, Celine mused. "No, not at all," she answered with a shake of her head. "If anything, relieved. He's up to his eyebrows in work, as always."

"That's Damien," Monica answered. "He works too hard. Don't you think?"

"Don't worry, Mom, we're taking plenty of video game breaks."

Her mother offered a wry glance. "He's happy here, right?" Monica fingered the edge of her napkin, tracing its outline.

"Yeah," Celine answered. "Yeah, he is. He enjoys living near the ocean. He takes a walk every morning along the beach. It's very relaxing for him, I think."

"That's good. And you? You're happy, right?"

Celine offered a confused smile. "Yes. Yes, I can honestly say I am very, very happy here."

Her mother exhaled a long sigh and nodded her head. "Good, that's… so good."

Celine narrowed her eyes. "Is everything okay?"

Their conversation was interrupted by the arrival of their food. The waitress set their plates down and asked if they needed anything before departing. Left alone to eat, Monica steered the conversation to other topics.

As the meal came to a close, Monica's agitation seemed to ramp up. She must be nervous about saying goodbye, Celine figured. As the waitress cleared their plates, Monica glanced at Celine with a smile. Celine returned the gesture.

The waitress sauntered away with a full tray, leaving the two women alone again. Monica took a sip of her water. Were her hands shaking, Celine wondered?

"What time does your train leave?" Celine inquired after a moment of silence.

"Oh, uh, three, I think," Monica answered.

Celine nodded. "Well, you have plenty of time then," Celine answered as the hotel's clock chimed one.

Monica gave her a tight-lipped smile and nodded. She opened her mouth to speak but closed it again, biting her lower lip. Celine noticed her eyes turn glassy. She'd never known Monica Benson to be this emotional. Perhaps the distance and time separation affected her more than Celine realized.

Monica reached across the table and grasped Celine's hand. She squeezed it as a tear fell to her cheek. She wiped it away with her other hand.

"Mom," Celine soothed, "it's okay. You can visit anytime. We'd be happy to see you. Next time, warn us and we'll make sure we have plenty of time to spend with you."

Monica pursed her lips and shook her head. "No," she choked out as she held back a sob, "it's not that." She waved the comment away as she composed herself. After a deep inhale and long, slow exhale, she continued, her voice breaking as she spoke. "Do you have another few minutes? There's something I need to talk to you about."

"Yes, of course," Celine answered. She squeezed her mother's hand in a show of support.

"Would you mind if we spoke in private?" Monica inquired.

"Not at all," Celine said.

Monica nodded and stood from her chair. She smoothed her dress before she glanced at Celine. Celine offered her a smile and slid her arm around Monica's waist.

Monica wrapped her arm around Celine's shoulders as they walked from the cafe and through the empty hotel lobby. They climbed the stairs and Monica shoved her key into the lock of Room Six. She stepped inside and set the key on the table.

Celine followed her into the space. "This is cute," she said as she scanned the nautically themed suite.

"It is!" Monica agreed. "Very quaint."

They stood in silence for another moment before Monica spoke again. "Josie, when I came up here..." Her voice trailed off. She took Celine's hands in hers and stared at her. She tried again. "The reason I came is... "

Celine squeezed her hands. "Mom, whatever it is you're

trying to say, just say it. It's okay. It'll be okay. We'll make sure it is."

Monica nodded and licked her lips. "There's something I need to tell you."

"Okay," Celine prompted with a nod.

Monica pursed her lips and focused on Celine. "I think you'd better sit down."

CHAPTER 15

Damien wandered into the east wing. Light streamed from one door near the end of the hall. Damien passed the many closed doors as he approached Millie's lab. He wondered what was behind them. Bedrooms, most likely. Or something creepy, his mind added.

He shook the thought away and continued down the hall. His knuckles drummed against the door jamb as he peered into the lab.

"Damien!" Millie exclaimed as she spotted him. "Come in."

"Good morning, Damien," Alexander greeted him.

"Hey," Damien said. "I was going to come to find you after I checked in with Millie. Celine said you might be helpful in identifying the poison Doc found yesterday."

"He's beat you to it," Millie responded.

"Have you solved it yet?"

"Afraid not," Alexander admitted.

"No," Millie confirmed. "Though we have vetted several ideas and have a laundry list of things to try."

"Oh, good!" Damien exclaimed, hope filling his voice. "Did anything pan out in your experiments last night?"

"No," Millie answered. "I tried several common remedies to fight the poison. Unsurprisingly none of them worked."

"How's Celine's blood sample?"

"Worse than yesterday but not completely overwhelmed. See for yourself," Millie said, directing him to the microscope across the room.

Damien wandered to it and peered inside. More black cells floated around than he'd seen on the slide yesterday. "So, it's still progressing, but hasn't killed her yet."

"That appears to be the case," Millie answered.

"Which buys us some time," Alexander added.

"Anything I can help with?"

"Do you have any knowledge of chemistry?" Millie inquired.

"Uhhh," Damien hedged.

"For example, do you know how to use a pipette or prepare a sample slide for viewing?"

"Yes!" Damien exclaimed. "I know how to do that!"

"Then there is something you can do," Mille answered. "We're preparing several samples after exposing them to various antidotes suggested by Alexander's research."

"Let's get to it!" Damien declared.

* * *

Celine shoved her hands into the pockets of her cardigan, pulling it closer around her. Despite the sunny day, a chill passed through her. Her mind replayed the conversation with Monica over and over. Before beginning, Monica had warned her she may want to sit down. She wasn't kidding. Celine never expected to hear what she heard before leaving the town's hotel.

Monica's upset hadn't completely subsided after she imparted her news. Celine spent time after the conversation ensuring Monica felt well enough to return home and assuring her all was not lost. Now she had to assure herself of that fact. And she had to tell Damien.

Tears formed in her eyes as she considered that conversation. He had to know. Didn't he? Perhaps not.

Celine climbed the winding driveway leading to the Buckley house. She veered off at the path to the beach. She picked her way across the rocky beach and sank onto a large stone in the middle. The waves lapped at the rocks in front of her. They ebbed and flowed much like her thoughts.

She shook her head. She'd have to tell Damien. He deserved to know. Monica said she couldn't bring herself to tell him. That task would fall to Celine. A tear fell to her cheek. She wiped it away. Damien would survive this. She would make sure of it. They would get through it. The biggest obstacle was getting the words out to him and working through his initial reaction.

Celine rubbed the muscles in her neck as she contemplated the conversation. Her neck ached and her head pounded. This revelation couldn't have come at a worse time, she reflected. Her eyes narrowed as she considered the timing. She'd been poisoned shortly after Monica's arrival.

Celine set her jaw as she considered the chain of events. Marcus's warning rang through her mind. She shook her head as she drew the inevitable conclusion. This was the handiwork of Marcus Northcott.

Celine stood. She squeezed her eyes shut for a moment as an episode of dizziness swept over her. She shook it off and continued her way across the beach. She slipped into the darkened beach cave and used it to hike to the cliffs above.

As she exited the cave high above the beach, she veered off on a path leading away from the house. Within minutes, she set her sights on her target. Marcus Northcott's seaside house rose on the horizon in front of her. She stormed toward it.

As she climbed the steps to the porch, she blew the door open in front of her. It banged off the wall adjacent to it. She stomped into the sitting room where Marcus Northcott sat.

"Celine! What a pleasant surprise," he greeted her.

"Did you know?" she inquired.

"Did I know what, dear?" he questioned as he crossed the room to pour himself a brandy. He waved the decanter at her in a silent offer.

Celine ignored it. "Did you bring Monica Benson here? Just to create trouble?"

Marcus rolled his eyes as he settled back into his chair, brandy in hand. "Really, Celine, must you continue these theatrics?"

"Must you?" she shot back.

"I have no idea to what you are referring."

Celine raised her eyebrows at him though she remained silent.

"Oh, honestly, Celine. I am not responsible for *every* bad thing that happens despite what you believe. Besides, I thought you were overjoyed to visit with your human mother."

Another moment of silence passed before Marcus continued. "Well, are you going to continue to stare daggers at me or do you plan to share what it is you are accusing me of being responsible for?"

Celine shook her head. "It's not worth it," she responded. Pain shot across her forehead and her legs wobbled. She squeezed her eyes shut as she struggled to hold in a distressed moan. The moment did not slip past Marcus.

"Celine, are you quite all right?" Marcus inquired.

Celine's eyes popped open as he spoke. She fought to

maintain her composure. "Leave my family alone," Celine warned before turning on her heel and storming from the house.

Celine stumbled down the stairs, catching herself at the bottom as she swayed. She swallowed hard and steadied herself. She shook the odd feeling from her body before she started down the path toward the house.

Her mind swam with the conversation facing her. She considered putting it off. Perhaps tomorrow morning would provide a better perspective for her. No, she thought, it was best to get it over with. The sooner it was finished the better.

She pressed on, forcing herself to take the most direct path despite her desire to meander in the seclusion of the dense forest.

The gothic house loomed in front of her as she exited from the canopy of the trees. With a deep inhale, she strode toward it and pushed through the front door. As she stepped into the foyer, she spotted Damien emerging from a hall across the space.

"Hey!" he called to her with a smile.

Her heart sank the moment she made eye contact with him. "Hey, D," she said with a sigh.

His smile faded as he approached her. "That doesn't sound good. Did everything go okay with Aunt Monica?"

Celine's head bounced around, unsure if she should nod or shake her head. "She's home-bound," Celine began.

"Whew, that's a relief!" Damien exclaimed.

Celine nodded at his statement. "I found out why she was here," she began, her hands shoved tightly into her sweater pockets. She avoided eye contact with Damien, staring at the marbled floor below her feet. Her head pounded and her knees wobbled.

"Oh?" he prompted.

"Yeah," she hedged. She raised her eyes to meet his. Her forehead wrinkled as she spoke. "D, we need to talk."

"Okay?" he said, phrasing his response as a question.

Celine hesitated a moment, her mind fuzzy. She breathed deeply, her chin dipping to her chest before she caught it. She wiggled her shoulders as discomfort set into them. "Maybe we should head upstairs to your..." she began. Her voice slurred and trailed off.

"Celine?" Damien questioned.

Celine's chest heaved a few times. She blinked, her eyelids heavy and hard to open. Her limbs felt like lead. Her head lolled as her eyes rolled back. The world around her closed to a pinpoint and she felt her body slip to the cold floor below.

Damien fixed his gaze on Celine. Her behavior was odd. Had something happened with Aunt Monica? Celine said she left, so what was the problem? "We need to talk," she said before she hesitated.

Damien prompted her to continue. She fidgeted. She began to suggest they head upstairs before her voice slowed. Her eyelids fluttered and her breathing became labored.

Within an instant, her eyes rolled back, and she began to slump to the floor.

"Celine!" Damien exclaimed as he reached for her. He wrapped his arms around her before she hit the floor. "Celine?"

Damien's face pinched with concern as he held her limp body in his arms. He eased her to the floor and knelt beside her. "Celine?!" he repeated, giving her a light shake.

"SOMEBODY HELP!" he shouted, panic lacing his voice.

The doors to the sitting room burst open and Michael appeared. "What's wrong?" he questioned.

"It's Celine," Damien croaked. "She… she… she just collapsed!" A worried moan escaped his lips as he twisted to face her again.

Michael joined him, reaching down to take her pulse. "Pulse is still strong," he mentioned.

"Get somebody. Get Millie!" Damien entreated. "Ooooh, Celine."

Michael squeezed Damien's shoulder. "I'll get her. Stay with Celine and try to stay calm, buddy."

Damien groaned again as he clutched her hand. "Easier said than done. Just hurry."

Michael gave him a clap on the back as he raced across the foyer and disappeared into a hallway. "Come on, Celine," Damien murmured as he squeezed her hand. "Wake up." He had witnessed the effects of the poison on her system through a microscope. Her red blood cells were slowly being overwhelmed by the poison. That must be what was happening inside her body.

He glanced down at her. Behind that fair skin, her body waged a war. A war she may be losing. His forehead pinched further as he fought back the waterfall of emotions that threatened to spill over.

The front door swung open, and Gray entered. "Damien! What happened?" Gray questioned as he collapsed to his knees on Celine's other side.

"One minute we were talking and then she just collapsed!" Damien shouted, his nerves forcing his voice an octave higher.

Gray grasped her hand and felt her cheek. "She isn't feverish."

"Michael's getting Millie," Damien informed him.

Gray nodded. "Let's move her to the sitting room." He

scooped her limp form into his arms and carried her into the adjacent room, laying her on the sofa.

Damien paced the room's length. He raked his fingers through his hair. The vision of Celine's cells being eaten away by the poison danced in his mind.

Millie, Michael and Alexander hurried into the room. Millie spotted her on the couch and made her way to Celine's side. "Tell me what happened, leave out no details," she instructed as she focused her attention on Celine.

"She was on the floor when I came in," Gray answered. "Damien, were you with her when she collapsed?"

"Uh," Damien murmured as he collected his thoughts.

Alexander approached him with a brandy. "Take your time, Damien," he offered.

"Yeah, yes, I was with her." He swallowed hard. "Umm, she... she... one minute she was talking and the next she slumped to the floor. Mid-sentence she just stopped talking and then she went down."

"Did she hit her head?" Millie inquired as she pulled Celine's eyelids open.

"No, no," Damien said with a shake of his head. "I caught her before she hit the floor."

"Any sign of pain? Labored breathing? Groaning? Clutching at any body part?"

Damien considered it. "No. Wait, yes. Her breathing was labored," he recalled. "She didn't look like she was in pain. She just stopped speaking. Her voice slurred a little like she was weak or tired."

"What was she saying?" Gray asked.

"She said we needed to talk," Damien responded.

"About?" he fired back.

"I don't know. I asked her about Aunt Monica. She said she left but she found out the reason she made the sudden appearance. She said we needed to talk, and she was starting to suggest we go upstairs when she collapsed. She seemed upset."

"Upset as in a potential expression of illness or upset about the impending conversation?" Alexander inquired.

Damien shrugged. "I'm not sure. I guessed about the conversation. She was acting strange. But it could have been because she wasn't feeling well."

Millie stood from her crouch near Celine. "Let's get her to bed. I'd like to examine her further and see if we can wake her."

Gray nodded as he pulled Celine into his arms. The group followed him upstairs to their suite. Michael and Alexander waited in the sitting room area as Millie and Damien filed into the bedroom behind Gray.

Millie pulled open her medical bag. She began by drawing a new blood sample. The blood that oozed into the tube looked thick and dark. Damien's stomach turned over at the sight. The poison had progressed further in Celine's system.

Millie slipped the vial into her bag before she extracted her stethoscope. She pressed the diaphragm against Celine's chest in several places. She shined her light into Celine's eyes after pulling her eyelids open. She stuck a thermometer into her ear for a temperature reading. She stood as she finished her exam.

"Well?" Gray demanded.

"Her lungs are clear, but her breathing is a bit shallow. That could be because of her unconscious state. Her pulse and heart rate are slow but steady. Her pupils are reactive. Her body temperature is normal. There are no signs of serious concern with her physical condition yet outside of the unconscious state." Millie dug into her bag and pulled a small vial from it. "I'd like to see if we can wake her. Either way, I must get her blood to the lab and determine the extent of progression of the poison in her system."

Millie pulled the top from the vial of smelling salts. She waved the small tube under Celine's nostrils. After a few seconds, she pursed her lips as she shoved the cap back onto the item. "Nothing. Not even a flinch."

"What does that mean?" Damien asked.

"It means we can't force her out of this state. Her body must wake on its own," Millie answered. "If you'll excuse me, I'd like to prepare this sample. Inform me if there are any acute changes in her condition."

Damien nodded as Millie heaved her bag onto her forearm and swept past him. Michael and Alexander filed into the room as Millie departed. "Any news?" Alexander inquired.

Gray shook his head. "She couldn't wake her," he admitted. "Right now, there are no physical issues to be concerned with, but Millie drew a blood sample to analyze."

Damien sank onto the bed next to Celine. He took her hand in his. Her listless fingers grazed his palm. He pushed a lock of blonde hair from her pale skin and adjusted her covers. What would the blood results show, he wondered?

He could do nothing sitting here. He'd go help Millie, he decided. Damien leapt from the bed and hurried to the door.

"Where you going, man?" Michael inquired.

"To help Millie," he mumbled as he raced from the room.

Alexander followed him. "Damien, wait!" he called.

"Please tell me one of those antidotes we prepared this morning worked," Damien answered as Alexander caught up to him.

CHAPTER 16

Alexander drew his mouth into a thin line. "None of them showed much promise, though that could have changed by now. Let's hope we find one that has helped."

They remained silent as they wandered through the halls to Millie's lab. They found her inside, already preparing the new blood sample.

"How does that look?" Damien inquired as he motioned toward the vial of thickened, gooey dark red blood.

"I'll know more when I see it under the microscope," Millie answered.

"That's bull," Damien shouted. "You can tell something now. That doesn't look right. I'm not a doctor and even I know that."

Alexander placed his hand on Damien's shoulder. "Easy, Damien. She's doing the best she can."

"No, he's right," Millie said with a deep sigh. "The blood is dark, thickened and tarry. It does not look good."

"The poison is progressing. That's what's causing her coma-like symptom, isn't it?" Damien pressed.

"Without viewing the sample, I cannot say for certain, but yes, that would be my professional opinion at the moment."

"Any luck with the antidotes we tested earlier?" Alexander inquired.

"Nothing shows a strong ability to reverse the poison's course," Millie answered. "Though it is early, perhaps in time…"

"In time?!" Damien cried, interrupting Millie. "We don't have time!"

Millie shrugged. "I'm afraid there's not much we can do until we stumble upon something."

"Start trying the antidotes on her."

"That is unwise," Alexander responded.

"I concur," Mille agreed. "We have no idea what effect these may have. We do not want to make the situation worse."

"Worse? How could it get worse?!"

"It could accelerate the poison's spread. At the moment, Celine's condition is stable. I understand how vexing her unconscious state is for you, Damien, however, she is not declining at the moment. We must take solace in that as we continue to pursue a solution."

Damien closed his eyes and shook his head as he gathered his thoughts. "Fine, fine," Damien concurred, waving his hands in the air. "But if she gets worse…"

"If she gets worse," Millie interrupted, "we'll reassess the situation and take a more aggressive course."

Damien nodded in agreement. "I'm sorry, I'm just…"

"Upset," Alexander finished. "We realize that. And we understand."

"You mentioned Celine wanted to speak with you," Millie said as she created a slide from Celine's blood sample. "Do you have any idea what it concerned?"

Damien shrugged and shook his head. "No," he admitted.

"She was acting strange like I said, but that could have been her illness."

"Do you imagine it may have had to do with her illness? Some clue we could use to find a way forward?" Alexander inquired.

"I really am not sure," Damien answered. "I wish I could tell you more. She just said we needed to talk. I assumed it had to do with why Aunt Monica suddenly appeared in Bucksville. And she wanted to speak alone. She suggested we go upstairs."

"Hmm," Alexander murmured. "Perhaps it has nothing to do with the poison then."

"It seems not," Millie agreed. "Well, let's see what we have with this sample and determine if any progress has been made by our potential antidotes."

"Anything I can do?" Damien asked.

"Not at the moment," Millie replied. "Why don't you go sit with Celine? If I need any help, I'll call for you."

"Okay," Damien agreed with a sigh. "If you find anything..."

"We'll let everyone know right away," Millie assured him.

With another nod, he stalked from the room. He shoved his hands into his pockets as he navigated the ornate hallways to Celine's bedroom. The house seemed quiet, cold. If something happened to Celine...

No, he refused to allow his mind to go to that possibility. They would find an antidote. They would save her. She would be fine.

He slogged through the door into her suite. Michael paced the floor in the sitting room. "Hey, buddy, any news?"

Damien shook his head, unable to force any words from his lips.

Michael clapped a hand on his shoulder. "It'll be okay."

Damien's forehead creased as he fought back emotions. "Nothing's worked so far. Nothing Millie's tried has worked."

"We'll find a way," Michael assured him.

"You don't know that," Damien countered. "Did you spot the vial of blood Millie drew? It doesn't even look like blood. It looks like tar."

Michael pursed his lips.

"And don't say we've been through worse because we haven't. Celine's never been sick like this."

"No, but she's been missing, and we got through that. We'll get through this."

"Somehow that seemed so trivial compared to what we're facing now."

"Because it's over. It wasn't trivial when we were dealing with it. Not for her, not for you. Come on, man, don't give up hope yet."

"I'm not," Damien assured him. "I can't. I can't imagine her…" He shook his head, refusing to say the word.

"Good," Michael said with a nod. "Besides, if Celine had something to tell you, she's coming back to tell you."

The comment earned a chuckle from Damien. "Yeah," he replied. "Yeah, she'll just refuse to die because she had something to tell me."

"That'd be Celine."

Damien offered another laugh before he said, "I'm going to sit with her for a little while."

"Okay. I'll be right out here if you need anything."

"Thanks, man," he said before he slipped into Celine's room.

Gray sat at her bedside. He glanced behind him as Damien approached the foot of the bed. "How is she?" Damien inquired.

"No change," Gray answered.

Damien bit his lower lip as he stared at Celine. "Sit

down," Gray suggested, waving him to the opposite side of the bed. "She'd want you here."

Damien crossed to the bed's side and sank onto the edge. He slipped his hand around Celine's. He watched her chest as it rose and fell. He glanced at her face. If he didn't know better, he'd have thought she was merely asleep.

"Hang in there, Celine," he muttered.

* * *

Celine fell through blackness. She'd been in the foyer with Damien a moment ago. Now nothing but darkness rushed past her.

She landed with a thud on a cold, hard surface. A chill passed over her as she scrambled to stand. She glanced around, finding only nothingness surrounding her.

Distorted voices sounded overhead. She glanced upward. "Hello?" she called. She strained to make out the words they spoke. "Hello?" she called again.

No one answered.

More garbled voices reached her ears. Celine wandered around the darkened space as she searched for a place where she could make sense of the muttered words.

After a moment of wandering, the voices became clearer.

"Gray?" she shouted, her voice echoing in the space.

"Sit down. She'd want you here," Gray said to someone.

"Hang in there, Celine," Damien's voice echoed.

"Damien!" she called.

They couldn't hear her. She couldn't speak to them. What had happened? She glanced around again. Where was she?

A new voice resounded. Loud and echoing, she winced as it blasted her eardrums.

"Come to me, Celine," Tobias's voice said.

Celine arched an eyebrow as she spun in a circle, scanning the space for him.

"Come to me, Celine," he repeated. "I can make you happy."

"No," she said.

"Yes," he countered.

Celine shook her head, intent on resisting him. She spiraled as she searched for an exit. As the voice continued to speak, she flung herself into the darkness, trying to outrun it.

"You cannot run. You cannot hide," Tobias said. "You are mine, Celine. This time you are mine."

Celine ran but nothing changed. The voice remained with her, and she found no escape. Her lower lip quivered as she ceased her sprint. She bit her lip as she sank to the cold floor. She was trapped. Stuck. Here she would wait in darkness until someone found her. She hoped against hope that someone would not be Tobias Greene.

* * *

Michael paced the floor of Celine and Gray's sitting room. Damien disappeared into the room moments earlier. The worry on his face was obvious.

Michael had tried his best to assuage his fears. He hoped he had set his mind somewhat at ease, though he doubted he'd made a dent in Damien's concern.

Still, perhaps he'd alleviated some of his burden by assuring him he wasn't alone in this.

Michael spun to stalk in the opposite direction. Damien was right. They'd never seen Celine this sick. Even when she was still human as Josie, she hadn't been this sick.

But she couldn't die. She'd pull through. At least, he hoped so.

In any case, Michael decided, he couldn't leave now. Even

with the Monica Benson situation solved, he couldn't walk out. Not with Celine so direly ill and Damien on the brink of mind-numbing worry.

He'd stick by his friends. He had to. They needed him.

Perhaps he could do something to help right now. He'd offer to grab some food or coffee for Damien. Michael strode to the door, intent on doing what little he could to assist.

* * *

Damien sat on Celine's bed, clutching her hand and counting her breaths for two hours. Michael offered to bring coffee or another refreshment, but Damien declined. He wasn't sure food would sit well on his jittery stomach.

As afternoon turned to early evening, beads of sweat began to form on Celine's forehead. Damien squinted at them, wondering if his eyes were deceiving him. Her hand, still clasped in his, turned clammy. Gray paced the floor on the opposite side of the bed. "Hey, Gray," Damien said.

"What is it?" Gray asked, whipping to face him, and sinking onto the bed next to Celine. "Is there some change?"

"The sweat on her forehead," Damien said. Damien placed the back of his hand against Celine's colorless cheek. "She feels warm."

"We need to get Millie."

"Yeah, I'll tell Michael."

Damien rushed to the door and passed the message along. Michael hastened from the sitting room beyond the bedroom in a mad dash to locate Millie.

Damien returned to Celine's side. Her lips began to lose their color, fading into her fair skin. Damien checked her breathing. It remained steady. Small miracles, he ruminated.

The door burst open to the bedroom as he pondered Celine's decline.

"Celine?!" Celeste cried from the door, her blue eyes wide as she stared at the listless form in the bed. "Oh, Celine!"

Celeste flew across the room to her sister's side. She shoved in front of Gray to grasp Celine's hand. "How long has she been like this?"

"Since she returned home earlier this afternoon," Gray answered.

"And it's poison?"

"Yes," Gray answered.

Millie's arrival stunted any further inquiries from Celeste. Damien stepped back to allow Millie access to Celine. She performed an exam, checking all vitals including her temperature.

"Well?" Celeste demanded as Millie straightened from her bent position over Celine.

"I'm afraid you were correct," Millie said as she focused on Gray and Damien. "She's developed a fever."

Damien shook his head.

"While it is indicative of her body fighting, it is concerning," Millie continued. "The fever is a tad over one-hundred-and-one and her condition is worsening rather than improving."

"You have to do something," Gray insisted.

Millie nodded as she withdrew a vial and syringe from her medical bag. "What's that?" Damien questioned.

"A pain reliever. It should reduce her fever and alleviate any discomfort she is experiencing."

"That's it?" Damien questioned.

"That's all we can do at the moment," Millie answered.

Celeste raised her eyebrows, her eyes widening. "I agree with Damien! This seems an inappropriate solution."

"None of the antidotes we are testing have shown any promise in stopping or even slowing the poison," Alexander chimed in.

"None?" Celeste cried incredulously. "What have you tried?"

"Perhaps if you ask your master, Northcott, we can find a solution faster," Gray snapped.

"Marcus?" Celeste questioned. "What has he to do with this?"

"Everything," Gray retorted.

"I agree," Michael said. "This has his fingerprints all over it."

Celeste scoffed. "No," she said with a shake of her head.

"Of course, you'd defend him," Gray replied as he crossed his arms.

Celeste matched his stance, setting her jaw and raising her eyebrows. "I am not defending him, merely assuring you he has no hand in this."

"How are you so sure?" Michael questioned.

"Simple," Celeste responded. "He'd never harm Celine."

Gray burst into laughter. "Oh, that's rich!" He turned serious. "He's done nothing but harm Celine since she was sixteen years old."

Celeste shook her head. "Not like this. If I am not mistaken, she's dying, or close. He'd never kill her."

"Perhaps he didn't intend to kill her," Alexander suggested. "But the poison went further than he expected, or the situation got away from him."

"He'd never chance Celine's death. Marcus does not take unforeseen risks. No, this is not Marcus's work."

"You're sure?" Alexander inquired.

"Yes," Celeste answered without hesitation.

"How sure?" Damien pressed.

Celeste turned her steely blue eyes to him. "I'd stake my life on it."

"You're not staking your life, you're staking Celine's, so you'd better be right," Michael said.

"We are wasting time discussing improbable solutions," Celeste argued. "We must pursue another avenue."

"But what?" Damien asked. "We're making no progress on the antidote front."

"What is the poison?" Celeste questioned.

"Unidentified," Alexander answered. "We've formulated antidotes based on the symptoms Celine experienced and poisons that cause them."

"What have you tried thus far?"

Millie recited a list of antidotes being tested against the poison, adding that nothing had shown any promise in reversing the poison's effects. Celeste narrowed her eyes as she considered them. "Have you tried combining them?"

"No," Millie admitted. "But I will as soon as I return to the lab."

Millie remained in her spot for another moment. An expression of shock crossed Celeste's face. "Well, hop to it, doctor! This is not the time for delay."

Millie closed her doctor's bag and departed from the room.

"That was unnecessary. You don't give the orders here," Gray warned Celeste.

"I'm going back to my house to retrieve a few more references. Perhaps they will contain a clue," Alexander said.

"Just a moment," Celeste said before Alexander departed. "Before you leave, I would like to hear the entire story surrounding Celine's condition."

"The poison came from a rose that pricked her finger," Gray explained.

"When?"

"A few days ago. She began to experience symptoms, both physical and otherwise. She complained of a dull headache at first, then numb, tingly hands."

"And?"

"And she began to lose time," Gray continued.

"Lose time?" Celeste questioned.

"Yes," Gray answered, "she didn't realize it at first. She chalked it up to sleepwalking and a wandering mind. But the night Monica came to dinner, we found her sitting on her swing completely unresponsive."

"After that incident," Alexander added, "Damien and I began to research the symptoms she experienced. She visited during one of our research sessions. During that time, she experienced another incident. She became unresponsive and wandered to a bedroom here in the house. She only came out of it when she caught our reflection in a mirror."

"Then Millie hypnotized her," Gray said, "and she slipped into the same unresponsive state. Only this time," Gray added, "one of us spotted something."

All eyes turned to Damien. He swallowed hard as he became the center of everyone's attention. "Oh, right, yeah, ummm," he stammered. "She was out of it, but again, she caught our reflection in the mirror. We tried to draw her away from the mirror to snap her out of it. Before she stepped away, she smashed the mirror to pieces. And that's when I spotted it."

"Yes?" Celeste prodded.

"In the mirror shards, I saw something red moving. I pieced together a few of the intact pieces on the floor. The mirror shards weren't reflecting the room, though, they were showing a different picture. Celine was in a red dress and was dancing with someone. I couldn't tell who. Then, suddenly, a hand reached through the mirror at me. It terrified me and I fell backward before the mirror exploded."

"And this all started following the finger prick from the rose?"

"Yes," Gray answered.

Celeste bit her lower lip as she considered the information.

"We don't know much more than that," Gray admitted. "Celine cannot recall anything from her blackouts. The only piece of information that points to any clues is the snippet Damien witnessed in the mirror. Based on that, we identified the time period to be somewhere between the 1830s and the 1860s."

"Leading us to our only other suspect," Alexander stated. "Tobias Greene."

Celeste snapped her head toward Alexander. "What?" she asked incredulously. "Impossible!"

"Why?" Damien questioned.

Celeste answered, "He disappeared over a century ago without a trace."

"Who the hell is this guy and why does everyone act so strange when his name is mentioned?" Michael asked.

Celeste shook her head. "The details are unimportant. What is important is curing Celine first and finding out who did this to her second. It wasn't Marcus, but I'm unconvinced Tobias Greene has resurfaced."

"Then who?" Alexander asked.

Celeste shrugged.

"Are you unconvinced the culprit is Tobias because you've got someone else more probable in mind or because you'd prefer it isn't?" Gray barked.

Celeste tightened her jaw as she considered her response. A moan from Celine interrupted any further conversation. "Celine?" she burst as she hurried to her side.

The group gathered around her. "Is she coming to?" Damien asked with hope filling his voice.

A pained expression crossed Celine's face as she groaned again.

"I doubt it," Alexander said with a sigh.

Damien furrowed his brow and glanced at the man. Alexander stepped around Gray and twisted Celine's arm to show the underside. A network of blackened veins crept up her porcelain skin from her index finger toward her shoulder.

CHAPTER 17

"What is that?" Damien gasped as he stared at the black web crawling up Celine's forearm.

"An effect from the poison, no doubt," Alexander replied.

"And I'm assuming it's not a good one," Michael added.

Alexander shook his head. "No," he responded. "No, it's not."

Damien pursed his lips and combed his fingers through his hair. "We need a solution, and we need one fast."

"I agree," Alexander answered. "I'm going to retrieve a few more references, but I will share the news with Millie on my way."

"Please hurry," Damien entreated.

"I will, Damien."

Damien paced the length of the room as Alexander disappeared through the door. Within ten minutes, Millie rushed into the room. "Alexander informed me of the change in Celine's condition," she puffed.

"Yes," Celeste answered. "We must do something NOW!"

Millie examined Celine's arm. The blackened veins reached almost to her elbow, fading into gray just before the crook of her arm. "I agree this does not look good," Millie said.

"Is there anything you can do, Millie?" Gray questioned.

"Given the latest development, I propose we try the combination suggested by Celeste earlier. It is untested though it should do her no harm. It may also do her no good."

"SHOULD do her no harm or WILL do her no harm?" Damien inquired.

"Should. I cannot say for certain. I have no data on this treatment. What I can say is on their own they didn't accelerate the poison's effect. I would expect their combination wouldn't either, but I cannot say with any degree of certainty."

Millie rested her gaze on Gray, waiting for his decision. Gray rubbed his chin.

"Well?" Celeste demanded.

"Easy, Celeste," Michael said. "Give him a minute."

Gray glanced to Damien. "What do you think?" he inquired.

Damien swallowed hard. "It's your call," he said.

"What if it was yours?" Gray questioned. "You love her, Damien. I trust your judgment. What would you do?"

Damien bit his lower lip as he glanced at Celine's slack form. He studied her pale, colorless skin devoid of its normal rosiness, the web of blackened veins crawling up her arm, the beads of sweat on her feverish forehead.

He flicked his gaze to Gray. "I'd try it."

Gray nodded at him before he turned to Millie. "Give it to her," he instructed.

Millie gave him a nod before she pulled a syringe from her medical bag. Filled with a colorless solution, she injected it into the blackened vein at Celine's cubital.

Damien watched as Millie depressed the plunger. His

gaze fell on Celine's face, studying it for any sign of reaction to the injection. None showed.

Millie straightened as she withdrew the needle from Celine's arm. "Now, we wait," she said. "If there are any changes in her condition, notify me immediately."

"Where are you going?" Damien questioned.

"Back to the lab. We have no guarantee this will work. I plan to continue work on other options in the event we need them."

"I'll go with you," Celeste said. "I may be of some assistance."

Millie nodded in agreement and the two women left the room. Damien collapsed onto the bed next to Celine with a long exhale. "I hate waiting," he lamented.

Michael squeezed his shoulder. "Let's hope we won't be waiting much longer."

Damien nodded in response.

"Hey, how about some dinner for everyone?" Michael inquired.

Damien shook his head. "I couldn't eat."

"You've gotta try, buddy," Michael argued.

"He's right," Gray interjected. "You should eat. Maybe get some rest."

"I'm not leaving her!" Damien insisted.

"No problem. I'll bring something for everyone. We can eat right here."

Damien remained silent for a moment. "In fact," Michael added, "I'll run to the cafe. Grab some burgers and fries. Maybe the whiff of Bucksville fries will wake her up!"

The comment earned a chuckle from Damien. "You don't have to go into town. But I wouldn't turn down those fries."

"You got it, buddy. Burgers and fries coming right up."

* * *

Millie hurried from the room with the empty syringe clutched in her hand. She struggled to stop her hand from shaking. She'd just injected an untested serum into her patient's body.

She fought to maintain her calm, clearheaded composure but she was losing that battle. She hadn't made the final call. Gray and Damien had. Following her advice, she reminded herself.

What if she'd assisted in Celine's demise? No, her scientific mind told her. The most likely scenario was that this would not harm Celine. The most likely scenario was also that it would do her no good.

Millie had made little progress with curing Celine's poisoned body thus far. Nothing she tried worked. She'd tested, retested, reformulated and tried again. Nothing worked.

As she and Celeste strode down the long hallway leading to her lab, she swallowed hard and blinked back the tears stinging her eyes.

What kind of doctor was she if she couldn't help her patient? What was the sense in staying here if at the first sign of trouble, they couldn't count on her?

She pushed her shoulders back and strengthened her stride. She had to make progress, she told herself.

* * *

Michael returned in thirty minutes with food for everyone. Damien shoved a fry into his mouth as he pondered the situation. Celine exhibited no changes. That wasn't good, he reflected. It also wasn't bad, his mind argued.

Gray bit into a fry, his mouth turning into a grimace. "I can't believe you eat these," he murmured.

"You don't know what good food is," Michael countered.

Gray stared at the remaining half of a fry clutched between his fingers. "I consider that a blessing."

Millie checked in as they finished their meal. She completed an exam.

"Any changes?" Damien asked as she tossed the stethoscope around her neck.

Millie sighed, her jaw tight and her lips in a frown. "Only slight ones."

"That's good, right?" Michael inquired.

Millie shook her head. "No," she disagreed. "Her temperature has risen. I'm going to suggest we give another round of the fever reducer and to keep a cool cloth on her forehead."

"I'll get it," Damien exclaimed, leaping from the bed.

Millie administered another round of medication while Damien retrieved a bowl of cool water and a rag. He wet it, wrung it out and laid it carefully across her hot skin.

In a fiery red ball, the sun sank below the horizon. Damien continued to refresh the cool rag. It became warm within moments of being laid across Celine's forehead. As he retrieved another bowl of cool water, this time adding ice, Gray offered to take over the job.

"Why don't you get some rest, Damien," he suggested.

Damien shook his head. "I'm fine," he promised. "I want to stay with her."

"I realize that. Stay here but let me take over. Get some rest."

Damien grasped Celine's hand in his. He squeezed it, offering a silent prayer for her. Outside of the blackened veins on her left arm, which hadn't spread any further so far, she appeared healthy. Pale, but healthy. He hoped the antidote was working.

As evening turned to night, Damien slouched onto the pillow next to Celine. His eyes became heavy though he fought to keep them open. He counted her breaths, checking that they were steady and even. The rhythmic breathing lulled him into a sleepy state. After a few moments, his eyes closed, and he drifted to sleep.

When Damien awoke, the room was dark. He rubbed his eyes and squinted into the blackness as he tried to discern any details. He reached next to him for Celine but found her nowhere. "Gray? Michael?" he inquired. He received no response.

Damien reached to the lamp on the night table and flicked its switch. No light flared into the room; it remained pitch black. He tried it a few more times but produced no results.

A knot grew in the pit of his stomach. Why didn't the lights work? Where was Celine? Gray? Michael? If something happened to her, why hadn't they woken him?

He climbed from the bed. His feet touched the cold floor. The icy shock sent a shiver up his spine as he raised himself to stand. He trudged across the room and pulled the door open to the sitting room.

"Hey, where are you..." he began.

Damien stopped speaking mid-sentence as he witnessed his surroundings. Beyond Celine's bedroom was a seemingly endless hallway. Doors lined each side. Where had the sitting room gone?

"Hello?" Damien called down the hall, his voice echoing. "Gray? Michael? Alexander? Anyone?"

He took a few steps into the dark hall. The door to Celine's bedroom slammed behind him. He spun and twisted the doorknob. The door did not budge. He banged against it with his fist, but to no avail.

With a heaving sigh, Damien twisted and eyed the hallway again. He stood straighter and squared his shoulders. With a hard swallow, he started down the hall in search of anything or anyone familiar.

Damien eyed each door as he scoured his surroundings for something familiar. He found nothing he recognized. Had he sleepwalked to another wing? A wing he'd never seen before?

He twisted one of the ornate doorknobs in an attempt to open the door. He found it locked. He tried another, also locked. He continued down the hall, trying doors as he went.

He was about to give up when one of the doorknobs turned and the door popped open. "Finally," he murmured. He swung the door open and glanced inside. His jaw dropped and his eyes went wide as he witnessed the scene inside. A black wolf stood in the room's center. With teeth bared, it growled, its red eyes fixed on him. He grasped for the doorknob and pulled the door shut, securing it tightly against the jamb.

Damien blew out a sigh of relief as he rested against the door. What the hell was happening, he wondered? With a shake of his head, he pulled away from the door and continued down the hall. He found several more locked doors before another one gave way.

As it popped open, he held his breath. What would he find on the opposite side? He eased the door open a crack and peered inside. Bright lights lit the room. Music floated from inside. He inched the door open enough to stick his head inside and view the entire room.

He blinked a few times as he gaped at the spectacle. A red dress floated around the room as though dancing. He must be more tired than he thought! He closed his eyes for a moment before he peered at the room again. The red dress continued its swaying around the room. He narrowed his eyes at it. There was something familiar about it.

The realization that it was Celine's dress from the mirror hit him just as the commotion began. The lights in the room flickered and dimmed. The music slowed. Blackness crept from the corners toward the center of the room. A deafening shriek filled the air. He clapped his hands over his ears and squeezed his eyes shut.

He opened them to slits and gasped at what faced him. A floating hand reached toward him. A sudden sense of terror and dread filled him. With a frightened moan, Damien grasped the door handle and swung the door shut.

He gulped air as his heart returned to normal speed. He rubbed his neck as he stared down the corridor, fearing what may lay ahead. Another sound broke the silence as he considered continuing.

"Damien?" Celine's voice echoed.

"Celine!" he shouted, searching for the source of her voice.

"Damien!" she called.

"Celine?! Celine, I'm here!" Damien raced down the hall.

"Hurry, Damien. Hurry."

"I'm trying," he answered as he sprinted. The corridor continued. For every door he passed, six more appeared. He stopped and spun in a circle, searching for another exit.

"Damien, hurry," Celine urged.

"Celine, I'm trying but I can't find you!"

"You must find me, Damien. Find me."

Damien groaned in frustration. "I'm trying! This hall is endless! Keep talking, I'll follow the sound of your voice."

His request was met with silence. "Celine?" he inquired. "Celine, are you there?"

"Hurry, Damien," she answered. "Remember. The red dress, the ruby necklace, the cave. The red dress, the ruby necklace, the cave. The red dress, the ruby necklace, the cave."

Celine's voice continued to repeat the phrase over and over. Damien hurried down the hall but ceased walking when it became apparent the end was no nearer. He spun again, studying the doors for signs of Celine or an exit. He walked back toward her bedroom. He circled again. He lost track of where he started, unsure of which direction was which.

Celine's voice continued to drone on with the same words. Damien whirled in a dizzying circle. The walls began to blur. He felt woozy. His legs threatened to buckle. His stomach turned and bile crept up his throat. He groaned as he placed his hand on his forehead and stumbled forward.

After two steps, he collapsed to his knees. "Celine," he croaked before he collapsed to the floor.

CHAPTER 18

"Celine," Damien murmured. His brow pinched and he thrashed in the bed. "The red dress, the ruby necklace, the cave."

He shot up to sitting as he gasped for breath.

"Easy, Damien, easy," Gray whispered as he grasped him by the shoulders.

"Huh?" he cried. "Celine!"

He whipped his head to the side. Celine lay unmoving next to him, except for the rhythmic rise and fall of her chest.

"She's fine, Damien," Gray said. "Millie was just here. There's no change."

Damien exhaled a sigh of relief. He nodded. "I had a nightmare."

"That much is apparent. Everything is fine. Go back to sleep. Get some more rest."

Damien nodded and reached out for Celine's hand as he eased back into his pillow. He spent a few moments staring at her, assuring himself she was okay. He pushed the haunting memories of the dream from his mind. Nothing more than a nightmare, he told himself. Just a nightmare. He drifted to sleep repeating the mantra.

* * *

Millie bent over her patient. Celine laid unmoving in the bed. Damien, next to her, clutched her hand in his as he snored softly. Careful not to disturb him, Millie performed her exam.

Celine's temperature held steady at one-hundred-and-five. It hadn't risen in hours, but it hadn't reduced either. The blackening of the veins in her forearm had spread to her upper arm.

The medication wasn't working. The antidote was not reversing the poison's progression.

Millie placed the stethoscope's earpieces into her ears. She pressed the diaphragm against Celine's chest. The thud of her heartbeat sounded. Slow, but steady. Good, Millie noted. She moved the stethoscope to her lungs. No crackling, still clear.

Millie straightened and placed the stethoscope around her neck with a sigh. She felt Gray's stare boring into her back.

She turned to face him and joined him at the foot of the bed.

"No change," she said in a low voice.

Gray nodded in answer.

"I'll come back in a few hours to check again."

"Thanks, Millie," he answered.

Millie spun on her heel and stalked from the room. She shut the door behind her as she stepped into the suite's sitting room. She bit her lower lip as she crumpled against the door behind her.

Tears stung her eyes and she squeezed them shut. Celine's

lack of improvement frustrated her. She'd still made no progress to help her. Her condition remained unchanged and would likely worsen.

With a sniffle, Millie pulled away from the door and strode across the room. She couldn't afford this moment of weakness. Celine's life hung in the balance. She must continue working toward a solution.

She swept away a lone tear that escaped to her cheek and navigated the halls to her lab. Alexander crouched over the microscope. Millie crossed to her bag. She reached in, her fingers searching for a mirror.

"How is she?" Alexander inquired.

"No better, I'm afraid," she murmured, her voice trembling as tears threatened again.

"Millie?" Alexander asked as she doubled over her bag, now in search of a tissue.

"Yes?" she croaked as she attempted to hide her emotional outburst.

"Are you all right?"

"Fine," she said with a sniffle as she batted her eyelashes until the tears receded.

She felt a warm hand on her shoulder. "Are you quite sure?"

She spun to face him, sinking onto the stool behind her. She pressed her lips together. "Celine is not improving," Millie admitted.

"Has her condition worsened?"

"Not really. The blackened veins have expanded to her upper arm, though nothing else has changed."

Millie wiped at her face with the tissue and blew her nose. "Is there something you aren't telling us?" Alexander inquired.

"No," Millie answered with another sniffle. "I've been completely honest. Completely honest at how terrible of a doctor I am." Tears spilled to her cheeks again as she fought them.

"You're not a terrible doctor."

"I am. I cannot fix her. I cannot fix anything."

Alexander grasped her shoulders. "Millie, you're exhausted. You need rest. You should get some sleep."

Millie shook her head at him. "No, I must press on. We have no solutions. We..."

"No," Alexander insisted. "We have several tests running. There is nothing else to do at the moment. In the morning, we'll reassess things and move forward with what we've learned. Pressing on when you're this tired will not help."

"If we can't find a working antidote..."

"Yes, I know the stakes. All too well," Alexander answered. "But pressing on while you are in this state solves nothing. Rest for an hour or two at least. I'll wake you if anything changes here."

Millie swallowed hard and wiped at her cheeks with the back of her hand. She nodded. "All right. Don't let me sleep longer than two hours."

"I wouldn't dream of it," Alexander promised.

With a heavy sigh, Millie slogged to the chaise in the corner of her lab. She pulled the blanket draped across its back over her and closed her sore eyes. She drifted to sleep, praying this nap wasn't a mistake that cost Celine her life.

* * *

Damien awoke to a barrage of activity in the room. Half-asleep he stretched and rubbed his eyes. A strange raspy sound reached his ears. What was that noise, he wondered? Had they brought some machine into the room?

He opened his bleary eyes and glanced at Celine. His

heart skipped a beat as he realized the rattling noise came from her.

He noted the changes in her appearance in addition to the awful noise escaping her. Blackened veins crawled the length of her arm, disappearing under her top at her shoulder. Her previously colorless lips were now tinged blue. With every breath, a crackling rattle escaped from her mouth.

"Celine?" he gasped. He leapt from the bed, intent on retrieving Millie.

"Millie's already been here," Gray informed him.

"And?" Damien demanded, his voice an octave higher than normal.

"She's bringing another medication."

"That's it?"

Gray pursed his lips before speaking. "Her condition is worse. Her lungs are filling with fluid. Millie will try to drain it, but outside of that, she's not improving."

Damien shook his head as understanding refused to set in. "What are you saying?"

"He's saying you may want to prepare yourself," Michael chimed in.

Damien's face contorted into a mask of horror and upset. "I'm sorry, man," Michael said.

"No," he said, the crease in his forehead deepening. "No!"

"All hope isn't lost," Gray said. "Millie has another serum to try. But…"

"But if that doesn't work?" Damien questioned.

Gray pursed his lips and shook his head. Damien rubbed his neck and closed his eyes as he digested the news. Millie hastened into the room with a variety of medical equipment. She appeared frazzled. Her brunette hair escaped from her usually sleek bun at all angles. Alexander followed her.

"Would you mind giving me some room to work?" she asked.

"Do you need help?" Michael inquired.

"I'll assist her," Alexander assured them.

"We'll be outside," Gray answered.

With his hand pressed against his forehead, Damien continued to stare at Celine. "Come on, Damien," Gray prompted. "We'll wait out here. She's in good hands."

Worry pinched Damien's features. "Come on, buddy," Michael added, grabbing hold of Damien's shoulders. "Let Millie do her job."

"I can't leave her. I don't want to leave her," Damien cried.

"The faster we get out of Millie's way, the faster she gets her job done and the faster Celine recovers," Michael countered.

With Gray's assistance, the two men guided Damien from the room. Gray pulled the doors to the bedroom shut behind them. Damien paced the floor of the space. He raked his fingers through his hair and blew out a long breath. He rubbed at his neck as he spun to amble in the opposite direction.

"I can't take anymore," he said. "I need to get out of here for a minute."

He stepped toward the door. "I'll come with you," Michael offered.

"No," Damien said with a shake of his head. "No, I just need a minute alone."

"You sure?" Michael inquired.

"I don't need a babysitter," Damien snapped.

Michael held his hands up in surrender. Damien squeezed his eyes shut. "Sorry. I just... yeah, I'm fine, I just need some fresh air."

"Okay," Michael agreed.

Damien stepped from Celine's suite and wound through the halls to the front door. He pulled on his hoodie and stepped into the chilly morning air. Darkness still hung in the sky, though streaks of salmon-colored light had begun to show on the horizon.

Damien wandered toward the brightening horizon, stopping at the cliff's edge. The waves crashed against the rocks below. The sound, normally relaxing, brought him no comfort. He breathed in a lungful of salty sea air. It did little to soothe his frazzled mind.

He continued down the path hugging the cliffs, his path rambling into the wooded area. The trees enveloped him, but their canopy brought him no comfort either. He roamed with no direction in mind.

As the trees cleared, he stared at the location his feet had subconsciously driven him to. Duke Marcus Northcott's seaside home rose in front of him.

Damien stared at the house for a moment before he took a step toward it. His last visit here had ended with him changing his mind. This time he strode determinedly toward the house. He had no choice, he told himself. He must do it.

He climbed the steps to the house and banged on the door. After a moment, Dembe pulled the front door open.

"Good morning. May I help you?" the dark-skinned man answered in his quiet tone.

"I need to see him," Damien answered. He pushed past Dembe into the foyer before he received an answer.

"This way, please," Dembe said after closing the door. "Duke Northcott is finishing his breakfast."

He led Damien down the hall to the dining room. Duke Northcott sat at the table, a piping hot cup of tea in front of him. He perused a newspaper.

As Dembe announced Damien's presence, Marcus did a double take. He raised his eyebrows in surprise. "Damien! What an interesting surprise! What brings you by?"

He returned to studying his newspaper as Dembe excused himself from the room.

Damien remained silent for a moment, unsure where to begin. The Duke's presence suddenly overwhelmed him. Though he understood what he needed to do. He cleared his throat and stepped forward.

"What's the matter, Damien? Cat got your tongue?"

"It's Celine," he squeaked out.

"What about Celine?" Marcus inquired, his eyes never leaving his paper.

Damien's forehead wrinkled as he choked out the words. "She's dying."

CHAPTER 19

*M*arcus snapped his head toward Damien. He studied his face for answers. "She's what?" he asked, an incredulous tone to his voice.

Damien swallowed hard, choking back his emotions. "She's dying," he repeated.

"Impossible," Marcus retorted. He squashed the newspaper in his hands and discarded it on the table. "Explain yourself."

"She was poisoned. She's been sick ever since. No one realized how sick she was until she collapsed yesterday. She hasn't woken up. Then she developed a fever. And now she's barely breathing."

Marcus's eyes went wide.

"Millie gave her some kind of antidote but it's not working," Damien continued.

Marcus shook his head in disbelief. "Poisoned?" he hissed as he stared into space.

Damien gave a slight nod of his head. "Yeah," he breathed.

"By whom?" Marcus questioned, more to himself than to Damien. "And why did I not sense it?"

Damien shrugged. "We thought you at first," Damien responded.

"Never!" Marcus insisted, his eyes blazing into Damien.

Damien shrugged again. "The general consensus after we ruled you out was someone named Tobias Greene. I don't…"

"What?!" Marcus exclaimed as he shot from his chair to standing. "Take me to her at once."

"Do you expect you can save her?" Damien asked, hope shining in his voice.

"I'm going to damn well try," Marcus answered.

They stepped into the hall. "Dembe! I am leaving."

The small man appeared in the hallway as if waiting for a summons.

"Something has happened. Remain alert in the event I need you," Marcus continued.

"Yes, Duke," the man said with a nod.

"Come, Damien, you can explain the details on the way."

Marcus pulled the door open and ushered Damien out. They set a brisk pace as they wound their way along the path to the Buckley house. Damien explained the circumstances in detail as they traveled.

Damien pulled the front door open, and they stepped into the foyer. "This way," he said, motioning up the stairs.

He led Marcus through the halls and into Gray and Celine's suite. He found the sitting room empty. The door to the bedroom stood open. As he approached, he heard the raspy sound of Celine's breathing. Despite the horrific sound, it brought him a measure of comfort. Celine was still alive.

"She's in here," he said, stepping into the room.

He found Michael, Alexander, Millie, Celeste and Gray inside, grouped around the bed. Gray perched on the edge of it with Celine's hand clutched in his.

Michael spotted them first, his eyes going wide at the sight. "How is she?" Damien asked in a low voice.

"No change," Gray answered. "The latest serum doesn't seem effective." He twisted to face Damien, his jaw dropping as he spotted Damien's companion.

He leapt from his seat next to Celine. "What the hell is he doing here?" he fired, wagging his finger toward Marcus.

Damien shrugged. "I didn't know what else to do. I thought maybe he could help."

"Over my dead body," Gray growled, closing the gap between him and Marcus.

"That can be arranged," Marcus assured him.

"Let him!" Celeste exclaimed. Damien noticed the tear stains on her cheeks.

Alexander grasped Gray's arm. "Perhaps it isn't a terrible idea, cousin."

"I don't want him anywhere near Celine," Gray railed.

"I agree with Gray on this one," Michael chimed in. "We have no idea what his motives in this may be."

"Are you all kidding right now? She's dying!" Damien exclaimed. "Am I the only one who doesn't want that to happen?"

"Of course not, Damien," Alexander answered.

"Nothing we're doing is helping her. We don't have many other choices," Damien argued.

"Gray," Alexander said, "if he can help her…" His voice trailed off as his eyes connected with Gray's.

"Nothing else we've tried has helped," Millie added.

"I'm not surprised," Marcus taunted, "the Buckleys couldn't cure a headache with an aspirin."

Gray lunged at him. Alexander held him back. "If you've come to crack jokes while my wife lays dying…"

"I've come to help Celine," Marcus interrupted.

"Can we please stop the bickering and let him help her?" Damien said.

"Can you?" Michael inquired of Marcus.

"The probability is high," Marcus answered.

"I'll bet," Gray answered. "Since you're the one who did this to her."

Marcus set his jaw and narrowed his eyes. "I would never harm Celine."

Gray let out a harsh laugh. "Oh, that's rich."

"What do you need?" Millie questioned.

"I must examine her."

Gray set his jaw. "Fine," he agreed.

Michael pursed his lips and offered a shrug. Damien breathed a sigh of relief as Marcus pushed past the others in the room toward Celine.

He pressed the back of his hand against her cheek. "What is her temperature?" he inquired.

"One-oh-five," Millie answered. "She developed it yesterday and it has risen quickly. Nothing I give her counters it."

"Mmm," Marcus murmured as he studied her blackened veins. "And when did this appear?"

"Also yesterday," Millie said. "Prior to this, she complained of a dull headache and numb, tingly hands."

"And she's had episodes of blacking out? Wandering the estate and remembering none of it?"

"Yes," Damien confirmed.

Marcus pressed his ear against Celine's chest. "Have you detected fluid in her lungs?"

"Yes," Millie confirmed. She withdrew a container from her medical bag. "We withdrew this from her lungs less than an hour ago."

Damien gasped at the site. A thick, black substance sloshed inside the glass container.

"When did her breathing begin to deteriorate?" Marcus questioned.

"About two hours ago," Millie answered.

"And what have you administered to her?"

Millie rattled off a list of serum ingredients along with a list of failed experimental lab treatments she had explored. "None of them have had any effect."

Marcus nodded. "I'd like to see a sample of the poison."

"I have it in the lab downstairs," Millie said with a nod.

"Can you help her or not?" Gray demanded before they left the room.

"Assuming I am correct, and I usually am, yes. I will confirm my suspicions by examining the poison. And I will need a few specific items, one of which only I possess."

"How convenient," Gray barked.

"It is a rare ingredient that came into my possession in the latter part of the last century. Someone must retrieve it from my home. Dembe will know where to find it." Marcus scratched a note on a piece of paper and held it out.

"I'll go," Michael and Damien said simultaneously.

"You stay with Celine," Michael added.

"I can't sit still, I'll go. I'm the one who brought him here."

"I'm way faster than you," Michael answered. "You lose every race we run."

"You cheat," Damien countered.

"You wish," Michael answered. He snatched the paper from Duke Northcott's hand. "I'll come straight to the lab."

"Good," Marcus answered. "Lead the way, doctor." Michael jogged from the room.

"I'll go with you," Alexander said.

"Keep an eye on him," Gray whispered to Alexander before he departed.

"Absolutely," Alexander agreed.

The trio left the room with Millie in the lead. She steered

them through the halls to her lab. Millie slicked her hair back as she approached the microscope. She slid a slide onto the stage and motioned for the Duke to use the microscope.

He peered into the eyepieces. After a few moments, he pulled away. "As I suspected," he said.

Millie raised her eyebrows at him. "You're familiar with this poison?"

"Yes," he answered. "I shall take it from here, doctor."

"If you don't mind, I would like to stay and observe. And, hopefully, learn something. Since I have failed miserably in my own attempts," she retorted with a sigh.

Marcus wandered to the nearby counter and perused the items. He lifted the bag containing the withered rose and studied it. "Mmm, I wouldn't say that, doctor."

Millie knit her brow. "Celine is dying. I would assess my attempts as complete failures."

"Yes, she is," Marcus agreed. "Though had it not been for your treatments she would be dead already. While you lacked the ability to save her, you prolonged her life so I could."

Alexander squeezed Millie's arm. She raised her chin at the Duke's admission and squared her shoulders.

"And you're certain you can save her?" Alexander questioned.

"Yes," Marcus answered.

"How?"

"With a similar concoction to what the good doctor used," Marcus answered.

"But mine had little to no effect," Millie countered.

"Yes," he answered as he wandered around the room studying various items. "Because it was missing a key ingredient."

"The item you requested Michael to acquire?" Alexander asked.

Marcus flitted his eyes to Alexander and gave him a nod.

"What does the ingredient do?" Millie questioned.

"Presumably you have studied the structure of the poison molecules, doctor?" Marcus inquired.

"Of course," Millie responded.

"And undoubtedly you have studied the effects of your serums on the poison," Marcus said.

"Yes."

"And what were the failings of any serum you tried?"

"While they seemed to weaken the poison, they could not succeed in destroying the molecules. I hoped with the weakened state of the poison cells, Celine's system would destroy them on its own. Alas, that did not work."

"No, it wouldn't. Did you notice the spiked exterior?"

"Yes," Millie answered. "I've never seen a cell formation quite like it."

"It is unique, yes. It is also the feature that makes the cells almost impervious to destruction."

"And that is where your special ingredient comes in?" Alexander inquired.

"Correct."

"I'll begin preparing another batch of the serum I used this morning," Millie offered.

"Good. We'll make a few minor adjustments and add my antidote as soon as Michael arrives," Marcus answered.

With a plan in place, Millie bustled about the room. Michael arrived within a quarter-hour. He puffed with exertion as he handed the small vial to Marcus. "Good," Marcus answered as he accepted the item. "Now, doctor, let us put the finishing touches on this serum." He uncorked the small vial of thick, blue, viscous liquid. Millie used a pipette to carefully withdraw the fluid from the vial.

"Here goes," she said as the pipette hovered over the beaker.

"Stand back, doctor," Marcus warned. "The effect is quite eruptive."

Millie released the blue liquid into the beaker. In a spectacular display, a puff of smoke exploded from within, billowing into the air. The liquid in the beaker bubbled and churned.

Michael's eyes widened at the reaction. "Are we sure this is safe?" he inquired.

Marcus rolled his eyes at the statement as he continued to monitor the creation of the antidote. "I am no amateur, Mr. Carlyle."

"I mean, that just exploded and you're going to pump it into Celine's body. I'm just sayin'."

Marcus ceased his work and stared at Michael. "I realize you're accustomed to working with dilettantes so I will overlook your comments. But going forward, I will not tolerate these insults."

Michael held his hands up in defeat. "Sorry, continue."

Marcus and Millie finalized the antidote. It continued to froth and bubble as they prepared a syringe.

"Careful, doctor," Marcus warned.

With a shaky hand, Millie loaded the syringe. "Ready," she declared after loading the appropriate dose.

"We should not delay," Marcus said.

Millie nodded in agreement. The group hastened through the halls to Celine's bedroom. The rattling sound of Celine's breathing reached their ears the moment they entered the sitting room.

They continued into Celine's bedroom. "Inject it into the arm with the blackened veins," Marcus instructed.

Millie nodded and crossed to Celine. "Just a moment," Gray said as he stood from his perch on the bed. He eyed the frothing liquid in the syringe. "Is this safe?" He directed the question to Alexander.

Alexander shrugged.

"It is essentially the formula I used earlier," Millie informed him. "With a few minor tweaks to the amounts and one new ingredient."

"It basically exploded downstairs when they put the new ingredient in," Michael added.

"What?" Damien exclaimed. "Are you serious?"

"An expected reaction," Marcus assured them.

"What's the other ingredient?" Gray demanded.

"You wouldn't know it even if I told you," Marcus claimed.

"Try me," Gray answered, his eyes narrowed at the man.

"Fine. Neuroveleno."

"Never heard of it," Gray snapped.

"Shocking," Marcus mocked in a satiric tone. "Satisfied?"

"Not in the slightest. We have no idea what this may do to her."

"It will save her."

"Says you."

"Says your best chance at saving Celine. Now, we can continue to argue or allow the good doctor to administer the life-saving serum."

Gray locked eyes with Marcus. The two men stared at each other as tension built.

"If I may interject," Alexander chimed in. "What we are certain of is if we do nothing, she will die."

"He's right," Damien agreed.

"You're okay with taking the chance?" Gray asked of Damien.

Damien glanced at Marcus then to Celine's limp form. He swallowed hard and nodded. "Yeah," he said softly.

Gray turned to Millie and gave her a nod. She injected the fluid into Celine's arm.

"A wise choice. I've always maintained you were clever, Damien," Marcus said, clapping Damien on the shoulder.

"Don't push your luck, buddy," Michael warned.

As Millie pushed the plunger on the syringe, a slight groan escape Celine's lips. Her body shuddered and her facial muscles twinged as though in pain. Gray snapped his head toward Marcus. "A normal reaction to a volatile solution."

Her face relaxed as the last of the bubbling liquid entered her body. Her raspy breathing continued. "Now we wait," Millie said with a sigh.

Tension built with each passing moment. All eyes focused on Celine. Her labored breathing continued, a constant marker of both the passage of time and her living state. Damien sat at her side, her hand in his. Celeste held her other hand. Gray paced the floor. Michael stared with narrowed eyes at the bed. Millie continued to monitor vital signs. Alexander offered a consoling glance to Gray before returning his attention to Celine.

After thirty painstaking minutes, Celine's breathing changed. Her chest rose and fell in quick succession. She panted for air. A groan escaped her lips before she gasped again.

"What's happening?" Damien inquired, his voice raising in panic.

Celine's breathing continued to be labored. She struggled to gasp for each breath. "Allow the serum to work," Marcus advised.

They watched for several more tense moments as Celine's breathing continued to worsen. Millie checked her vitals. "Her pulse is slowing," she reported.

"Is that good?" Damien inquired.

"Celine?" Gray asked, rushing to her side.

Celine took a long, labored inhale before she croaked out a breath. The raspy sound of her breathing ceased. Her chest no longer rose and fell. She lay still and unmoving. Her pale skin, framed by her blonde curls, appeared gray. The blackened network of veins still marked her body.

"Celine?!" Gray exclaimed.

Damien's eyes widened and he hastened toward her. "No, no, no, no, Celine? Celine!" he cried. He shook her. Her body flopped back to the bed when he let go, pulled away by Marcus Northcott.

"Leave her," Marcus instructed.

Celeste leapt from the bed, turning away from Celine as she wept.

"Oh my God," Gray choked out. "She's dead. You've killed her! Celine is dead!"

CHAPTER 20

Gray leapt from the bed and raced toward Marcus. He grasped him by the collar, dragging him backward. "You bastard! You killed her!"

"Unhand me, you dimwitted cretin!" Marcus demanded. "Before I lose my patience."

"Gentlemen! Please!" Alexander shouted. "At a time like this, we must..."

"Wait!" Damien exclaimed. He stared at Celine then crept closer to her. His eyes narrowed and he turned his ear toward her.

"What is it, Damien?" Michael questioned.

"That noise, do you hear it?"

The room plunged into silence as everyone strained to listen. "It's like a hissing sound," Damien whispered.

"Yes," Celeste breathed, "yes, I hear it. It sounds like..."

"Like it's coming from Celine," Damien finished for her.

The hissing noise ceased. Celine laid quiet for a second. Without warning, Celine's eyes shot open. They stared upward at the ceiling before she gulped in a full breath. Her back arched upward at a horrifying angle. Her arms dangled at her sides as her stomach curved toward the ceiling.

Gray released Marcus and turned his attention to Celine. Millie backed from the bed. Damien's lips formed a grimace as he witnessed the hair-raising scene. Celine's body collapsed back down to the bed. Her head and chest rose. Her unseeing eyes stared ahead as her mouth opened wider than normal.

Marcus grasped Damien and dragged him backward away from the bed. From Celine's open mouth, a black nebula poured out. It continued for half a minute before she collapsed back into the pillows. Her mouth and eyes closed again.

The black cloud rose toward the ceiling, dissipating into thin air as it climbed.

"Wh-wh-what the hell was that?" Damien gasped in a shaky breath.

"Yeah," Michael echoed, "someone want to clue us in on what just happened?"

"I must admit, I have never witnessed anything like that in my centuries of living," Alexander answered.

"Look!" Millie exclaimed as she inched toward the bed.

Damien's jaw went slack as he witnessed what Millie pointed out. Rosy cheeks graced Celine's porcelain complexion. Pink lips replaced her blue-tinged mouth. The black veins that crawled under her skin moments ago disappeared.

Marcus adjusted his collar. "She has expelled the poison from her system."

Gray stared at him, his eyes narrowed.

"Well, go ahead and take a blood sample and find out for yourself if you don't believe me," Marcus added.

Millie pulled her stethoscope from around her neck. She listened to Celine's heart and lungs. She took her temperature and felt for a pulse.

"Well?" Gray inquired as Millie pulled a syringe and tube from her bag for a blood sample.

"My physical exam shows her the picture of perfect health," Millie admitted.

She wrapped a tourniquet around Celine's upper arm and jabbed the needle into her vein. Healthy, red blood flowed into the tube.

"This is certainly promising," Millie said as she eyed it. "I'll examine it in the lab to be certain."

"Let us know the results as soon as you have them," Gray said.

Millie nodded as she hurried from the room with the blood sample in her hands.

"So, is she cured?" Damien inquired.

"From the poison, yes," Marcus answered.

"Then why hasn't she woken up yet?" Gray demanded.

"She is cured physically of the poison," Marcus repeated. "Her mental status is another matter entirely."

"What does that mean?" Michael questioned.

"It means she is trapped somewhere," Marcus answered. "By the man who poisoned her."

"What?" Damien asked.

"Your assumptions proved correct. The poison was formulated and sent to Celine by Tobias Greene."

"How do you know?" Alexander asked.

"The poison contained traces of an element Tobias uses often."

Alexander and Gray glanced at each other. "Maybe someone can clue us in on who this guy is," Michael said.

"He is a Zieleneter," Marcus answered.

Damien's face scrunched in confusion at the phrase.

"A soul eater," Marcus added.

"A what?" Michael inquired.

"A warlock who draws power by gathering the souls of others," Alexander explained.

Damien mulled over the information. "How is that any different from you?" he asked Marcus.

"You must be joking," Marcus said.

"Well, you wanted Celine to sign her soul to you."

"To sign her soul to my cause, yes. I did not extinguish her life so as to control her soul to gain in my own power." Marcus rolled his eyes at Damien's innocence.

"Technically, they are different," Alexander assured him. "Warlocks like Tobias destroy their victims to gain power."

"But she's fine now, right? The poison is gone," Damien answered.

"Physically, at the moment, yes," Marcus replied.

"Will everyone please stop talking in circles and explain this straight?" Michael asked.

"Tobias poisoned Celine to weaken her enough to draw her to him. I am not surprised she hasn't awoken yet. Her consciousness is likely trapped somewhere with him."

Damien's eyes widened. "So, what good was the antidote?"

"She will not die from the poison," Marcus said.

"But?" Damien questioned.

"But she will remain unresponsive with her consciousness trapped wherever he has taken it and eventually will fade away once he acquires her soul completely."

"Fade away?" Damien asked.

"A fate similar to death," Marcus explained.

"So, this guy eats souls?" Michael inquired.

"Not literally," Gray said.

"No, the term is rather a misnomer," Alexander said.

"Okay, so, this Tobias Greene guy poisons her to weaken her enough to trap her consciousness and then he'll basically just suck the life out of her?" Michael asked.

"Correct," Marcus said.

"Can we save her?" Damien asked.

"Yes, if we find where he has drawn her."

"Well, where is that? How can we tell?" Damien inquired.

"My best guess is," Marcus began.

"1842," Alexander, Marcus and Gray answered simultaneously.

"1842?" Damien questioned. "Why then? How?"

"Tobias Greene attacked her in this time once before. He nearly captured her soul then. He fell short," Gray explained.

"Yes, but with newly acquired power, he may not fall short this time," Marcus warned.

"How do you know he has more power? And if he's got newly acquired power, why not attack her now?" Michael asked.

"He has the power to draw her to another place, so he's acquired new talents and strong power, likely the result of gathering more souls. So why put in double the work? The groundwork is laid in 1842. He can continue the work to its fruition," Alexander said.

"So, how can we save her?" Damien questioned. "Just head back to 1842 and stop him?"

Gray let out a derisive laugh.

"Stopping him will be a feat," Celeste chimed in. "He is extraordinarily powerful. We cannot defeat him outright."

"We have to try!" Damien exclaimed.

"In order to do so, we must travel back to 1842," Marcus said.

Michael sighed. "Of course. Once, just once, I'd really like to solve a problem right here in the good old twenty-first century."

"Don't go," Gray said. "We'll handle this."

Marcus scoffed. "You couldn't handle one-quarter of what Tobias can do. You'd be useless to defeat him."

"I'd like to go," Damien said.

"And I'm not letting you go alone," Michael said. "Hatred for time travel or not, we're a team."

"You two would be more useless than us at defeating a soul eater," Gray said.

"Untrue," Marcus said. "As humans, they will be perceived as less of a threat by Tobias. Buckley will pose the most direct threat. As such, he has the largest target on him. Damien's relationship with Celine will be useful to reach her and draw her back should we need it, and he may be able to escape Tobias's scrutiny. Further, we should not leave Celine unguarded. She is safer here, though, so the task should be manageable for you two with Celeste's assistance, despite your obvious lacking in talent and Celeste's distress."

Damien paced the floor as he rubbed his chin. He considered the information. The odds seemed insurmountable. An undefeatable warlock? One outside of even the Duke's capabilities? Could they win?

"Why would you assume you'd go? You're the worst person to go," Gray argued.

"You can't defeat him either," Alexander pointed out. "Therefore, it doesn't matter who goes back, does it?"

"Not outright, but I possess far better skills to ensure an acceptable outcome."

"If we're so lacking, perhaps you should stay here and ensure nothing happens to her in this time," Gray countered.

"Yes, I am obviously the best choice in both circumstances. I cannot tear myself in two, so you'll have to fill in the gap in the situation that provides the least taxing complications."

Damien's eyes widened at the last statement. "Wait," he said as his mind formulated a thought. "What did you say?"

"I said I clearly would be the best choice in both circumstances, but I cannot tear myself in two…"

Damien snapped his fingers. "That's it!"

"I'm all for tearing him in two, also, Damien," Gray said.

"No, not that," Damien said with a shake of his head. "You said you can't tear yourself in two, but you can. Sort of."

"What are you getting at, Damien?" Alexander questioned.

"If you go back in time to a time in which you already exist," Damien said to Marcus, "what happens? Do you meld into the body that already exists in that time or are there two of you?"

Marcus raised his eyebrows and smirked. "There are two of me," he said.

"Okay, that's what I assumed. Now, you said you can't defeat him outright. But could two of you?"

Marcus considered the idea. "It's possible."

"Possible is the best we're going to get," Damien said. "So that settles it. He goes back, you stay here."

"The decision isn't yours," Gray grumbled.

"Do you have any better ideas?" Michael asked.

Gray stared at Celine's form in the bed. He crossed his arms and set his jaw. "No," he admitted.

"If it's any consolation, I'm not pleased with this plan either," Alexander said.

"If it saves Celine, that's all that matters," Damien argued.

"I'm uncomfortable sending the two of you with him," Gray said.

"Celine did it to save us. Now we can return the favor," Damien answered.

"Let's hope you live through it."

"Are we agreed then?" Marcus questioned.

The men glanced around at each other. Nods circulated through the group. "Then we should prepare," Marcus said. "The sooner we leave, the better."

* * *

Damien stared down at Celine's sleeping form. She looked better than she had only hours ago. Her porcelain skin remained rosy, her lips pink. Her blonde curls spilled around her on the pillow. She was the picture of perfect health.

Millie had confirmed Celine's physical health after completing a full blood panel workup. Her blood lacked any trace of the poison that wreaked havoc on it mere hours earlier.

Now only her mental health needed saving. True to his word, Duke Marcus Northcott had saved Celine, eradicating the poison from her system. He'd then informed them she suffered from a different ailment. One that required them to return to another era to rescue her.

In his old-fashioned clothing, Damien tugged at his collar before he sank onto the bed next to her. He took her hand in his. "We're coming to save you, Celine," he whispered as his thumb rubbed the back of her hand.

As he issued the promise, his mind swam with questions and worries. What were they facing? A soul-consuming warlock? One that even the Duke couldn't defeat? Though the Duke's powers were not unmatched, the idea of another evil entity who could outmaneuver him worried Damien.

They were heading to save Celine. But could they pull it off? Or, facing insurmountable odds, were they staring down their own doom and sealing Celine's fate?

"She'd hate what you're about to do," Gray said as he strode into the room.

Damien snorted a laugh. "Yeah, she would," he admitted. "Good thing she's unconscious. I mean… that's not what I meant… it's not good it's just…"

Gray clapped him on the shoulder. "I understand what

you mean," he said, then whispered, "and you're right. If she was awake, you'd be getting a tongue-lashing."

Damien nodded in agreement as his gaze fell back to a sleeping Celine. A few moments of silence passed between them before Gray spoke again.

"You know, what you did, going to the Duke, was incredibly stupid."

Damien's lips formed a frown. "But also," Gray continued, "incredibly brave. And incredibly selfless."

Damien shook his head. "It was neither. My stomach was doing backflips the minute I walked into his house."

"Don't discount it, Damien. You did what needed to be done to save Celine. My pride wouldn't have allowed me. I could have cost Celine her life."

"You never would have done that," Damien disagreed.

"I'm glad you have such a high opinion of me," Gray said.

"It's true. You wouldn't have risked Celine's life. Even if it meant turning to the Duke for help."

Gray shook his head and frowned. "I hate that it came to that."

"So do I, but I have to admit, he came through. In spades. She's the picture of health."

"I'll admit I'm glad to see her back to normal. I still hate the way we achieved that."

"Let's hope we can get her fully back to normal."

Gray nodded. "As much as I want that, Damien, watch your back with the Duke. Even though he helped her, that doesn't mean he can be trusted."

Damien gave Gray a nod as Michael entered the room in his 1842 finery. "Don't worry about that," he said as he finished fastening his cufflink. "I've got my eyes all over him. He won't get away with anything on my watch."

"Hey, I'm watching him, too," Damien said. "It's not like I trust him either!"

"No, but you're too naive, Damien," Michael answered.

"He's right," Gray agreed. "You give that man far too much credit. Not everyone is as nice as you."

"I'm not *that* nice," Damien countered.

Michael knit his eyebrows and stared at him.

"What? I'm not! Once I cut in line at an amusement park."

"Oh-ho, wow," Michael said with a chuckle. "Damien, you're a Boy Scout!"

"Like you're so street smart," Damien argued.

"More so than you. I grew up with constant deception. It's easy for me to spot."

"Oh, yeah, in the viper den of Carlyle Industries, huh?"

"Something like that," Michael said.

Damien offered a wry glance, unconvinced.

"Both my father and grandfather are shrewd business-men. Sometimes they bend the laws a little."

"Uh-huh," Damien answered.

"And beyond that," Michael continued, "my parents were constantly lying to each other. There were countless affairs. They told the truth less than they lied. Spotting deception is ingrained in me."

"Okay, okay, you win," Damien said. "Deception-spotting skills or not, I'm glad you're going with me. Truth be told, I'd rather not go anywhere alone with him."

"Should my ears be burning?" Marcus inquired as he stepped into the room.

"Huh? What? No! We weren't just talking about you," Damien babbled nervously.

Marcus arched an eyebrow at Damien's chattering. "Gentlemen, are we ready?"

"Yep, totally ready."

"Born ready," Michael said, narrowing his eyes at Marcus.

Marcus smirked. "We'll see about that when you're staring into the eyes of a soul eater."

"Just do what you have to do and get straight back here," Gray warned.

"Believe me, I don't want to spend another minute with this guy than we have to," Michael said, shoving his thumb in Marcus's direction.

"Plus, I want to see Celine the moment she wakes up!" Damien exclaimed.

Alexander entered the room. "Oh, good, I caught you before you left," he said.

"We were just about to go," Damien answered.

"Millie prepared a second dose of the antidote in case you should need it," Alexander said as he handed the vial to Damien.

"Thanks," Damien said, placing it in his pocket.

"Good luck," Alexander said, sticking his hand out. "We're all looking forward to your return."

"So are we," Michael replied.

"We should depart from another location. So as not to disturb Celine," Marcus suggested.

Damien nodded. He gave Celine's hand one final squeeze and made a silent promise to return to her. They shuffled from the room. Damien's stomach somersaulted as they stepped out of the comfort of Celine's room.

"We shall depart outside," Marcus said as they descended the stairs into the foyer.

They followed him to a clearing in the woods outside the main house. "When I open the time portal, go through immediately, do not wait for me. I shall follow."

Michael knit his eyebrows. "Why shouldn't we wait for you?"

Marcus returned the gesture. "Because I said not to."

"Ohhhh, right. We should just trust you."

Marcus sighed and frowned at him. "Fine, I shall explain it as if you were a child. If you should dally, I may pass you in the time portal, which will already be closing. If that happens, I would emerge in 1842. You would not. You would be trapped in the time-space continuum with no way to escape. While that idea holds a certain appeal to me, it is not my primary objective given the situation."

Michael's jaw tensed at the lecture.

"Fine, we'll go straight through. Got it," Damien conceded.

"Gentlemen, if this arrangement is to work, we must work together not fight against each other."

"Forgive me if I don't exactly trust you," Michael said, his eyes narrowed at Marcus.

"A sentiment you'll have to put aside," Marcus argued.

"Easier said than done," Michael retorted.

Marcus narrowed his eyes at Michael and the two men glared at each other. "Okay, come on, guys," Damien interjected as he stepped between them. "Let's just agree to get along and semi-trust each other in this instance. For Celine's sake. Huh?"

"For Celine's sake," Marcus answered, his eyes unwavering from Michael's.

"Fine, anything for Celine," Michael answered, continuing his stare down. "But I'm keeping my eye on you."

"Duly noted," Marcus growled as he rolled his eyes. "Now, shall we proceed?"

"Yes, please, let us proceed," Damien said with a sigh of relief.

Marcus raised his arms to open the time portal. The leaves rustled on the trees as the wind picked up. A small black dot appeared in front of them. The branches swayed and bowed as the sparkling opening grew in size.

"The portal is open, go!" Marcus shouted over the din.

"Come on," Damien said to Michael as he stepped forward.

CHAPTER 21

The two men climbed into the shimmering hole, passing into complete darkness. They stumbled for a moment before their eyes adjusted.

Damien blinked a few times. Moonlight streamed down through the trees. He glanced around. "I guess we made it."

"Yes, guess so," Michael said.

"Hey," Damien said as he twisted to face Michael, "before he gets here, can we take the bickering down a notch?"

"Sorry, buddy, but I don't trust this guy."

"I realize that," Damien said. "Neither do I. But I'm more concerned with saving Celine."

"I'm concerned with that, too, but we need to be smart about it."

Damien stared down at the ground.

"I'll tone it down," Michael promised as Marcus stepped through the portal behind them. The shimmering hole snapped shut behind him.

"Okay, where do we start?" Damien asked.

"Perhaps we should…" Marcus began.

"Get down!" Michael hissed, shoving them behind a large tree.

A dark figure approached on the path near where they had stood moments ago. The familiar form of Stefano bobbed along under the trees, whistling as he walked.

"Close call," Damien whispered.

"Yeah, with that horrible whistling, I heard him coming from a mile away," Michael said in a low tone.

Stefano stopped steps away from them. He stared up at the moonlight as the shrill whistling continued.

"What's he doing? This is the last thing we need! We have to get to Celine and find out what's going on."

"I don't know," Michael answered. "Move it along, Bub."

"He's meeting someone," Marcus breathed.

"Who? Who would he be meeting in the middle of the woods at night?" Damien questioned.

"Ohhh, of course," Michael groaned as a second figure approached.

Marcus raised his eyebrows at them, a smirk on his lips. The 1842 version of Marcus Northcott strode toward them.

"This is bizarre," Damien whispered.

"It's downright frightening if you ask me," Michael added.

"No one asked you," Marcus said. "And don't be a spoil-sport, Damien. I'm rather enjoying it."

"Of course, you would," Michael grumbled.

1842 Marcus stepped from beneath the canopy of trees into the moonlight. The cascading silver beams cast deep shadows across his chiseled face.

"Rather a handsome devil, wouldn't you agree?" Marcus joked to Michael and Damien.

"I'd agree with fifty percent of that statement," Michael retorted.

"And I'd bet it's not the handsome part," Damien clarified.

* * *

"Duke Northcott," Stefano greeted him.

"Have you completed the task?"

"Yes, of course," Stefano replied.

"Good."

"I'm confused, though, Duke," Stefano began.

The nineteenth-century Duke's face conveyed annoyance. "I am not surprised."

"Why did we…"

The Duke held up his hand to stop Stefano. "My reasons are my own. Let us leave it at that."

"But…"

"Stefano, I haven't the time nor the inclination to explain my motives to you. Come, we have much to attend to."

Stefano shrugged. "All right, Duke."

The two men disappeared into the darkness under the canopy of the trees.

* * *

"What was that about?" Michael questioned as they stood.

"Never mind," Marcus said. "We have many things to attend to."

"So does the other you, apparently," Damien answered.

"Undoubtedly. If I am correct, and I always am, we've arrived just as things with Tobias are about to accelerate."

Michael rolled his eyes at the statement. Marcus stared at him with narrowed eyes. Michael held up his hands in defeat. "All right, what's the plan?"

"We must part ways," Marcus began.

"Whoa, wait just a minute," Michael said. "No way."

Marcus offered an unimpressed stare. Damien glanced between the two of them. "Okay, come on, we need a plan.

And maybe it's best we don't split up. If this soul eater guy is running around here, we shouldn't be alone, right?"

Marcus explained, "The first thing you must do is find Celine. I judge that's best done between you and Michael. The best place to begin would be the Buckleys' home. I cannot imagine in any era I would be well received there. The task is best left to the two of you."

Damien nodded. He had a point. They'd have to go to the main house. They couldn't appear there with the Duke in tow. "Fine," he conceded. "Point taken. But what are you going to do?"

"I shall go into town and determine if Tobias has arrived yet. We shall meet afterward near the gazebo."

"What time?" Michael questioned.

"I shall be no more than two hours," Marcus answered. "Though I suspect you may be longer."

"Fine," Michael said. "We meet at the gazebo in two hours."

"Good luck, gentlemen," Marcus said. He spun on his heel and strode away toward Bucksville.

Damien and Michael stared after him as he departed. "I really hate this," Michael lamented.

Damien clapped him on the back. "I know, buddy," he answered. "With any luck, we'll be back in our time soon."

Michael shook his head. "Not that. I mean, I hate that, too. But I'm talking about working with him." He thumbed toward the diminishing figure of Marcus Northcott.

"Oh, right," Damien answered. "I'm not too keen on it either. I feel like we're one double-cross away from death."

"Or two," Michael said. "We've got to keep our eye on him AND the other him."

"Good point," Damien agreed. "Though the other Duke is probably more dangerous than this Duke. This Duke realizes the situation and seems like he wants to help. The other Duke hates us."

"True. And he really detests us now after we stole both his book and the portrait of Celine."

"Yep. If we run into him, we're doomed."

"How will we tell?" Michael inquired.

Damien's jaw dropped and his eyebrows raised. "Oh, good question. We should have marked this Duke somehow."

"I don't think that was an option."

"Probably not. We'll have to wing it and hope for the best."

"I'll keep my fingers crossed. Oh, and while we're on the subject, don't believe for a second if the right opportunity presents itself, he won't sell us and Celine down the river."

Damien shrugged. "I'd agree he'd sell us out. I'm not as convinced he'd do it to Celine."

"I'm less convinced than you. Let's hope the right opportunity doesn't present itself so we don't have to find out."

"Okay," Damien answered. "We'd better get going."

Michael nodded and the two set off on the path toward the main house on the property. They trudged through the forested path toward the lights shining in the distance.

"So," Damien ventured as they walked. "Still considering leaving Bucksville?"

Michael gave him a sideways glance. "I've kind of put that decision on hold given the current situation."

Damien nodded. "Oh."

"Look, Damien," Michael began when a new noise cut him off.

A distinctive click of a revolver being cocked sounded. "Don't move," a voice greeted them. "My husband has taught me well how to shoot. I will not miss."

Michael and Damien's steps ground to a halt. They raised their hands in the air.

"Turn around, slowly," the voice instructed.

They both spun slowly around until they faced their assailant. Damien's shoulders rose to his ears in a shrug, and he offered a lopsided smile.

Their attacker lowered her weapon. A smile crept over her face. "Michael and Damien Carlyle?" Celine questioned, her accent now completely American.

"In the flesh," Michael answered.

The grin on her face widened and she threw her arms around them. "It's wonderful to see you!"

They offered her a return embrace. "Good to see you, too," Damien answered.

"What's with the gun?" Michael questioned.

Celine waved the revolver around. "Gray insisted."

Damien's brows furrowed. "Why? Can't you just use a fireball?"

Celine shrugged her shoulders. "Yes. Though we're trying to blend in. Rumors spread quickly in a small town like this."

"Ahhhh," Damien said as understanding dawned. "Got it."

Celine shook her head, dismissing the conversation. "What are you doing here?" she inquired.

"Oh, just checking in on you. We were in town and figured we'd visit."

Celine's eyebrows crept upward. "Oh? Is this your time?"

"No," Damien answered as Michael said, "Yes."

They glanced at each other. "Yes," Damien replied as Michael said, "No."

Celine's lips formed a confused frown. "What we're trying to say is, that might not be something we should share," Michael answered.

Celine nodded. "I understand. Well, are you staying in town, or can I convince you to stay at the house?"

"We'd love to stay at the house if you're offering," Damien answered.

"Of course, I am! Let us go now and I'll have your rooms set up while your luggage is retrieved."

"Oh, ah, no luggage," Michael said.

"Again?" Celine said with a chuckle.

"Again," Damien admitted.

She continued her giggle. "I'll get you some clothes, too."

"Thanks," Michael said.

"What business brings you to Bucksville?" Celine inquired as the glow from the house emerged through the tree branches.

"Ahhhh," Damien stammered.

"Following up on a business lead given to us by a friend," Michael dodged.

Celine slid her gaze sideways as they reached the house but did not push further. She pushed through the doors into the foyer. Odd, Damien mused as he glanced around the space, how little things changed.

"Anderson," Celine said to a tall, wiry, salt-and-pepper-haired man who descended the stairs.

"Yes, Mrs. Buckley?" he answered, standing straight as a rail, his hands clasped behind him.

"Could you see that two rooms are made up near my suite for Mr. Carlyle and his brother?"

"At once, madam. And shall I send for the luggage?"

"No," Celine answered, "that won't be necessary. They've had it sent on. It should arrive soon."

"I will see it is sorted properly when it does."

Michael waved his hand at the man. "Thank you, but we'll handle it."

"Very good, sir," the man said with a nod of his head.

"Thank you, Anderson."

"Of course, Mrs. Buckley. Also, a package has arrived for you. I set it there." He motioned toward the large, wooden table near the fireplace.

"Thank you," Celine repeated. The man bowed his head again and spun on his heel to disappear down a hallway. "While we wait, let us see what has arrived for me!"

She wandered to the table where a large box rested. A note with her name scrawled on it sat on top of the white box. She slid the envelope open and pulled the note from inside.

Damien peered over her shoulder at it.

In scrawled writing, the note read

Dearest Celine - I have been delayed in Boston. I've sent your dress on ahead of me as I know you're eager to receive it. I hope to arrive in Bucksville day after tomorrow at the latest.

All my love, my dearest, Grayson

"Gray's in Boston?" Damien inquired.

"Yes," Celine said with a bob of her head. "On some business. I am dismayed about the delay in Gray's return, but I am thrilled he has sent my dress on!"

"You always did like fashion!" Damien said with a chuckle.

Celine lifted a shoulder to him and offered a grin as she pulled the box's lid off. After removing the paper wrapping the dress, she pulled the gown from the box.

"Oh!" she exclaimed. "It is *lovely!*"

Damien sucked in air as the fabric flowed from the box.

"What do you think?" she asked the men as she held the dress in front of her. "Is it not exquisite?"

"Very pretty," Michael answered.

Damien swallowed hard. "Yep, nice," Damien choked out.

His heart pounded in his chest and his pulse raced. He stared at the bright red dress. He recognized it. He'd seen it before. In the mirror. The dress Celine admired was the same dress he'd seen her wearing as she danced in the mirror.

"Oh!" Celine cried as she returned the dress to the box. "How impolite of me! I'm certain you must be hungry. I'll arrange food for you while you wait for your rooms."

Michael began to shake his head when Damien smacked him with the back of his hand. "Starved," he said. "Thanks."

"Of course. You can wait in the sitting room. I shall return in a moment with sustenance!"

"Oh, before you go, Celine, is Alexander here?"

"No, I'm afraid not," she answered. "He plans to return from London in one month."

"Oh, that's too bad. I hoped to see him."

"My apologies," Celine said with a sigh. "What I can provide is a meal, though! I shall return soon."

Damien smiled and nodded as she crossed the room.

"Are you really that hungry?" Michael asked as they sauntered to the sitting room.

"No, I just needed a moment."

"A moment? From what? She seems fine. I'm encouraged, actually. I thought we'd find something far worse happening here."

"The dress," Damien choked out.

Michael's eyebrows scrunched down. "What about it?"

"It's *the* dress."

Michael narrowed his eyes as he tried to follow Damien's cryptic conversation. "*The* dress, Michael. The dress I saw in the mirror."

CHAPTER 22

"Ohhhhh," Michael murmured as realization dawned on him.

"Yeah, ohhhhh," Damien repeated. "It's started. The red dress, the ruby necklace, the cave. Part one of Celine's prophecy. Couldn't even get one night before it started."

Michael puffed out his lips as he blew out a long breath. "It actually started when we had to come back with the Duke."

Damien paced the floor as he rubbed the back of his neck. "Yeah, I know. I know. I don't like it either, but we have no choice. We have to win this time. The stakes have never been higher."

Michael nodded. "Yeah, I get it. But we need to keep a sharp mind. You can't fall apart, man."

"I know!" Damien cried, frustration showing through his voice. "I just…" He paused for a moment and shook his head. "If we fail…"

"I know, Damien," Michael interrupted.

"Do you? If we fail, no more Celine. That's it!"

Michael nodded.

"And," Damien continued, "we're about to meet a soul eater. One that not even the Duke can defeat! The odds aren't good!"

"A real man makes his own luck," Michael responded.

"Stop quoting Billy Zane! This is serious!"

"Sorry, Damien. Just trying to lighten the mood. Look, we've been down and out before…"

"But never with the stakes this high and never with an opponent we couldn't defeat."

"That's not true. When Celine went missing, the stakes were high. We couldn't defeat the Duke, but we did it. We found her. And we'll win again. We just need to stay sharp and watch each other's backs."

"I wish I had your confidence," Damien lamented as he finger-combed his hair.

Michael offered a half-grin. "It's my strong suit. I'll make up for your lack of it. Now, let's get some food, meet the Duke, get the lay of the land and come up with a plan. Sound good?"

Damien puffed out a breath and bobbed his head up and down. "Sounds good," he answered.

"That's the spirit," Michael said as he clapped him on the back.

Celine returned with sandwiches for them before showing them to their rooms. She placed them in the same rooms they had in their own time. Also, the same ones they used in 1791. They said their thank yous as Celine left them to rest.

Within minutes, Michael knocked on Damien's door. "We're going to be late," he said as he stepped into Damien's room. "Is it weird that we're always in the same rooms?"

Damien considered the question as he shoved the clothes Celine delivered to them into a drawer. He shrugged. "Do you want to switch?"

Michael pursed his lips. "No, better not. Don't want to ruin our streak."

"Right," Damien agreed. "Besides, I find it comforting."

"I find nothing about this comforting. Including who we're about to go meet."

"I agree. We'd better get going. You were right, we're going to be late."

Michael inched the door open and peered into the hallway. "Coast's clear," he whispered. "Let's go."

They hurried from the room through the back halls and into the cool night air. "I'm glad we live here and know the back halls," Damien said as the gravel on the drive crunched under their feet as they crossed into the woods.

They approached the gazebo. Moonlight limned the familiar form of Duke Marcus Northcott. Michael offered an audible grumble as he came into view.

"Gentlemen," Marcus called as they closed the distance between them. "You are late."

Michael bit his tongue and squeezed his lips shut, giving a shake of his head.

"We know," Damien puffed as he hurried the final few steps. "Sorry. Took longer than we expected."

Marcus raised his eyebrows. Damien offered a nod. Marcus's jaw unhinged. "And how was Celine?" he prompted when neither of them spoke.

"Oh, Celine, right," Damien said. "She's good. Fine, actually."

Marcus arched one eyebrow high in the air.

"Nothing seems to have happened yet, though she did receive the red dress," Michael filled in.

"The red dress?" Marcus repeated.

"Yeah, before we left, she kept saying one phrase over and over. The first part was the red dress. The red dress she received today is the same one I saw her in during her mirror waltz."

"So it begins," Marcus said.

"And what about your little trip?" Michael inquired.

"The news is as expected," Marcus answered. "Tobias Greene arrived in town earlier this evening. I expect him to present himself tomorrow."

"Should we be there? For Celine?" Damien questioned. "Both Gray and Alexander are out of town."

"I would not recommend it," Marcus answered.

"But shouldn't we be stopping him from doing something to her?"

"No," Marcus counseled. "As painful as it may be to witness, we must allow events to run their course. Once he has drawn her into his web, we shall stop him and rescue her. Otherwise, this does not work."

"Sorry, but that sounds like the worst plan ever," Michael argued.

"Oh?" Marcus retorted, his eyebrows rising high. "Perhaps you'd care to suggest another."

"Stop him right now before he gets to Celine."

"Ah, yes. Let us flesh out the details of that plan, shall we? We shall stop him from meeting Celine. How do you propose we do that? And even if we succeed, how do we return Celine's mind to her current body? It is in limbo awaiting his call at this moment. There is no guarantee it will not become lost."

Damien wrinkled his brow. His eyes shifted back and forth as he parsed through the Duke's comments. "But…"

"An oddity of time travel," Marcus answered before he could vocalize his thoughts.

"Right, yeah, this time travel stuff is super confusing," Damien answered.

"I have no doubt for you it is," Marcus retorted.

"Why did you bring us here, then? Why not send us to when we can help her?" Michael questioned.

Marcus's face set in stone. "For several reasons which I should not have to explain but since this will likely lead to yet another argument I shall. Please pay attention so your feeble mind can comprehend this on the first pass."

Michael narrowed his eyes at him, his jaw set.

"This chain of events may play out differently than it did in the first iteration. Tobias has acquired additional powers and information. He is somehow spanning the centuries. I did not wish to arrive too late to save Celine. We have a limited window in which we can salvage her mental capacity. I do not wish to miss that opportunity.

"So, I chose to arrive just before Tobias inserted himself into her life. This way we shall be prepared in the event that the timeline moves faster than it did in the first sequence of events.

"In addition, there are several components I must put into place to defeat him. This is delicate work. It must be done properly or we shall not succeed."

"How did the timeline move the first time?" Damien inquired.

"Tobias arrived and introduced himself to the family who promptly invited him to stay at the house. Shortly after, Celine began to lose time. Other members of the family began to suffer from strange fits. Evan Buckley, the current owner of the property, became bed-ridden. Buckley returned from Boston within a week of Tobias's arrival. This event interrupted Tobias's attack on Celine. It weakened the potency of his assault, and we were able to drive him away."

"A week?" Michael asked. "Gray's note to Celine said he'd be home day after tomorrow."

"He will be delayed. At least, he was in the first chain of

events. I expect the assault to move at a faster rate this time. He will likely not risk Buckley's return ruining his plans."

"Oh, great," Damien groused. "That's perfect. An invincible soul eater with an accelerated attack on Celine. Neither Grayson nor Alexander is here to help. This is setting up to be a wonderful time."

"Difficult, yes. Invincible, no," Marcus argued. "I would also argue the Buckleys can do little to help."

"Grayson's arrival interrupted his attack and weakened it. Your words," Damien countered. "We need him."

"We do not," Marcus retorted.

"Really? His attack this time will be faster and more powerful. Explain to me how we don't need Gray!"

"Simple," Marcus answered. "We have you."

"What's that supposed to mean? I don't have any supernatural powers," Damien responded.

"It is not Buckley's supernatural ability that hindered Tobias's attack. It was his personal connection with Celine. A personal connection you possess with her as well."

"Not *that* kind of personal connection," Damien said. His mind reeled. Did he possess the ability to draw Celine back from a powerful soul eater? He wasn't certain, though he wasn't sure he wanted to find out. Celine's fate resting entirely on his shoulders made him nervous. His head began to ache, and his shoulders tensed.

Marcus shook his head. "She came to Shadow World and asked me for help to save your life, Damien. Your connection is extraordinarily strong. You are the key to saving her. If Buckley arrives, fine, it won't hurt. But we do not need him. We need you."

Damien blew out a breath as he scanned the horizon in search of answers. His mind churned. Michael clapped him on the back. "He's right, buddy. You can do this."

"Yes, though to that end, we must remain vigilant. You

should avoid any and all contact with Tobias Greene. Should he even suspect your connection he will attack you."

"That doesn't sound pleasant," Michael said. "I'll keep an eye out for him."

"That is an understatement. His attack will be relentless. He will destroy Damien. As a human, you will be even more susceptible. We must ensure your safety."

Michael nodded in agreement. "Got it."

"I'm starting to think it would have been better to bring Gray and Alexander," Damien said in a shaky voice.

"He would destroy them, too, given the chance. And we could not leave Celine unprotected."

"She had Celeste," Damien countered.

"It is of no consequence. They are not impervious to his attacks. And, in fact, he'd launch them sooner knowing they pose a threat as warlocks."

Damien sighed but argued no further. The decision had been made, for better or worse.

After a pause, Marcus said, "All right, gentlemen, I suppose then our business is concluded for the evening. You should get a good night's rest. You will undoubtedly need it. The next step is to carefully monitor the situation with Celine while avoiding contact with Tobias. We shall regroup in the morning."

"Wait, where are you going?" Damien inquired, finding his voice again.

"I shall find lodging for the evening."

"Come on, buddy. Let's get to bed," Michael encouraged.

Damien nodded and they retreated a few steps toward the house. Damien lingered a moment on the path before continuing.

"What's wrong?" Michael inquired.

Damien glanced back toward the gazebo. "Should we offer him somewhere to stay?"

"Are you kidding me?" Michael asked. "Did the time travel screw up your brain?"

"No," Damien argued. "I just… I dunno, I feel bad."

"For him?" Michael spat out, his voice incredulous.

Damien shrugged.

"Listen, even if I agree, and NOT because I feel bad, but because I'd rather keep tabs on this guy, I don't see any option here. What do you propose we do? Run him up to the house and ask if Celine minds if he stays with her?"

"No, obviously not. We'd have to sneak him in."

"I'm not sure that's the best idea," Michael countered.

"Well, like you said, we could keep an eye on him. And he could keep an eye on us. You know, so this Tobias guy doesn't kill us in our sleep or something."

Michael rolled his eyes. "I really hate this," he lamented. "Come on."

They stalked back toward Marcus. "Is there a problem?" Marcus inquired.

Damien and Michael shared a glance. "Maybe it'd be better if you came with us," Damien suggested.

"To stay in the Buckley house? Have you gone mad?"

Damien held back a frustrated sigh. "No, but perhaps it's best we stick together. We'll sneak you in…"

"No," Marcus interrupted him.

"Oh? You have somewhere else to be?" Michael questioned.

"It is unwise for me to stay in the Buckley home. Should Celine find me there, it may wreck her trust in you. We cannot risk it."

"He has a point," Damien groaned.

"Fine by me. I'd rather part ways. Though I don't trust you." Michael waved his finger at Marcus.

"Good night, gentlemen," Marcus said. He spun on his heel and strode away from them.

"Well, that's that," Damien said as his hands slapped his sides. "Let's go."

Michael and Damien returned to the house, slipping in through a side door and parting ways into their individual rooms. Damien changed into the nightclothes Celine provided though he did not climb into bed. Instead, he paced the floor. His mind frothed with worry.

He settled near the window, cracking it open to let the sounds of the ocean inside. He leaned against the wall and stared out into the night. Could he handle what the Duke thrust upon him? He had traveled into Shadow World once before to save Celine. That world took an extreme physical toll on him. He withstood it. He did it for Celine. He would take any risk if it meant saving those he cared about.

But this situation seemed entirely different. Could he reach Celine? Could he pull her back from the brink? He worried he couldn't. But he'd damn well try, he decided.

With that settled he crawled into bed for a restless night. He tossed and turned. When he did sleep, nightmares haunted his dreams.

* * *

Bright sunshine streamed through the window early the next morning. Damien blinked against it as his eyes fluttered open. For a moment, he laid in bed, his mind at ease. He inhaled a deep breath as he stared at the cloudless sky.

He yawned and stretched, glancing around the room. His muscles tensed as he noticed the missing door. No bathroom. He recalled his current circumstances. He wasn't at home; he was in 1842. Facing insurmountable odds.

An invisible rubber band squeezed his head as tension crept over him. He crawled from his bed and pulled on his clothes. He had no desire to face the day, but he had little choice.

A knock sounded on his door as he fiddled with his tie. "Yeah?" he called.

"Sleeping in?" Michael inquired as he pushed through the door.

"Forgot where I was for a second," Damien answered as he put the final touches on his centuries-old outfit.

"Did you sleep?"

Damien lifted a shoulder before letting it drop. "Not really. I tossed and turned most of the night. When I woke up, my overtired mind thought we were at home. Then I remembered when I saw the missing bathroom."

"Ugh, please don't remind me of the missing bathroom," Michael lamented.

"We should get out of here and meet the Duke," Damien suggested.

"Yeah, before the creepy soul eater arrives," Michael said.

"Wonder if we can sneak into the dining room and grab some scones before we go."

"I'm not sure I want to chance that," Michael said.

"Meet the Duke on an empty stomach?" Damien asked.

"Fine, fine," Michael gave in. "If the dining room is empty, we'll pocket some scones."

Damien nodded as they crept from the room into the hall. They navigated to the dining room. Michael peered into the large space. "Coast's clear," he whispered.

"Good," Damien said, skirting around Michael and to the sideboard. "We're in luck!"

He perused the offerings before pouring a cup of coffee.

"Hey, we're not supposed to be sticking around," Michael reminded him.

"I know," Damien answered between gulps of coffee. "Just a little fuel before we go."

"Pour me one," Michael instructed, holding a cup out. Damien obliged him and filled the cup. Michael sipped it as Damien shoved a scone into his mouth and pocketed another few.

He slurped another sip of coffee. "Okay, I'm good," he mumbled with a full mouth.

Michael took another long gulp from his cup. "Let's go," he said as he set the cup on the sideboard.

They hurried from the dining room. "Sneak out the side door?" Damien suggested.

"Yep," Michael agreed.

They ducked down a side hall. Voices floated from around the corner. They stopped short. "Sounds like Celine's voice," Damien whispered.

Michael nodded. He signaled for them to go back the way they came. They spun and hurried down the hall and past the dining room. They emerged in the main foyer. The two men peeked into the vast space, scanning it for people.

They found it empty. "Let's make a run for the front door," Michael breathed.

Damien nodded in response. They hastened from the hall, making it a quarter of the way across the room before Celine emerged from another hall. "Go back! Go back!" Damien whispered.

They spun around and tried to return to the hallway, but their progress was stopped by Celine's voice.

"Michael! Damien!" she called to them.

They ground to a halt. Damien winced and shot a glance at Michael. He returned the expression. They twisted to face Celine. "Celine!" Damien said, fake surprise in his voice. "Didn't see you there."

Celine sauntered across the foyer to them. "Did you sleep well? I worried I had missed you!"

"Oh, yes," Damien fibbed. "Like a baby. So great. I slept

really well. I couldn't have been more comfortable. It really was…"

Michael gave him a jolt to quiet him.

"I am so pleased. And very pleased I did not miss you this morning!"

"Oh?" Michael inquired.

"Yes! We have a guest on the estate. I wanted you to meet him."

"Oh, well, we were just on our way out," Michael began.

"And we're running late. I overslept," Damien chimed in.

"We really should be going. Perhaps later."

"You cannot spare a few moments?" Celine questioned. Her brow furrowed and her lips formed a pout. Michael and Damien recognized the familiar expression of disappointment.

"Well…" Damien began.

"Please, it will only take a few moments! A quick introduction!"

Michael plastered a smile on his face. "A brief hello," he answered. "Then we really must be going. We are late to meet our associate."

"Wonderful!" Celine said with a clap of her hands. "I promise it will only take a moment. And you can offer my apologies to your colleague."

Michael nodded as Celine led them across the foyer and into the sitting room. A man stood across the room; his arm perched on the mantel. He stared into the fire. As they entered, he spun to face them. A broad grin crossed his angular face. His deep-set dark brown eyes studied them. A tangle of dark, curly hair topped his head.

A chill passed over Damien. "Ah, you've found them," he said, his white teeth gleaming against his medium-toned skin.

"I have," Celine said with a smile. "They were on their way

out so I'm afraid the introduction shall be brief. Nonetheless, it can be made. Michael and Damien Carlyle, please meet Tobias Greene.

"Tobias, Michael and Damien Carlyle, cousins of mine."

He thrust his hand out as he approached them. "What a pleasure," he said, his accent sounding British.

They each shook his hand. "I'm sorry, Mr. Greene," Michael said as they shook. "Have we met before?"

Tobias frowned and glanced upward in a dramatic display of searching his memory. "I do not believe so. I am quite good with names and faces."

"Hmm," Michael murmured, "what did you say your business is, again?"

He offered another grin. "I didn't," he answered.

"A secret, then?" Michael pushed as Tobias turned his attention to Damien.

"Not at all," he assured them. "I own several shipping vessels that travel to the Far East. I am eager to discuss a partnership with the Buckleys."

"Ah," Michael said with a nod.

Damien licked his lips and offered a nervous chuckle as he gripped the man's hand. The warm flesh sent a shiver down his spine. His brown eyes bore into Damien and a bead of sweat formed on Damien's brow.

CHAPTER 23

*D*amien struggled to stay upright as the eyes of Tobias Greene fell upon him.

Michael clapped him on the shoulder. "Well, we should be going. We are late for a business discussion of our own."

"And what is your business, Mr. Carlyle?" Tobias questioned.

"Railroads," Michael lied.

Tobias offered a tight-lipped grin and an unimpressed nod. "Well, we should be on our way," Michael added. "Celine, we may not return until late. Please do not wait on us for dinner."

Michael turned on his heel and strode from the room. He reached back to tug Damien along with him. They exited the sitting room and pushed through the front door into the cool, late morning air.

"I didn't think you were going to leave," Michael said as they ambled down the drive.

Damien shrugged. "I didn't think I could move until you pulled me," Damien admitted.

"Really?" Michael questioned.

"Yeah. Maybe it was imagined, but I felt like he had some pull on me. Like he was probing my mind while he stood there smiling at me."

"Hmm," Michael murmured.

"You didn't feel that?"

"Nope," Michael admitted.

"Maybe because you were too busy with your interrogation."

"I figured better to know what we're dealing with," Michael said.

"I figured better to not tick this guy off," Damien retorted.

"I guess. Well, this morning's conversation should go really well. The one thing the Duke told us not to do, we've already failed at."

"Yep. Avoid Tobias at all costs," Damien imitated. "And we run into the guy less than twelve hours after he tells us that."

They continued the rest of the journey in silence. They approached the gazebo near the cliff's edge. Michael sighed as they approached the waiting figure of the Duke.

"You're late," he said as they closed the distance.

"Yeah, sorry, we ran into a delay," Michael answered.

"Have you spoken with Celine?"

"Yes," Michael answered.

"And?"

"And she…" Michael began.

"We tried to avoid her, but we ran into her and she insisted on introducing us to Tobias," Damien burst out.

Marcus's jaw fell open and he blinked his widened eyes at them. "You what? You met him?"

"Yeah, we did," Michael admitted.

"Unbelievable," Marcus retorted, shaking his head and closing his eyes. "I warned you about one thing…"

"Yeah, yeah, yeah, we know," Michael retorted. "Look, we

didn't exactly have a choice. Celine strong-armed us into it. We're doing the best we can here."

Marcus offered an unimpressed stare.

"She's pretty persuasive," Damien added.

"So she is," Marcus grumbled. "Never mind. It's done. Avoid him in the future at all costs."

"Definitely," Damien said with a shiver.

"What's our plan for the day? Do we just go back to the house, avoid Tobias and wait for him to attack Celine?"

"No," Marcus answered. "We shall follow him today and see what we can learn about him."

Michael wrinkled his forehead. "Wait, avoid him at all costs, but we're going to follow him?"

"If you are too cowardly, I can manage the task myself."

"We're not, I'm just asking," Michael said.

"Then follow me. We shall await his departure from the house." Marcus strode up the path toward the Buckleys' main house. He twisted to face them. "And by the way, I do not plan on running into him, merely following him."

Michael and Damien shared a glance and a sigh before following Marcus. They veered off the path as the house came into view. The trio crept through the trees, shoving branches and prickly limbs aside. They came to a stop just inside the wooded area.

"Now, we wait," Marcus announced.

The three men stared at the doorway in anticipation. As the sun rose overhead, Michael and Damien's attention waned. Michael puffed out a long breath as he leaned his back against a tree trunk.

Damien kicked a pinecone around, creating a small divot in the dirt.

"Bored, gentlemen?" Marcus taunted.

"I just figured he'd be gone by now," Michael answered as he stared up at the sun overhead.

"Really," Damien said. "It's been hours! What's he doing in there?"

A few silent moments passed before Damien dug into his pocket. He pulled out a blueberry scone and nibbled it. "Scone?" he asked as he pulled two more from his pocket.

"Thanks," Michael said, accepting the baked treat.

Damien waved the other at Marcus and raised his eyebrows in a silent question. Marcus's expression conveyed disgust. "No," he said flatly in response.

"Suit yourself," Damien said with a shrug and shoved the scone back into his pocket.

Marcus frowned at them as they continued to consume the baked goods. He rolled his eyes and returned his focus to the front door.

Their efforts were rewarded moments later. Tobias Greene strode into the afternoon sun. He pulled his time-piece from his pocket and checked it before striding down the pathway.

"There," Marcus announced, calling their attention to him.

"Oh, yeah," Damien mumbled with a mouthful of scone.

"Finally," Michael added, also with a full mouth.

"Where's he going?" Damien muttered.

"Hasn't anyone ever told you not to speak with your mouth full?" Marcus chided.

"Sorry," Damien said with a shrug. He wiped crumbs from his lips with the back of his hand.

"Are you worried about our bad manners or where he's going?" Michael questioned, his finger pointing after the disappearing form of Tobias Greene.

Marcus narrowed his eyes at Michael. With a roll of his eyes, he tromped through the trees, keeping the figure in front of him. Michael and Damien continued behind him, fighting through branches and dodging trees as the woods thickened. Marcus moved like a lithe cat, easily navigating through the thickened brush.

"Hurry, gentlemen!" he called over his shoulder. "We must not lose him."

"Yeah, yeah," Michael answered as he pushed a pine branch aside.

Tobias descended the drive toward Bucksville.

"Is he going to town?" Damien pondered aloud.

"Maybe he's got some business there," Michael suggested.

"Checking on some ships?" Damien suggested.

"Got a ship coming in?" Michael conjectured.

"Looking at the Buckley fleet?"

"Will you two stop babbling?" Marcus barked.

Michael and Damien shared another glance. Michael rolled his eyes. They continued in silence.

Tobias followed the drive to the road below then ambled toward town. Before reaching the small village, Tobias slipped down a side street. He disappeared into a small shanty on stilts.

The men approached cautiously and peered through the windows. No trace of the man existed. They gathered behind a grove of trees behind the cottage.

"He's not downstairs," Damien said.

"Nope. What's he doing here? This place looks deserted," Michael replied.

Marcus scanned the upper windows. A figure moved near one of the windows.

"We'll never know what he's doing up there," Damien lamented with a sigh.

Marcus peered around at the nearby trees. A small bird flitted in one of the branches. It chirped and tweeted as it leapt from branch to branch. Marcus focused on the tiny creature.

Michael and Damien followed his gaze. "Taking up bird watching?" Michael inquired.

"Something like that," Marcus answered. He whistled at the bird. It titled its head, one eye studying him. Marcus held his hand out, fingers extended. He whistled again.

The little black-headed bird fluttered its wings and floated down to land on Marcus's finger.

Damien's jaw dropped open as Marcus pulled the little chickadee toward him. He stroked the bird's tiny head with one finger.

"What are you going to do with that?" Michael questioned.

Damien winced. "Or do we not want to know?"

Marcus offered an unimpressed stare. "Our small friend will allow us to witness what's happening in that room."

Marcus plucked a tiny feather from its body. He pulled the bird close to his lips and whispered a few words. He extended his arm again and the bird flew toward the window. It fluttered outside it before settling on the ledge. The bird hopped closer, peering into the room.

Marcus waved the feather in the air and an image began to form.

A lantern glowed inside a dark corner. Tobias sat cross-legged in front of it. He held his hands outstretched, palms resting on his knees and facing upward. His eyes pinched closed and his mouth murmured unintelligible words. The image floated in the air for a moment before dissolving away.

"What is he doing?" Damien questioned.

"Communicating," Marcus answered. "Likely with a version of himself in the future. So, that's how he's getting his information."

"I am never going to look at birds the same way," Michael mumbled.

"We shall wait here until he makes his next move," Marcus said.

They waited an hour before Tobias wandered from the house and retraced his steps toward the Buckley property.

"Heading home after his meditation session?" Michael said.

Tobias veered off the road and into the woods again. "Nope," Damien answered.

They entered the woods behind him. Tobias continued through the trees toward the beach beyond. They reached the beach moments behind him.

Damien scanned the area but spotted nothing. "Where is he?"

Marcus pushed into the clearing and onto the beach. He spun in a circle, searching the area. His brow wrinkled in confusion.

"Maybe he realized we were following him and turned off before he reached the beach," Michael suggested.

Marcus frowned as he completed his search. "No, he did not turn off."

"Then where is he?"

Marcus's frown deepened and he did not respond.

"Great!" Damien shouted. "Outsmarted already by a simple walk in the woods!"

Marcus grimaced again. "You should return to the Buckley house and await his return."

"What? That's it?" Michael questioned. "Just go home?"

"Do you have another suggestion?" Marcus inquired. "At this hour, he will likely return for dinner and stay afterward to regale the family with his tales of travel. There is nothing more to be done today."

"What are you going to do?" Damien asked.

"I shall try to determine where he disappeared to," Marcus answered. "We shall meet tomorrow morning again."

"Fine," Michael said. "Let's go, Damien."

Damien hesitated a moment before he followed Michael from the beach. As they stepped onto the path toward the house, Damien vented his frustration.

"Well, this is going great so far."

"Yep," Michael answered.

Damien kicked a stone on the path, his agitation surfacing.

"Am I the only one still creeped out by the bird thing?" Michael said after a moment.

"Nope," Damien responded. "Every time I see a bird flying around me, I'm going to wonder if a picture is forming in front of the Duke."

Michael grimaced. "Yeah."

"Hey, I'm starved. All we had for lunch was scones."

"Me too. Wonder if we can get a few sandwiches at the house?"

"I hope so. I'm not planning on dining with Tobias Greene but I'd hate to miss dinner. I've only got two scones left in my pocket!"

They continued to the house, slipping in through a side door. After a quick trip to the kitchen, surprising a few members of the household staff, they obtained sandwiches and carried them up to Damien's bedroom.

They slipped inside without running into anyone. As they ate, they discussed the situation so far and their lack of progress. Frustrated, they called it a night and parted ways to get some rest.

* * *

Damien shivered as the cold struck him. He stood in a long hallway. Doors lined each side.

"Hello?" he called.

He spun in a circle, searching for something familiar. He found nothing.

Damien crept down the hall. He eyed each door, afraid to open them.

"Hello?" he shouted again. His voice echoed off the empty space but he received no response.

The lights overhead flickered and went out. The hallway plunged into darkness. Damien groaned as he let his eyes adjust to the blackness. "Hello?" he croaked for a third time.

This time he received a response. A roaring noise whooshed through the hall. Wind blasted him, blowing him back a few steps.

"DAMIEN," a male voice growled.

He gulped as he steadied himself against the wind gust. His eyes reduced to slits. He held a hand in front of his face as he peered forward. Light glowed at the end of the hall.

The wind died down and Damien ventured forward. He squinted as he tried to discern the light's source. As he approached, he made out the shape of an open door.

He inched toward it. The door flung open. "DAMIEN," the voice roared again from inside the room.

Damien stopped his slow crawl and peered into the light.

"DAMIEN," the voice repeated.

Damien gulped again and glanced behind him as he considered a retreat.

"Damien."

Damien's brow wrinkled and he twisted to face the open door again. This voice was different.

"Damien," the second voice repeated.

"Celine?" he questioned.

He took another step toward the glowing light.

"Damien!" Celine called.

"Celine!" he shouted in return. "Celine, I'm coming!"

He raced toward the room, skittered over the threshold

and inside. He blinked against the bright light as he peered around the room.

"Celine?"

He took another few steps into the room.

"Celine?!"

A laugh greeted his calls. A deep, maniacal laugh. He spun in search of the sound. The door to the room slammed shut. Damien gasped as his only exit was cut off. He raced toward the closed door and twisted the doorknob. He tugged at it. It didn't budge.

He whipped around and pressed his back against the door as he scoured the room. A figure stepped forward. He recognized Tobias Greene. The man spoke to him though his lips did not move, and no sound came from his mouth.

"Damien," he communicated as his eyes burned a hole into Damien's mind.

Damien squeezed his eyes shut in an attempt to shut the man out. He grimaced as a searing pain shot across his forehead. When he risked another glance into the room, the man was gone.

A sigh of relief escaped his lips, and he released his white-knuckled grasp on the doorknob. He gulped in air before his eyes shot around the room, searching for an escape. Suddenly, the man reappeared directly in front of him.

Damien leapt back, banging into the door behind him. The man gripped his throat and shoved his chin toward the ceiling. "Leave, Damien. Leave Celine to me."

"No," Damien choked out.

"She is mine," he communicated. His dark eyes smoldered at Damien.

Damien struggled to move under the man's chokehold. He managed a slight shake of his head.

"No, never," he spat.

Tobias's grip tightened around his throat. His grasp lifted

Damien off the floor. His legs dangled as Tobias choked the life from him. His vision clouded as he struggled to breathe. He tugged at the man's hand but could not loosen his fingers. His vision narrowed to a pinpoint before blackness engulfed him.

255

CHAPTER 24

*D*amien gasped for breath and clutched at his pillows. He moaned in his sleep before shooting to sitting. He gulped in air as he acclimated to his surroundings. He glanced around the room before his gaze fell on the landscape outside the window.

Damien rolled out of bed and stumbled to the window. He pushed it open and gulped deep breaths of the sea air. The ocean slapped against the rocks on the nearby coast. He allowed the sound to lull him into a more peaceful state.

The dream replayed itself in Damien's head. He shivered as he recalled Tobias's grip tightening around his throat. He chewed his lower lip as he recalled the man's demand. Celine. She is mine, he said. Damien shook his head. "No," he said aloud. "No, you can't have her!"

He stalked back to his bed and perched on the edge. They needed a plan. And they needed it fast. They couldn't leave this up to chance. "You can't have her," he repeated.

* * *

A knock sounded at Damien's door the next morning. Damien pulled it open immediately. "Hey, good morning, that was quick," Michael greeted him from the hallway.

"Come in," Damien said, waving him into the room.

Michael entered and closed the door behind him. "You ready for another day of this?"

"Yes," Damien answered. "I've been up for hours."

"Did you get any sleep?" Michael inquired.

"Some. Until I had a nightmare in which Tobias informed me to stay out of his way so he could have Celine."

Michael's eyebrows shot skyward. "Really?"

"Really," Damien said with a sigh. "We need to step up our game."

"How?" Michael inquired.

Damien remained silent for a moment. "I don't know. I've been up for hours, and I can't come up with anything. But I think we need to keep a better eye on Celine. We need to be there the moment he tries anything with her."

"I don't know, man. The Duke told us to stay off his radar and quite frankly, for once, I agree with him."

"After my dream last night, I agree we need to stay away from Tobias Greene, but we need to watch Celine. Stalking around in the woods with the Duke isn't our best use of time."

"All right," Michael agreed. "We'll do what you think is best."

"We'll have to slip out and tell him, but after that, straight back here!"

"Okay, sounds like a plan."

With a nod, Damien pulled his door open and peeked into the hall. "Coast's clear. Oh, could we grab some scones on the way?"

Michael chuckled and clapped him on the shoulder. "Sure, buddy."

They navigated the halls, retrieved the scones and were about to slip out a side door when a voice stopped them. Both men froze and Damien gulped. They twisted to glance behind them.

"Gentlemen," Tobias repeated. "How fortunate I am to have caught you before you sneaked from the house."

"Sneaked?" Damien inquired with a nervous chuckle. "No one's sneaking."

Michael squared his shoulders and narrowed his eyes at Tobias. "Hardly sneaking," he answered. "Just on our way to an important meeting."

Tobias arched one eyebrow. "Business?"

"Yes," Michael replied.

"Thinking of bringing a railway through Bucksville?"

Michael offered a smirk. "I like to keep all the options available."

Tobias shifted his gaze to Damien. Damien swallowed hard. The man's eyes narrowed, and he smirked at Damien. Damien's head began to ache. A dull throb pounded at each temple. He resisted the urge to squeeze his eyes shut. His knees wobbled and he fought to stay upright.

"If you're finished with your interrogation, we really do need to be going," Michael said, stepping between Damien and Tobias.

The overwhelming feeling passed from Damien as Tobias's gaze was averted.

The man offered an upside-down smile. "No interrogation. I merely hoped to speak with you. We missed you at dinner last night and I hoped to ensure your attendance this evening."

"Well..." Michael began.

"For Celine. She seemed so very glum when you didn't appear."

Michael offered a brief smile. "We'll do our best."

The man's teeth gleamed as he offered a broad smile. "Excellent. Well, I shall let you get to your business. Good day, gentlemen." He turned on his heel and strode down the hall.

Michael nodded as they turned to exit to the fresh air.

"Oh, gentlemen," Tobias said, twisting back to face them. "Did I see you wandering in the woods yesterday?"

Michael offered a confused glance. He frowned and shook his head. "No."

"Hmm," Tobias said with a wiggle of his eyebrows. "I must have been mistaken."

He spun away and ambled down the hall, whistling as he went.

Damien and Michael pushed through the door into the morning air. Gray clouds rolled through the sky and a cool breeze gusted past them. Damien gulped it in.

"Hey, you okay?" Michael questioned as Damien squeezed his eyes shut as he drank in the air.

Damien nodded before his head bobbing turned into a shake. "No," he admitted.

"What's going on?"

"Every time he looks at me, something happens to me."

"Something happens to you?" Michael questioned.

"Yeah. This time as soon as he looked at me, I got a headache. Then I started to feel woozy. If you wouldn't have stepped between us, I may have passed out."

"Wow," Michael said. "I'm glad I did. Some urge just came over me and I felt I needed to get between you."

"I'm glad it did."

"I think the Duke's right. We need to stay away from him."

"But can we?"

"We have to!"

"The thing about Celine and dinner… it sounded like a threat."

Michael heaved a sigh. "But we're no match for him."

"Clearly I'm not," Damien lamented. "But we can't leave Celine alone with this guy."

Michael tensed his jaw. "Well, we're already all over his radar. He didn't ask us if we were in the woods yesterday for fun. He spotted us. And he wants us to know it."

Damien shivered as his nerves began to settle. "Yeah. Not good news. Maybe we should avoid the dinner."

"As much as I hate that these words are coming out of my mouth, perhaps we should discuss this with the Duke."

Damien shook his head but agreed. "You're right. And yes, as bizarre as it sounds, he's our best asset right now."

"Do you feel okay to walk?"

"Yeah, I can walk. The feeling's passed now."

"Okay, we should get going. We're going to be late. Again."

The two men set off on the path, directing their aim toward the familiar gazebo. The Duke stood nearby staring at the cloudy sky.

"You're late," he stated as they approached. "Again."

Michael rolled his eyes. "Yeah, sorry, we had a bit of a situation. Again."

"How is Celine?"

"We didn't see her," Damien said.

Marcus's eyebrow shot skyward. "Then what was the situation?"

Michael's lips formed a half-frown. "We ran into Tobias Greene this morning."

Marcus's jaw unhinged. "You what?"

"We couldn't avoid it!" Michael countered.

"Yeah," Damien added, "we tried to sneak out of the house, and he caught us."

Marcus closed his eyes and shook his head. "I have given you one directive during this venture. To avoid Tobias

Greene. And you've bungled it. Twice you have managed to become entangled with him."

"It's not our fault."

"Yeah, it's not like we WANT to run into him," Damien argued. "The guy makes me sick. Literally."

Marcus cocked his head. "Explain."

"Yesterday when we met him, it felt like he was probing my brain. And today, when he looked at me, I got a pounding headache and started to feel like I was going to pass out. Not to mention the nightmare I had last night."

Marcus sighed and shook his head again.

"And he seems intent on keeping tabs on us," Michael added. "Today he tracked us down to make sure he'd see us at dinner tonight. He mentioned how sad Celine was that we weren't there last night."

Damien nodded in agreement. "And he asked if we were in the woods yesterday. Said he thought he saw us."

Marcus puckered his lips. "The situation is devolving faster than I expected."

"What should we do?" Damien questioned.

Marcus's brow furrowed as he dissected the situation. "You must avoid Tobias," he stated.

"But how?" Damien countered. "If we avoid him, we can't keep tabs on Celine."

"Plus, the guy seems intent on inserting himself wherever we are," Michael added.

Marcus's jaw tensed. "Damn it!" he shouted. "My hands are tied. I can't freely parade around the Buckley home yet you cannot be left there alone since you are incapable of remaining unseen."

"We're going to have to sneak you in," Damien said. "And you're going to have to just lurk around in the shadows while we make the contact with Celine and Tobias."

"I'm afraid we have no other choice," Marcus lamented.

"That'll work. You're an expert at lurking," Michael said to him.

He offered Michael an unimpressed glance.

"There's a secret passage in the sitting room. If I remember correctly, it goes past the dining room and into another wing of the house. It should provide you access to hear our inescapable dinner conversation," Damien said.

"That's right. Max showed us where it is. We'll sneak you in and hide you in there."

Marcus agreed with a sigh. "Fine. As there appears to be no other options, I suppose that will do."

They agreed to the plan, deciding to spend the morning hidden outside and return after the lunch hour. The trio made their way through a cave to the beach where Damien claimed a spot on a rock to wait out the morning hours.

"You okay, buddy?" Michael inquired, joining him on the large stone slab.

"Honestly, I'm still feeling a little rough. And I'm tired."

"Maybe you can catch a nap before dinner," Michael suggested.

Damien shrugged. "Yeah, maybe. I'm almost afraid to close my eyes again."

"You and Celine really suffer from those nightmares."

"Yep. And we're not even related."

"Yet still so much alike."

Damien smiled at the comparison. He picked up a small stone and tossed it toward the rolling ocean. It skittered across the rocky beach and came to a rest just outside the waves' reach.

"We should have gone to Alexander's," Damien said.

"He's out of town," Michael replied.

"Maybe he left his doors unlocked. We could have hung out there."

"Great idea, as long as we don't get caught."

"You're right. Maybe we should stay put."

The sun rose overhead, still obscured by the gray clouds. Conversation between them waned as they waited out the morning. Damien rose and paced the beach.

Tension mounted as conversation dwindled and worry overcame each man. As Damien made his fifteenth loop, he spun to face the wooded area they emerged from yesterday. He stopped in his tracks.

"Look!" he breathed. He pointed a finger toward the woods on the opposite end of the beach. Michael stood from the rock and peered around an outcropping in the direction Damien indicated. Marcus joined them, glancing over Damien's shoulder into the distance.

Michael's eyes grew wide as Tobias Greene emerged from under the canopy of the trees. "Perhaps we should hide?" Damien questioned.

"Good idea," Michael answered.

They hurried to the rocky outcropping and ducked behind it. Michael chanced a glance around the large stone. His brows knit and he shifted his glance to Damien.

"What is it?"

"He's gone," Michael reported.

"What?" Marcus asked. He shoved the two men aside and leaned to peer around the rocks.

"Well?" Damien inquired.

"Michael is correct. He's gone."

Damien stood and stalked around the rock. He searched the area, spinning to check behind him and then back to the woods. "Where did he go?"

"Maybe back into the woods," Michael conjectured.

"That's the second time he's disappeared," Damien said.

They strode down the beach and searched for any sign of Tobias. They found none.

"He's not here," Michael said after fifteen minutes of searching.

"Nope."

"Maybe we should take advantage of him being out of the house and sneak back in."

"Good idea," Damien agreed. "With any luck, we'll beat him back there."

Michael, Damien and Marcus retraced their steps through the cave to the cliffs above. They took a direct path back to the house. After circling it, they entered through the front entrance and hurried into the sitting room.

Michael closed the doors behind them as Damien jogged across the room and pulled open the secret panel. He motioned for Marcus to enter.

"If you hang a right at the…"

"I can find my way to the dining room when I need to," Marcus retorted as he slid into the dark hole.

"Do you need a candle or something?" Michael questioned.

Marcus cupped his hand and formed a fireball in it.

"Right," Michael said with a nod. "Okay, see ya!" Michael shoved the panel closed and dusted his hands. "Come on, let's head upstairs."

Damien nodded and the two men navigated upstairs to the bedroom, avoiding contact with any other household members. They pushed through the door into Damien's room and bolted it behind them.

"Whew," Damien said as he leaned against the locked door.

"At least we're rid of you-know-who," Michael said.

Damien nodded with a sigh as he slogged to his bed. He sank onto the edge. "Yeah," he answered. "This whole situation is starting to wear on me."

"Maybe you should try a nap. We'll need the energy if we're going to have dinner with Tobias Greene."

"At least the rest of the family should be there," Damien answered with a yawn.

They were quiet for a moment before Damien added. "If you don't mind, I'm going to take you up on that nap."

"No problem," Michael answered. "Hey, do you mind if I stay here? I really don't want to hang out in my room alone."

"You don't want to join the Duke, and lurk around in the secret passage."

"Hard pass," Michael said.

Damien offered a chuckle as he fell into the pillow. After sinking into the chair, Michael propped his feet on the sill. He glanced over at the bed. Damien's form curled in a ball, breathing rhythmically. "Sleep well, Damien," Michael breathed as he turned his attention back to the scenery outside.

* * *

Michael's head lolled and his chin rolled down toward his chest. He snapped it up, sniffing deeply. He yawned and glanced around. He must have nodded off. He checked his watch. It was mid-afternoon. They had a bit more time before their dreaded dinner.

He swung his eyes toward Damien's bed. Damien laid on his back, asleep. Michael relaxed back into the armchair and closed his eyes. Within seconds, he snapped them open. He glanced toward Damien again. His brows knit together, and he dropped his feet to the floor.

He squinted toward Damien. His chest rose and fell rapidly. Too rapidly. Michael leapt from his chair and hurried toward the bed. "Damien?" he called.

Damien panted, his fingers gripping the sheets around

him in a tight ball. Sweat beaded across his forehead. "Damien!" Michael shouted again. He grabbed hold of his shoulders and shook him. Damien did not respond. Michael felt the heat through Damien's clothes. He pressed his hand against Damien's forehead. His skin burned.

Michael ran his fingers through his sandy blonde hair. He swallowed hard. He needed help.

CHAPTER 25

Michael couldn't rouse Damien. Damien's labored breathing and raised body temperature added to his worry. His mind scanned through his options.

He raced into the hallway, determined to find someone to help. As he burst through the door he ran into Celine.

"Michael!" Celine greeted him. "Have you returned for dinner? I hope to see you there this evening."

Michael gasped. "I need your help."

The smile waned on Celine's face. "What is wrong?"

Michael grabbed her arm and tugged her toward Damien's room. "Damien fell asleep earlier and when I checked on him, he's feverish and breathing hard."

Celine pulled away from Michael and rushed toward the bed to check Damien. "He is warm, yes," she said. "Damien?" She patted him on the cheeks.

Damien groaned and thrashed his head back and forth. "Damien?" Michael inquired.

"I'll retrieve a cool cloth for his head," Celine said as she darted from the room.

Michael collapsed onto the bed. "Damien, can you hear me?"

Damien moaned again. A pained expression crossed his face. Celine returned moments later with a washbasin and cloth. She wet and wrung the cloth, placing it across his forehead.

Damien's breathing relaxed as Celine tended to him. Ten minutes passed before Damien issued another groan. His eyes fluttered open, and he stared at the ceiling for a few moments.

"Damien?" Celine inquired. "Can you hear us?"

Damien did not respond.

"Come on, buddy. Talk to us," Michael said.

Damien's eyes scanned the room and he squirmed before he swallowed and spoke. "Hey," he said.

"Hey, buddy, you feel okay?"

Damien began to sit up. "Easy, Damien," Celine warned.

"I'm okay," he assured them as he pushed to sitting. He stared at the cloth clutched in Celine's hand.

"You seemed feverish," she explained. She felt his forehead with the back of her hand. "It seems to have passed."

Michael blew out a long breath.

"Still," Celine continued. "Perhaps you should remain abed. I will request dinner to be sent…"

"No, no, no," Damien insisted. "I'm fine. We missed dinner last evening. I'd like to attend tonight."

"There is no obligation. Please do not feel duty-bound."

"Maybe we should skip it," Michael suggested.

Damien shook his head. "No. I'm fine! Just overheated. I should have removed my jacket before laying down."

"Are you certain you feel up to it?" Celine inquired.

"Definitely," Damien said with a nod. "Looking forward to it!"

Celine smiled at him. "I shall see you soon, then." She rose and excused herself from the room, pulling the door shut behind her.

Damien sank back into his pillows with a long sigh.

"Why did you rope us into that dinner again?" Michael questioned.

"We can't leave Celine alone there!" Damien argued.

Michael's shoulders slumped. "Are you sure you're up to it?"

Damien nodded. "Yeah. I'm a little tired, but I can make it." Damien pulled himself to sitting and swung his legs over the side of the bed. He stood and collapsed back to the bed.

"Really?" Michael asked, his eyebrows rising high.

Damien took a deep breath. "I'm fine," Damien answered. "I don't feel ill at all."

"I don't know, man," Michael said. "You weren't looking too good a few minutes ago. You were feverish, sweating, panting and I couldn't wake you."

"I was having a nightmare," Damien admitted.

"Again?"

"Yep, again. Same thing as before."

"Are you sure this is a good idea? Another nightmare with physical side effects? This might not be the best idea."

"We should stick to the plan," Damien said. "The nightmare is another threat. We can't leave her alone with that monster. Plus, we've got the Duke hidden as the ace up our sleeves."

"I really hate that he is our ace. All right," Michael agreed, "we'll go to dinner."

The two men waited on pins and needles, pacing the floor to pass the time before dinner. When the hour arrived, they trudged downstairs. Neither looked forward to the meal. Damien's stomach churned and threatened to disagree with any food he ingested.

They crossed the foyer and entered the sitting room.

"Damien! Michael!" Celine greeted them with a broad smile. "I am so glad you were able to attend."

An older man shifted in his chair to eye them. "Are these your cousins, Celine?" he questioned.

"Yes, Evan, please meet Michael and Damien Carlyle. Michael, Damien, please meet Mr. Evan Buckley, Gray's cousin."

"Pleased to meet you, sir," Michael said, his hand extended.

Evan rose and shook hands with each of them. "Welcome to our home. Please meet my wife, Rebecca." He motioned toward a woman sitting on a loveseat across from them.

They offered their greeting as Tobias crossed the room toward them. "So glad you could join us this evening, gentlemen," he said with this characteristic wide grin.

"Ah, you've already met, Tobias?" Evan asked him.

"Yes. I was fortunate enough to make their acquaintance yesterday after my arrival."

The butler arrived to announce dinner and pass a message along to Celine.

"What is it?" Evan questioned as Celine read it. Her face betrayed a problem.

"Gray has been delayed again."

"Oh, how unfortunate!"

Celine nodded. "A terrible shame, particularly with Mr. Greene awaiting his return so eagerly."

"I shall not complain about spending additional time with this lovely family," Tobias responded. He offered his arm to Celine to escort her to dinner.

She accepted and Michael and Damien trailed behind them to the dining room. Michael stared at the dark paneled walls of the large space, wondering behind which the Duke crept.

Light conversation centered around town life as they ate

their first course. By the second, Rebecca and Evan discussed their children.

Damien slouched in his chair and pushed the food around on his plate in between bites. His head throbbed and jitters filled his stomach. Each bite of food tasted sour, and he worried it would not stay down.

"And how is the railroad business coming?" Tobias directed the question toward Michael.

"We cannot complain," he answered.

Damien kept his eyes fixed on his plate as he pushed the peas around.

"And how are you finding Bucksville?" Tobias inquired, his gaze settling on Damien.

Michael glanced at him, noticing the blank stare in Damien's eyes and the sweat beading on his forehead.

"We're enjoying it," Michael answered for him. "And, of course, it's lovely to visit with Celine."

"And you, Damien?" Tobias pressed.

Damien's fork clattered to his plate as it slipped from his grip. He shut his eyes a moment as he gathered his strength. He swallowed hard. "I'm really enjoying it, too," he answered, his voice just above a whisper.

Tobias grinned at him. "Wonderful."

Damien exhaled a relieved sigh as Evan directed a question to Tobias and Tobias's stare shifted away from him.

Michael kicked him under the table. Damien lifted his eyes to Michael's face. He struggled to maintain his composure as the room swayed. He offered a weak nod and a fleeting upturn of his lips.

By the dessert course, Damien's skin crawled as though he was feverish. He shifted in his seat, fidgeting to seek a comfortable spot.

Celine leaned closer to him and whispered, "Damien, are you feeling ill again?"

He shook his head. "I'm okay," he breathed.

"Ill?" Tobias inquired. "Were you ill?"

"No," Michael answered for him. "He struggles to sleep in new locations. I expect it will settle after a good night's rest."

"Oh, good, I would hate to see one of you ill."

Michael narrowed his eyes at the man, not believing a word he said.

"You know, I have been feeling a bit worse for wear myself. Perhaps nightcaps are in order," Evan suggested.

"Oh, wonderful," Rebecca said. "Shall we?"

"Indeed," Tobias agreed.

The group made their way to the sitting room for a post-dinner drink. Evan and Rebecca excused themselves after one brandy. Damien hoped the party would break up soon.

"Celine, would you like to go for a stroll before retiring?" Michael inquired.

"That sounds lovely," Celine agreed.

"Oh," Tobias interjected, "would it inconvenience you to wait a few moments? I had a gift I hoped to impart to you."

"A gift?" Celine questioned.

"Yes. I had hoped to present it to both you and Gray. Given the news of his delay, though, coupled with the fact that the gift is primarily intended for you, I shall pass it along now."

Celine glanced at Michael and Damien. "We can wait," Michael said.

Tobias reached into his pocket and withdrew a velvet box. He held it toward Celine before he popped open the lid. Celine's eyes widened. Inside, limned by the black velvet, a teardrop ruby necklace laid.

Damien struggled not to groan out loud as he eyed the ruby. The ruby necklace, his mind repeated. The second piece of Celine's ominous prediction. Or was it a recollection not a prediction because it happened in the past not the future? Or was this the future? Damien's mind melted as it spun in a thousand different directions. His temples throbbed and his dinner threatened to make a reappearance. He struggled to focus on the current events. The timeline was moving forward. They'd need to keep their wits about them.

"How lovely!" Celine exclaimed.

"I had hoped you were keen on it. It is a small piece from a Chinese emperor's collection. I came across it in my travels."

"Surely you prefer to save it for a future sweetheart," Celine suggested.

"My beautiful Celine, I cannot fathom a more appropriate person to offer this to than you."

Celine cocked her head and arched an eyebrow.

"Oh, please do not misunderstand the gesture! I mean nothing untoward."

Celine offered a gracious smile. "The gesture is lovely and appreciated."

"May I?" he questioned as he withdrew the item from the box.

Celine offered a closed-mouth smile as she swept away any tendrils of hair from her neck. He positioned the necklace around her slender neck. The teardrop fell from the choker-style necklace into the hollow of her throat. She grasped it between her index finger and thumb as she ambled to a mirror to gaze at it.

"It is stunning," she murmured.

"I am so pleased you find it so," Tobias answered as he positioned himself behind her. "I hope it will grace your neck on many occasions."

They stood staring into the mirror together for another few moments. Celine seemed lost in her reflection. Tobias stared into her reflection's eyes. Were they communicating, Damien wondered?

"Well," Tobias said after a moment, "I shall leave you to your evening walk with these fine gentlemen. Good evening, everyone."

With a nod of his head, Tobias stalked from the room. Celine continued to admire the necklace after he left.

"Celine?" Michael inquired. He caressed her forearm. "Celine?"

She blinked her eyes and swung her head toward him. Her brow furrowed as her eyes flitted around the room. "Yes?" she questioned.

"You seemed lost in thought. Are you ready for our walk?"

"Oh!" Celine replied as though she just remembered. "Would you mind waiting while I grab a wrap? I'm afraid the night air may be cool."

"Of course," Michael answered.

Celine nodded and scooted from the room.

Damien let his head drop into his hands and groaned.

"The ruby necklace," Michael announced.

"Yep," Damien moaned.

"How are you holding up?"

"My brain feels like it's on fire," Damien admitted. "Hey, maybe you should follow Celine. I'd go myself but I'm saving my strength."

"Are you sure? She said she'd be right back, and I'm concerned about you."

"I'll be fine now that Tobias left. Just make sure Celine is okay."

Michael nodded. "All right. I'll be right back." Michael hastened from the room.

Damien slouched further forward and rubbed his temples. He covered his face with his hands after a moment and sighed. As he raised his head, he fidgeted in his seat. He pulled himself to standing and wandered across the room. He stared at an object on the baby grand piano in the corner.

After a breath, he grabbed hold of the heavy glass vase. He swung his arm, striking the vase against the piano's side. It shattered into pieces. Broken glass rained to the floor.

Damien clutched one piece in his hand. He stared down at it. Its splintered edge gleamed in the room's lights. Damien pressed the sharp edge against the inside of his wrist. His face pinched as the razor-sharp edge drew the first drop of blood.

CHAPTER 26

"Stop, Damien!" Marcus shouted from across the room. He emerged from the concealed passage and hurried toward him. He grasped Damien's arm and pulled the glass away from his wrist.

Damien wrestled against him for a moment, though he was no match for Marcus's supernatural strength. Marcus squeezed his wrist until his hand opened and dropped the shard of glass.

"What the hell is going on?" Michael inquired as he rushed into the room. He glanced to the broken glass scattered across the floor then at Marcus and Damien.

Marcus guided Damien to a chair to sit. Damien collapsed onto it and gulped in a deep breath. "He saved my life." Michael shoved the doors to the foyer closed.

"What?" Michael inquired as his eyebrows pinched.

"He tried to slit his wrist with the glass," Marcus said.

"I don't know what came over me," Damien said. "I just… it was like I had no control over my own mind or body. I don't even remember breaking the vase and pressing it to my wrist."

Damien flashed the underside of his arm. A small trail of blood flowed down to his hand. Marcus offered a handkerchief to Damien. He accepted it, pressing it against the small wound.

Michael stood in silence, stunned by the revelation. He shook his head as he tried to formulate words, but none came.

"This is the work of Tobias Greene," Marcus said. "Damien cannot be left alone. He is in grave danger."

The doorknob twisted. "Michael, Damien?" Celine called.

Michael held the door shut. "Just a second!" he shouted.

"Oh," Damien groaned. "You need to hide."

Marcus hurried across the room and stepped back into the passage, pulling the panel shut behind him.

"Are you okay?" Michael mouthed to Damien.

Damien nodded. "Yeah, I feel fine now. Headache and everything is gone."

With a nod, Michael pulled the doors open to the foyer. Celine stood on the other side, a shawl wrapped around her shoulders.

"Don't come in," Michael warned.

Celine screwed up her face. "What?"

"We've had a little accident. I'm so embarrassed," Damien said. "I am so clumsy. I knocked the vase from the piano and broke it." He winced as he motioned toward the broken glass.

Celine frowned at it as she pushed past Michael into the room.

"I'm really sorry," Damien lamented.

"We'll pay for a replacement," Michael offered.

Celine shook her head. "It was a wedding present to Rebecca," Celine explained. "A one-of-a-kind."

Damien's shoulders slumped at the admission.

"It is nothing to fret over," Celine assured them. "I shall fix it." She extended her arm over the broken glass on the floor and stretched her fingers. The glass pieces rose from the floor and reassembled themselves before the finished vase flew into her hand. "There, good as new." She grinned and set the vase on the piano.

Damien's eyebrows lifted. "Wow, that's impressive."

She offered a wider grin. "Shall we walk?"

"Yes," Damien said as he rose.

Michael eyed him. He offered a silent message to Damien to determine if he was well enough to walk. Damien offered a slight nod.

"Looks like a clear night. It should be an enjoyable stroll," Michael said.

"Oh," Damien said before they exited into the night air, "should you be wearing that necklace?"

Celine offered a confused glance as her fingertips found the teardrop ruby.

"We wouldn't want you to lose it," Michael added.

"It seems quite secure. I'm certain it will be fine. Shall we?"

They stepped outside. Moonlight lit the path and cast the trees in eerie shadows. The trio wandered to the cliffs overlooking the ocean before circling back to the house.

They said their goodnights before Michael and Damien slipped into Damien's room. They spied Celine continue down the hall and disappear into her room.

"Come on, let's go," Damien said as he pulled the door open. They slipped from the room and back to the sitting room. Michael eased the doors shut behind them.

"You can come out now," Michael said as he spun to face the interior of the room.

The panel hinged open from across the room and Marcus stepped from inside. "How is Celine?" he inquired.

"For all intents and purposes, she seems fine," Michael answered.

Marcus eyed Damien. "And you?"

Damien shrugged.

"Can we move this conversation before someone stumbles upon us?" Michael suggested.

"Good idea," Damien said. "Let's go upstairs."

"Follow us," Michael said.

Michael peered into the foyer. "Coast's clear," he whispered.

Michael pulled the door open and raced across the foyer and up the stairs. They wound through the halls toward their bedrooms.

They slipped through the door to Damien's bedroom. Damien blew out a long, shaky breath as he sank onto the bed.

"What a night," he lamented.

"Yeah," Michael agreed. "Are you sure you're okay?"

"I feel okay now, more or less. Though I'm still shaken up by the idea that I nearly slit my own wrist. If it hadn't have been for… " Damien motioned toward Marcus. "Thank you. I owe you my life."

"I could not let you die," Marcus said. Damien's expression softened toward the man. "I need you to save Celine."

Michael rolled his eyes and Damien pushed out his lips as he shook his head.

"On that note, you cannot be left alone. It is far too dangerous," Marcus added.

"I agree. I'll sleep in here tonight. Well, I'll try not to sleep so I can keep an eye on you."

"No, you need sleep, too," Damien argued.

"I'll never be able to rest while you're being attacked by this guy!"

"This is an impossible situation," Damien lamented.

"You are overlooking the obvious solution," Marcus said.

"What?" Michael and Damien said simultaneously.

Marcus held his arms out to the side, presenting himself as the solution.

"Oh, you've got to be kidding," Michael said with a chuckle. "You? Trust you to watch Damien?"

Marcus set his jaw. "May I remind you I have saved his life once already?"

"Because it was convenient for you. What happens next time when it's more convenient to let him die?" Michael questioned. "Besides, I thought you couldn't stay in the Buckley house in case someone discovers you?"

"Stop it!" Damien exclaimed.

"Sorry, buddy, I just…" Michael began.

"Shh," Damien shushed him.

Michael cocked his head as Damien waved them into silence. He tapped his index finger in the air toward the door.

All attention turned to the closed door. Another door banged shut down the hall. A voice carried from the opposite end.

"Come to me, Celine," Tobias said.

Michael crept across the room and inched the door open. Damien and Marcus followed him. The three men piled against the door, closer than any of them would have preferred.

Through the crack in the door, they spotted Celine. She wore her red dinner dress. The ruby necklace still hung around her neck. Her eyes remained fixed on the opposite end of the hallway.

"Come, Celine," he prodded again.

Celine straggled down the hall. She moved as though she was in a trance. They leaned away from the door as she passed, though her eyes never strayed from Tobias.

Marcus offered a growling sigh.

Damien motioned for them to follow her. Michael offered a quizzical shrug. Damien gave a vehement nod.

"What are you two fools gesturing about?" Marcus breathed.

"We should follow her," Damien whispered.

"No way. It's way too dangerous," Michael countered.

"For who? Isn't it dangerous for Celine?" Damien argued.

"Still…" Michael began.

"We're losing her!" Damien said.

"I agree, we should keep tabs on this," Marcus chimed in.

"Two against one, I win," Damien said as he pulled the door open wider.

"I can't believe this. I lost an argument because you sided with the Duke," Michael muttered as he followed the two men down the hall in the direction Celine had gone moments earlier.

They sneaked to the end of the corridor and peeked around the corner. Celine wandered down another hall. Damien crept into the hallway behind her.

"Don't!" Michael warned in a hushed tone. He tugged Damien back around the corner. "She'll spot you!"

"I don't think she can see anything. She's in a daze," Damien argued.

"While she may be in a trance," Marcus interjected, "we should keep our distance. Better safe than sorry."

Damien frowned as Michael motioned a "thank you" toward Marcus. "Feel better now?" Damien whispered while they waited for Celine to disappear around the corner. "Now you've won an argument because of the Duke."

Michael rolled his eyes and shook his head at Damien. Celine rounded the corner into another hallway.

"Let's go, she's around the bend," Damien said as he darted from their hallway into the next. They hurried down the hall and retrained their eyes on Celine.

She led them through various corridors, eventually leading them to a hallway containing a series of bedrooms. Light glowed from one doorway.

"Isn't this the hall she kept going to in our time?" Michael questioned.

"Yeah," Damien responded, "and it looks like she's going to the same bedroom she kept wandering to also."

Celine staggered to the lit door halfway down the hall and entered the room.

"Come on, let's get closer," Damien said. Before Michael could stop him, Damien sprinted down the hall and positioned himself near the open door.

Michael and Marcus followed, gathering near the opening, and remaining as hidden as possible. Celine stood inside with Tobias. He smiled at her. "Hello, Celine," he said.

Celine did not respond. She stood stiff with her eyes unwavering.

"I am glad you came. I have something I'd like to show you. Come." He motioned for her to follow him.

Tobias guided her across the room to the full-length mirror. He positioned her in front of it. Celine stared at her reflection, though Damien wasn't certain if she could see anything or not. Tobias gazed over her shoulder into the mirror, his hands clutched at her arms.

"Tell me what you see, Celine."

"I see my reflection," Celine murmured.

He smirked and shifted her position. "Look closer."

Celine's brow furrowed. "I see..." she began but paused.

"Keep looking, Celine. Look beyond the simple reflection and tell me what you see."

"Me," she answered again.

"Describe what you see," he prodded.

"Blonde curls, blue eyes, fair skin," she started.

"Do you want to know what I see?" he questioned as he paced the floor behind her.

She cocked her head as she continued to stare into the glass.

"I see a frightened child," he said. "Robbed of her innocence. Thrust into a life she never should have led. I see the shell of a desperate woman, clinging to any shred of happiness she can find. I see a life ravaged by misery."

He ceased his pacing and positioned himself behind her again. "Do you see it, Celine? Do you see what I see?"

Damien squinted toward the mirror, gauging Celine's response. Her reflection changed. Her plump pink cheeks turned sunken and ashy. Her fair skin shriveled to become gray and wrinkled. Her blonde hair whitened. Her blue eyes faded, and dark circles formed under them.

A tear escaped onto Celine's cheek as she witnessed the altered reflection.

"Whoa, what the hell?" Michael whispered.

"He is taunting her," Marcus breathed. "Attempting to sway her to his side."

"By making her horrified?" Damien questioned.

"Yes, and then offering her a way out," Marcus explained. He signaled for them to continue watching.

"Oh, do not cry, my beautiful Celine," he chided. He wiped his thumb across her cheek to remove the tear. "I can help you."

The image in the mirror faded, replaced by Celine's reflection. She twisted to face him. He caressed her chin with his hand before turning her head toward the mirror again.

"Look, Celine. Look into the mirror and see what I can offer you."

Celine gazed into the reflective surface. Her expression softened and a smile formed on her lips.

"What does she see?" Damien questioned.

"Whatever she wants," Marcus explained. "Whatever makes her happy and at peace."

"Why can't we see it?" Michael asked.

"Because it exists only in her mind. He will draw her into her own mind so far she will cease to function and eventually to exist, leaving him free access to her soul."

"Do you see it, Celine?" Tobias inquired.

"Yes," she murmured.

"What do you see?"

"Happiness."

"And do you desire it?"

"Yes."

"Then allow me to help you," he said, grasping her arms. "Will you?"

The crease between her brows deepened.

"That's it, Celine, tell him where to go!" Damien hissed.

"There is no need to answer now," Tobias said. "Consider it. Rest now, Celine."

The smile formed on her lips again. She offered him a slow nod.

"Good night, Celine," he said.

"Time to take our leave, gentlemen," Marcus said as he backed from the door.

Michael and Damien nodded, and they retraced their steps back to Damien's room. The group trudged inside. Damien collapsed onto the bed while Michael slumped into the chair.

"This is a nightmare," Damien said with a sigh.

"Yeah. How can we fight against this?" Michael inquired.

Marcus rolled his eyes. "Even Buckley managed to do it once. I have every faith in your abilities."

"Come on! We're up against a guy who's promising her eternal happiness and a way out of a life she never wanted. A life she hated enough that she did escape from once, I might add," Damien lamented.

"I didn't say it would be easy," Marcus replied. "But it can be done."

"For once, I hope you're right," Michael said.

"Should we start working on Celine now? Maybe we can snap her out of it before this really sets in," Damien asked.

"You can try," Marcus replied. The expression on his face conveyed his skepticism about them achieving their goal.

"What's that mean?" Michael questioned.

"It means you are welcome to try."

"But?" Michael added.

"But I doubt you will succeed."

"Thanks for the vote of confidence," Michael groaned.

"Why won't this work?" Damien questioned.

"She will not recall anything that just happened. In fact, she will likely consider you mad for suggesting anything is amiss."

"We can get through to her, I know it," Damien responded.

Marcus raised his eyebrows. "Do you recall stalking across the sitting room, smashing a vase and attempting to slit your wrist?"

Damien's shoulders slumped as he answered a dejected, "No."

"Celine's experiences are similar. She will not recall this incident. She will wonder what you are referring to."

"So, how can we beat this?" Damien cried.

"While she has regressed into herself. Only then can she be reached."

"So, while she's in the state we just saw her in?" Michael questioned.

"Correct," Marcus replied.

"Every time she's in that state, Tobias will be there," Michael said.

"Not necessarily. She will fall into and out of the state. Though Tobias may not be far behind. Combined with the threat to Damien, it is risky."

"Where are we on defeating this guy?" Michael questioned.

"I am making progress toward the goal. Though I am now delayed as I must guard you both this evening."

"Right, blame us," Michael groaned. "Look, I'll guard Damien and you go make your progress."

"You both need rest. You are both human," Marcus argued.

"We'll be fine," Michael snapped.

"Will you? Are you willing to bet Damien's life on it? Should you fall asleep for even seconds, it could spell disaster. Are you willing to chance it?"

Michael tensed his jaw. "You're right," he said, holding his hands up in defeat.

Silence fell over the group for a few moments before Michael spoke again. "Not to be weird but… would anyone mind if I slept in here? I really have no desire to be alone right now."

"Not at all, buddy. I'd feel better if you did," Damien assured him. "This Tobias guy scares the heck out of me."

"I suggest you gentlemen get some rest now. The next several days will undoubtedly prove to be very trying."

CHAPTER 27

*D*amien spent the evening tossing and turning. He slipped in and out of sleep. He glanced around the room while awake. The presence of the Duke brought him some small measure of comfort. The oddness of the situation did not escape him. Relying on the Duke as their largest form of protection was bizarre. And possibly stupid, his tired brain surmised.

His eyes flitted to the sleeping form of Michael. It turned the corners of his mouth upward. At least they were in this together. Two pals, fighting the darkness. At least some things hadn't changed.

Damien let his head fall back to the pillow behind him. His heavy eyelids closed, and he drifted off into a fitful sleep.

* * *

Damien awoke to bright sunrise streaming through the window. Marcus stood staring out. Damien yawned and stretched as he climbed from his bed.

"Oh good, you're finally awake," Marcus said as Damien shuffled across the room.

Michael startled awake from the armchair. "What happened? What's wrong?" he shouted as he leapt to his feet.

"Nothing," Damien answered. "I just woke up."

"Oh," Michael answered. "Right." He ran his fingers through his hair. "Good morning."

"Now that you two are awake, I must depart. I'd recommend you stay here and out of sight."

"Where are you going?" Michael questioned.

"To settle things. As I informed you yesterday, I must plan to remove Tobias from the situation. I am already behind schedule thanks to Tobias's attacks on Damien."

Michael rolled his eyes. "Fine, go."

"Are you certain you're both able to stay awake and watch each other?"

Damien nodded. "Yep, I'm good."

"Me too," Michael said.

"Fine. Stay out of sight. Stay away from Tobias."

The two men nodded. Marcus strode to the door, inched it open, and checked the hallway. He slipped out the door, pulling it shut behind him, and disappeared.

Michael blew out a long breath as he stalked to the window. "How do you feel? Did you get any sleep?" he asked as he gazed out over the scenery below.

"A little. Weird to have the Duke watching over us."

"Yeah, tell me about it," Michael answered.

They spent a few moments in silence before Damien spoke. "Man, I'm starving."

"Me too," Michael admitted.

"Do you think you can sneak down for some breakfast?"

Michael made a face. "Should I? I feel like the Duke was really emphatic about sticking together."

"Come on," Damien implored, "it'll take five minutes. And better for me to stay out of sight, right?"

Michael considered it. "Okay," he agreed. "I'll hurry. Don't leave this room."

Damien nodded. "Deal." Michael pulled the door open and stepped into the hall. "Get some scones for later!"

Damien paced the floor as he waited for Michael to return. After a few minutes, he began to worry. What if Michael ran into someone? What if Tobias appeared in his room? Was this a mistake? His grumbling stomach disagreed. But his mind concocted scenario after scenario where it was better if they missed a meal.

After what seemed like an eternity, Michael returned. He ducked into the room, his arms full of his bounty. He juggled two plates piled with eggs, toast and scones. In one hand, he clutched two coffee cups. Dark liquid sloshed as he pushed into the room.

Damien hurried to relieve him of some items. "Feels like you've been gone forever. I thought something happened to you."

"Nope," Michael admitted. "Clear path to and from. Didn't see a soul."

"Or a soul eater," Damien said with a chuckle as he piled eggs onto his fork.

"Mmm-hmm," Michael agreed as he sipped his coffee.

They ate in silence for a few minutes before they discussed their situation. They came to no new conclusions over their meal.

As they finished the food, piling their plates on a dresser, Damien paced the floor.

"Wonder how long the Duke will be with his plan," he questioned.

"No idea. If that's what he's doing," Michael said.

"You think he's double-crossing us?"

"I really hope not. Because we don't stand a chance if he switches sides."

"Tell me about it. I'm worried about pulling this off WITH his help."

The sound of a door closing reached their ears. "Wonder if that's Celine?" Damien questioned. He hurried across the room and eased the door open.

"Is it?" Michael asked as he joined Damien at the door. They peered through the crack. Celine wandered down the hall. Her eyes stared ahead, fixed and unmoving.

"Yeah," Damien whispered. "And she's in another trance."

"It's getting worse."

"We should try talking to her," Damien said. He pulled the door open wider.

"No," Michael said, barring the door from opening any further. "We can't risk it. We can't run into Tobias."

"He's not around," Damien argued. "We have to try!"

Michael pursed his lips before he released the door. "Okay, let's do it."

Damien swung the door open and raced into the hall. He scurried around Celine and held out his hands to stop her forward progress. She halted, standing stick straight and staring blankly ahead of her.

"Celine!" Damien said. He grasped her arms and shook her. "Celine, are you there?"

She did not respond.

"Try again," Michael said.

Damien nodded. He gave Celine another slight shake. "Celine, can you hear me?"

"Yes," she murmured.

Damien breathed a sigh of relief. "Celine, you've got to fight him. You've got to snap out of this."

Celine's brow furrowed though she made no eye contact with either man.

"Fight, Celine. You don't want to do this."

"I want to be happy," she said.

"Then you have to snap out of this."

"He can make me happy," she responded. She tried to push past them. Damien stopped her again.

"No, Celine. No, he can't. Come on, Celine, snap out of it. Fight!"

"Celine? Where are you?" Tobias called from around the corner.

Michael's eyes went wide. "We gotta go!"

"No, wait!" Damien said.

Michael grasped Damien's arm and tugged him toward his bedroom. "Come on! We can't get caught."

"Ugh," Damien groaned as he let go of Celine. She wandered around the corner.

"There you are," they heard Tobias call.

They hastened to the ajar bedroom door and raced inside, slamming the door behind them.

"Damn it!" Damien exclaimed.

Michael rubbed the back of his neck. "That didn't go over well," he agreed.

"Well? It didn't go over at all! Not even a glimmer of recognition in her eyes."

"We didn't have very much time with her. Maybe if we had longer with her… " Michael began.

Damien shook his head. "How are we going to pull that off? Tobias is lurking around every corner, especially when she's in that state."

Michael parsed through the information. "Maybe the Duke can help."

"It's scary that he's our best hope."

Michael snorted a laugh. "Yeah."

"But you're right. He's our best hope. Perhaps he can give us more time with Celine."

"So, we've got to sit here and wait for him to come back. And hope she's still in the goofy state."

Damien shook his head in disagreement. "No, we can't wait. We need to go find him."

"He told us not to leave," Michael argued.

"We know where Tobias is! We can get out safely."

Michael scrunched his eyebrows. "Okay, good point. Let's go for it."

They hurried from their room, creeping through the halls and slipping out the front door. They darted away from the house, heading for the cover of the wooded path. Once the trees enveloped them, they slowed their pace.

"Whew," Damien said as he glanced back toward the house. "You know, I feel better just being out of that house."

"Was Tobias getting to you again?" Michael questioned.

"No. At least, not that I can recall. But I felt trapped in there."

"I know what you mean," Michael replied. "Enjoy the fresh air."

"I'm trying to, though my mind is wandering to where the Duke might be."

"Seaside house?"

"That's a good place to start," Damien agreed.

They navigated the paths to the house by the sea, stopping just inside the safety of the woods. They stared at the outline of the house hugging the shoreline.

No movement betrayed anyone on the premises. "Looks like no one's home," Michael said after a few minutes.

Damien frowned. "Yep."

"Wait!" Michael exclaimed. "There!" He pointed toward the front door.

It swung open and a figure stepped onto the porch.

"I can't believe I'm hoping to see the Duke," Damien said.

Both men groaned after the figure stepped forward on

the porch. Stefano ambled down the porch's length before sinking into a rocker. He puffed on a cigar as he stretched his legs, perching his feet on the railing.

"He's not there," Michael said.

"Nope. Stefano would never put his feet on the railing if the Duke was there."

They stood from their refuge behind a large bush. "Now where?" Damien questioned.

"Town?" Michael said with a shrug.

"I guess that's as good a place to try as any."

They ambled through the woods and to the edge of the Buckley property. They strolled down the road into the small town. They began their search at the local pub but found it almost empty at this hour. They tried the town's hotel and cafe. No traces of the Duke existed in either location. They searched a few additional locations, also finding nothing. They even tried the house they had followed Tobias to but found it abandoned.

Michael flung his hands in the air. "Now what?" he questioned.

Damien sighed. He shrugged with his hands on his hips. "I don't know. Where could he be?"

"Maybe he went back to the house," Michael suggested.

"Maybe. I guess we can head back there. I can't think of any other places to check. And by this point, he may be finished with whatever he's doing."

"I really wish we knew what that was."

"Me too. I hate working with him period. Especially since he's so secretive."

"We don't have much choice," Michael replied.

"Nope," Damien agreed. "Well, shall we?"

Michael motioned for Damien to proceed before him. They traversed down the dirt alley toward town before turning toward the Buckley estate. The men veered off on a path leading to the house via the beach. They spent a few minutes brooding as they watched the rolling ocean.

"I guess we should get back," Michael said.

"Yeah," Damien agreed. "Felt good not to be near all the drama for a minute, but we should get back."

They climbed to the cliffs above on a rocky path. As they entered the shade provided by the trees, they spotted a man approaching them. Even at a distance, they recognized the form of Marcus Northcott.

Damien breathed a sigh of relief and both men quickened their pace toward him.

"Boy, are we glad to see you," Damien said.

"Yeah," Michael agreed, "as strange as it is to say that, there it is. We've been searching and searching for you."

Marcus's eyes flitted between the two of them. His brow furrowed and the corners of his mouth turned downward. He did not appear pleased. Likely angry because they left the room after he instructed them not to, Damien surmised.

"Something happened with Celine," Damien began in an attempt to explain.

"Michael and Damien Carlyle?" Marcus questioned. "What an interesting surprise."

"Surprise?" Michael questioned, his gaze falling to the ground as he processed the statement.

"You don't happen to have my book, do you? Or perhaps Celine's portrait?"

Damien's eyes went wide. "Uhhhh," he murmured. He shook his head as he blindly reached out to grasp Michael's arm. "Wrong one, wrong one." He began to inch backward, pulling Michael with him.

"Leaving? So soon? I think not!" He cupped a fireball in his hand as he lifted an eyebrow at them.

He flung the fireball in their direction. Michael recoiled.

Damien squeezed his eyes shut as he prepared for the painful and paralyzing effects.

A fiery explosion erupted inches from their face as another fireball slammed into Marcus's. Michael winced as tiny sparks crackled and charred the ground. Damien opened one eye then the other. He glanced behind them, expecting to find Celine storming toward them.

Instead, his eyes grew wide again as he witnessed an unexpected figure stalking in their direction.

"Now, now, let's not be hasty," Marcus said as he approached his 1842 counterpart.

"This is weird," Damien whispered.

"Uh-huh," Michael murmured as they eyed the odd exchange.

The other Marcus raised his eyebrows high as he stared at his future self. "These two men stole *The Book of the Dead* and disappeared with it. They then assisted Celine in stealing her portrait back! They have much to answer for."

"Perhaps, though, now is not the time."

"I find no better time than the present." Marcus readied to launch another fireball.

His future form dispatched another fireball, knocking the fiery weapon from his past self's hand.

The two versions of Marcus stared at each other, both of them offering the other an unimpressed stare.

"I said no," Marcus retorted to his former self.

The 1842-era Marcus opened his mouth to protest but Marcus cut him off. "They are vital to my plan."

"Perhaps you should explain."

Fire burned from future Marcus's eyes and he tensed his jaw. "I haven't the time nor the inclination. Stop this nonsense and get to work on the task you have been given."

The exasperated former Duke matched the tensed jaw gesture but relented. "Fine."

"Wow," Damien whispered. "He's even mean to himself."

Michael agreed with a silent nod.

Marcus circa 1842 pushed between Michael and Damien, knocking them both aside as he passed. He stormed down the path, disappearing into the sunshine beyond the tree cover.

"Well, that was creepy," Michael said as the situation defused.

"Yeah," Damien agreed. "Thanks for the save. We thought he was you." He nodded to Marcus.

"What are you two imbeciles doing roaming the property?" Marcus retorted.

Michael shook his head at the statement as Damien responded. "Celine had another one of those episodes. We tried to talk to her, but it was useless."

"I am not surprised. Tobias's pull on her is strong."

"We were interrupted by him," Damien said. "So, we didn't have much time to try."

Marcus closed his eyes for a moment and sighed. "Fools."

"He didn't see us!" Damien protested. "But anyway, we wanted to find you and let you know."

"And ask if you could come back and keep Tobias occupied while we try again," Michael added.

"Right," Damien agreed with a nod.

"I may have been better to have brought the Buckleys," Marcus lamented with a sigh. "Come along, we shall return to the house."

They trudged back to the Buckley house, hiding in the woods outside until they could safely enter and sneak to Damien's room.

"All right," Damien said once inside. "How do we do this?"

"We do not," Marcus retorted.

"What?" Michael questioned. "I thought that's why you said to come back?"

"No," Marcus corrected. "It is not."

"But we need to help Celine! We need to try to get through to her before things get worse."

"I do not disagree, though it will be easier once Tobias has been removed from the equation."

Michael's eyebrows shot up. "When will that be?"

"Tomorrow night," Marcus answered, "if things go to plan. And if you two can manage to contain yourselves and remain out of sight."

"We already explained that," Michael retorted.

Marcus strode to the door. "I am going out to finish the details for tomorrow. Remain here in this room. Do not gallivant around. Stay away from Tobias. Await my return."

Michael rolled his eyes as Marcus disappeared into the hallway. "Have I mentioned how much I hate that guy?"

Damien leapt to his feet and paced the floor. After an hour he sank into the armchair next to Michael.

"You okay?" Michael questioned.

"Yeah," Damien said. "Just a headache."

"Headache? Anything else? Any weird thoughts or other symptoms similar to what happened yesterday before you… you know?" Michael motioned to his wrist.

"No," Damien confirmed. "I'm just starving."

"Me, too," Michael admitted.

"Run down for some food?"

"I'll run down," Michael offered.

"I'll go, too. We shouldn't split up."

"If we run into someone, you can't chance another dinner with Tobias. Stay out of sight and wait for me here."

"Fine, fine. I'll hide here while you get us dinner."

"You're not hiding, you're just being smart." Michael nodded to him and let himself out the door. He returned twenty minutes later with food in hand.

"Any trouble?" Damien inquired as he perused the selection.

Michael rolled his eyes. "Ran into Tobias."

"Are you serious?" Damien questioned as he dropped his spoon into his soup bowl.

Michael nodded sheepishly. "Yes," he admitted.

"What happened? Are you okay?"

"Yeah, I'm fine. He doesn't get to me like he does with you," Michael said with a shrug.

"What did he say?"

"He asked if we were going to dinner. I said no, we had a mountain of work to discuss. He pretended to be upset. Then he gave me this." Michael pulled a small bronze figure of a train from his pocket. He shrugged and set it on the nearby table before he grabbed a warm roll and bit into it.

"A bronze train?" Damien inquired as he grabbed a scone from the tray.

"Because we're train builders or whatever they're called."

"Oh, right," Damien said with a nod. "Usually we're ship builders."

"Yeah, I figured, new century, new business," Michael said with a laugh.

The two finished their dinner, devouring everything on the tray including the leftover scones Michael had swiped from the kitchen.

Both full, they relaxed back into their armchairs. "Wonder how Celine's doing?" Damien asked.

Michael shook his head. "I don't know. I wish we could find out."

"Me too. Maybe we should..." Damien began when the door popped open.

Marcus Northcott strode into the room.

"Oh!" he exclaimed. "You've managed to stay put! I am impressed."

Michael tensed his jaw. He made no mention of the quick trip to retrieve dinner.

They settled into a tense silence as the night wore on. Michael fidgeted in his chair after a time.

"Stiff?" Damien inquired.

"Eh," Michael answered. "I guess." He raised and lowered his right shoulder. "My shoulder is killing me."

Damien narrowed his eyes. Michael fidgeted again, raising his hand and wiggling his fingers. "Hand's numb," he said as he noticed Damien's gaze. "And is it cold in here?"

"Cold? No," Damien answered. "Your hand is numb?

"Yeah," Michael confirmed as he grimaced.

Damien swallowed hard as he climbed from his seat. He approached Michael and grabbed his hand. He pulled it toward him and twisted his palm upright. Damien shoved Michael's sleeve up. He gasped at what he saw.

Michael's eyes went wide. "Oh, no," he lamented. His eyes raised to Damien's. Raw fear shone in them.

Damien gulped as his shoulders sagged. He stared at the blackened web of veins crawling up Michael's forearm.

"What are you two buffoons carrying on about?" Marcus asked as he stalked away from his post at the window.

"He's been poisoned," Damien said.

CHAPTER 28

Marcus glanced at Michael's blackened arm. "How did this happen?"

Michael swallowed hard. "Earlier tonight, I went out to grab us some dinner," Michael began.

Marcus sighed and shook his head at the admission.

"I-I ran into Tobias. It must have happened then."

Damien glanced at the small train figurine on the table. He pointed to it, remaining silent.

"You fools," Marcus chided. He turned to Damien. "Do you still have the antidote from the doctor?"

Damien reached into his pocket and pulled out the syringe. "Yeah," he said.

"Good. It may save him."

"May?" Damien questioned.

"Yes, may. If we caught it in time. Quickly, administer it."

"Like inject it into his vein?" Damien cried, blanching at the idea.

Marcus tensed his jaw and closed his eyes. "Yes, into his vein. Where else?"

Damien opened his mouth to answer. Marcus cut him off. "Don't answer, just inject it."

Michael rolled up his sleeve. He winced as Damien shoved the needle into a black squiggle on his arm. "Sorry," Damien lamented. He shoved the plunger down. The volatile serum entered Michael's bloodstream.

Within seconds, Michael gasped. He clutched his right arm and yelped in pain. Damien's eyes widened and he backed up a step. His mouth formed a grimace and he glanced to Marcus for help.

"Should this be happening?" he inquired, fear lacing his voice.

"An expected reaction," Marcus said.

Michael groaned in pain, gritting his teeth. Damien put his hand on Michael's back. Worry creased Damien's face. Michael's face reddened and his body trembled. His eyes rolled back in his head, and he pitched forward, sprawling on the floor.

"Michael!" Damien yelled. He fell to his knees next to him on the floor.

"Let's get him into bed," Marcus said.

Damien nodded, his hands shaking as he helped Marcus lift Michael and settle him in his bed.

Michael's head beaded with sweat. He groaned as they eased him onto the bed. Damien covered him with the blanket. Michael thrashed his head back and forth before his eyes flitted open.

"Michael?" Damien asked. "Hey, buddy, you okay?"

Michael trembled under the blanket. "C-c-cold," he stuttered.

Damien tore off his suit jacket and covered Michael.

Michael forced a crooked smile on his face. "Th-Th-Thanks." His lips quivered. He fought to stay conscious. Pain wracked through his body. It felt like every fiber of him ached. He shivered from fever and his stomach turned over. His eyelids felt heavy. He struggled to keep them open, afraid if he closed them, it would be for the last time.

Damien monitored Michael for three hours. His skin turned ashy. His fever continued to rise. Damien could feel the heat from Michael's skin even at a distance. He lamented not being able to gather a basin of cool water and rag to help temper the fever.

"It would do no good," Marcus assured him. "And we cannot chance you running into anyone."

"But… "

"But nothing. You will do as I say."

Damien's shoulders slumped as he returned his eyes to Michael. "Take solace, Damien. It has been hours and he is alive. The poison should have killed him by now."

Damien nodded, clinging to that small shred of hope.

Another hour passed. "Shouldn't he have spit out all that black stuff already?" Damien inquired. "Celine was much faster than this."

"Celine is an extraordinary woman. Her body needed a tiny push, his needs a colossal push."

Damien licked his lips as he returned his gaze to Michael. Was the antidote enough of a push?

"What if the serum isn't strong enough for him as a human?" he voiced.

"Then he will die."

Damien leapt from the bed and paced the floor.

"Again, Damien, he has survived this long. It's likely he will live."

Damien sank onto the bed and stared at Michael. After thirty more minutes, Michael squirmed in the bed. He thrashed and groaned. His moaning turned to cries of pain.

"Come on, buddy," Damien said. "Fight."

Michael's grunting died down as his breathing became

labored. He panted and gasped for breath. His breathing turned from rhythmic to intermittent. He drew in shaky, raspy breaths at random moments.

Damien clutched his hand. "Fight, Michael."

After twenty minutes of sporadic breaths, Michael sucked in a long breath. He held it a moment. Damien hoped he was turning the corner. Michael blew out the breath.

Damien waited for him to take another. "Michael?" Damien jiggled his body. "Michael?!" Damien groaned and glanced wide-eyed at Marcus. "He stopped breathing!"

Marcus narrowed his eyes at Michael. He touched his skin and checked his eyes.

"No, Michael, come on, buddy. You can't die." Damien grasped hold of his friend. He shook his body. "Come on, Michael!"

Marcus grasped Damien by the collar and dragged him back a few steps.

"No," Damien cried. "No! We have to do something! We can't let him die! We can't…"

Damien stopped dead as Michael's body twitched. It jerked a second time before his chest rose. His back arched like Celine's before he collapsed back to the bed. His eyes flew open, and his mouth gaped. Black detritus spewed from his mouth. It billowed toward the ceiling before dissipating.

Michael collapsed back to the bed. His breathing returned to normal. Marcus released his grasp on Damien, who rushed back to Michael's side. He checked his arm, finding the black veins gone.

He watched his breathing, now rhythmic and easy. After an hour, Michael's fever reduced. As the sun crested the horizon, Michael's eyes opened. With a sigh, he glanced around.

"What happened?" he asked, his voice raspy and weak.

"You're okay, buddy," Damien answered. "The poison's gone."

Michael offered a weak smile.

"How do you feel?"

"Tired," he answered.

"You should both rest," Marcus suggested.

"I should get him some food," Damien said. "He needs his strength."

Marcus grumbled. "You should not be roaming about the house."

"He needs sustenance!" Damien argued.

Marcus shook his head and rose from his armchair. "Wait here."

He disappeared through the door, returning minutes later. He unraveled a towel revealing several scones and two hard-boiled eggs. "Now stop whining."

"Thanks," Damien said as he peeled the egg and passed it to Michael.

Michael sat up with Damien's help and took a few bites of the egg before grabbing a scone.

Damien munched on a scone while he peeled his egg.

"Mmm, this is good," Michael said.

"Yeah," Damien mumbled with a mouthful of scone.

"I can't believe how much better I feel," Michael said as he finished the egg. He shoved back the covers.

"Whoa, wait a minute," Damien said.

"I feel better," Michael insisted. "Like I wasn't even sick." He swung his legs over the side of the bed.

"I wouldn't if I were you," Marcus said.

Michael stood and collapsed back onto the bed.

"Okay, maybe I should rest a bit more."

"You both should. Tonight is far too important to risk ruining," Marcus answered.

"You take the bed, buddy. I'll hang out in the armchair."

"I slept all night, we can switch," Michael suggested.

"Nope," Damien said as he rose and sauntered to the armchair. "I'm good. You rest."

"Thanks, buddy," Michael answered. He climbed under the covers and laid back.

Both men fell asleep within minutes, spending most of the day resting. They awoke as the sun descended in the sky and evening approached.

Damien stretched and glanced to Michael who also stirred.

"Oh, good, you're awake," Marcus said.

"Did you sleep?" Damien asked.

"Yes, like the dead. Oh, bad wording," Michael said with a wince. "You?"

"I did. How do you feel?"

"Like nothing happened to me," Michael admitted. He rose from the bed and stretched.

"If you are finished discussing your wellbeing, I must be going. Are you able to stay awake?"

"Yes," Damien said. Marcus glanced to Michael. He nodded and offered an affirmative response.

"Good. Now, if all goes to plan, and I'd be shocked if it didn't, Tobias Greene will be removed from this earth tonight. Stay here. Stay out of sight. I shall return by midnight."

"What if you don't return?" Damien inquired.

"Run." With that, Marcus pulled the door open and disappeared into the hallway beyond.

"Well, that was dramatic," Michael said after Marcus departed.

"Yeah," Damien answered. "And now we're stuck here, waiting again. I feel like a kid whose been grounded."

Michael sank into the armchair near the window with a sigh. Silence passed between them for a few moments before

Damien spoke.

"What if he doesn't succeed?"

"Run," Michael said in his best Duke imitation.

Damien rolled his eyes. "Yes, perfect answer. We'll run away in a time we're not from with no money and no idea how to make a living. That makes perfect sense!" Damien threw his arms into the air as he slumped into the armchair across from Michael.

Michael shrugged. "Let's hope he succeeds."

"But what if he doesn't? What if it's too late for Celine? What if Tobias wins? What if we're stuck here? What if…"

"You really need to cool it with the 'what ifs,' man," Michael said.

"I can't help it!" Damien exclaimed. He leapt from his chair and paced the floor. "We're stuck here in the worst situation of our lives, if things go wrong, it could cost us our lives and will definitely cost Celine hers, and we're at the mercy of the Duke of all people."

"No one is more uncomfortable with this than me. But we don't have many other choices. If he doesn't succeed tonight, we need to rethink our plan. But for now, let's give him a few hours to see what he comes up with."

"Maybe we should spend this time going over another plan so we're ready to roll if we need to go to plan B."

"Okay, good idea."

Damien nodded and sank into his chair. They spent the next several hours trading ideas, vetting options, and making suggestions. In the end, they agreed the best plan on the table still relied on the Duke's success.

Damien slouched in his chair as they admitted none of their plans topped Marcus's. "Well, that helped us with nothing."

"It passed a few hours at least." He glanced out the

window and noted the fiery ball as it sank in the sky. "Almost dusk."

"How much longer?" Damien whined.

Michael stood and stretched before he paced the length of the room. Damien let his head fall back onto the chair behind him.

"You feeling okay?" Michael asked.

"Yeah," Damien responded. "I just have a killer headache."

Michael rushed toward him. "Is your mind clouding up or anything? Do you feel sick?"

"No," Damien said with a shake of his head. "No, nothing like that. I think I'm just hungry."

"Missing lunch and dinner didn't help," Michael admitted.

Michael resumed his pacing. He stopped moments later. "I'm starved, too."

"We can't go to dinner."

"No, but maybe I can sneak down for some food from the kitchen. Everyone should be in the dining room right now."

"You're right," Damien said with a nod. "You shouldn't run into anyone. You can snatch some food and run right back up without any trouble!"

Michael snapped his fingers and pointed to Damien. "I'll be right back. Wait, you're sure you feel okay?"

"Yes. I feel nothing like I did last night at dinner."

"Okay," Michael said with a nod. "I'll hurry."

"See if there are any more scones!" Damien called as Michael disappeared through the door.

Damien gazed at the closed door for a moment before he leapt from his chair. He paced the room before settling in front of the window. He stared at the trees, basked in the red glow of the setting sun.

How was Celine, he wondered? How was she handling dinner? Did Tobias attend? Was he pleased Michael and Damien did not? Did he assume he'd won? What was the

Duke's plan? How much longer would it take? Right now, Tobias was likely rubbing elbows with the Buckleys and assuming Celine was his. How would Marcus handle this?

His mind spun through questions but found no answers. Instead, his headache worsened. He wondered where Michael was with the food. He hoped nourishment eased the tension building at his temples.

He turned to face the room's interior. An ache built between his shoulders. His skin began to crawl. He fidgeted in his jacket as he massaged his neck. His saliva turned thick and salty. His eyes glazed over. His mind numbed. The questions disappeared. He found he could only focus on one thing.

That one thought pervaded his brain. His brow wrinkled as he focused on it. He dropped his arms to his sides and crossed the room.

* * *

Michael sneaked down a back stairway to the main floor. He darted toward the kitchen. As he passed the hallway containing the dining room he peered at the open doors. The sound of conversation floated down the hall. He heard Tobias's laugh.

Michael nodded to himself, and his lips formed a half-smile. Tobias was accounted for. He should be able to make it to the kitchen unscathed. He continued down the hall and entered through a back door.

The kitchen staff bustled around the room.

"Hello," Michael said to a woman wearing an apron. "We aren't able to dine with the family tonight and I hoped to request a sandwich for me and my brother."

"Of course, sir," the cook said. "Anna, prepare a plate of sandwiches from the roast beef."

"And if it's not too much, do you happen to have any breakfast scones left over?"

The cook offered him a smile. "I've got something even better for you," she promised before she bustled away.

After a few moments, she whipped together a large tray containing sandwiches, two bowls of beef broth and two slices of blueberry pie.

"This looks perfect, thank you!" Michael said to her as he lifted the large wooden tray and spun to leave the room.

"Enjoy, sir," the cook called after him.

He darted from the warm kitchen and into the hall, eyeing his bounty. No scones, but the blueberry pie should make up for that, he surmised.

Michael hurried through the halls and up the stairs to the second floor. He threaded through two hallways before he approached the one containing their bedrooms. He balanced the tray on one forearm as he approached Damien's door.

"No scones, but I think you'll be pleased," he announced as he entered the room. He stopped two steps into the room.

His eyes searched the empty space.

"Damien?" he questioned. His heart sped up, pounding against his ribs. His mouth went dry, and his knees wobbled. "Oh, no," he groaned breathlessly.

He spun to leave the room as the tray fell from his arm. The sound of the dishes clattering to the floor echoed in the hall as he sprinted down it.

* * *

Damien stalked into the brisk evening air. The cloudless, dusky sky rose overhead. A gentle night breeze rustled the tree leaves.

Damien felt none of it. His body numbed to his

surroundings. His mind focused on one goal. With unblinking eyes, he stumbled down the drive.

Each step brought him closer to his goal. He focused on moving his feet. One in front of the other. Closer. Closer. Closer. Each brought him closer to his goal.

He had to make it. His mind pushed him forward. One thought echoed in it.

He must succeed. He must not fail.

CHAPTER 29

Michael sprinted through the halls. He searched for any signs of Damien but found none.

"Where are you, Damien?" he murmured as he reached the landing overlooking the foyer.

He spun in a circle as he raked his fingers through his hair. He moaned as he grasped hold of the railing and squeezed it in frustration. "Come on, think, Michael, think," he urged to himself.

He hurried down the stairs and across the massive foyer. Michael swung the doors open to the sitting room. He searched the space for Damien. His eyes fell upon the vase Damien had broken yesterday. It remained intact.

He pulled the doors shut. A cool breeze brushed across his cheek. As he leaned against the wooden panels, his gaze landed on the front door. It stood open. His jaw slackened and he raced toward it.

"Damien!" he shouted as he careened through the door. He skittered to a stop on the driveway and searched in every direction.

"Which way?" he questioned himself.

He spent thirty seconds with his head on a swivel, gulping in air as his distraught mind decided on a course of action.

He darted toward the sound of the waves crashing in the distance. As he entered the cover of the trees, a figure approached. Michael ran toward him.

"Have you seen Damien?" he shouted as he met Marcus Northcott on the path.

"Damien? No? Why are you wandering about?"

"He's gone. Damien's gone. I went to get us dinner and…"

Marcus's eyes went wide, and he inquired, "You left him?"

"For a few minutes, yes. We figured it was safe with Tobias accounted for and we were hungry. Look, there's no time to explain. He's gone. I can't find him. We have to find him before…" Michael's voice trailed off. "Never mind. We have to find him."

"Why would you expect I would know where he is?"

"I don't know," Michael answered, his voice harried. "Can't you… I don't know, ask a bird or something?"

Marcus rolled his eyes and sighed. "Find him," he implored.

Michael nodded. "I'll go this way and you can…"

Marcus shook his head. "No, I am late. If things do not go to plan, all will be lost."

Michael swallowed hard and groaned. He grimaced and chewed his lower lip. Marcus grabbed hold of him by the shoulders. "Find him. If you do not find him, we cannot save Celine. Now get hold of yourself and think. You know him. You know where he may go."

Michael nodded. "If I find him…"

"WHEN you find him, take him back to his room and wait for me there. Do not leave for any reason. We cannot afford any additional foul-ups."

"When, right," Michael said. "Okay. I'll find him."

Marcus nodded to him before striding away.

Michael glanced around the wooded area. The clearing in the trees Damien and Celine loved was just ahead. He'd try there on the way to the cliffs overlooking the ocean. He didn't know where he'd search after that. He hoped he didn't need to find out.

"Come on, Damien, be there," Michael said as he jogged toward the clearing. He arrived moments later and found the spot empty.

A sinking feeling grew in the pit of his stomach and a lump formed in his throat. His legs turned to jelly as he continued onward. If Damien wasn't at the cliff's edge, he had no idea where to check next. He could be anywhere, especially if Tobias had a hold of his mind. And if he didn't find Damien soon… No, he refused to consider the thought. He had to find him.

"Damien, come on, man, be okay," he murmured as he hastened down the path.

* * *

Damien stood on the cliffs overlooking the raging ocean. The waves pounded against the rocks. His eyes lowered to the craggy beach below. Sharp edges jutted at every angle.

A piece of driftwood floated on the water's top as the ocean swelled again. The water pushed the weathered wood toward the shore. It smashed against the rocks, splintering into pieces before the waves dragged it back to sea.

That's what would happen to him if he stepped from the cliff's edge. His body would plummet to the rocks below. It would smash against them, breaking bones and damaging organs. Then the ocean would drag him to a watery grave.

Yes, his mind reflected, if he just stepped forward, that would be his fate. One more step to his death.

"Step forward, Damien," Tobias's voice rang in his head.

Damien lifted his foot and pushed it out. It hung in the air over the rocks. He shifted his weight until he felt himself falling forward.

* * *

Michael cleared the trees and eyed the cliffs ahead. In the dim light, he spotted a figure on the edge.

"Damien!" he called.

Damien's body swayed as he peered to the rocks below.

Michael quickened his pace. "Damien!" he shouted again.

Damien ignored him as though he was unable to hear his calls. He raised his leg and stuck his foot over the void. After a moment, Damien pitched his weight forward and began to fall.

Michael stretched his hand in front of him as he ran headlong toward Damien. "DAMIEN, NO!" he screamed.

Michael leapt into the air and dove toward Damien's falling form. He grasped hold of Damien's arm as his body shifted into the fall. The force of Damien's fall hurtled him toward the edge. He slid forward on his belly as he dug his legs and feet in to stop his forward motion.

He ground to a halt as his arm dangled over the side. Damien hung below him. Michael puffed with exertion as he glanced over the edge at Damien.

Damien swung from his arm. He cried out, as he flailed his legs. He glanced up to Michael. His mouth formed a terrified grimace.

"Help," Damien whimpered.

"I'm not going to let you go, Damien," Michael grunted. "Give me your other hand."

Damien nodded and tried to reach up toward Michael. As he did, Michael's grip on his sleeve slipped. Damien dropped a few inches before Michael tightened his grip around Damien's wrist.

"Whoa!" Damien exclaimed, his voice filled with fear.

Michael struggled to hang on to his dangling form. Sweat beaded on his forehead as he groaned with effort.

Damien's bottom lip quivered as he glanced up to Michael. "Don't let me die," he pleaded.

"Not going to happen," Michael promised him. "Now reach!"

Michael steadied himself and swung his other hand out as Damien reached up. He grasped his hand and squeezed tight.

"I'm going to try to pull you up," Michael said. He flexed his muscles as he labored to pull Damien up. As he tightened his biceps, his weight shifted forward. He slid closer to the cliff's edge. Damien dropped further. Michael froze and his slide ceased. Damien jarred to a stop.

"Ahhhhhh," he exclaimed as he glanced up toward Michael.

"I can't pull you up," Michael said. "I'm slipping. You're going to have to climb. See if you can steady your feet against the cliff."

"Okay," Damien said, his voice quaking. He swung his legs toward the rock. His feet slipped as he tried to brace against the slippery stone. He swung away from the cliff as Michael struggled and stretched to hold him.

Michael grumbled with effort. Damien kicked again but his shoes slid down the rock's face.

"We're going to have to try something else," Michael groaned.

"Give me one more try," Damien said. "I think I found a foothold."

"Okay, go for it," Michael strained.

Damien nodded and raised his foot toward the stone. He stuck his foot sideways on a small outcropping. He shimmied it toward the cliff and wedged it. "Got it!" he called.

"Okay, good," Michael answered.

"I'm looking for another one."

Michael continued to hold him steady while Damien scanned the rock for a second foothold. "Found one!"

Damien raised his leg and stepped onto the rock. It crumbled away under his weight. He slipped and struggled to steady himself as Michael clung to him.

He swallowed hard. "I'm going to try again," he said in a shaky voice.

"Okay," Michael grunted.

Damien lifted his foot and searched for a foothold. He found another and tested it. It held when he applied pressure. He allowed his weight to shift to it.

"You steady?" Michael asked.

"Yeah, I've got my feet braced. If you pull, I can try to scramble up."

Michael nodded. "Here goes."

Michael curled his arms upward as he tried to inch back. With some of Damien's weight braced, he was able to make progress. He pulled Damien to the cliff's edge. As Damien rose, he grasped the cliff's edge with one hand while keeping his other firmly clutched around Michael's. He inched his feet upward, blindly searching for another groove in the rock. He found one and pushed against it. He rose higher and Michael shifted the grip on his free arm to Damien's shoulder. He pulled Damien further up.

As Damien's chest flattened against the stone, Michael grasped him around the waist and tugged. Damien crawled onto the clifftop next to Michael. He collapsed in a heap, his breathing heavy. Michael rolled onto his back. His chest heaved as he gulped in air.

They laid in silence for a moment as they both recovered from the experience.

After a few moments, Damien rolled onto his back and breathed a sigh of relief. "Ahhh," he murmured. "That was…"

"Don't say it," Michael answered as he pushed himself up to sitting. He hung his head as he wiped his brow.

Damien pulled himself up. He clapped Michael on the shoulder. "Thanks, man. If you wouldn't have found me…" His voice faded. "Thanks."

"No problem," Michael said as he wrapped his arm around Damien's shoulders. "I wasn't letting you go."

"Because you need me to save Celine?" Damien questioned.

"No, I'm not a heartless bastard like the Duke," Michael answered.

They listened to the ocean's surf pound against the rocks below. "All I heard was Tobias's voice telling me to jump," Damien said.

"I hope the Duke's plan works and this guy is toast soon."

Damien nodded.

"Anyway," Michael groaned as he climbed to his feet, "we should get you back to the house. I ran into the Duke while I searched for you and he said to go straight back there once I found you. And this time I'm not leaving you alone."

Michael held his hand out to pull Damien to standing. Damien accepted it and rose to his feet. They trudged to the path leading toward the house.

"Sorry I messed up our dinner."

"Yeah, about that," Michael said, "I panicked when I found your room empty. So, we've got some cleaning up to do when we get back."

Damien raised his eyebrows.

"I dumped it," Michael added. "Like all over the floor."

"Maybe we can save the scones. Did you get the scones?"

Michael shook his head. "No. But I got blueberry pie. Which is probably smeared across the hardwood now."

Damien frowned. "Maybe we can salvage some," he said with hope in his voice.

A figure approached as they continued up the path.

"Oh, great," Michael complained. "This night keeps getting better and better."

"Which one is it?" Damien inquired as he squinted into the waning light.

"Gentlemen," Marcus Northcott greeted them, "we meet again."

"The worse one," Michael answered.

Marcus shook his head at them. "Aren't you two supposed to be cowering under your beds?"

Michael tensed his jaw as he bit his tongue.

Marcus continued, "I would recommend after this situation is resolved, you do just that."

"Oh?" Michael inquired.

"Yes. Because I will be searching for you. And I will not be as generous as I was in our last encounter. Now run along, children. The adults are at work." He shooed them away with his hand as he continued down the path.

"I really hate that guy," Damien confessed as they followed his receding form.

"In all his forms," Michael added. "Hey, maybe we should get off the path. I'm not so sure we want to run into anyone else."

"Good idea," Damien agreed.

They stepped off the path and returned to their journey. The moon rose overhead, providing dim light as they threaded through the woods. As they closed the distance to the house, a rustling sounded on the nearby path.

"Now what?" Michael groaned.

They ceased their walking and hid themselves behind a large tree.

A figure stalked down the path toward their hidden location.

CHAPTER 30

The moonlight shining through the trees reflected off Celine's blonde curls.

"It's Celine!" Damien whispered.

Celine wandered mere feet from them. Her eyes stared blankly ahead. Her arms hung limply at her sides. She shuffled in a slow, plodding fashion. Damien noted the ruby necklace hanging around her neck.

"She's in another trance," Michael breathed.

"Yeah," Damien answered. "We need to try to reach her."

"No," Michael countered. "No way!"

"We may not have another chance! We have to try!"

"You almost threw yourself off a cliff ten minutes ago! We need to get back to the house and lay low!"

"I'm not going to hide under my bed like the Duke said!"

"He might have a point this time," Michael argued.

Damien shook his head as Celine passed them. "It's too important."

Damien darted onto the path. Michael lunged to stop him but missed his arm. With a groan, he followed his friend.

Damien rushed toward Celine, scooting around her and spinning to face her.

"Celine!" he entreated. "Celine, stop!"

Celine continued her journey forward, ignoring Damien.

"Celine! Where are you going? You've got to stop. He can't help you. Tobias can't help you."

Celine stalked ahead, still in her non-responsive state.

"She's not responding," Damien groaned.

"No, it's like she can't even hear you," Michael said.

Damien held his hands in front of him in an attempt to stop Celine's movement. "Celine, stop," he begged.

She continued forward.

"What should I do?" he inquired. "Should I slap her?"

"Really?" Michael questioned.

Damien shrugged as he continued to walk backward to stay in front of Celine. "It works in the movies!"

Michael considered it. "Okay, if you want, go ahead and try it."

Damien nodded. He raised his hand and firmed his jaw. After a moment, he let his hand fall. "I can't," he admitted. Instead, he patted her cheeks in an attempt to snap her out of the trance. "Come on, Celine."

She paid no attention to his attempts to reach her. Celine stalked forward, driving Damien and Michael further back.

"Celine, stop," Damien said. He pushed back against her. She stopped, bouncing off his hands. It ceased her forward motion and she stumbled back a step. She stood motionless for a moment before she began walking forward again. She brushed past Damien as she continued down the path.

"All right, that's it," Damien said. "Grab her."

"Grab her?" Michael questioned.

Damien nodded. "Yeah. We'll just grab her and take her back to the house."

"Grab her. Right," Michael said with a nod. "On three."

Michael began the count. "One."

Michael continued, "Two."

Damien prepared to grasp her arm as he opened his mouth to give the final number in the count.

"Shoot!" Michael hissed. Damien's brow furrowed as Michael veered away from Celine and shoved Damien off the path. Damien stumbled and fell backward onto the trees. Michael dove into the woods behind him.

"What the hell, man? What are you doing? She's getting away!"

Damien climbed to his feet lunged toward the path. Michael grasped hold of his arm and tugged him back. He pressed a finger to his lips and pointed toward a fork in the path.

Damien followed his finger, his eyes going wide. At the end of the pathway stood Tobias Greene. In the moonlight, his smirk appeared more devilish than in normal light.

"Come to me, Celine," he called, his arms outstretched.

"We have to stop her!" Damien said.

"We can't!" Michael contended. "You can't get anywhere near Tobias!"

Celine joined Tobias. "Come, Celine. To where you can rest and be happy," he promised.

Damien sighed and flung his arms in the air. "She's getting away," he cried. "Ugh!"

"Come on, buddy," Michael said as he squeezed Damien's shoulder. "We'll get her next time."

"I hope there is a next time," Damien mumbled as they turned toward the house.

They trudged back to the house and slogged through the front door, heading straight to Damien's room. The door stood open. A mess laid just over the threshold. Damien stared at it as he skirted it to enter the room.

The top of one sandwich had skittered across the floor,

landing near the bed and leaving a trail of crumbs in its wake. A piece of roast beef stuck to the floor. The plate that contained them lay upside down near the tray. The other sandwich had toppled but remained on its plate. Most of the beef broth had sloshed out of the bowls, leaving a soppy mess on the tray. Both pieces of pie slid and formed a gooey pile, though both dessert plates had miraculously stayed on the tray.

Damien peeled the beef slice off the floor and snatched up the bread. He set them on the upturned plate as he eyed the pie.

"Sorry, buddy," Michael said. "The pie looked good. Before I dropped it."

Damien shrugged. "It kinda still does."

"You serious? It's all smashed."

"It'll get all smashed in my stomach anyway."

Damien lifted the tray and set it on the nearby dresser. He swiped a fork and a plate of flattened pie before stalking to his bed and sinking onto it. He scooped up a forkful of the dessert and shoveled it into his mouth.

"Still good," he mumbled with his mouth full.

Michael eyed him for a moment before he glanced at the second piece of pie. With a shrug, he grasped a fork and the second plate. He joined Damien on the bed, both of them teetering on the edge as they enjoyed the destroyed yet delicious dessert.

They spent the next few moments in silence as they downed the pie.

"Mmm," Damien said as he scraped the last bits of blueberry filling from the plate.

"Yeah, it was good," Michael agreed.

"Ugh, what I wouldn't give for two of Millie's pain relievers and my twenty-first-century bed," Damien lamented.

"Do I actually hear Damien Sherwood complaining about the non-modern amenities in a previous era?"

Damien shrugged, eliciting a groan and a wince. "After my near header off the cliffs, I ache from head to toe."

Michael shifted his shoulders back and forth. "I wouldn't complain about being offered two painkillers with a nice long nap, either."

Damien stood and stalked back and forth in front of the bed.

"Maybe you should try to get some rest," Michael suggested.

"No," Damien said, dismissing the idea, "no, I can't sleep. I'm wired. Where was he taking Celine?"

"I'm not sure," Michael answered. "But, for once, I really hope the Duke succeeds."

Damien snorted and shook his head. "What kind of lives are we leading to have to hope he wins?"

"I've been asking myself that question since the start of this."

Damien settled in front of the window. He stared at darkened skies. "Let's hope this is over soon."

* * *

Marcus milled around on the path toward the Buckley house. He waited to enact the first portion of his plan. He hated waiting. He used the time to ponder his recent encounter with Michael. Hysterical, Michael informed him he'd lost track of Damien. He shook his head. The fool.

If Michael Carlyle's incompetence cost them the ability to save Celine, he would single-handedly snuff out his life. Ridding the world of Tobias Greene comprised only one part of his plan. The second was far more important. Saving Celine was all that mattered. He needed Damien Sherwood for that. As awkward and ungainly as the boy was, he could reach Celine, even in her regressed state. They shared some unknown connection.

Movement caught his eye. A figure approached in the distance. Marcus shoved his thoughts aside to focus on the task at hand. His eyes narrowed at the form of Tobias Greene as he hid in the shadows. A smirk formed on his face as he reminded himself this would serve as the man's last night on earth.

As Tobias approached, Marcus stepped into the moonlight.

Tobias slowed and cocked his head. He raised his eyebrows. "Marcus Northcott!"

"In the flesh," Marcus replied.

"I had heard you were skulking around the area."

"I'd hardly call it skulking," Marcus countered.

"Hmm," Tobias murmured. "Yet here you are lurking in the shadows. Lying in wait to spring out at me."

"Perhaps you would have preferred an engraved invitation."

Tobias chuckled as he paced the path in front of Marcus. "Oh, I believe it is you, Marcus, who desires an invitation. You see, I am welcome at the Buckley estate as an honored guest. Yet you, a Duke, has been spurned. Reduced to prowling the grounds, confined to the dark shadows."

Marcus flexed his jaw as he swallowed his anger over the last statement. He could not wait to witness the man's demise. A voice echoed within his head. He ignored it.

"You have misunderstood. You see, I have laid in wait, as you put it, for a very special reason!"

"Oh?" Tobias inquired. "And what, pray tell, is that?"

"Your demise."

Tobias burst into loud laughter. He clapped his hands

after a moment as his chuckles died down. "Oh, bravo, Marcus. You prove most entertaining this evening!"

"Yes, I agree, the evening should provide a good deal of entertainment."

Tobias sneered at him. "You are overconfident, Marcus. You cannot defeat me."

Marcus pretended to weigh the statement in his mind. He formed an upside-down smile with his lips. "Alone, no. Though I am not alone."

"Oh? Who have you persuaded to your side, hmm?" He narrowed his eyes at Marcus and glanced at him sideways. "The Buckleys?" He chuckled. "They cannot help you."

The voice sounded in his mind again.

"Not quite. And you can cease your ridiculous attacks on me, they have no effect," Marcus replied. He readied for the strike. He wiggled his fingers as they cracked with electricity.

"This is all really a lovely show, Marcus, but ineffective."

"Not if my power is doubled."

"Doubled? Impossible. Unless you have persuaded someone with Celine's level of talent to your side. Though I know you have not persuaded Celine, your powers have not multiplied."

"Think again," a voice said from behind Tobias.

The 1842 version of Marcus stepped into the path.

Tobias swiveled to face him. His brow furrowed and his eyes widened as he spotted the second Marcus. He twisted to face the original man then swung back toward the prior version.

"How?" he questioned as both men launched their attack on him. His voice trailed off as the electricity jolted through him. He dropped to his knees as his body convulsed. The combined attack paralyzed him. He dropped to the ground face down, alive but immobilized. Hands lifted him under his arms. He bumped along the rocky dirt path as they dragged him away.

Tobias slumped to the dirt floor. Slipping in and out of consciousness as both Marcuses dragged him to an unknown location, Tobias fought to stay alert. The double volleyed attack had left him stunned and reeling.

Marcus crouched beside him. He slapped his cheek. "Time to wake up, Tobias," he said.

Tobias startled to full consciousness. He peered around at his surroundings. A windowless space met his gaze. Wooden stairs led up to a closed door. He narrowed his eyes at it. Marcus followed his gaze.

"You won't make it," he promised.

Tobias shifted his gaze to Marcus. He stared at him, his eyes burning with intensity.

Marcus smirked. "Your so-called attacks have little effect on me. Other than to amuse me."

Tobias grimaced as his eyes searched the space again. They appeared to be alone. The second version of Marcus was nowhere to be found. Did he exist? Or was that a figment of his imagination? No, Marcus could not have stunned him the way he did alone. Who was the other man? And where was he?

A small doorway on the far side of the room led to another space. He'd never make it there if he ran, though alone, Marcus could not defeat him outright. Not without his doppelgänger. Still, it proved too much of a gamble. He'd try another method.

"You have gained some impressive skills, Marcus," he said.

"Indeed," Marcus replied.

Tobias raised his eyebrows. "I, too, am a man of considerable skills."

Marcus did not respond. Tobias continued, "Perhaps we can come to some arrangement?"

"Arrangement?" Marcus scoffed.

"Yes," Tobias suggested. "Our strengths may complement each other well. I propose an alliance."

Marcus lifted his eyebrows, an amused expression crossing his features.

"I wouldn't dismiss it out of hand, Marcus. My talents combined with yours can prove to open new worlds."

Marcus smirked. "I have a proposition of my own."

"Oh?" Tobias inquired. "I am all ears."

Marcus wrapped his hands around the man's throat, throttling him as he wrestled him to the floor. "I would propose you go to Hell."

Tobias grasped Marcus's hands in an attempt to pull them away. After a moment, Marcus released his grip. Tobias choked and coughed as he pushed himself to his hands and knees. He swallowed hard as he attempted to decide his next move.

"To that end," Marcus continued, "I have provided a means by which you can accommodate my request."

"Marcus," Tobias choked out in a strained voice, "consider the possibilities."

"There is no need. I've no desire to join forces with you. Not after what you've attempted to do to my Celine."

Tobias sneered at him as he attempted to rise to his feet. "She will never be your Celine. And I haven't attempted it. I'm hours away from pulling it off."

Marcus knocked Tobias onto his side with a fireball. "We'll see about that."

"Abandon this foolishness, Marcus," Tobias said as he righted himself. "You cannot destroy me. Not even with your twin friend."

As if on cue, the other Marcus strode into the room. He nodded his head to his identical counterpart. Tobias climbed to his feet.

"We shall see," Marcus said to him.

Tobias's brow crinkled at the statement. He followed the other Marcus as he strode into the room. His eyes flitted to the doorway he'd used to enter. Movement caught his eye. He knit his brows further. What was it? The figure dragged itself along as though injured. His mind pondered what Marcus might have conjured and how it could pose a threat to him.

CHAPTER 31

"Come, Bazios," Marcus called across the room. "See what sacrifice we have brought you."

"Bazios?" Tobias questioned. "No, you couldn't…"

"Yet, I did," Marcus retorted.

Tobias swallowed hard as he focused on the figure sliding through the doorway. Formed from the brown dirt making up the floor, the serpentine figure slithered its way toward him. The giant snake's body was topped with a human face graced with large goat-like horns protruding from its forehead.

"What have you to show me, Marcus?" the giant snake hissed.

"A Zieleneter," Marcus said as he motioned toward Tobias.

The snake slithered a circle around Tobias. "And of what interest is this Zieleneter to me?"

"None," Tobias burst. "There is no reason I should concern you."

"I disagree," Marcus said.

"State your case," Bazios said, his forked tongue flicking in and out of his mouth as his snake eyes peered at Tobias.

"He threatens one intended to be yours."

"Intended to be yours?" Tobias countered. "Celine will never bend to your will. She is a lost cause."

"She is only lost if you consume her soul," Marcus argued.

"SILENCE!" Bazios spat.

He continued his slow crawl around Tobias.

"He has grown drunk with power," Marcus continued. "He threatens your coven. You should take action, Bazios."

"I do no such thing," Tobias said in his defense. "In fact, only moments ago, I offered an alliance with Marcus. Our combined powers can achieve things no one else can. Imagine the possibilities, Bazios. Surely a creature as shrewd and progressive as yourself can spot the benefits of such a joining."

"You insult me, Tobias Greene, even as you attempt to win me over," Bazios growled.

"No!" Tobias insisted. "No, I meant every word I uttered."

The snake flicked his tongue at him. His eyes turned red. "There can be no alliance," he stated.

"Please," Tobias began.

"You are worthless to us," Bazios interrupted. "Soul consumption is the antithesis of our goal. You are an enemy, not an ally."

"Surely, we can come to some arrangement," Tobias tried again.

"Yes," Bazios hissed, "I believe we can. Your destruction is the arrangement I seek."

Tobias's eyes grew wide. "No," he countered with a quick shake of his head. "No, there is another way."

"SILENCE!" the snake spat.

Tobias scanned the room for any source of escape. Sweat

beaded on his brow as his eyes darted to the doorway. It provided the only means for him to get away.

He dashed toward it. The snake followed in hot pursuit. Steps from the opening, the giant serpent caught up to him. It reared back, its colossal mouth yawning wide and thrust forward. Bazios devoured Tobias's screaming form within seconds.

His forked tongue flicked as silence filled the room after the deafening screams. He slid in a circle, slithering back to the two Marcuses.

"Your pathway is cleared, Marcus. I expect results."

"You shall have them," Marcus promised.

The snake wound its way across the floor, disintegrating into the dirt before reaching the doorway.

* * *

Damien spun on his heel and crossed the floorboards of his room in the opposite direction.

"Will you stop that pacing?" Michael requested. "It's making me nervous." He tugged at his collar as he leaned forward and let his forearms rest on his thighs.

"Sorry," Damien exclaimed, flinging his arms out at his sides. "I can't help it! What's taking so long? Where is he?"

"Probably doing something nefarious," Michael murmured.

Damien sank into the other armchair. "Do you think he's double-crossing us?"

"Man, I really hope not," Michael said with a sigh.

Damien's leg bobbed up and down for several moments before he leapt from the chair again. He stalked the length of the room before returning along the same path. Michael rubbed his face with his hands.

The door popped open. Damien spun to face it and

Michael stood from his chair. Marcus Northcott slipped into the room and closed the door behind him.

"Finally!" Damien exclaimed.

"Yeah, where the hell have you been?" Michael questioned.

Marcus raised his eyebrows as his jaw dropped open. He shook his head as he blinked several times. "Ridding us of Tobias Greene," he responded after a moment.

"Really?" Damien questioned.

"Did it work?" Michael added.

"Yes."

Damien's eyes went wide, and he glanced to Michael.

"Just like that, huh? He's just… gone?" Michael inquired.

Marcus tensed his jaw and narrowed his eyes. "No, not 'just like that,'" he answered. "It took delicate work, but the task is complete. We are rid of him."

Damien blew out a sigh of relief. "Thank God," he exclaimed.

"And I see you completed your task," Marcus said to Michael.

"Yeah," Michael answered.

"And we are no worse for the wear?" Marcus questioned as he eyed Damien from head to toe.

"More or less," Damien answered. "Unless you count dangling from a cliff for a few minutes worse for the wear."

"Thankfully, we are rid of the man who drove you to such lengths. Now we must focus on Celine."

"I agree," Damien said.

"Wait, with Tobias gone, won't she just be cured?" Michael questioned.

"It depends on the state she was in when he met his end."

"What does that mean?" Michael inquired.

"If she was not in a trance, she may have no lasting effects."

"And if she was?" Damien asked.

"We may need to take more extreme measures to pull her out of it."

"Oh, great," Damien lamented, "that doesn't sound good."

"Where is she?" Marcus inquired.

"No idea," Damien answered.

"You mean you have no idea where Celine may be?" Marcus asked.

"Nope," Damien admitted. "The last we saw her, she was wandering around in a daze outside. We tried to stop her, but Tobias showed up. I don't know where she went after that."

Marcus closed his eyes and shook his head. "We must search for her at once."

"But where?" Michael inquired.

"Maybe she snapped out of the trance and came back here," Michael suggested.

Damien considered it. "No, or if she did, she hasn't come back to her room. We'd have heard her."

"Where was she when you last saw her?"

"On the path near the cliffs," Michael answered.

"We shall begin our search there," Marcus said. He pulled the door open. He and Michael stepped into the hallway. Damien did not move.

"You coming?" Michael questioned.

Damien stood still for a moment, his brow crinkled.

"What is it, Damien? What's wrong?" Michael asked.

"The cave," Damien said.

"Huh?" Michael asked.

"The cave," Damien repeated. "We should search for her in the cave."

Realization dawned on Michael. "The red dress, the ruby necklace..." he began.

"The cave," Michael and Damien said simultaneously.

Damien nodded, a half-smile on his face. "Yes, Celine's prediction. The cave was the last piece. I'll bet that's where she is."

"All right, gentlemen, let us not waste any additional time," Marcus said. "Come along."

They hurried through the halls and outside, taking the most direct path to the cave leading to the beach. Marcus illuminated the interior with a fireball as they began their search. They probed every nook and cranny, finding nothing.

Damien took a final glance around the stony space before he retreated onto the beach. He sank onto a rock, his mind clouded and worry crossing his face.

"Sorry, man," Michael said. "I thought she'd be there, too."

Damien puffed out a sigh. "Now what?" he murmured.

"Try another cave? What about that one you stuck Celine in when you kidnapped her?" Michael inquired of Marcus.

"Perhaps we should try there," Marcus agreed.

Michael nodded and they turned to leave. Again, Damien did not move. He stared out at the stormy sea. "She's not there," he said.

"How do you know?" Michael asked.

Damien shrugged. "Just a feeling."

"Come on, man, I know you're worried, but we'll find her," Michael said. "But we have to keep looking, we can't just sit here."

Damien pursed his lips and nodded. "Okay," he said as he climbed to standing with a sigh. He glanced down the beach before he turned toward the sea cave. He took two steps before he stopped again. His face pinched. He spun to face the beach.

"Damien?" Michael queried.

Damien stared down the beach for a moment before he twisted to face Michael and Marcus. "It doesn't make sense."

"What?"

"If they were going to the other cave, why did they take the cliff path?"

Michael shrugged. "Celine was in a daze, just wandering. I don't think she was carefully choosing the most direct route."

"But Tobias was guiding her. And he might."

"So, what are you saying?" Michael asked.

Damien considered Michael's question. "I'm not sure. I just… " His voice trailed off as he tried to formulate his thoughts.

Marcus narrowed his eyes at Damien. "Something holds you back from leaving this spot. What is it?"

Damien shrugged. "Gut feeling. Celine's clue was the cave. Tobias and Celine were right there on the cliff path."

"Where on the cliff path, specifically?" Marcus inquired.

"At the fork," Michael answered.

"So, they could have gone either way," Damien added.

"Why go the opposite way?" Michael inquired. "There are no caves that way."

Damien shook his head. "No, but…"

"But what?" Michael inquired.

"We spotted Tobias on that side of the beach twice. And he disappeared both times."

"There's no cave down there," Michael argued.

Marcus narrowed his eyes and pursed his lips. "It's worth considering."

Damien nodded. He and Marcus strode down the beach, skirting around the rocky outcropping and making their way toward the spot they had lost Tobias.

Michael held his hands out to his sides. "Really? That's the second time!"

Michael shook his head but hurried after them. They approached the cliff face.

"I don't get it," Michael said. "There are no caves here. We were here during the day. You'd see it."

"It could be hidden," Damien suggested.

"Or enchanted," Marcus added.

Marcus scanned the area. He pressed his hand against the cold rock making up the sheer cliffs. With his hand pressed against the stone, he strode down the beach. As he approached the middle, a spark of electricity shot from the rocks. His lips formed a half-smirk.

"And here it is," he said.

Damien's and Michael's jaws dropped open at the sight. "You found it?!" Damien asked.

"Yes," Marcus confirmed.

Damien rushed forward. "How do we get in?"

"Careful," Marcus said a moment too late. Damien reached forward to press against the stone. The jolt he received blew him backward. He landed hard on the sand, skittering to a halt at the water's edge.

"Damien!" Michael shouted, racing to him. He knelt at his side. "Are you okay?"

"Yeah," Damien said in a weak voice. He shook his hand. "Wow, that stings!"

Marcus eyed the enchanted rock as Michael pulled Damien to his feet.

"Don't touch it again," Marcus warned as they approached.

"No kidding," Damien said.

"You could have warned us," Michael complained.

"I tried. I had no idea he'd be dimwitted enough to touch it."

Michael rolled his eyes at the statement.

"Just concentrate on removing it so we can get to her," Damien said.

Marcus offered a frustrated sigh but refrained from

making any comment. He returned to studying the rock wall. He eyed it from several different angles. His eyes narrowed as he pressed his cheek against the cliff wall. He reached out with one finger toward the enchanted rock. Sparks flew as he came into contact with it.

He grimaced as he retracted his hand. He spent several more moments inspecting the wall.

"Well?" Michael asked after five minutes. "What's the verdict?"

"Can you open it or not?" Damien added.

"Patience, gentlemen. This is delicate work."

"In other words, you can't," Michael spat.

"Of course, I can. Though I must decipher the enchantment first and ensure I open it properly."

"Can you decipher faster?" Damien asked.

Marcus shot him an unimpressed glance.

"Just sayin'," Damien said with a shrug.

After another five minutes passed, Marcus spoke again. "Stand back."

"Why?" Michael questioned.

Marcus frowned at him. "Or don't. It's your life."

"Maybe we should listen to him," Damien said as he tugged Michael backward a few steps toward the ocean.

Marcus stretched his arms out in front of him. He spread his fingers wide. He murmured a few unintelligible words before he snapped his fingers closed, balling his hands into fists. Sparks flew from the rock onto the beach. A doorway-shaped rectangle coursed with electricity, giving the rock an eerie white-blue glow.

Marcus pulled his hands closer toward him. The glowing door-shaped entity lifted from the rock face. It floated in the air several inches from the rockface. A loud hum reverberated against the surrounding rocks. Some shattered to pieces and the beach shook from the vibrations.

Damien pressed his hands over his ears. Michael followed suit.

Marcus pushed his fists together in a slow, deliberate manner. He grimaced as though fighting against some unseen force to shove them toward the center of his body. As his fists touched, a brilliant burst of light seared Michael's and Damien's eyes. They each squeezed their eyes shut against the blinding light as they spun away. A supersonic boom sounded, and air whooshed around them.

Damien popped one eye open, risking a glance at the cliff. The beach had returned to normal. Marcus stood in front of a roughly hewn opening in the cliff face. Damien released his hands from his ears and tapped Michael's shoulder.

Michael glanced toward him before dropping his hands.

"Gentlemen," Marcus said, twisting to face them, "the way is opened."

Damien raced forward, navigating the rocky beach as best he could at his fast pace.

"Damien, careful!" Michael called as he hurried after him.

Damien paused for a moment outside the cave's entrance. He gulped as he crept into the dark opening. Michael followed him. Marcus entered last, illuminating the space with a fireball.

Damien scanned the interior. His eyes fell to the ground. They widened as he spotted red fabric.

"Celine!" he shouted as he rushed to her side. He skidded to a stop, dropping to his knees next to her huddled form. He pulled her limp body into his arms.

Marcus hastened to them and felt Celine's cheek with the back of his hand. He lifted one of her eyelids.

"Is she…" Michael began, unable to finish.

"She is alive," Marcus answered. "Barely."

"Barely?" Damien cried.

Marcus stood. "It is worse than I anticipated. Her mind has regressed further than I expected."

Damien glanced down at Celine's inanimate form. "We can still save her, right?" he squeaked.

"Yes, though it will require an intense effort."

"I can do it," Damien promised. "I'm ready. Just tell me what I need to do."

"We must enter her mind space and draw her back."

"Huh?" Michael questioned. "Enter her mind space?"

"Yes," Marcus answered. "We must make a connection with her mind. She is lost in it somewhere, likely hiding. We must find her and convince her to return."

"Okay," Damien agreed. "But how?"

"I can make the connection and guide you there. Michael you must remain here to monitor Damien. I shall make an incision in my hand and Celine's and use it to connect to Celine's mind. I will make a similar incision in my other hand and yours and pull you through."

Michael nodded. "Okay," he said. "What am I monitoring him for?"

"The journey into Celine's mind will be taxing on him. After we enter her cognizance, he will begin to turn blue. He may experience convulsions, he may murmur unintelligible words, or his posture may become stiff. That is normal. If he turns purple suddenly, or begins to turn green, pull his hand from mine immediately to revive him. Do not wait, do not dally. One second too long could mean his life."

Michael swallowed hard but offered a shaky nod.

Damien eased Celine to the ground before he stood. He wiped his sweaty palms against his jacket. "Okay," he said in a shaky voice, "I'm ready."

Michael approached him. "Good luck."

"Thanks," Damien said with a nod. "See you on the flip side."

"Yeah," Michael said, forcing a smile onto his face, "yeah, see you after you save Celine."

Damien offered a nod and a smile. Marcus eased himself to sitting next to Celine. He pulled a knife from his pocket and sliced a wide cut into Celine's hand then one in his hand. Red blood spattered across the dirt below.

Damien joined him in a seated position. He held his hand out and Marcus wasted no time in slicing it open. Damien winced as the knife penetrated his flesh. Michael cringed as red blood flowed from Damien's hand. Marcus made the final slice in his left hand.

"Ready?" he inquired.

Damien nodded. "Yeah," he murmured in a soft voice.

Marcus grasped Celine's hand then held out the other for Damien. Damien grabbed hold of it. Marcus closed his eyes. Damien stared at him for a moment. Michael kept a close watch.

"I don't..." Damien whispered before an unseen force jolted him. His eyes widened and his muscles stiffened before he slumped back onto the dirt floor. His eyes closed and he lay still. Michael rushed to his side and peered closely at him. His lips began to tinge blue. He reminded himself this was normal.

"Good luck, Damien," he whispered. "Good luck."

CHAPTER 32

*D*amien opened his eyes. He stood in a vast, dark space. He glanced around, not recognizing anything.

"Welcome," Marcus's voice said behind him, echoing off the darkened walls.

He spun to face it.

"Wh-where are we?" he questioned as a chill passed over him.

"Inside Celine's mind."

Damien's eyes darted around again. They stood in a circular chamber. Hallways jutted from it in various locations. Doorways lined them. Other halls disappeared around corners.

"This is Celine's mind?" Damien questioned. "It's like a maze!"

Damien continued his survey of the space. His gaze settled on an object in the center of the chamber. Illuminated by a dark red light, an hourglass stood on a pedestal. Damien approached it. Grains of sand tumbled through the opening.

"What is this?" he asked Marcus.

"This," Marcus answered, "is how much time we have remaining to save Celine."

Damien's jaw dropped. "What? It's already halfway empty on top!"

"Then I suggest we do not dally." Marcus strode toward the chamber's side. "Come along, Damien."

Damien hurried after him. "How can we find Celine in this? What are all these doors?"

"They represent Celine's memories," Marcus answered. "We must navigate her mind space. She is hiding somewhere here. We must find the location then convince her to return."

Damien glanced back to the falling sands. "And all before that runs out."

"Correct. Where shall we begin?"

Damien spun in a circle. "I don't know!" he said with a shrug.

Marcus rolled his eyes. "Think, Damien. You know her best. Pick a spot and begin."

Damien nodded, his eyes scanning the room. "Here," he said, pointing to a long hall.

They stepped into the darkened space. Damien approached the first door.

"I'm almost afraid to open this," he admitted. He swallowed hard, steeling his nerves. He twisted the doorknob and swung the door open.

Inside, a scene played out. Marcus and Celine stood on a beach. Damien recognized it as the beach near the van Woodsen home.

"Leave me alone, Marcus," Celine shouted. She raised her hand and slapped him across the face before storming away.

"Yikes!" Damien said as he pulled the door shut. "She's not in there!"

He shuffled a few steps across the hall and tried another door.

"I will never give in to you!" Celine shouted at Marcus in a large sitting room. She pulled her hand back and issued a crack across his cheek.

Damien grimaced as he closed the door. He continued down the hall. He pushed the next door open. Another shouting match. Another slap.

Across the hall, he witnessed a similar event. He tried a fifth door and witnessed yet another scene ending with a slap across Marcus's face.

He furrowed his brow as he gazed down the long hallway. There had to be over one hundred doors in it. "Is this hall really just devoted to all Celine's memories of slapping you?"

"Does it matter? We are clearly in the wrong location. We should return to the center and try another direction."

Damien nodded. Before he retreated, he stared down the length of the hall. "There's just so many," he murmured.

"Come along, Damien, don't dally," Marcus called, already approaching the central chamber. After one last glance, Damien hurried after Marcus. They emerged into the round chamber.

"Pick another hall," Marcus said.

"Ummm," Damien murmured as he scanned the selections. "That one." He pointed across the room. "The one furthest from slap city."

They crossed the room. Damien's eyes shot to the hourglass. The sands paraded through the opening, draining faster than he preferred. He tore his eyes from it, determined to find Celine.

They entered the corridor. Damien approached the first door and pulled it open.

Celine sashayed down a large, curved stairway in a blush pink gown. Her curls were piled on top of her head. She smiled widely at the group awaiting her at the bottom of the stairs.

Marcus crinkled his brow as he watched the scene unfold.

Damien swung the door shut. "She's not in there."

"What was that memory?"

"Senior prom. When she was Josie."

Damien crossed the hall and tried another door. In this room, a pony-tailed, sweatpants-clad Josie pounded her thumbs against a game controller. She elbowed Damien with a grin on her face. "I'm going to kick your butt again," she said.

"Not if I can help it," the figment of Damien said as the real Damien repeated it alongside him.

Damien smiled at the memory, recalling how simple their lives had been before Josie discovered her true self. He stood for an extra moment, viewing the heartwarming scene. He pulled himself away from it, swinging the door shut.

He tried several more doors, all containing memories of Josie. He shook his head and shrugged his shoulders. "This is impossible. There are millions of doors. How can we find her?"

"Think, Damien," Marcus answered. "Where is the most likely place Celine would go to retreat from the world?"

Damien considered the question. "I don't know!" he exclaimed. "Josie seemed happy, would she come here?" He stared down the length of the seemingly endless hall. "But we can't search through all these doors!"

"She would be near her happiest memories. Are they in this hall? Are they when she was Josie?"

Damien's face clouded as he frowned. "I don't know. I don't… Let's try another hall."

They retraced their steps and selected another corridor. Damien opened the first door in it. A sixteen-year-old Celine raced through a cave, a book clutched in her hand. Damien shook his head as he pulled the door closed.

He tried another door in the hall for good measure. It

contained the disturbing memory of Celine being stabbed in the gut by a seaman in the beachside caves in Martinique.

"No," Damien said. "This is definitely the wrong place."

Damien slogged back to the main chamber. He bit his lower lip as he stared at the ever-emptying hourglass. With a sigh, he ran his fingers through his hair.

"We're running out of time," Damien said.

"We are. And you are wasting time."

"I don't know where she is!" Damien cried.

"Think, Damien."

"Perhaps we should go back to the Josie corridor. Maybe she's there," Damien conjectured.

"Your gut says no."

"No, it doesn't. It doesn't say anything," Damien claimed.

"You would not have left that hall if you suspected she was there."

Damien scrunched his face as he pondered the situation. "We haven't seen any memories of Gray yet. Maybe she's there," he postulated.

"Perhaps. Yet she sought to escape even from him."

Damien sighed as he raked his hands through his hair.

"I did not mean that to sound as unhelpful as it did," Marcus admitted.

"No," Damien said with a shake of his head. "You have a point." He gave it another few moments of thought. "She was happy with Gray, but she did choose to leave even him to escape her life. And when she was Josie, she had to have realized subconsciously who she really was. That's why she so readily accepted Gray when he showed up."

Damien paced around the chamber. "So, neither of those make sense as her happiest memories. What does that leave?"

Damien continued his ambling as he thought. "We're going to have to check each of these corridors and see what they hold."

Damien stalked through the entrance to another hallway. He pulled open the first door. Celine held her hand out to a smiling Grayson at a large ball.

"Found Gray!" Damien called.

"Wonderful," Marcus groaned.

Damien crossed to another hall. He pulled a door open. Inside, Celine and Damien sat across from Monica Benson in the cafe in Bucksville.

"Nope," Damien mumbled as he pulled the door closed.

He hurried to the next hall. Damien swung the first door open. The scene inside played out in a large dining room. Celine sat across the table from Michael and Damien. They wore clothes from another era. A man entered the room with his hand held behind his back.

Damien recognized the scene. He recalled it being the night Celine's father gave her the gold music box. The night Duke Northcott ordered a seaman to rob him of his life.

He pulled the door shut but his hand lingered on the doorknob. His brow furrowed. He pushed the door open again. The memory replayed. Damien stared at the expression on Celine's young face. He eased the door shut as he considered it.

Marcus joined him. "What is it?"

"I'm not sure," Damien said as he wandered across the hall.

He peered into the next room. Another memory played out with Marquis Devereaux. He hurried down the hall to another memory chamber. It showed Celine strolling the back garden at her Martinique home.

A smile spread across Damien's face.

"What is it?" Marcus repeated.

"I think we may be close." He continued down the hall. He opened a few doors here and there. He broke into a run, barreling down the dark corridor. He searched for any sign of Celine.

As his head swiveled, he caught sight of a glowing light shining under a door. He skidded to a halt as the light beckoned from the end of another corridor branching off the main hall.

"There!" he shouted.

He raced headlong toward it. Marcus followed him.

Damien came to a halt outside the room. He pulled open the door. A sunny, warm day glowed inside. Spring flowers bloomed in a garden. An enormous tree with light pink leaves rose in the middle of the space. A broad wooden swing hung from two thick ropes.

Celine sat on the swing. Her blonde curls blew in the breeze as she pumped her legs to force the swing higher. Her bare feet reached toward the sky. Her white dress ruffled around her.

"There she is!" Damien whispered.

"Quickly, Damien," Marcus encouraged. "You must speak with her and convince her to return to the real world."

Damien glanced around the space. "Tall order."

"Go, Damien. We are running out of time."

Damien nodded and stepped onto the lush green grass. He inched closer to Celine. He swallowed hard as he planned what he would say to her to convince her. He glanced back toward the darkened hall.

Marcus motioned for him to continue. Damien nodded and spun back toward Celine.

He cleared his throat and said, "Celine?"

Celine ignored him. Perhaps she had not heard him. "Celine!" he said again in a louder tone.

Celine twisted to face him, a surprised expression on her face. She leapt from the swing and stared at him.

He took a tentative step toward her and smiled. "Hey, Celine."

She backed a step away. "Who are you?"

* * *

Michael paced the dirt floor of the cave. He studied the three bodies lying in front of him.

Celine's and Marcus's appearances remained unchanged. Damien, however, suffered from an austere transformation. His skin turned ashen. His lips were tinged blue as were his fingernails. His breathing seemed labored.

Michael bent closer toward him. He grasped his hand and squinted at his fingertips. Were they green or blue? He inspected his lips. He moved his gaze to Damien's bloodied hand, pressed against Marcus's. Should he pull him out of it?

He pondered it a moment. If Damien hadn't completed his task yet, he'd never forgive him the interruption. But what if Damien was in danger? He studied his lips and fingertips again. Blue, he decided. He'd wait longer and give Damien time to work.

Michael stood and resumed his pacing. A moment later, a groan emanated from Damien's blue lips. Michael dropped to his knees again. Damien convulsed, his body shaking hard enough to bang his head off the dirt floor.

"Damien?" Michael called. He braced him against the ground, so he didn't injure himself.

Damien's convulsions ceased, replaced by a mild trembling. His lips opened and closed before his voice sounded.

"Problem," he said. "Problem, problem, problem, problem, problem."

Michael's face scrunched with concern. "Damien?" he repeated.

He checked Damien's coloring as he muttered to himself,

"Does this mean I need to pull you out or not?" Damien's lips and fingertips remained bright blue.

"Not purple, not green," Michael said aloud. "He's fine. The Duke said this could happen. He's fine."

Damien's voice faded away again as Michael reassured himself of Damien's wellbeing.

"Come on, buddy," he murmured. "Get Celine and get out of there."

* * *

Damien stopped and swallowed hard. Celine didn't recognize him. How could he convince her to return to the real world when she didn't know him?

"It's me, Damien," Damien answered.

Celine narrowed her eyes at him.

"You know me, Celine," Damien insisted. "I'm your cousin. Well, sort of. I'm Josie's cousin. Do you remember being Josie?"

"Josie? I know of no Josie," Celine insisted.

Damien glanced back toward Marcus. He twisted to face Celine again. His mind spun as he searched for a solution. He shook his head. "Wait here," he entreated.

He raced back toward the dark hall.

"We have a problem," he breathed to Marcus.

"What?"

"Celine doesn't remember me. She doesn't remember being Josie. I can't do this."

Marcus stared at him for a moment. "You must, Damien. There is no one else. You must find a way to reach her."

Damien eyed Celine. She extended her finger to the sky as a dove descended and perched on it.

Marcus grasped Damien's shoulders, calling his attention

back to him. "Focus, Damien. You must succeed. There are no alternatives."

Damien nodded and sucked in a few deep breaths. "Okay," he said. He strode back to Celine.

The bird fluttered away as she gazed after it. "Celine," Damien tried again. "What do you remember about your life?"

Celine cocked her head. "I remember…" She paused. Her forehead wrinkled. Her eyes slid sideways. She pursed her lips together. "I remember…" she tried again. Her breathing became heavy as she struggled to search for a memory. "I am happy here."

"What about Gray? Do you remember Gray?"

"Gray?" she questioned, her brow deeply furrowed.

"Gray, your husband."

"I have no husband."

"You do!" Damien insisted. "He's sitting at your bedside right now. You're sick. Dying in fact! If you don't snap out of this, you're not going to survive!"

Celine considered his statement. "No," she said after a moment, "no, I am happy here."

"But you're going to die. You don't have long left!"

"No!" she insisted. "No, I will not."

"Yes, this is an illusion, Celine. It's not real."

Celine's eyes flitted around the space. Her expression became troubled as she pondered his statements.

"Okay," Damien tried again. "You had a father, right? What is your father's name?"

"Yes," Celine answered. "Yes, of course, I had a father."

"What's his name?" Damien repeated.

"His name is…" Celine stopped dead. "It is… " She pursed her lips, the crease in her brow deepening. Her breathing turned labored as she struggled to recall the details of her life.

She snapped her head up to face Damien. She gave it a hard shake. "No," she shouted, "you must leave."

She stalked several steps away from him, her arms wrapped around her midriff. A few pink leaves fluttered to the ground from the tree overhead.

Damien followed her. "Celine," he implored.

"No!" she interrupted. She inched backward as he reached out to her. She dodged away from his grasp.

"Celine, please!" Damien pleaded. He reached toward her again, grasping her by the arms.

Her body jolted as he touched her. Goosebumps covered her flesh and her forehead crinkled as if in pain.

Her eyes rose to meet his gaze. "D-Damien?" she questioned.

Damien gasped in relief. "Yes!" he exclaimed.

Celine sucked in a breath. More leaves fell from the tree behind her, littering the grass below. The flowers near Damien wilted. A wide crack formed in the cloudless azure sky.

Celine's brow furrowed as she sought to regain her memory. A voice reverberated throughout the space. "Hang in there, Celine. Damien and Michael are going to help you."

"Gray," Celine breathed. She glanced to the fractured sky. An image of his face formed there.

"Yes, that's it, Celine, remember," Damien encouraged.

Images flitted across the sky in rapid succession as Celine's memory returned. With every memory that passed, another leaf fell to the ground and the tear in the sky grew wider. The flowers continued to wilt and shrivel, and the grass began to turn brown.

She turned to face him, now attired in the red dress and ruby necklace he'd found her wearing in the cave.

"It's all right, D," a voice said from his right side.

While keeping hold of Celine's hands, he twisted his neck

to ascertain the source of the voice. Another version of Celine stood next to him. She wore a pair of jeans, a light blue tunic and a hoodie. Her gaze fell on the previous iteration of herself.

"We know what we must do," current Celine said.

Tears sprang to Damien's eyes at the sight of her. "Celine!" he exclaimed, relief apparent in his voice.

She turned to face him, grasping his hand and squeezing it. "Thanks, D," she said, pulling him into a hug. "I've got it from here."

"Are you sure?" Damien asked as he pulled back.

Celine nodded. "Yes. You need to go, right away. You have to be gone from my mind space before my memories collate completely. Otherwise, you'll be trapped here."

"Okay," Damien said with a nod. "I love you, Celine."

He gave her another brief embrace.

"I love you, too, D. Now go."

He gave her another nod before he hurried to the door. He glanced back once. Modern Celine held her former self's hand. The red-clad woman reached to her neck and ripped off the ruby necklace. It crumbled into black dust and blew away. Modern Celine offered him a smile and a wave.

He noticed the tree's leaves were nearly gone and the blue sky had almost turned black. He ducked through the doorway and into the dark hall beyond.

"Well?" Marcus questioned.

"She's reassembling herself," Damien reported.

A cracking boom sounded overhead. Damien shrank away from it.

"We must leave. Otherwise…"

"We'll be trapped. Yeah, Celine told me."

"We must get to the central chamber."

Damien nodded. "Okay. Come on."

He started down the hall as the lights flickered. Another

crash reverberated. Doors banged open and shut. A boulder crashed down in front of them, blocking their path.

Damien skidded to a halt. He searched the area.

"Here," Marcus said, pointing to a hallway branching off.

Damien dove toward it as the floor below him splintered. Marcus pulled him to standing and they raced down the hallway. They turned the corner.

The floor dropped off to a black void. Damien skidded to a halt, teetering on the edge. Marcus grasped his jacket and pulled him away from the ledge.

"We must go back," Marcus said.

"If we can," Damien groaned.

Marcus dragged him back down the hall. They found another corridor jutting off a few paces from the collapsed floor. They plunged into it, hoping it led back to the main chamber.

Red light glowed at the end of the hall, indicating the central room.

"There!" Damien pointed. He pushed his body to run faster. As he approached the hall's end, a large chunk of the floor fell away. A gaping hole stared back. Damien estimated it to be at least twelve feet across.

Damien's jaw dropped as he slid to a halt. "Oh no," he lamented. Creaks and groans sounded as Celine's memories continued to compile. "We'll never make it if we have to go back."

"I do not plan on going back," Marcus said.

"We can't jump that," Damien exclaimed. "It's too wide!"

"I can," Marcus said.

He backed up a few steps. He ran forward, grasped Damien by the collar, and flung himself across the void. With the grace of a cat, he landed on his feet. He set Damien down next to him. "Let's go."

Damien stood for a second, his breathing still shaky

before he followed Marcus to the round chamber. The hourglass still stood on the central pedestal. The grains of sand no longer moved. Instead, they remained frozen in whatever configuration had existed when Celine snapped out of her trance.

Marcus grabbed Damien's arm and pulled him toward the room's center. He grasped the hourglass and flung it to the floor. It smashed into pieces as the world blackened around them. The floor dropped away, and Damien experienced the sensation of falling.

CHAPTER 33

$\mathcal{M}$ichael spun and stalked in the opposite direction on his umpteenth pass across the cave's interior. His constant movement had worn a groove into the dirt beneath him. He glanced at the three bodies sprawled in front of him. Still no signs of return from anyone.

Michael finished his trek across the cave and twirled to retrace his steps. His eyes slid to the side as he passed Damien. He stopped dead. Did he detect a slight difference in Damien's breathing?

Michael hurried to his side. "Damien?" he questioned as he fell to his knees next to him.

Damien's breathing increased. He panted and quivered, his muscles twitching. Michael studied his pale skin searching for any sign of distress. His hand hovered over the clutched hands of Damien and Marcus.

He bit his lower lip as he tried to assess the situation. His coloring remained blue. He'd give him a few more minutes then he'd pull him from the trance or whatever he was in,

Michael decided. He collapsed onto his rear and checked his watch.

"Five more minutes," he warned. "Then I'm pulling you out of there."

Damien's breathing continued to be labored. After a moment, the Duke's muscles began to twitch. Celine remained still. What did it mean, Michael wondered?

His eyes flitted between the two men. He pressed his lips together as he checked his watch. "Three minutes," he announced, his voice echoing off the cave walls.

Damien issued a groan, his blue mouth forming a frown. Seconds later, his limbs went stiff. Both his and Marcus's bodies launched from the ground remaining airborne for several seconds before descending back to the dirt below. Michael scrambled backward away from them, his eyes wide. He rose to his feet, his own breathing now becoming intermittent. He stared at Damien and Marcus. What had just happened? Why had their bodies floated in the air?

He reached a trembling hand toward Damien, intent on pulling him from the trance. Before he could make contact, Marcus gasped and shot up to sitting. He blinked his eyes and glanced around the cave. He released his grip on Celine's and Damien's hands.

Michael snapped his hand back and glanced at Damien. He jerked his head to face Marcus. "Why isn't he back yet?" he demanded.

As he finished the question, Damien sucked in air and groaned. He wriggled on the ground before his eyes fluttered open. He blinked a few times before he sat up.

"Damien!" Michael exclaimed. He breathed a sigh of relief.

"Hey, buddy," Damien answered in a weak voice. He winced as he pulled his hand toward him, glancing down at the large gash.

"Did it work?" Michael questioned, his eyes flitting to Celine's still inanimate form.

"Yeah," Damien confirmed. "She should be back any minute, I think. Right?"

He glanced to Marcus who pulled himself to standing. He offered Damien a handkerchief for his bloody hand. "Yes," Marcus confirmed. "As soon as her memories finish integrating. I should not be here when she wakes."

"Right," Damien said as Michael pulled him to standing. He wrapped his hand with the handkerchief.

"When you have settled Celine, meet me at the beach cave. Then we will return home."

Damien nodded to him before he disappeared into the night air.

Michael clapped him on the shoulder. "You okay?"

The blue tinge around Damien's lips had already disappeared but he remained ashen.

"Yeah," Damien said with a nod as he wiggled the fingers on his injured hand and winced.

"You sure?"

He nodded again. "Yeah. It was… intense," he admitted. "Celine's mind is like a maze of rooms in a massive, horrible, scary hotel."

"Really? Just like corridors filled with rooms?"

"Yeah. And halls branching everywhere. There was an entire hallway of memories of her slapping the Duke. Like hundreds of them."

Michael raised his eyebrows. "I'd have paid to see that."

Damien chuckled. "I probably opened a few too many doors in that hall, but I couldn't help myself."

"It sounds pretty horrible. I'm glad you're back."

"Thanks. It was frightening in some ways, but we did it."

"I can imagine. And *you* did it. I'll bet the Duke was of little help."

Damien shrugged. "He obviously wasn't much help in convincing Celine. The mere sight of him probably would have caused her to disappear forever."

"I figured as much."

"But I wouldn't have made it back without him. Did you know he can fly?"

"He can fly?"

"Sort of. He jumped a gap in the floor that had to be at least twelve feet across. Thankfully, he dragged me with him so we could escape in time."

A small moan escaped from Celine.

"Celine?" Damien inquired, hurrying to her side, and kneeling next to her. Michael circled around her and dropped to one knee on her other side.

She shifted her position and thrashed her head from side to side. Damien clutched her now-healed hand. Her eyelids fluttered open. She gazed around the space, her eyes falling onto Damien.

"Damien," she said with a soft smile. She shifted her gaze. "Michael."

"We're here, Celine," Damien said. "How do you feel?"

"Weak," she admitted, "but overall fine."

Damien patted her hand. "Let's get you back to the house where you can rest."

She nodded and allowed them to pull her to standing.

"Can you walk?" Michael questioned.

"Yes," she said.

The trio returned to the Buckley house. Grayson rushed from the sitting room. "Celine!"

"Gray!" she said as she flung her arms around his neck.

"Where were you? When I returned, I found you missing."

"Yes, something terrible happened. It will take a bit of explaining but rest assured I am fine now. I am alive thanks to Michael and Damien."

Gray glanced behind Celine at the two men. "Michael and Damien Carlyle," he said.

"Hello, again," Damien said with a wave.

"Well," Gray said, "if Celine credits you with saving her, I suppose I am in your debt."

"Think nothing of it," Michael answered.

"I shall explain everything to you," Celine said, "but first I would very much like to change and rest."

"Of course, dear," Gray answered.

"Michael, Damien," Celine said, turning to address them, "can I have anything sent up for you? Perhaps a meal or brandy?"

"No," Damien answered.

"We have to be going," Michael added.

"So soon?" Celine inquired. "Are you certain?"

"Yes," Michael said.

Celine furrowed her brow. "I am not certain I can open a time portal given my recent experience, but I shall try."

"There's no need," Michael said. "We can return to our home on our own."

Celine's eyebrows pinched further together.

"Trust us," Damien said as he grasped her hand and squeezed it.

"All right," she answered. "Then I shall say goodbye to you once again. And hope to see you again soon."

"Same," Damien said. "Take care, Celine."

"Wait," Celine said. She pulled them both into an embrace. "Thank you. Both of you."

They each returned her smile. "You're welcome," Damien said.

Damien and Michael left the foyer, entering the clear night air. Damien gave one final glance back, noticing the ruby necklace was missing from around Celine's neck. He recalled her cognizance removing it while her memories compiled. He smiled, glad she was rid of the cursed object.

"Let's get back and make sure our Celine is also fine," Michael said.

"I can't wait."

"And rid ourselves of the Duke."

"Again, I can't wait."

They hurried down the path and navigated through the beach cave. The Duke awaited them on the beach, gazing out over the surf as it pounded the rocky shoreline.

"Is Celine settled?"

"Yep," Damien reported. "Left her with Gray. He'll take good care of her."

"Forgive me if that statement fails to bring me any comfort. Shall we proceed home?"

Damien rolled his eyes.

"Yes," Michael answered. "Let's get out of here."

Marcus opened the time portal, ushering Michael and Damien through it before he followed them. They emerged on the beach in their own time.

"Ahhh, the good old twenty-first century," Michael said as they climbed to the cliffs above with Marcus trailing behind them.

"Yes," Damien agreed, "the one with only one Duke."

"Race you to the house?"

"You're on," Damien said.

The two men scrambled down the path toward the house. They arrived winded but in a cloud of laughter as Michael beat Damien by a hair.

"I win!" Michael exclaimed. "Again!"

"You cheated! You started running before I agreed to the race."

"No way, man, I gave you a head start. I am officially faster than you. I won!"

"Actually, gentlemen," Marcus said as he leaned against the house's stone facade, "I won. I beat you both."

Michael and Damien shared a glance. "Now, I know you cheated," Damien said as he pointed at the Duke.

Marcus shrugged. "Whoever said cheaters never win, didn't know how to properly cheat."

"Come on, let's go check on Celine," Damien answered as they pushed through the doors into the foyer. "I hope she's awake already."

"Uncle Michael!" Max shouted from across the colossal space.

"Uncle Damien!" Maddy added.

Both children raced across the room toward the men. Michael squatted down and opened his arms for Max while Damien scooped up Maddy.

"Hey, guys!" Michael said.

"We missed you!" Maddy exclaimed as she flung her arms around Damien.

"Aww, we missed you, too!" Damien said. "How was the beach?"

"Hot," Max grumbled.

"Hot? Beaches are supposed to be hot," Michael said.

"Our beaches here aren't hot," Max countered.

"No, but you've already seen that kind. It's nice to try something new. Did you get a lot of pictures?" Michael asked.

"I sure did!" Max answered. "Wanna see 'em? I can show you over lunch tomorrow."

"That sounds perfect," Michael agreed.

"How about you?" Damien asked Maddy. "Did you get any pictures?"

Maddy shook her head. "No. I don't have a camera, silly."

"Oh, right, that might make it tricky," Damien answered.

Maddy giggled. "But I did get something for you."

"Oh, yeah, what?" Damien asked.

"Seashells! I got one for each of you."

"Oh boy! I can't wait to see mine!" Damien answered.

Maddy reached into her pocket and pulled out a handful of shells. She stared at them for a moment before she picked out a tan-colored conch shell. "This one is for Uncle Michael," she said as she passed it to him.

"Aw, thanks!" Michael said. "I love it. How did you know I was looking for this kind?"

"Lucky guess," she said.

"She had another one for you," Max chimed in, "but it had a hermit crab in it, and she screamed and threw it away."

"I would have screamed, too," Damien said.

"Wimps," Max said.

"Are not!" Maddy shouted.

"Are too!" Max insisted.

"Okay, okay," Michael said, stopping the argument between them. "Easy there, you two." Max grimaced but the children ceased their bickering.

Maddy returned to her shells. For Damien, she picked out a speckled cone. "This one is for you."

She placed it in his palm. "Oh, wow! I like it very much, thank you!"

Maddy beamed at him. She cocked her head and glanced behind them. "Who are you?" she questioned, pointing a finger at Marcus.

"Duke Marcus Northcott," Marcus answered, frowning at the child.

"What kind of name is that?" Max asked.

"One that implies I am a powerful man," Marcus answered.

Max scrunched up his face. "You don't look very powerful."

Marcus looked down his nose at him, his eyes narrowed. "Neither do you."

"I'm pretty tough. I bet I could beat you thumb wrestling."

"Let's not test that theory, buddy," Michael said.

"Do you want a seashell?" Maddy asked.

Marcus raised an eyebrow as he stared at her as though she were a bug. Maddy picked out a white coffee bean shaped shell. "Here," she said, holding it out toward him.

Michael lifted Marcus's hand up and Maddy dropped the shell into it. Michael pushed his fingers shut around it. "Aww, look, he's so happy, he's speechless! He'll treasure it forever."

Maddy giggled and gave him a broad grin, pleased with her efforts.

Marcus crinkled his nose at the scene.

"Are they passing out the shells they found for you?" Avery called from the landing above them.

"Yeah," Michael answered as she descended the stairs.

Avery giggled. "She's been carrying those around since we got home. How was your trip?"

"Successful," Michael reported. "Yours?"

"Those are the best kind. Mine was relaxing."

"Hey, is Celine awake yet? Do you know?" Damien asked.

"I haven't heard. Uncle Gray told us she was sick but doing better when we returned. I'm afraid the unpacking took me longer than I expected, and I haven't had a chance to check back with him. Sorry." She shrugged.

"That's okay, we're just heading up to check on her now."

"All right, you two," Avery said to the children. "Let's let Uncle Michael and Uncle Damien and their friend go check on Aunt Celine, okay?"

"Oh, ah, right," Michael said. "Avery, this is Marcus Northcott."

Avery plastered on a smile and stuck her hand out to Marcus. "Avery Hughes."

Marcus shook her hand. "Duke Marcus Northcott," he said.

Avery gave him a nod. "Well, kids, come on, you've still got a few things to put away."

"Awww, come on, Mom," Max complained, "I'd rather play a game."

"Yeah, me, too," Maddy grumbled as Damien set her on the floor.

Avery grabbed their hands. "I'll bet you do," she said as she led them away. "But life isn't all fun and games…" Her voice trailed off as she led them into a hallway at the rear of the foyer.

"Thought you might like to meet some of the people you love to torment," Michael said to Marcus.

"Come on," Damien said, "let's go check on Celine."

He started up the stairs. Marcus remained stationary for a moment.

"What should I do with this?" Marcus questioned. He opened his hand to reveal the small shell.

"Keep it," Michael said, clapping him on the shoulder before following Damien. "It was like gold to that little girl, and she gave it to you. Remember that."

Marcus's brow furrowed as he stared at the small white object.

"You coming?" Damien called to him.

Marcus shoved the shell into his pocket and followed them upstairs. They navigated to Celine and Gray's suite. Damien hurried across the room and through the open door into the bedroom.

CHAPTER 34

"She's not awake yet?" he questioned as he rounded the bed and sank onto it.

"Welcome back," Gray said as they all entered the room. "No, not yet. Did you succeed in 1842?"

"Yes," Damien answered. "At least I thought we did." His brow furrowed as he stared at Celine's still sleeping form. He glanced around the room.

"Welcome home," Alexander said.

"Thanks. Where is everyone else?" he inquired.

"Millie's getting some rest. Celeste ran home for some rose water. She thought it might soothe Celine."

"Soothe her? Has she been sick again?"

"No, but earlier she seemed to be fading. Her breathing was shallow, and she was pale."

Damien considered his statement. Had it been when he'd heard Gray's voice echo in Celine's mind space?

He squeezed her hand. "Come on, Celine. Wake up."

"It may take her mind some time to catch up," Marcus chimed in.

Gray closed his eyes and stretched his neck. "I see you brought him back."

"I'd like to see it through if you don't mind."

"I do," Gray shouted, leaping from the bed.

"Easy, man," Michael said. "We're all here for Celine."

Gray pursed his lips and nodded. "Fine." He sank to the edge of the bed and grabbed Celine's hand again.

Together, they waited for thirty tedious minutes before Celine showed any signs of stirring. Finally, the fingers of her hand quivered and she stretched them. She readjusted her body in the bed with a slight moan.

"Celine?" Gray questioned, leaping to his feet and leaning over her. "Get Millie."

Alexander nodded and hurried from the room.

"Celine? Can you hear us?" Gray asked.

She offered a sigh before her heavy eyelids blinked open and closed. She stared at the ceiling for a moment before her eyes scanned the room.

"Celine!" Gray said with a smile and teary eyes. "Welcome back, darling." He clutched her hand to his chest.

"Thank you." She smiled at him. Her eyes shifted to Damien. "Hi," she whispered.

"Hey," he said with a grin.

Celine pushed herself up to sitting and drew Gray and Damien into an embrace. She squeezed her eyes shut as she held them close.

"It's good to see you awake," Damien said.

She nodded before opening her eyes. Her gaze fell upon the other two men in the room. Michael and Marcus stood at the foot of the bed. She gave them a nod and extended her hands out toward both of them.

Michael grasped it, giving it a squeeze. Marcus's brow furrowed. He stared at her porcelain hand extended toward him. He reached out and grasped it. She wrapped her fingers around his hand and squeezed.

"Thank you," she mouthed.

Moments later, Millie swept into the room with Alexander.

"All right, gentlemen, let's give the patient some room to breathe, please!" she instructed. Damien and Gray pulled away to allow Millie access to Celine.

She kicked them out in short order to examine her patient. After she was satisfied Celine sustained no lingering ill effects, she allowed them to rejoin her for a brief time before insisting she rest.

Damien and Michael descended the stairs to the foyer with Marcus Northcott in tow.

"Drink?" Michael asked.

"Yes, please," Damien said. He yawned. "I'm exhausted, but there's no way I'm going to sleep."

"Same here," Michael answered as he strode to the sitting room.

"Gentlemen, I shall take my leave," Marcus said. "My work here is done."

"Oh, you're leaving?" Damien asked. "Oh, okay. Well..." He stuck his hand out at the man. "Thanks for your help."

Marcus stared at it for a moment before accepting it. "I would do anything for Celine," he responded.

Damien nodded at the remark. "Me too," he said. "Though I guess you owed it to her. What with your warning and everything. You knew it was coming and you did nothing to stop it."

Marcus raised his eyebrows at Damien. "I was as blind-sided by the reappearance of Tobias Greene as you were."

Damien knit his brows. "But..."

"Now," Marcus continued, cutting off Damien's rebuttal, "I shall be going. Before you hurl any additional insults."

Damien winced. "I'll let you know how she is once she's back on her feet."

"I shall look forward to the update. Good night."

Marcus spun on his heel and strode from the house. Damien gazed after his disappearing form as he wandered down the path toward the cliffs.

Michael returned, two brandies in his hands. He handed one to Damien. "Wow," he muttered.

"Yeah, most awkward conversation ever."

"Yep," Michael agreed. "I'm glad he's gone, though."

"Me too," Damien admitted. "Though he did help Celine. He saved her life."

"Yeah," Michael said, "he did."

"Hmm," Damien murmured.

"Come on," Michael said. "Let's head inside and sit down. I want to hear more about the hall of slaps inside Celine's mind."

Damien offered a chuckle. "Okay," he agreed.

* * *

Celine climbed from her bed late the following morning. She stretched and wandered to her dresser, pulling a sweater from the middle drawer.

"And just what do you think you're doing?" Gray inquired as he leaned against the door jamb.

"I think I've been in bed long enough," Celine answered.

"You should be resting."

Celine guffawed. "Again, I think I've rested long enough."

"Celine, you've just been through hell. Again. You can take a day off."

"I need to talk to Damien," she answered.

"It can wait."

She shook her head. A frown formed on her lips and her forehead pinched.

"Hey," Gray said, approaching her and wrapping her in his arms, "what's that look for? Are you sick?"

She shook her head. "No. No, I just…"

"What? Listen, if you're dragging yourself out of bed to thank Damien, he knows how grateful you are. And he wouldn't want you pushing yourself either."

"It's not that."

"Then what?"

Celine stared into his stormy blue eyes. "Before Monica left, she told me the reason she'd come."

"Which is?"

Celine bit her lower lip. "I need to talk to Damien about it first."

Gray raised his eyebrows at her.

"Please understand. It involves him. He deserves to know. And he deserves to know first."

"All right," Gray agreed. "We'll discuss it after you've spoken to Damien. But I still believe this can wait a day or two."

"No," Celine disagreed with a vehement shake of her head. "No, I don't want to put it off. Gray, I can't. I can't keep this inside. I have to tell him."

Gray pushed a lock of her blonde hair from her face. "All right, Celine." He kissed the tip of her nose.

She leaned in to him. "How about a proper kiss?" she asked.

"I won't say no," Gray said with a grin.

Celine brushed his lips with hers. "I missed you," she said.

"I love you, Celine Devereaux," Gray answered.

"And I love you, Grayson Buckley."

"Now, go have your conversation with Damien."

Celine raised her eyebrows at him.

"I can see the worry etched in those crystal blue eyes. Go."

She smiled at him. "Thanks, Gray."

Celine pulled on a change of clothes and made her way downstairs. She found Damien in the sitting room, clacking around on his keyboard.

"Hey!" she said. "Am I interrupting?"

"Celine!" Damien exclaimed, bobbling the laptop as he hurried to stand. "No, you're not, just doing some work. Should you be up?"

"I'm fine," Celine insisted. "And what about you? I'm sure what you went through wasn't much better."

Damien shook his head. "I'm okay," he answered.

"Damien, you had to wander through the maze of my mind. That couldn't have been easy."

"It wasn't that bad. Though your mind is a hot mess, Celine."

Celine offered a giggle at the statement. "Sorry, I'll try to have it cleaned up next time you visit."

"Let's hope there isn't a next time."

"Fingers crossed," Celine said. She glanced up at him. "And Tobias..." She paused. "Did he..."

"No lasting effects," Damien answered before she could finish.

"No lasting effects? What effects did you have while you were there?" Celine inquired.

Damien shrugged. He frowned while shaking his head. "Not much, we tried to avoid him mostly."

"Damien," Celine said. She stared at him.

He shrugged again. "Really, it wasn't that bad."

She raised her eyebrows at him. "Damien," she repeated, "you know I can tell when you're avoiding a question, right?"

Damien gulped. "Some stuff happened, but we came through it."

"What stuff?" Celine asked.

Damien hedged. "You know, he tried to mess with my mind and stuff."

Celine hiked her eyebrows again.

"And I… almost killed myself… twice."

"Damien!" Celine exclaimed, her jaw agape. She shook her head.

"I didn't! Obviously!"

"But you could have!" She sighed. "What happened?"

Damien shrugged. "He kept getting into my head. It started small, with him telling me you were his. When we didn't leave it alone, he'd keep pestering at me and pestering at me until I couldn't think straight."

Celine shook her head. "Oh, D, I'm starting to think this life is too dangerous for you and Michael both."

"No," Damien insisted. "No, I'm fine. It's okay!"

"It's not okay. Damien, you could have died!"

"So could you!" Damien countered. "We all look out for each other, right? We're a team!"

Celine sighed. "I guess. I just feel terrible that I wasn't able to look out for you this time."

"Don't worry. Michael did. He pulled me back when I almost jumped off the cliff. And the Duke saved me once, too, weirdly."

"Caring about someone else's life. That must have been a new sensation for him."

"Yeah, I owe him my life. He stopped me from slitting my wrist. Then he told me he only did it because he needed me to save you." Damien rolled his eyes.

"Always charming, that's Marcus."

"Yep," Damien said with a chuckle. "Anyway, stop worrying. I'm fine. It's like a bad dream now that Tobias is gone. You, on the other hand, really went through it. We almost lost you. Twice. It wouldn't be a terrible idea to hang out in bed for the day."

"I'm fine, D," Celine assured him. "And really glad Tobias is gone. How did Marcus pull that off, I wonder?"

Damien shrugged. "I'm not sure. He was pretty secretive about it."

"Not surprising."

Damien shook his head. "Hey, did you know he can talk to birds?"

"What?"

"Yeah, he can talk to birds and use them to spy on people."

"Oh, do you mean to use them as an eye? Yes, an interesting trick. Sometimes useful. Anyway, we need to talk. I don't want to put this off." She swallowed hard as she avoided his gaze.

"Okay?"

Celine bit her lower lip and took a deep breath.

"Hey, if this is about me going to the Duke to begin with when you were sick, I was really upset and I didn't see another way to…"

Celine shook her head. "No, it's not. Though about that. Damien, that was an incredibly brave but very, very stupid thing to do. Thank you."

"Anytime," he said with a smile.

"I mean it," she answered. "Thank you. I hate that you went to him for help. I hate it more that you went alone. But if you hadn't… "

"Let's not discuss that. I did. He helped. It's done. Although…"

"Although what?" Celine asked.

"I told him he owed it to you since he knew it was coming and did nothing. He claimed the warning he gave you had nothing to do with Tobias Greene and he was as blindsided as we were."

Celine's brow furrowed as she considered the statement. "So, then what was his warning about?"

Damien shrugged. "We're still in the dark on that one. Guess we'll tackle that problem next."

Celine shook her head and sighed.

"Did you hear Maddy gave him a seashell?" Damien inquired as a change of subject.

Celine offered him a stunned expression.

"Yeah," Damien said with a chuckle. "When we got home the kids were here. She gave Michael and me a seashell from their trip. Then she offered him one. I don't think he knew what to do."

"Did he take it?"

"Yeah, Michael made him take it and keep it."

"Wow," Celine said as she pondered it. "I can't imagine Marcus even knowing what to say to a child."

"We told her he was stunned into silence by her gift. It was rather comical," Damien admitted.

Celine chuckled before silence fell between them.

"Anyway," Damien said. "You said you wanted to talk to me? Although, I'm one hundred percent sure it can wait if you're not up to it."

Celine shook her head. "No, it can't."

"Okay?"

"We should sit down."

"Umm," Damien said, shifting his weight from side to side, "this sounds terrible. Is it really that bad?"

Celine didn't answer.

"Celine, what is it?" Damien asked. "Is there something wrong with you? After everything Tobias did? Are you still sick or is there some lasting effect from his attack on you?"

"No," Celine said with a shake of her head. "No, it's not me."

She gave Damien a consoling glance.

"Before I got sick," she continued, "I told you Monica told me the reason she came to Bucksville."

Damien nodded. "Yeah?"

Celine's forehead wrinkled. "She confessed something to me. She couldn't tell you herself. I told her I would tell you. She couldn't face you."

Damien and Celine sank onto the couch. Damien's brows knit and he stared at Celine.

"Is-Is Aunt Monica sick?" he questioned, anxiety clear in his voice.

"No," Celine admitted. "No, it's nothing like that."

"Uncle Trevor?" Damien queried.

"No, it's not that," Celine said. "Both of them are fine, D."

"Then what is it?"

Celine hesitated. "I don't know how to say this," she began.

"Hey," Damien said, grasping her hand and offering her a half-smile, "I've been in a time with two Dukes. I can handle anything!"

Celine offered a chuckle, though the concern remained inscribed in her features.

"The thing is, Damien," Celine said before pausing. She continued after a breath, "You were adopted."

Damien's expression blanched. "What?"

Celine nodded as she grasped his hand in hers. "Monica said she's known all your life and never said anything. She said it wasn't her secret to tell but given the recent events with me, she felt it was best to say something.

"She said it's been bothering her since we moved and she finally got up the nerve to say the words. She planned to tell me at our lunch but then you came along with me. The moment she saw you, she didn't think she could tell you. She realized how upsetting it would be for you. She couldn't look into your eyes and tell you that you weren't your parents' child."

Damien leapt from his seat and paced the floor.

"Say something, D," Celine said after a moment.

He shrugged. "What's there to say?"

"Talk to me, D. Tell me what you're thinking, what you're feeling." Celine followed him across the room and put her hand on his shoulder.

"There's nothing to think about. So, I was adopted, so what? So, I'm just nobody. I'm not a Sherwood. I'm not your cousin. I was sort of Josie's but now I'm not even that."

"It's okay, D. I mean, I thought I was adopted, too, after Monica told me. It didn't change anything for me. Monica and Trevor were still my parents."

Damien nodded. "Yeah, you thought you were adopted for all of two seconds. And you were still pretty upset about it. Though you figured yours out pretty quickly. There are just so many questions when you hear something like this. I'd just like to know who I really am since I'm no longer who I thought I was. Why did my parents get rid of me?" Damien pressed his hands against the mantel and stared into the fire.

"We'll figure it out for you, too, D," Celine promised. "It's okay to be upset."

She rubbed her hand up and down his back.

"Hey, have you seen my…" Michael shouted as he strolled into the room. "Oh! Whoa, sorry," he said, witnessing the scene near the fireplace, "didn't realize you were in here. I'll leave you to it."

"No, don't leave on my account," Damien said. He spun to stalk across the room. "Come on in. Join in the fun."

Michael side-eyed him. "You okay, man?"

"Sure," Damien said, his voice dripping in sarcasm, "just perfect."

Michael shifted his eyes to Celine. "Could you give us a minute?" she requested.

"No, no, don't leave. Stay!"

"D…" Celine began.

"No, really, Celine," Damien said. "He's going to find out sooner or later. Why not sooner."

"Find out what?'

Damien poured himself a brandy and sipped it. "Find out that I've got no more business being here than you."

"Huh?"

"You told me you didn't belong here," Damien reminded Michael, "because you had no ties to the Buckleys. Well, turns out, neither do I!"

"You're Celine's cousin."

"Nope. I'm not."

"That's splitting hairs, Damien," Michael contended. "Celine WAS Josie. You were her cousin."

"Not really," Damien said. "Turns out, I was adopted, too. I'm not really a Sherwood."

Michael's eyes widened and his eyebrows shot toward his hairline. He glanced to Celine who nodded.

"That's why Monica came," he surmised.

"Yes," Celine said with a nod.

"Wow, sorry, man. That's…"

"A surprise," Damien said.

"Yeah," Michael agreed. "But it doesn't change anything, really."

Damien shot him a glance. Michael shrugged. "It doesn't," he insisted. "You're still you. You and Josie were still raised together. You're still cousins."

Damien nodded as he glowered into his brandy. "It's still a shock. Who am I?"

"We're going to find out," Michael promised.

"Before or after you take off?" Damien questioned.

"I'm not going anywhere, buddy," Michael said with a half-smile.

"You don't have to stay because I got some unexpected news," Damien said.

Michael shook his head. "I'm not."

Damien furrowed his brow. "So, you're leaving?"

"Nope," Michael said. "I'm staying and it's not because of your news. I made my decision while you were dangling from the cliff." Michael strode across the room and snatched a manila folder from the coffee table. "That's what I came in here for. My contracts. I decided. I'm staying."

"Why?" Damien asked. "Not that I'm complaining."

Michael flicked the folder open and shuffled through the papers. "Because we're a team, right?" He grabbed a pen and scribbled his name across the paperwork. He spun to face them, holding his hands out to his sides. "We're the Shadow Slayers, right?"

"That we are," Celine agreed with a half-smile. She approached Michael and Damien. She circled her arm around Damien's waist. "We'll find your real parents, D."

"Yeah, man," Michael agreed. "It'll be the next thing we solve."

"So, you're really sure about this?" Damien asked, motioning toward the papers sprawled across the table.

"Yep, and here's my signature to prove it." Michael held up the signed paper.

Celine stared at Michael's signature scrawled under his father's signature. Something about the paper struck her. Damien's voice drew her attention away from it.

"I'm glad you're staying," Damien said.

"We've been through too much together. I can't bail," Michael said. "It doesn't matter how we came together, we're a team. We stick together. And besides, you guys can't get by without me." He offered a devilish grin at his last statement.

Damien nodded. "Yes, we do. And, no, we can't!"

"Now, what do you say we celebrate in town with a few drinks? We can discuss our latest conquest and our plan to find your family."

"Sounds good. You up for it tonight?" Damien asked.

"Yep," Michael confirmed. "How about you, Celine? You feel well enough for a trip to the bar?"

"To celebrate ridding ourselves of Tobias Greene? You bet!"

EPILOGUE

Celine, Michael and Damien sat at a corner table of Bucksville's oldest and most popular pub, The Thirsty Seal. Celine glanced out the nearby window. Dense fog rolled in from the harbor. Shadowy figures meandered through the gray soup as they traversed the sidewalks, heading to their destinations.

Two amber ales sat in front of Michael and Damien. Celine sipped at her ginger ale.

"So, Monica didn't give any indication of who Damien's parents might be?" Michael inquired.

Celine shook her head. "No," she answered. "She was beside herself when she started to tell me. She was so concerned Damien would hate her for keeping this from him."

"I don't hate her," Damien said. "But I'm still in shock. It's weird to find out your entire life has been a lie."

"It hasn't been a lie, D," Celine assuaged. "Your parents loved you and so did Monica and Trevor."

Damien nodded. "Yeah, I know but…"

"But?" Michael questioned as he sipped his beer.

Damien shrugged again. "I'm grateful for the life I led. I'm grateful my parents adopted me. I'm grateful when they died Aunt Monica and Uncle Trevor took me in. I had a wonderful life with a wonderful family." He reached out to grab and squeeze Celine's hand. "But I can't stop thinking about who I really am. Where did I come from? And why did my parents dump me?"

"Could be as simple as an unplanned pregnancy, Damien," Michael said. "There may be nothing nefarious about it."

"I'm not suggesting it was nefarious. Maybe my birth mom was some sixteen-year-old kid who couldn't raise me on her own."

Michael nodded in agreement.

"But I'd still like to know," he added.

Celine squeezed his hand. "We'll find out, D."

"And Monica had no records or no information from her sister about this? Adopting a child is a pretty major undertaking."

Celine shook her head. "She said it was a closed adoption and Lucy and Nathan were barred from speaking about it entirely."

"So, since I'm the child, can I request it be opened?"

"Monica said no. She said the records are sealed and private. Even you can't request access to learn the identity of your birth parents."

Damien hung his head for a moment. "Ugh," he murmured.

"It's okay, man," Michael said. "We'll find a way."

"What way?" Damien inquired.

"Carlyle Industries has a lot of money and a lot of influence. I'll bribe a judge if I have to." Michael grinned at him.

"Thanks, buddy, I appreciate that," Damien said. "Though maybe we can find a more legal route to pursue first."

"Monica did say one thing that might help."

"What's that?" Michael inquired.

"She said something about Damien being named after his father, but not really."

Michael furrowed his brow and Damien scrunched up his face. "What the heck does that mean?" Damien asked.

Celine shrugged her shoulders. "I don't know. That's all she knew. I asked her about it, and she said she didn't have any other information. Just that Lucy told her Damien was named after his father, but not really."

"Well, that's not a lot to go on," Michael said.

"Nope," Damien agreed.

Silence fell between them for several moments as they contemplated the problem.

"How about a change of subject?" Michael asked.

"Sounds good to me," Damien agreed. "To what?"

"How about how awesome we are? So awesome that we kicked that soul eater's butt and saved Celine!" Michael said, raising his beer high.

Celine smiled at the remark as she lifted her glass. Damien followed suit. "To the Shadow Slayers!" Michael exclaimed.

"To the Shadow Slayers," Celine and Damien said.

Michael set down his glass after taking a sip, a smile plastered on his face. He shook his head. "I still look at birds weird."

Damien burst into laughter. "Right? And who knew the Duke could fly?"

"Wow," Michael said with a chuckle. "I'm not sure I would have believed it even if I saw it. And he just snatched you from the ground and jumped?"

"Yep!" Damien said. "Got a running start, grabbed me mid-run, and sailed across like a twelve-foot hole like he was hopping over a crack!"

"Tell me again about all the slaps in that one hallway," Michael said.

Damien agreed with a laugh.

The bar's door opened as a new patron entered. A chilly gust of wind swept in. It sent a shiver down Celine's spine. She glanced to the new occupant who sashayed to the bar. She froze. Her muscles stiffened and she sat straighter in her seat.

She swallowed hard as she followed the dark-haired woman who approached the bar. Michael and Damien's conversation faded into the background, turning into unintelligible chatter as the hairs on the back of her neck stood up.

"What do you think, Celine?" Damien questioned. He raised his eyebrows at her. "Celine?"

"Hey, Celine!" Michael tried.

"Hello?!" Damien said as he waved his hand in front of her face.

She did not flinch. Her eyes remained fixed on the figure at the bar.

"Celine? What's wrong What is it?" Damien asked as he glanced around, trying to ascertain the target of her stare. He swung back to face her.

Celine wore a troubled expression. Her brow pinched, her crystal blue eyes turned stormy. Goosebumps pocked her flesh and her bottom lip trembled. She now understood Marcus's ominous warning all too well. She swallowed hard and uttered a single word in answer to Damien's question. "Trouble."

Continue the series with *Darkness Rising,* Book 5 in the Shadow Slayers Series.

A NOTE FROM THE AUTHOR

Dear Reader,

Thank you for reading this book! *Trouble* is Book 4 of the Shadow Slayers saga. It's quite different from Book 3 of the series, but I wanted to bring a lightness to the story for a moment. I hope Monica Benson's appearance followed by the Slayers comical shenanigans did just that!

I hope you enjoyed reading this book as much as I did writing it! If you loved it, please consider leaving a review and help get the book into the hands of other interested readers.

Shadow Slayers Book 5 isn't available yet, but look for it coming in 2023! In the meantime, try *Death of a Duchess* for another great supernatural read!

If you'd like to stay up to date with all my news, be the first to find out about new releases first, sales and get free offers, join the Nellie H. Steele's Mystery Readers' Group! Or sign up for my newsletter now!

All the best, Nellie

DEATH OF A DUCHESS SYNOPSIS

An unexpected marriage proposal from a Duke blindsides her. Will it lead to a fairytale ending or certain death?

Lenora expected her unique ability would condemn her to a life of solitude, shunned by society. But when she receives an unexpected marriage proposal hinging on it, Lenora is shocked. All she must do in exchange for the life of a duchess is use her communicative skills to determine the reason for the former Duchess of Blackmoore's suicide.

Beyond the strange blackening on the stones of Blackmoore Castle, Lenora discovers another darkness lurks in her new Scottish Highlands home. The secrets housed within the castle walls chill Lenora to the bone... and threaten her own life.

Will Lenora discover the hidden truth behind the death of the former duchess? Or will she, too, fall prey to a similar fate?

Indies Today calls *Death of a Duchess* "wildly entertaining," and "a grand mystery with a paranormal undercurrent and glamorous overtones."

Find out why in *Death of a Duchess,* book one in the gripping *Duchess of Blackmoore Mysteries* series!

DEATH OF A DUCHESS EXCERPT

The imposing silhouette of Blackmoore Castle rose from the mist, standing in stark contrast against the ominous gray sky. Its grand towers and turrets with banners waving rose high above the landscape. The castle, perched on the cliffs, beckoned me home as my carriage trundled up the path toward it.

It still had the power to take my breath away as it did when I first laid eyes upon it, drenched in moonlight, some three months ago when I arrived. I recalled the journey into the Scottish Highlands as though it were yesterday. Filled with a mix of excitement and trepidation of what would become of me, I rode in silence with my traveling companion, Henry Langford, a middle-aged estate agent with a kind face in the service of Duke Blackmoore, the castle's proprietor.

The foreboding façade of the castle may have sent shivers up the spine of most women my age. However, the turmoil of my short life of eighteen years and two months created within me a façade almost as formidable as the castle's, if not more so. Instead, the brooding castle with its gothic design and blackened stones generated a stirring of home inside me. And despite my questioning mind regarding what would become of me, I feared not what secrets the ominous castle held within its walls.

As the carriage bounced over the rocky pathway to the castle, I closed my eyes, recalling the night I had first arrived. My day had started like any other, with no indication of difference from the days before it. At the orphanage, my home for ten years, six months and three weeks, days were rarely unique. Mundaneness and routine thrived at the orphanage above all things. I passed most of my time reading and learning. I had, in fact, been returning from the orphanage's paltry library on that morning when I overheard the tail end of the conversation between Duke Blackmoore's man and the headmistress. I shall make clear one thing: I was not eavesdropping. However, upon passing through the foyer to the staircase leading to bedrooms, I overheard my name. Naturally intrigued, I stopped to listen.

Headmistress Williamson protested, "There are far better girls beyond Miss Hastings in this orphanage for this sort of thing."

"Far better for what?" my mind questioned. Though her comment did not surprise me. Her dislike for me was well known. She despised my quick wit among other aspects of my personality. As much as she hoped to rid herself of me, she sabotaged every possibility of my departure. I had long since resigned myself to becoming a teacher at the orphanage.

I did not recognize the voice that answered her. "Miss Williamson, I am not here to ask your opinion, merely to pay for any expenses Miss Hastings accumulated during her time at your facility and to retrieve her," he argued.

My brow furrowed at the mention of retrieving me. Who was this mystery man, I wondered, and what right of claim did he have to me? He wasn't my father, of this much I was sure. An uncle, perhaps. My mind wandered from possibility to possibility as the doors to Headmistress Williamson's office flung open.

Headmistress Williamson spotted me in an instant, her eyes wide as she noted my proximity to her office doors. Her mouth set itself into its usual scowl as her eyes settled on me. Her mousy brown hair, pulled back into its low bun at the nape of her neck, added to the dour expression on her face.

"Miss Hastings," she growled, glowering at me with those fiery emerald eyes, "how fortuitous to find you here. Mr. Langford," she said, motioning to the man who stepped behind her to fill the doorway, "is here to collect you."

I glanced to the man, exploring his features as I searched them for an answer. None came. Instead of explanations, what came was a quick swat on my upper arm. "Do not stand there dumbfounded, girl!" Headmistress Williamson exclaimed. "Mr. Langford does not have all day. He'd like to get as early a start as possible!"

The headmistress offering a contrite glance to Mr. Langford before spinning me on my feet and shoving me up the stairs. She huffed as we hurried down the hall toward the bedroom I occupied with seven other girls. "Quickly, now, Lenora, pack your things. You won't be needing this." She ripped the book still clutched in my hands away, discarding it on a nearby dresser.

I had come to the orphanage with a small, well-worn suitcase which I kept shoved under my sagging mattress. Retrieving it from its hiding spot, I placed it on the bed and set about gathering the few possessions I had accumulated over the years. My meager belongings, consisting of a second dress, a tarnished gold hair comb missing the jewels that once adorned it and a well-worn copy of *Frankenstein* gifted to me by a former teacher, were packed within minutes. I pulled on a tattered pair of gloves and secured a frayed cape at my neck.

"Well, I suppose this is goodbye… for now," the headmistress replied as I stood in my cape, suitcase in my hand.

"For now?" I questioned.

"I wouldn't be surprised if you are not returned within a month's time," she commented, a skeptical expression clouding her features as she considered my journey.

I heaved a sigh and stepped past her, making my way to the doorway. There I turned, giving one last glance at my home for just over a decade. I held no melancholy in my heart despite the extended time I had spent here. Without a word, I continued through the doorway, descending the stairs to the waiting man below. Headmistress Williamson followed on my heels. "I do apologize for the wait, Mr. Langford. And please, if Miss Hastings does not work out for any reason, do not hesitate to contact me. I am certain we can suggest a more appropriate placement for you and Duke Blackmoore."

The vote of confidence in my ability was staggering, and I fought to restrain my tongue. "I am certain there will be no need for that," Mr. Langford replied with a curt smile. He shifted his gaze to me. "Come, Miss Hastings. We've a long journey ahead of us. Good day, Headmistress Williamson." He placed his hat on his head, tipping it to her and extending his arm to usher me from the building. I nodded to him, eager to leave the place behind.

Outside, a carriage awaited, drawn by four large horses. As we exited into the street, Mr. Langford lifted the suitcase from my hands. I opened my mouth to protest, but he insisted, passing my case off to the coachman. The man held it as he opened the carriage door, offering his hand to assist me into the contraption. I climbed inside followed by Mr. Langford and the door was closed behind us. The coachman set about securing my case to the rear of the carriage with what I assumed to be Mr. Langford's luggage.

I glanced to Mr. Langford, who fiddled with the latch on an attaché case. After clearing my throat, I inquired, "May I ask where we are going?"

"Blackmoore Castle. Highlands of Scotland. Settle in, Miss Hastings, we've a long journey ahead of us," he replied, removing a stack of papers and fixing a pair of spectacles to his nose.

Though I had more questions, I quieted my tongue. Mr. Langford's focus on the papers in front of him made it clear my queries were unwelcome at present.

The buggy shimmied as the coachmen climbed into his seat, taking hold of the reins. The carriage lurched forward and the characteristic sound of horseshoes on cobblestones filled my ears. I leaned forward, peering from the window at the orphanage as it slid away from my view.

I folded by hands, placing them in my lap as I continued to watch the city fade away. After several hours, rolling green hills dotted with autumn foliage filled the view in all directions. The scene, though charming, became monotonous after a time and I nodded off, soothed by the swaying motion of the carriage ride.

When I woke, the moon, already high in the darkened sky, glowed brightly. Mountainous terrain now surrounded us, and I assumed we had entered the Scottish Highlands, though having never traveled there, I could not be sure.

I straightened in my seat, drawing my threadbare cape closer around me. The air, markedly cooler and damper here, penetrated my bones. Heavy mists clung to the moors, obscuring some of them completely. The large white moon glowed over the land, casting an eerie image across the landscape.

The carriage slowed, and I was pitched backward as we

began to climb. "We're nearly there, Lenora," Mr. Langford said with a smile. It was the first time he'd used my first name. I noted he was devoid of his paperwork, likely unable to view it as the light waned to darkness. "All that remains is the climb to the castle."

I gazed out the window as the carriage lurched around a bend, noticing the large structure perched on the top of the moor. Lit by moonlight, I distinguished multiple features of the castle looming above us. Turrets and towers jutted from various areas of the sprawling framework. The moonlit castle struck an imposing silhouette against the night sky.

I returned my gaze to Mr. Langford. "Am I to be a governess?" I inquired.

An amused smile crossed the man's face. "No, you are not to be a governess."

"A companion, then? A ladies' maid?" I continued, not understanding what my new role was to be when we arrived.

"No, Lenora," he answered, "Duke Blackmoore has far better uses for your special skills in mind. He has far bigger plans for you." I furrowed my brow in confusion at his answer as he continued. "You, my dear Lenora, are to be a duchess!"

* * *

My mind snapped back to the present as the carriage slowed to a halt outside the castle. I waited inside as the coachman dismounted from his driving perch and opened the door, unfurling the steps and offering his hand for me to disembark. How quickly one becomes used to the genteel things, my mind contemplated during my short wait. Accepting his hand, I stepped out onto the gravel drive below, pulling my fur-trimmed velvet cape closer around me to keep out the winter chill.

For a moment, I glanced up at the castle's exterior, recalling my thoughts just three months prior when I arrived. The odd blackening on some parts of the stones, always a source of local gossip, cast a sinister countenance on what would otherwise pass for a fairytale castle. Some of the more levelheaded townsfolk attributed the blackening to some internal quality of the stones used or the growth of local flora. Still others insisted it represented the veins of the castle. As though, somehow, the castle had become alive and its very soul was blackening as a result of the strange goings-on here. Or perhaps because it defiled some ancient sacred ground.

I paid little attention to the histrionics of most of the locals, many of whom warned me to flee before I should meet a gruesome end. I had grown accustomed to people like this in my life and had learned to ignore them at a very young age. They based most of their opinion on lack of knowledge, understanding, superstition and a general sense of foolishness.

When I arrived three months ago, the castle, lit by moonlight, its network of blackened veins crawling through the stones, conjured no apprehensive reactions but only contentment. The serenity and peace I felt that night had never waned, it had only grown. Each time I returned here, I experienced the same emotion, as though I had found my place in the world.

Three months later, the only change in my emotion was the lack of curiosity in my heart over my new life. I now possessed a firm understanding of what my life would become and what my role was here.

The gravel crunched under my feet as I stepped toward my home, ready to continue my odyssey within the castle walls.

At this moment, it occurs to me that I haven't properly

introduced myself to you, dear reader. Now seems an opportune moment to make a proper introduction before we continue together.

My name is Lenora Fletcher. I am the Duchess of Blackmoore. And I can communicate with the dead. Within these pages, dear reader, I have recorded one of my stories.

Want to read more? Find out what strings were attached to Lenora's marriage proposal and delve into her world. Click here to read!

OTHER SERIES BY NELLIE H. STEELE

Cozy Mystery Series

Cate Kensie Mysteries
Lily & Cassie by the Sea Mysteries
Pearl Party Mysteries
Middle Age is Murder Cozy Mysteries

Supernatural Suspense/Urban Fantasy

Shadow Slayers Stories
Duchess of Blackmoore Mysteries

Adventure

Maggie Edwards Adventures
Clif & Ri on the Sea